Proposals

What woman could resist a proposal from these rugged Outback men?

Three passionate novels!

In June 2006 Mills & Boon bring back two of their classic collections, each featuring three favourite romances by our bestselling authors…

OUTBACK PROPOSALS

Outback Mistress
by Lindsay Armstrong
Outback Baby by Barbara Hannay
Wedding at Waverley Creek
by Jessica Hart

BABY LOVE

Marriage and Maternity
by Gill Sanderson
The Midwife's Secret
by Fiona McArthur
The Midwife Bride by Janet Ferguson

Outback Proposals

OUTBACK MISTRESS
by
Lindsay Armstrong

OUTBACK BABY
by
Barbara Hannay

WEDDING AT WAVERLEY CREEK
by
Jessica Hart

MILLS & BOON®

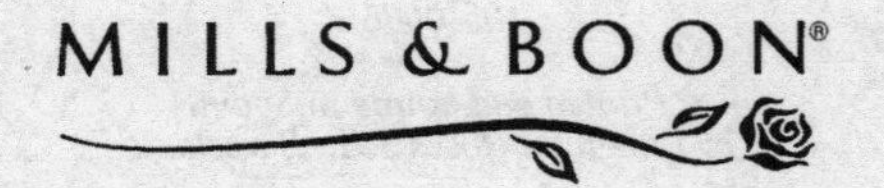

DID YOU PURCHASE THIS BOOK WITHOUT A COVER?
If you did, you should be aware it is **stolen property** as it was reported *unsold and destroyed* by a retailer. Neither the author nor the publisher has received any payment for this book.

All the characters in this book have no existence outside the imagination of the author, and have no relation whatsoever to anyone bearing the same name or names. They are not even distantly inspired by any individual known or unknown to the author, and all the incidents are pure invention.

MILLS & BOON and MILLS & BOON with the Rose Device are registered trademarks of the publisher.
Harlequin Mills & Boon Limited,
Eton House, 18-24 Paradise Road, Richmond, Surrey, TW9 1SR

OUTBACK PROPOSALS

Outback Mistress, Outback Baby and *Wedding at Waverley Creek* were first published in Great Britain by Harlequin Mills & Boon Limited in separate, single volumes.

ISBN 0 263 84962 7

05-0606

Printed and bound in Spain
by Litografia Rosés S.A., Barcelona

OUTBACK MISTRESS

by

Lindsay Armstrong

Lindsay Armstrong was born in South Africa but now lives in Australia with her New Zealand-born husband and their five children. They have lived in nearly every state of Australia and have tried their hand at some unusual – for them – occupations, such as farming and horse-training – all grist to the mill for a writer! Lindsay started writing romances when their youngest child began school and she was left feeling at a loose end. She is still doing it and loving it.

CHAPTER ONE

OLIVIA LOCKHART pushed the damp tendrils of fair hair off her face and flapped the front of her red and cream checked blouse. She was sitting on a fence in the feed shed, an open-sided structure with a corrugated-iron roof, and there were four children gathered around her. 'So,' she said, 'we need to be extra careful—'

She paused as two more children ran up panting—twins, a boy and a girl with identical gingery curls, freckles and gap-toothed smiles as well as a reputation for being able to get into more trouble than Flash Gordon, as the saying went on the station. 'What have you two been up to?' she asked resignedly.

'Nothing! Nothing *bad*,' Ryan Whyte replied with an injured air and turned to his sister Sonia for confirmation.

She nodded her head energetically. 'But, Livvie—'

'Not now, Sonia; let me finish first—we can't afford to waste water—'

'But, Livvie—'

'Sonia, just do as you're told for once—where have you been anyway?'

'Down in the horse paddock, and—'

'Well, you shouldn't be down there on your own. Your father would be very cross. Where was I?' She paused and scanned the faces of the youngsters she was giving this lecture on water conservation to, all children of families who lived and worked on the cattle station. 'That's right—until it rains again we *really* have to—'

'But, Livvie, we found a man,' Sonia said stubbornly.

'We really have to be very careful we don't waste water and—'

'He's dead!' Ryan said.

It took a moment for this to sink in then Olivia jumped off the fence and said warningly, 'If you two are making this up—'

'No, Livvie, he's lying on the ground and he's bleeding. He won't move. We poked him with a stick but nothing happened.'

'He's not dead,' Olivia said thankfully as she knelt in the dusty paddock beneath a burning blue sky. 'But he is unconscious and he's got a nasty gash on his temple.' She reached for a dressing from the first-aid kit they'd brought. 'Who on earth is he and how did he get here?'

Jack Bentley, who was the station foreman, removed his broad-brimmed hat and scratched his head. 'Never seen him in my life before. But we'd better get him up to the homestead and get some attention for him. It's not even as if there's a stray horse around.' He put his hand above his eyes and scanned the paddock.

'Curiouser and curiouser,' Olivia murmured. 'Here, I'll take his feet.'

But it was quite an effort. The stranger was at least

six feet tall and well-built and although they were as careful as could be it was not that easy to ease him onto the back of the Land Rover. He remained deeply unconscious, however.

Olivia climbed into the back with him while Jack drove them to the house and she studied the man narrowly at the same time. She thought he would be in his early thirties and she got the feeling his eyes would be blue—he had thick black hair but a fair, though sunburnt complexion. His face, grimy, bloodstained and cut though it was, was good-looking in a lean way, smooth now but giving a hint of being arresting…

The rest of him, clad in a torn khaki boiler suit, was equally impressive—long and strong-looking but with not an ounce of extra flesh.

Olivia frowned then began cautiously to feel through his pockets but apart from some money and a handkerchief they yielded nothing. She shook her head and murmured, 'Whoever you are, I hope you don't have amnesia because it's almost as if you dropped in from another planet!'

Two hours later, the flying doctor straightened and regarded the strange man with a frown. They'd put him in a guest bedroom and between them, Jack and the doctor, they'd removed his boiler suit and, with Olivia's help, washed him. Then the doctor had stitched his temple but nothing they'd done had caused him to stir.

'Is he in a coma?' Olivia asked worriedly as she

regarded the recumbent figure on the wide bed beneath a clean white sheet.

'Looks like it. He's also got a bump on the head as big as the Opera House but all his vital signs are OK. Uh—I'd say he's a bit dehydrated so I'm going to have to set up a drip— Hang on!'

They all moved closer as the man stirred, muttered something and his eyelids fluttered open.

They *were* blue, Olivia noted—a deep blue but also completely blank. 'Where—the hell am I?' he said with an effort.

It was the doctor who explained, adding ruefully, 'The thing is, we don't know how you came to be here.'

'What…what state?'

'Queensland—Central Queensland. Does that ring a bell?'

But those blue eyes blinked dazedly then the man said, 'Would you believe, I can't seem to remember my name…?' And he struggled suddenly to sit up at the same time as Olivia felt a start of guilt, almost as if she'd wished amnesia on this man.

They had an urgent conference on the veranda.

'Only temporary amnesia, I'd hazard,' the doctor said. 'He has had an almighty bump on the head. If that's the case it will come back to him gradually and we have no real problems. We'll have to keep the fluids up to him and keep him quiet; he's bound to have concussion—think you can cope, Livvie?'

'Of course but—' Olivia gestured a little helplessly

'—what if it isn't temporary? Shouldn't we airlift him to a hospital?'

'I honestly don't think it's necessary at this stage and, to complicate matters, we're really stretched at the moment. I was on my way to pick up someone with a badly broken leg when I intercepted your call and the other aircraft has gone to check out a suspected outbreak of meningitis. But if nothing comes back in a day or two that's what we will do. If you're worried, don't hesitate to call, though. Somehow or other we'll work something out—is your uncle home?'

'No, he's in Japan with a beef marketing delegation but—' she shook her head '—Jack can help me if I need it. We'll have to alert the police, though.' She paused and frowned. 'He must have ridden over from a neighbouring property and his horse—perhaps it threw him and bolted home?'

'Sounds reasonable,' Jack agreed. 'I'll get on to it.'

'Are you a nurse?'

Olivia straightened and looked down at her patient. 'No. But I've had extensive first-aid training—how do you feel?' She smoothed the sheet and sat down beside the bed.

'Terrible,' he said with a wry smile twitching his lips. 'A king-size headache, hot all over, aching like the devil and my tongue seems to be twice its normal size.'

'That's because you're dehydrated and sunburnt—you really shouldn't wander around this countryside without a hat—and the headache comes from a spectacular bump on your head and three stitches in your temple. Otherwise you're fine, apparently.'

He grimaced and winced. 'What about this *fog* I'm living in?'

'Temporary amnesia,' Olivia said promptly and with more assurance than she actually felt. 'The doctor reckons it'll all come back to you gradually.'

'I hope to hell he's right.' He moved restlessly and Olivia got up to plump up his pillows so he could be more comfortable. It was late afternoon and rays from the setting sun were creeping in through the veranda doors and giving a gilded outline to the bed and the lovely old pieces of furniture in the high-ceilinged room. The clock-clocking of a couple of guinea fowl could be heard as they rustled amongst flowering shrubs below the wooden veranda. And Olivia herself was gilded by the rays of the sun.

He studied her, taking in the fair, flyaway hair escaping from the knot at the back of her head and worn with a fringe, the clear-cut sweep of her jaw and slender neck, her grey eyes and creamy skin, her capable hands and outfit of red and cream checked shirt and long khaki trousers. And something crossed those blue eyes although she couldn't read it.

He said, 'Could you tell me a bit more about yourself and this place?'

'If you drink all of this first.' She picked up a glass from the bedside table and offered it to him.

He wrinkled his brow. 'It tastes awful!'

'It's an electrolyte solution to replace all the minerals and salts you lost—look at it this way, you could be hooked up to a drip instead.'

'And you *should* have been a nurse,' he countered with a wicked little glint in his eye.

'Take it or leave it!' she said, but with a grin.

He drank the lot and pulled a face.

Olivia sat down again. 'Well, I'm Olivia Lockhart and you're on Wattle Creek Station. My uncle owns it—he's overseas at the moment—but I've lived here all my life and I help to run it—'

'How old are you?'

'Twenty-five—and we breed—'

He broke in again, with a frown this time. 'Haven't you done anything else? I must say you don't look like the essential jillaroo.'

'Nevertheless I am.' She paused and eyed him.

'What?' he asked gravely but with his eyes laughing at her.

'I just wondered whether you were going to keep interrupting me, Mr...well...whatever your name is.'

'We might have to invent one for the time being. I don't really relish being cast as the man with no name,' he said whimsically.

Olivia considered. 'How would it be if I called you...well, you could have a choice—Tom, Dick or Harry?'

He looked hurt. 'Surely you can do better than that—that would *really* make me feel like a stray mongrel!'

She laughed then sobered. 'Have you *no*...? No, strike that, I—'

'No idea? I really don't,' he said pensively, 'and it's a bloody awful feeling if you must know.'

'Don't strain yourself,' Olivia said contritely. 'I'm

sure it's better to let it come naturally and you're right, I can do better than Tom, Dick or Harry. I'll start at the top of the alphabet,' she said humorously. 'Let's see. Adam, Adrian, Alexander—you couldn't feel like a stray with that name, uh—Arnold, Alfred—'

'Hang on,' he said abruptly. 'Arnold—you know I do believe my name is Benedict…Ben…Ben…' But nothing else came and he swore and collapsed against the pillows.

'That's terrific,' Olivia enthused. 'It shows your memory is coming back. Ben, short for Benedict! But you just relax now,' she ordered.

'Yes, ma'am,' he murmured wryly. 'If you go on telling me about yourself.'

'There's not a lot more to tell—'

'There must be,' he interrupted. 'How come you're not all dry and crinkled?'

'I…' Olivia paused and discovered she felt self-conscious as that blue gaze roamed her face and figure again then came back to her face. 'I've always taken good care of my skin—' she shrugged '—used sun-block and a hat, long sleeves et cetera. My mother used to do the same. But—' her lips curved '—I'm as tough as any other jillaroo underneath it.'

'And you haven't ever done anything else?' he queried.

'Yes, and I still do.' She folded her hands but didn't elaborate.

'If you don't tell me,' he murmured, 'I'll get all hot and bothered again.'

She looked at him narrowly. 'I've got the feeling

you're a genius at getting your own way, Benedict Arnold—that's something you don't seem to have forgotten.'

But he only gazed at her innocently.

She sighed. 'Heaven knows why it's of any interest—'

'It's not every day I get nursed by someone as attractive as you, Olivia Lockhart.'

She bit her lip then saw that glint of wicked amusement in his eyes again. 'OK. I spent three years at university doing an arts course and I paint and design greeting cards if you must know. I've also all but restored Wattle Creek homestead—' she looked around '—to its former glory. I'm passionate about old homes and old things. That's all there is to it. Satisfied, Ben?' she asked laconically.

'No. But certainly interested—what kind of greeting cards?'

'Ones with outback scenes on them or the local flora and fauna; those kind.'

'I'm impressed,' he said. 'You seem to live a very useful and productive life. Is there a Mr Olivia Lockhart?' His gaze strayed to her bare left hand. 'Ah, I see not, unless you don't wear your ring all the time.'

'There is no Mr Olivia Lockhart,' Olivia said coolly, and stopped as whispers and footsteps made themselves heard on the veranda. She listened for a moment then stood up and regarded her patient a little maliciously. 'But I'm sure you wouldn't mind reassuring those who found you that you're not dead.

I'm told that when they poked you with a stick you didn't respond so they thought you were.'

An inward tremor of laughter shook her as she saw his eyes almost cross at this revelation. Then she said, 'Come in, Ryan and Sonia! This is Ben.'

The twins tiptoed in and came to the bedside.

'Glory be,' the man called Ben said, 'what have we here? A case of double trouble if ever I saw one.'

'You're not wrong,' Olivia murmured.

'They're not yours, are they?'

'No. Their parents work on the property.'

'He can talk,' Ryan said to Sonia. 'You couldn't talk when we found you,' he said reproachfully to Ben.

'We thought you were dead!' Sonia added. 'You frightened six months out of us.'

'I do apologize. I must have knocked myself out somehow or other. But I'm very grateful you found me, extremely grateful.'

The twins looked gratified and Ryan said, 'That means we won't get a belting for being in the horse paddock. Doesn't it, Livvie?' He turned to Olivia for reassurance.

'Ryan, you know very well you don't get belted. Your dad just worries about your safety. There could be snakes, anything out there.'

'He can make it feel like a belting even if he doesn't do it, Livvie,' Sonia said earnestly. 'He can make you feel this high.' She demonstrated a distance of about an inch between her thumb and forefinger.

'And that's why you take so much notice of him,' Olivia said sternly although she was trying not to laugh. 'But in this instance we'll forget about it. Off you go!'

'Bye, Mr Ben!' they chorused, and scampered out.

'This paddock with the snakes and—anything in it; how do you think I got there?' Ben asked perplexedly.

'The only thing I can think of is that you rode over from a neighbouring property and your horse—' she shrugged '—got a fright and threw you then bolted home.'

'I've never been thrown by a horse in my life—well, not since I was ten!'

'How do you know?' Olivia asked.

'I…just know,' he said frustratedly.

'But it can happen to anyone,' Olivia objected. 'I mean it *could* have been a snake. Anyway Jack, our station foreman, is making enquiries. He's also getting in touch with the police— Look, you don't look too well again. Why don't you rest?'

'I don't feel well!' He moved uncomfortably and his face contorted with pain.

'Then I'll give you one of these pills; it'll help—now don't make a fuss,' she recommended smoothly. 'I know men can be dreadful patients but it doesn't become you.'

Dark blue eyes stared into hers, angry dark blue eyes, and their owner said, 'Bloody hell—how old do you take me for, Olivia Lockhart?'

'Thirty-something? All the more reason to behave yourself.' She handed him the pill and poured some water into the glass from a jug and handed him that, and simply watched him calmly.

He hesitated then swallowed the pill with the help of the water.

'Good.' She took the glass back and indicated a little silver bell on the bedside table. 'I'm going to start dinner but if you need anything just ring that. Don't you dare get out of bed; is that understood?'

'I was wrong,' Ben said bitterly. 'You should have been a major-general.'

She smiled faintly and placed a cool hand on his forehead. 'Go to sleep, I'm sure things will look better when you wake up.'

He slept through dinner and beyond.

Jack Bentley came up as she was eating her meal at the kitchen table and she invited him to have coffee with her. 'Any news?' she asked as she took two cups and saucers down from the old-fashioned dresser.

'Not a skerrick. No one in the district seems to know him or have anyone unaccounted for. The police are making enquiries; I gave them a description—by the way, Livvie, there is one possibility that's of interest. They've had heavy rain in the next shire, a couple of inches in three hours, and there are a few roads cut. It could be that he got bogged, decided to walk somewhere and got bushed, but—'

'Oh, Jack,' she breathed, 'is it headed this way?'

'Sure is!' He nodded enthusiastically. 'There's a low pressure system that might just do the trick but—' he gestured '—you know how capricious they can be! Good rain fifty miles away doesn't mean it'll hit here although it will seep down eventually which is good news.'

'Let's hold thumbs.' Olivia poured some fragrant coffee from the yellow enamel pot that had been bubbling on the Aga. 'I was just lecturing all the kids about wasting water this afternoon.' She stopped and sighed. 'Another drought would be the last thing we need on top of, well, all else.'

'Low beef prices, currency fluctuations, you name it,' he said.

'Still, Wattle Creek has survived for a long time,' Olivia said, and brushed back her fringe.

'Uh-huh,' Jack murmured noncommittally. 'Doesn't get us much further forward with this bloke, though. How is he?'

'Out like a light—but he's OK. I've been checking his pulse regularly. He can remember his name—his first name anyway. It's Benedict.'

'Got the feeling it might be something fancy.'

'Oh. Did you?' Olivia looked a question at him over the rim of her cup.

'He sounded kinda upper class.' Jack shrugged.

She grimaced. 'I suppose so. He's also quite sure no horse would be game to throw him.'

Jack grinned. 'Cocky as well?'

'Rather sure of himself despite his lack of memory—yes, you could say so,' Olivia responded with a certain amount of feeling.

Jack raised an eyebrow. 'Need a hand? I can stay up here tonight.'

'No, but thanks all the same, Jack.' She stopped as the kitchen door swung and the curtains flapped. 'The wind is getting up.' She put her hands to the side of her head. 'Let's pray it's blowing that depression this way.'

Jack got up. 'I'd best get going then and check everything's tied down and covered up. See you in the morning, Livvie. Don't forget to give me a call if Mr Benedict gets to be a handful.'

Olivia did the dishes and tidied the kitchen.

It was a large, old-fashioned kitchen dominated by the huge old dresser with its colourful display of crockery. There was also a big table and a wooden airing rack suspended from the ceiling where she hung pots and baskets and upside-down bunches of flowers, herbs and leaves she was drying.

The walls were pale yellow, the curtains yellow with white daisies, and at the opposite end to the dresser there was a long narrow table against the wall upon which stood her collection of old implements, an old mincer, a wooden box grinder, a set of brass scales, old biscuit and other tins from a bygone era and her collection of blue and white Spode Regency plates. The floor was green-tiled and the ladder-backed chairs at the table had rush seats.

Although Wattle Creek homestead had other, more formal rooms, the kitchen was the nerve centre of the house.

Then she stepped outside and sniffed the air. It was definitely a restless night, and to her infinite satisfaction, clouds obscured the moon. She went back inside and did a tour through the old homestead, closing doors that led onto the verandas.

And she went to check her patient.

She'd left a lamp on in his room but shaded the bed side of it with a small towel. She could see that he was still asleep although it was a restless kind of sleep and she stared down at him thoughtfully. He wore a pair of her uncle's pyjamas but they were too short and too wide for him and were twisted and rucked around him—her uncle had a large girth, which this man did not, but there was nothing she could do about that. So she concentrated on his face with its lean lines, sunburnt skin and dark shadows on his jaw.

And she thought that he looked vulnerable in this uneasy sleep but, given the things he'd said, she had the feeling that vulnerable was not a state that normally applied to him. Yet, for some reason, she found that she was touched by this man, and she put a hand out and laid it gently on his brow.

He muttered unintelligibly then reached up and grasped her wrist and pulled her hand down to his mouth, and kissed her palm. At the same time his blue eyes fluttered open and he said, 'Sweetheart, I…' And stopped abruptly.

Olivia froze and tried to pull away but his fingers tightened on her wrist.

Then he released a breath and said, 'If it isn't Major-General Lockhart.'

'None other,' she replied tartly. 'Sorry to disappoint you.'

'I didn't say that. Can't think of anyone else I'd rather have soothing my fevered brow at the moment.'

'Will you let me go?'

'Have I offended you?' he countered.

'No… I mean, no, of course not.' She reclaimed her hand.

'You looked entirely disapproving, however,' he commented.

'Who knows how far you could have gone under the misapprehension I was a ''sweetheart'' of some kind?' she murmured dryly, and pulled a chair up. 'How do you feel?'

He studied her enigmatically for a moment and ignored the question. 'Ever been a ''sweetheart'' of any kind, Olivia?'

'That's none of your business,' she said evenly. 'Let's just concentrate on how you are.'

He raised an eyebrow. 'Do I detect a reservation on the subject of your love life? As if it mightn't have been that pleasurable an experience?'

Olivia breathed exasperatedly. 'Look, you may as well be the man in the moon for all I know—you don't, surely, expect me to tell you my life story!'

'I may as well be the man in the moon for all *I* know,' he said with a sudden frown. But added with a wry twist of his lips, 'It would help to pass the time.'

'Then you're destined to be disappointed—I have no intention of passing the time that way with you. Will you tell me how you *are* or will I get Jack Bentley up to take over from me?'

'The man who wasn't the doctor?'

'None other,' she said sweetly. 'He's our station foreman and I can assure you he has a heart of gold but–' she gestured '—well, he's very good at roping and throwing calves, I'm just not sure how gentle he is with patients.'

'You wouldn't do that to me, would you, Olivia?' He looked at her reproachfully.

'I most certainly would. So just get your mind off my love life, Mr Benedict Arnold, and tell me how you are!'

He laughed softly. 'Yes, ma'am. Apologies, ma'am! You know, I don't know about Benedict Arnold; he was a traitor if you care to recall.'

'It's not my fault your first name is Benedict,' she retorted, and went to stand up.

'Uh—how am I?' he said hastily. 'Slightly better in some areas than when I reported to you last. My headache has eased a bit and I even appear to be a bit hungry.'

She sank back. 'That's good. I kept some dinner for you. Thirsty?'

'Uh—yes,' he said cautiously. 'However, that presents another problem.'

'I don't think so, you should be thirsty—'

'On the other hand, the copious amounts of liquid you've forced down me have made me highly uncomfortable in another area, I regret to say. May I get up?'

'Oh, that,' Olivia said matter-of-factly. 'No, you may not. I'll—'

'Olivia, I have to tell you that I may be the man from the moon but I do have some modesty—you could be the woman from the moon for all I know.'

'I have no intention of making you blush,' Olivia said with a wicked little glint of her own. 'But the doctor warned me not to let you get up too soon because if you black out I will have the devil's own job to get you back to bed—apart from any further injury you may do to yourself.'

'I see.' The man called Ben eyed her with suspicion. 'So what do you suggest?'

'That I bring you a receptacle, then retire discreetly,' she answered serenely.

'How very practical,' he murmured.

'I told you—well, I didn't go into details, but I did do an extensive first-aid course while I was at university because it's so handy when you live beyond the black stump. I even had hospital experience as a nursing aide.'

'I see,' he said again.

'What now?' she enquired as his eyes lingered on her thoughtfully.

'Nothing. Other than a reinforcement of my earlier sentiment on how useful and productive a person you are. So, I don't have to worry about outraging *your* maidenly modesty?'

'No.'

'That *was* another reason for my reticence—'

'Can I tell you something?' Olivia interrupted, and proceeded to do so. 'You talk too much. Heaven alone knows what you're like when you're fully fit!' And she walked out.

Half an hour later, she brought him a light meal.

He struggled to sit up and she put some more pillows behind him. 'I'm as weak as a kitten,' he said with considerable irritation.

'Some food will help. There's soup and a ragout of chicken.' She lifted the covers off the two dishes.

'Mmm.' He inhaled with evident pleasure. 'I guess cooking is another of your skills.'

'A lot of people cook,' she responded, and handed him a napkin.

'Tell me a bit more about Wattle—Creek, is it?'

Olivia hesitated then sat down beside the bed. 'Yes, well, it's been in the Lockhart family for a hundred years. My uncle runs it now; my father was his brother but he and my mother were killed in a car accident when I was twelve.'

'Do you have a share in it?'

Olivia hesitated again then thought that this had to be better than discussing her love life with a perfect stranger. 'Yes, but my father was a younger brother so my uncle has the controlling share.'

'Central Queensland,' Ben said musingly. 'I've got the feeling I know a lot about it but I can't think why. So…' he paused and turned his attention to the chicken '…in a hundred years I imagine Wattle Creek has had its fair share of drought, flood, pestilence, fire—as well as the good times?'

'It's survived,' Olivia said with simple pride, 'and will go on surviving.'

He lifted his blue gaze to her and frowned. 'Sometimes it can be a whole new ball game; things change,' he said slowly.

'I'm sure they can,' she conceded, 'but we Lockharts are a tough bunch.'

'Tell me a bit more about your uncle. Does he have an heir?'

'Yes, me at the moment,' she said, and grinned. 'He never married. He's a crusty old curmudgeon when he wants to be but I love him dearly.'

'There won't be a Lockhart to carry on the family name?'

She shrugged. 'Not unless I can persuade any future husband of mine to change his name, no. But there'll still be Lockhart blood in our children.'

'Would you do that?' he asked curiously.

'What?'

'Get a future husband to change his name?'

She regarded him gravely. 'Why not?'

'It seems an extreme length to go to—family pride can be, well, too much of it can be dangerous.'

'You say that because you're a man.'

He looked at her quizzically. 'And you could get a reputation for wearing the pants.'

'I probably have that reputation already,' she said prosaically.

He raised an eyebrow. 'You don't mind?'

She smiled coolly at him but reflected inwardly that, while it had never crossed her mind to ask a future husband to change his name until this man had suspected it of her, the lack of a man in her life could just have something to do with an unfeminine, no doubt, unwillingness to have to rely on any man.

'What does that mean?' he queried.

'I—' she shrugged '—like being independent.'

'I believe you.'

Her lips twitched. 'I wouldn't be surprised if you're extremely independent.'

He looked comically surprised. 'What makes you say that?'

'I don't know.' She wrinkled her brow. 'Just a feeling I get, that's all. Perhaps it's because you're so sure no horse would be game enough to throw you.'

He pushed his plate away and lay back against the pillows. 'I've got the feeling you could be right.'

'As well as being a right handful,' Olivia commented.

'I'm sure I don't know what gave you that impression!'

She laughed. 'You don't fool me for a moment, Ben.'

'I wasn't aware that I was trying to but I shall remember that for future reference,' he said ruefully.

'Like a cup of coffee—or perhaps you ought to have tea? Coffee might keep you awake.'

'No, thanks; I don't drink either.'

Olivia raised an eyebrow.

'Don't ask me how I know,' he said frustratedly, 'I just do.'

'I wasn't—going to ask you that. It just seems strange. Do you remember what you do drink?'

'Well, I don't think I'm a teetotaller; a nice cold beer wouldn't go astray—'

'No chance,' she said.

'You are? A teetotaller? Is this a dry establishment?' he asked with some foreboding.

'Not at all. But beer is a diuretic and since we're trying to achieve the opposite it's out of the question. How about a long cold glass of milk?'

'Now that,' he said slowly, 'sounds lovely.'

Olivia regarded him with a mixture of amusement and wryness. 'You're a bundle of surprises, Ben!' She got up, took the tray and went to get him a glass of milk.

'What now?' he asked when he'd finished it.

'Sleep,' she said promptly. 'I don't know about you but I've been up since the crack of dawn—' She stopped and raised her head. 'Was that thunder?'

'It sounded like it.'

'Glory be—and rain!' She walked to the veranda door and peered outside. Big droplets were pattering on the tin roof.

'You need rain?'

She turned back to him. 'Desperately if we're to have a good season. Our dams and creeks are drying up, the feed in the paddocks is withering—oh, do we need rain.'

He looked at her narrowly and seemed about to say something then appeared to change his mind. At least his manner changed and he said lightly, 'Perhaps I've brought you good luck, Olivia.'

She grimaced. 'Perhaps you have, Ben. OK—is there anything else I can do for you? If you're not feeling sleepy would you like to read for a while or—'

'No, thanks.' He yawned suddenly and lay back against the pillows. 'Heaven knows why but I feel extremely sleepy.'

'Good. Now, I'm just next door and I'll leave my door open so don't hesitate to call or ring your bell if you have any problems. Goodnight.'

'Goodnight, Florence Nightingale,' he murmured, but when she looked fleetingly annoyed he said,

'Don't be cross, Olivia. I think you're magnificent and I'm extremely grateful to you.'

She hesitated then walked out with a faint shrug.

She had a shower and sat at her dressing table to brush her hair in a thoughtful, slightly keyed-up mood although she wasn't sure why she should be keyed up. Unless, she mused, it's the wonderful sound of good, heavy rain on the roof?

She put her silver-backed brush down and looked around her bedroom. It had been her parents' bedroom so the bed was double and had lovely curved, cherry-wood ends. The walls were papered in blue and white, a delicate tracery of blue tendrils and flowers on a white background, and the bedspread and curtains matched. She'd found and restored a cherry-wood dressing table with a cheval-mirror and there was a marvellous tallboy chest of drawers.

The carpet was sapphire-blue and there were framed miniatures on the walls that she'd painted herself, framed photos, some of them sepia with age, and a collection of silver and glass perfume bottles on the tallboy. Two big pillows covered in Battenberg lace sat at the head of the bed.

But her bedroom didn't afford her the usual satisfaction and she turned back to the mirror with a sigh. Be honest, Livvie, she told herself. It was the look in his eye when he told you you were magnificent that's caused you to feel keyed up.

She grimaced at her reflection but it didn't alter the distinct impression she'd got that he hadn't been alluding to her nursing skills when he'd said it.

Somehow or other he'd managed to combine a tribute to her face and figure in that lazy blue glance.

She looked down at her hands then forced herself to study herself in the mirror.

True, her skin was good, the colour of her hair was like ripe wheat, her grey eyes were clear, her lashes long and dark-tipped, her neck long and her figure lithe and trim. True, when she took the trouble, she could look elegant and—someone had once told her—refined. But she'd never considered herself especially attractive. And she rarely bothered to dress up… Always too busy doing something else, she reflected with a spark of amusement.

But she sobered almost immediately. And nearly always too busy to worry much about men, she added to herself. So *why* should a perfect stranger suddenly produce this reaction?

Anyway, how dare he, when all he can remember is his first name, be sending me those kind of looks?

She got up and smoothed her navy pyjamas piped with white, and got into bed. Think about the rain, she commanded herself. Don't let it stop too soon—if the power of thought can do it!

CHAPTER TWO

A COUPLE of hours later she was woken by a crash.

She flew out of bed and saw light flood into the passage from the guest bedroom. 'Don't tell me you've fallen out of bed,' she muttered, and raced into the next room.

But Ben was sitting up dazedly in bed with his hand still on the lamp switch—and the cause of the crash became obvious. One of the veranda doors was swinging dementedly as rain blew into the room.

'Damn! I mustn't have closed it properly when I looked out earlier.' She ran across the room and with an effort pushed the door closed against the wind and latched it. 'Sorry.' She turned to the bed and shook raindrops off herself. 'That's probably the last thing you needed—things that go bang in the night.'

'I...' he lay back '...couldn't work out where the hell I was. That's quite a storm.'

'Yes. I just hope it's not all talk—you all right? You look pale.' She stood beside the bed and frowned down at him.

'I'm OK—well, relatively.'

'How about—how about a nip of brandy? I think I could do with one myself. I thought the roof was falling in.'

'What a fine suggestion, Olivia.'

So she got two nips in crystal tumblers and sat down beside the bed.

'Storms don't bother you?' he queried.

'No.' She took a sip of brandy. 'I like them.'

'Silly question,' he murmured.

'Do they bother you?' Olivia asked.

'Contrary to all manly norms, they do a bit. I once saw a bolt of lightning strike a horse and I've never been the same since. Although I don't have to scuttle under beds these days.'

Olivia laughed. 'I don't believe you.'

'You should.'

'Where was this horse?'

He screwed up his face. 'I can't remember but—'

'Don't try,' she said immediately. 'Sorry I asked. Have some brandy instead.'

He looked at her ruefully then his eyes changed. 'There is one thing better than scuttling under a bed in a storm.'

'What's that?'

'Having someone *in* bed with you who you can cuddle up to.'

Olivia blinked, and in the pause that developed as his gaze roamed over her navy pyjamas and her loose hair she was astounded to have a clear image in her mind of—just that. She swallowed and coughed. 'You—you're an incredibly quick worker, Benedict Arnold!'

'Seize the moment—someone said. I think it would be rather nice. Might just get me off to sleep again, which isn't going to happen otherwise,' he added pointedly.

'Oh, yes, it is. I'll give you another of those pills.'

'Dear Olivia, don't do that to me,' he said plaintively. 'I hate being drugged. You have no idea how lousy you feel when you wake out of it.'

'Well, I'm certainly not getting into bed with you—you must be mad,' she said helplessly.

He smiled slightly and although his scratches were visible, his lips dry and cracked, and despite the dark shadows on his jaw, it was, Olivia found herself thinking, one of the most arresting, vital faces she'd ever seen.

He said, 'Considering that I am wounded, that I've lost my memory and hate storms—' he winced at a crack of thunder '—could you stay and talk to me for just a bit? You do look thoroughly wide awake yourself.'

'I—' She bit her lip and contemplated that she was thoroughly wide awake, as well as thinking how awful it might be to be lying awake in the dark wondering who you were. 'All right. Just for a bit, though. I'll go and get a dressing gown.'

'To curb any further improper suggestions I might make?' he queried gravely.

'Because I'm cold, but that too,' she retorted, and marched out.

She came back wearing a white terry towelling robe and with socks on and a tartan rug over her arm. She pulled a more comfortable armchair up to the bed, and a footstool, stretched herself out and put the rug over her. Then she picked up her brandy and said, 'Sure you're warm enough?'

'Quite, thank you,' he said politely.

'What shall we talk about?'

'Well, there's nothing I can tell you about me so it will have to be you.'

'I've told you all I intend to tell you about me.' Olivia shot him a cutting little grey glance.

'Not even in general terms?' he said. 'Your ambitions, your plans—unless they *are* all bound up with Wattle Creek?'

She sighed and laid her head back. 'You don't have to make it sound so…limited.'

'Did I? My apologies. How old did you say you were, Olivia?'

'Twenty-five. What's that got to do with anything?'

'Nothing *per se* but isn't it about time you thought of providing those heirs for Wattle Creek?'

'You don't need to concern yourself along those lines, Ben.' She studied the amber liquid in the crystal glass then raised her grey eyes to his. 'In fact I find it insufferably prying of you.'

He shrugged but wasn't noticeably dashed. 'Have you ever thought, has it ever occurred to you that men might see you quite differently from how you see yourself?'

Olivia frowned. 'I don't know what you mean.'

'Well, a lot of women don't realize just what men see in them.'

'If I knew what this was leading to I might be able to agree or disagree,' she said humorously. 'But if you're expecting me to ask you how you see me it doesn't bother me one way or the other.'

'No,' he mused. 'Far too independent for that but

I'll tell you anyway. I see a girl a man could take seriously—provided he could ever get to first base. And…' he paused and looked at her with his lips twitching '…for heirs to ensue one needs to do that at least.'

'How do you know no one has done just that?'

'Have they?' He looked at her alertly.

Olivia finished her brandy. 'That's personal not general, Ben.'

'You brought it up!'

'Only because you led me into it— Look,' she said goadedly, 'I'll tell you what I feel then perhaps we can get some relief from this subject! Love is *fine*. I've fallen in love a couple of times and it was—all the things it should be. Except that it didn't last and that was without the pressures of marriage, children and so on. Or the pressure of a bossy boots like me,' she added blithely.

He grinned. But a moment later he said soberly, 'If you ever lost Wattle Creek, though—and these things can happen—what would you do with your life?'

'I'd fight tooth and nail *not* to lose Wattle Creek,' she responded tartly. 'They'd have to drag me off kicking and screaming!' She grimaced. 'But if they did manage to achieve it I've always got my painting and—who knows? I could take up nursing impossibly curious amnesia victims.'

'Thank you,' he murmured.

She gazed at him, opened her mouth then closed it.

'Do tell me, Olivia.' He looked amused.

'I shouldn't really but I couldn't help wondering

whether, amongst the things you *do* remember, there is an attitude towards love and marriage?'

He drained his glass, set it on the table and slipped down the pillows. 'I think it's a fine institution in general. Like you, though, I tend to wonder how the spark stays in it under all the pressures you mentioned, but that could be because neither of us has really fallen in love yet.'

'So you don't think you could be married?'

'I have…no recollection of a wife.' He paused and frowned.

'I keep doing it,' Olivia said contritely. 'Look, I'm sure by tomorrow—well, today—the police will come up with who you are.'

'Let's hope so. In general terms, though, what kind of a wife do you think you'd make?'

'I have no idea—what kind of a husband do you think you'd make?'

'I think I'd be rather good at it,' he said pensively. 'I'm house-trained, I like children and I like women—'

'Not more than one at a time, I hope. That wouldn't make you a good husband.'

'Well, all this is on the basis of having found the *right* one, naturally, but when I say I like women I mean that their little foibles don't irritate me unduly.'

'Such as?' Olivia asked ominously but the glint of laughter in her grey eyes gave her away.

'Their preoccupation with clothes for example. Women are much nicer when they've got the right things to wear and their hair is to their satisfaction et cetera for all that they may not understand the basics are what men still see.'

'Do you know, Benedict Arnold, that's a very superior attitude?'

He grinned. 'It's also a wise one, Olivia Lockhart. So, all in all, *I* think I'd make a nice husband.'

'Your faith in yourself is monumental. *I* think you'd make a real handful of a husband, Ben.'

'I don't know why you persist with this "handful" tag,' he murmured.

'Call it feminine intuition,' she said wryly. 'Not all of us are so taken up with clothes et cetera that we can't see past the end of our noses.'

He looked thoughtful. 'Is there anything about men that drives you mad?'

'I—' she paused '—get on very well with men as it happens.'

'That could be because you're not one of those ultra-feminine women.'

For a moment her expression defied description then she started to laugh. 'Many would take exception to that remark, Ben.'

'Let me explain—'

'I think it would be a good idea—you are a bit dependent on my goodwill at the moment, you know.'

'Well, there are women you can only think of in terms of having sex with. I mean to say you really can't find a lot to talk to them about—'

'What you *really* shouldn't do is go to bed with women you can't talk to, Ben. There are some very unkind labels for that kind of man.'

'Unfortunately it's one of the hazards of being a

man, Olivia,' he countered wickedly. 'A predisposition to think along those lines. However, what I was trying to say is that you very obviously have a mind of your own that would be interesting to explore and you don't give off vibes of being sultry and seductive, which is quite a relief, and all in all, as I said earlier, you're a woman a man could take seriously in a variety of ways. Which is to say in bed and out of it.'

She regarded him fixedly for a time. Then she blinked and said, 'You've only known me for a matter of hours!'

'If there's one good thing to be said for having a blank mind it's that it's very receptive to new impressions.'

'And you don't have any qualms about making these kind of declarations to a complete stranger? Don't answer; that was a rhetorical question.'

He grinned. 'Oh, well, Olivia, I've got the feeling I'm not one for beating about the bush.'

'So have I,' she said dryly. 'But here's something for you to think about—any more of this kind of talk and I'll go to bed.'

'Right. Tell me what kind of cattle you breed, how many head you run, what the acreage of Wattle Creek is, capacity, et cetera.'

She opened her mouth but his expression was grave and polite. Her lips twisted, then curved into a reluctant smile. 'Don't think you fool me for a moment but—you asked for it.'

'I'm really interested,' he protested.

Olivia drained the last of her brandy, laid her head back, and started to tell him.

He asked some surprisingly intelligent questions along the way until Olivia was moved to say, 'I think you may know something about this business, Ben.'

'I think I may,' he responded. 'Why and wherefore is another matter.' He stopped and yawned.

'Good time to go to sleep,' she suggested.

'Are you going to abandon me?'

She studied him then said, 'There is something you may not know about me.'

He lifted a sleepy eyebrow.

'I sing,' she said. 'How would it be if I sang you to sleep?'

A look of wariness descended across his expression that made her want to laugh. 'I'll do it very quietly,' she assured him, and started off. '"Git along, little dogie..."'

Her voice was clear and soft and as she sang that old cowboy song she saw him look surprised then relax and within minutes he was asleep.

She contemplated getting up, switching off the lamp and going to bed but discovered she was quite comfortable and feeling sleepy herself. I'll do it in a few minutes, when he's properly asleep, she thought—and that's the last thing she remembered.

It was Jack Bentley who woke them the next morning.

'Livvie—oh, there you are!'

Olivia struggled up in the armchair and Ben opened his eyes.

'What's the problem, Livvie?' Jack asked anxiously, coming into the room and looking at her bewilderedly. 'Has he had—is there…are you OK, mate?' He turned to Ben.

Olivia stood up and stretched. 'He's fine, Jack. Well, he was last night, just couldn't sleep so I kept him company for a while. Any news? Glory be, it's still raining!'

'Not only that but it's flooding,' Jack said. 'We're going to have to move a bit of stock about.'

'Any other news?' Ben said, sitting up with a contorted expression as if he had any number of aches and pains.

'Well, mate, if it means anything to you, there's a flap on about a bloke who went missing in his light aircraft—think it could be you?'

Olivia gasped.

Whereas Ben said slowly, 'Bloody hell. So that's what happened. Yes, I remember now. I had to make an emergency landing in the middle of nowhere; the fuel pump seemed to have gone on the blink. But…but…'

'So the name Bradshaw doesn't mean anything to you?' Jack asked acutely.

'Bradshaw. Bradshaw,' Ben said slowly, and that frown Olivia was coming to know well creased his brow.

'Never mind, it'll come,' she said comfortingly, and turned to Jack with more urgency. 'Just let me get dressed and I'll— Jack, would you mind helping Ben with whatever he needs at the moment? I'll call the police and let them know he's safe and sound. Then we can have a conference.' She gathered up the rug and padded out of the room.

Jack Bentley and Ben Bradshaw watched her go then looked at each other ruefully.

'That is one very capable lady,' Ben said.

'You're not wrong, mate. And very much esteemed on Wattle Creek,' he added with a suddenly straight glance.

'I...get the picture,' Ben Bradshaw said slowly.

'Yep, wouldn't do to try and take advantage of her.'

The patient raised an eyebrow. 'I don't think there's any danger of that; she seems to have her feet firmly planted on the ground.'

'Maybe. Just thought I'd pass it on,' Jack said urbanely. 'So your memory's coming back? Any idea where you made this emergency landing? Not that there's a lot we can do at the moment.'

Ben lay back. 'Not only did the fuel pump pack up but I had a complete electrical failure, so my GPS lost power, and the radio. I do remember hiking for bloody hours. That's right, I'd flown over the homestead a couple of hours earlier so I set off in the direction I remembered it to be in. South-east, so the plane should be north-west of here roughly.'

'Can you remember why you were flying in these parts?'

'I—' But he broke off as Olivia came in. She was dressed in jodhpurs, an oilskin jacket and had a broad-brimmed hat in her hands.

'Ben, you took off from Longreach yesterday morning and you filed a flight plan to return to Longreach in the afternoon. The authorities are getting in touch with your next of kin or whatever but it looks as if you might be stuck with us for a day or two. There's extensive flooding, roads are impassable and telephone lines are cut everywhere and people are stranded, our airstrip is under water and our only form of communication at the moment is the satellite phone.'

'I see. I—'

But Olivia swept on. 'How do you feel?' And she reached for his wrist to check his pulse against her watch.

'A lot better other than a few stiff muscles.'

'No severe headaches, double vision or nausea?' She watched him narrowly as he shook his head, and presented him with a thermometer. 'Open up.'

He did so ruefully.

'No internal pains, no waterworks problems?'

He shook his head again and she pinched the skin of his forearm, appeared satisfied with the result and gently removed the dressing over the stitches on his temple. 'Good,' she said briskly, and applied a fresh one. Then she removed the thermometer and murmured, 'Pretty normal. All the same, stay in bed.'

'Oh, I—'

'Just do as you're told, Benedict Arnold,' Olivia recommended. 'I'm going to have to leave you for a few hours but I'm putting you on your honour. Kay, Jack's wife, is coming up to cook you breakfast and so on—don't give her any trouble. And the flying doctor is going to ring so you can tell him exactly how you feel and how your memory is coming back.'

'Yes, ma'am!' Ben replied, and for some reason cast Jack a bitter little glance.

'What's that supposed to mean?' she enquired.

'Nothing...' They said it together but Jack looked amused.

'Ready, then, Jack?'

'Whenever you are, Livvie.'

They walked out together and Ben Bradshaw watched them go then shook his head somewhat bemusedly. A homely face presently intruded upon his reflections and Kay Bentley came into the room with his breakfast.

It was four-thirty in the afternoon before Olivia returned to the homestead. It was still pouring.

'How is he?' she asked Kay as she came wearily and wetly into the kitchen.

'Good as gold,' Kay said. 'He's been dozing quite a lot but the flying doctor said he could get up later—by the way, Livvie, the satellite phone dropped out.'

Olivia swore beneath her breath.

'I took it down to Davo; he said he'd try and fix it—but he's a lovely man—Ben, I mean,' Kay continued enthusiastically. 'Really grateful with beautiful manners and he made me laugh too.'

'He obviously didn't—' Olivia broke off. Suggest you go to bed with him, she'd been going to say, but thought better of it.

'And I went down and got some of Graham's clothes for him,' Kay continued. Graham was their twenty-year-old son. 'Your uncle's things are miles too wide and short for him,' she added with a chuckle.

'That was kind of you, Kay.' Olivia sat down at the kitchen table. 'You wouldn't believe it but yesterday I was worried about a drought; now I'm worried about too much rain.'

'It's always either a feast or a famine on the land but it can't do any harm in the long run,' Kay offered.

'No, but half-drowned stock in the short term is a problem.'

'I'll make you a cuppa. Eaten anything today?'

Olivia roused herself. 'Not a lot. A bite of breakfast in passing.'

Kay got busy immediately and shortly a cup of tea and plate of cheese and tomato sandwiches were set in front of Olivia.

'Thanks, Kay, you're a brick.'

'I also made you a casserole for dinner. You just need to heat it up. When is your uncle due back?'

'Not for a week. Still, I'm sure we can cope—you wouldn't believe the wretched phone going on the blink!'

'Why don't you relax for a while?' Kay said sympathetically. 'I can hold the fort for an hour or so.'

'I think I'll do just that!'

She didn't actually rest but she had a long hot bath and changed into slim black trousers and a rich tawny shirt with long sleeves. She put her hair up in a knot and thought about trimming her fringe but couldn't be bothered. Then she remembered Ben Bradshaw and as well as smoothing moisturizer into her skin she put on some frosted, bronzey lipstick.

I must be mad, she thought, with a slight smile. What am I trying to do? Prove that I'm not all sober, serious and unseductive?

But he wasn't in the guest bedroom and she found him seated alone at the kitchen table.

'Are you sure—?' she started to say.

'Quite sure,' he broke in, and got up. 'I even have the blessing of the doctor.'

'So Kay said,' she murmured, and studied him. He wore a pair of navy blue jeans and a blue and white checked shirt. His thick, dark hair was brushed and he'd shaved although rather sketchily because of the stitches and scratches on his face. His sunburn was fading.

'You look tired,' he commented.

She grimaced. 'A day in the saddle on top of a broken night can do that to you but I'll be fine.'

'I feel guilty—I not only kept you up but I seem to have brought you too much rain.'

'Time will tell.' She moved past him. 'Country life is a bit like that—either a feast or a famine, as Kay remarked earlier. The problem is there has been rain to the north and although it kept missing us it was flowing into the channels and creeping down towards us. That's why this downpour has caused them to flood.'

'Banjo Paterson country.'

'Yes.' She pulled out a chair. 'But tell me about your day.'

'I didn't accomplish much,' he said ruefully. 'I spoke to the flying doctor then the police but the satellite phone dropped out at that point, I'm sorry to have to tell you, Olivia.'

'So Kay said.' Olivia grimaced. 'It never rains but pours but Davo, our resident mechanic, is a bit of a genius so here's hoping he can fix it. Did you get the chance to find out anything from the police?'

'Well, yes. I am Ben Bradshaw, I work for a pastoralist company, I'm thirty-three, I was on my way to Campbell Downs and I'm based at Charleville.'

Olivia stared at him then got up and took a bottle of wine from the fridge and got two glasses out. 'Congratulations! So there is no fog any more?'

He frowned. 'There are still blank patches but it's starting to get clearer.'

'Thank goodness.' She handed him a corkscrew. 'You do drink wine, don't you?'

'I do.'

'Open that, then, and I'll just pop Kay's casserole in the oven.' She opened the Aga oven with a padded glove and slid the dish in.

'What about family and friends?' she asked as she sat down again and accepted a glass of golden chardonnay from him. 'Cheers, by the way. You're lucky you weren't killed, one way or another.'

'Cheers. And many thanks,' he responded.

'So?'

He raised an eyebrow at her.

'Family and friends,' she reminded him wryly.

'My next of kin, they tell me, is my mother and she's overseas—I remember her—but I guess they'll get in touch with anyone else who might need reassuring—that was when the phone cut out.'

'So you don't have a wife?'

'Apparently not.' But his eyes were amused. 'Why do you ask?'

'She might be horrified to know how your mind works under the influence of temporary amnesia.'

'I didn't think I was that bad.'

It was her turn to look amused. 'You know very well you were.'

'Could be I took one look at you and was slayed, Olivia.'

'I doubt it. I'm twenty-five and I don't usually have that effect on men—as you took pains to explain why to me.'

He sat back and played with the stem of his wine-glass. Then he raised those deep blue eyes to hers. 'I think you look tired but lovely tonight.'

She felt herself colour and found herself speechless for a moment or two. Then she looked away and said, 'Thanks, but I'd rather you said no more.'

'All right. How many head of cattle did you have to move?'

They discussed the situation on the station in detail then the country in general and it took them through Kay's delicious beef and mushroom casserole. Then he asked if she'd show him the homestead.

'With pleasure,' she said warmly.

It was a rambling old house with a huge lounge and dining room separated by a graceful wooden arch. The walls were forest-green, the couches and chairs covered in ruby brocade and the round dining-room table was an early Australian antique. Gold-framed pictures hung on the walls, there was a magnificent grandfather clock and, above the fireplace, the portrait of a fair woman.

'My mother,' Olivia said sadly.

'That must have been dreadful.'

'It was.'

'You look a lot like her.'

'Thanks. But I remember thinking she was truly beautiful. This is my father.' She moved to a smaller portrait in the dining room. 'And this is my uncle Garth.'

'I would—uh—he looks like a tough customer.'

'He is. I could do with him right now.'

'Did you—? No, you couldn't have painted these.'

'No. But, apart from being too young, I'll tell you why when we get to my studio.'

He glanced at her then paused in the doorway to look back at the lovely room. 'You certainly have a knack for decorating.'

She shrugged. 'I had some lovely stuff to work with and you don't find rooms with these proportions so readily these days. This is the morning room, much more modern, and this—' she moved to another doorway '—is my studio. I glassed in a veranda, conservatory style, to give me plenty of light, not that you can appreciate it at the moment.'

In fact rain was beating heavily on the glass but the overhead light was strong and revealed an uncluttered room with a wooden floor, a big table and a couple of stools, a sink and two easels.

'You were going to tell me something,' he said as he wandered over to the easels.

'Ah, yes. For some reason I paint best in miniature. That's why greeting cards suit me so well.'

He turned to her. 'That's…curious.'

'I know. It's inexplicable actually. My mind's eye must have a miniaturizing effect on my brain.'

'But these are good.' He studied a small canvas resting on one easel and a sketch pad on the other. The canvas, in oils, was a scene of ghost gums on a creek bank, while the pad bore a delicate and faithful watercolour reproduction of a pink and grey galah on a branch. 'And this is accurate—are you a naturalist too?'

'In a way. I like to get them right.' She brushed back her fringe. 'I sometimes think that a hundred years ago that's what I might have been, you know, wandering around in a long white dress with a high neck and a cameo brooch, a big hat and a sketch pad.'

'I think that even a hundred years ago you'd have been too energetic for that.'

'Perhaps,' she conceded wryly. 'But ladies were expected to be ladies in those days.'

'I don't think there's much doubt that you're a lady, Olivia.'

She looked at him wryly. 'How can you tell?'

'Well—' he leant against a wall and folded his arms '—you have a certain born-to-command air—'

'You told me yesterday that could be misconstrued as a desire to wear the pants.'

'I've changed my mind about that. You do it—rather regally in fact. Then there's the way you handle impossibly curious, not to mention importuning strangers.'

'I don't know about that either,' Olivia commented ruefully. 'You got me to discuss things with you that

I would normally never dream of discussing with a strange man.'

'That could be because of the electricity between us,' he said idly, but went on before she could take issue. 'All the same, there was still a lot of reserve about you. And you paint, you decorate, you cook like a dream—'

'I didn't cook tonight. That was Kay.'

'But you did last night. Yes.' He straightened. 'I think I'd take you for a lady.'

'I— Some of the best cooks have been men,' she said, irrelevantly, she felt, but she was oddly breathless, she discovered. And unable to tear her gaze from his. But she forced herself to breathe evenly, and to respond more in kind. 'You—I don't know about being a gentleman—but you sound rather upper class, Ben.'

The faintest smile twisted his lips. 'Do I?'

'Yes. Jack was the first to notice it.'

She paused and studied him reflectively. 'But now I come to think of it, you sound very well educated, you speak refinedly and you certainly are quite unabashed by anything, even under the influence of temporary amnesia. That kind of self-possession is often associated with a privileged background. You're born and bred to it, in other words, even if you can't remember it.'

'My mother would be delighted to hear you say so, Olivia, but in fact my father was a blacksmith.'

She blinked.

He looked at her wickedly. 'I'm sorry if I've disappointed you—'

'Of course you haven't. I mean to say—' she heard herself sounding flustered and was sure she looked it '—it means nothing—Oh! Now I feel like a terrible snob which I'm *not*. How did you do this to me?'

He laughed and came to stand right in front of her. 'All *I* was trying to do was compliment you on your class, Olivia.'

'To make up for earlier telling me how unseductive I was,' she remarked dismally.

'That wasn't what I said at all; I'm sorry if I hit a nerve but I *meant* that there was a lot more to you.'

'Heaven alone knows why you should have hit a nerve,' she replied ruefully. 'I don't know you—'

'From a bar of soap,' he finished with a little glint of devilry in his eyes. 'Perhaps this is the reason.'

All he did was touch the back of his hand to her cheek but she was transfixed.

The uproar of the rain on the roof, the familiar setting of her studio, the cares of a cattle station all but under water faded and it was just the two of them standing in a pool of light. But that contact of his hand on her cheek was magnetic and seemed to transmit an awareness of all that was vital, attractive and tantalizing about Ben Bradshaw.

The intensity of it startled her so that her eyes widened because she could never before remember being so physically conscious of a man, so instantly attracted not only to the lean, lithe length of him and his broad shoulders but his wicked sense of humour and the odd little things that she'd learnt about him—that he liked milk, not tea or coffee, that he disliked thunderstorms, his insouciance when all he'd been able to remember was his first name.

Silly things really but for some reason they added up to produce a feeling of tenderness in her as well as the electricity that was sparking between them.

And she couldn't doubt that it was, as his blue gaze roamed down her tawny shirt then lingered on the hollows at the base of her throat. Because it was as if his long fingers were stroking her skin, touching secret, sensitive parts of her body, and it was as if the only relief from the sweet torture of it would be to be in his arms.

I don't believe this, she thought, but her heart was beating heavily under the tawny silk and her breasts started to tingle as his curiously heavy-lidded gaze rested on them. How can I be so aware of him? How can my body respond to a mere touch on my cheek and the way he's looking at me?

'No…' It was the barest whisper but he dropped his hand as she said it, and she moved a step backwards.

'I agree,' he said quietly.

Olivia blinked and swallowed and found her voice. '*What* do we agree about?'

'That we shouldn't rush into anything,' he murmured with some irony.

'Rush…I…you didn't expect…' She closed her mouth.

He raised a wry eyebrow. 'Didn't expect that, although it's what we both want, you would come to bed with me? No. Nor would I ask you. It could just get my face slapped,' he said gravely.

'Don't...don't joke about it,' she warned intensely.

He sobered. 'Then will you tell me what you would like to do, Olivia?'

She stared at him and brushed her fringe aside with her fingers. 'Nothing, Ben. Not until I get to know you better, at least, but I don't even know if that will happen.'

'Why not?'

'Well—' she looked at him a little helplessly '—we don't know whether our lives will run parallel at all.'

He narrowed his eyes. 'Do you mean whether my life will run parallel with Wattle Creek?'

She shrugged defensively. 'I am here and you are in Charleville.'

'That's not what I meant, Olivia, and I think you know it.'

'Ben—' she rubbed her eyes suddenly and shook her head '—I can't...please... This has sprung up out of nothing!'

He stared down at her inscrutably for a long moment then he touched her cheek again but this time it was the briefest touch of his fingers. 'Go to bed. But we *were* in agreement—about not rushing into anything.'

'I...yes. But I just can't go to bed like that. Anyway you should be the one—'

'What did you propose doing?'

'The dishes for one thing, closing up, turning out lights, and I was going to do the ironing—'

'You're not serious?'

'Well...' she hesitated and her shoulders slumped

'...perhaps not the ironing tonight; it could wait but the rest can't.'

'I can do all the rest.'

She opened her mouth then frowned. '*You're* not serious?'

'Perfectly. I told you I was house-trained.'

'I know but...' She trailed off.

'I've also spent most of the day *in* bed and I wouldn't be able to sleep yet. Whereas you are out on your feet. By the way, that's one thing I forgot to add to the list of your ladylike virtues: you sing too. Really well.'

She smiled suddenly. 'If you could have seen your face when I offered to.'

'You did take me by surprise,' he said ruefully.

'I certainly won't need any singing to sleep. Then—' she hesitated again '—if you're sure?'

'Quite sure I can cope with a few dishes and turning the lights out, Olivia.' He watched her with some irony.

She blushed unaccountably but recovered almost immediately. 'Goodnight, Mr Arnold, then,' she said humorously, and offered him her hand.

'Goodnight, Miss Lockhart,' he responded, and they shook hands.

'Don't do too much, though,' she warned. 'I'm sure one should treat a bump that caused even temporary amnesia with care.'

'I'm sure one should and I'll be very careful.'

He let her hand go and they stared at each other for a long moment. Until Olivia turned away.

CHAPTER THREE

SHE fell asleep almost immediately but woke at two in the morning. It was still raining.

The continuing rain didn't occupy her mind as she lay in her parents' bed beneath the blue and white coverlet; Ben Bradshaw did.

What kind of a man is he really? she wondered. I know I attributed his sang-froid to a privileged background but that's not necessarily the way it may be. Anyway, a privileged background is no guarantee of anything. But he is a charming, attractive stranger and the big question is—how indiscriminately does he use that charm? I'd hate to be one of a long line of conquests and his *modus operandi* has to be somewhat suspect—doesn't it?

She moved and frowned in the darkness. It was a long time, she realized, since she'd been attracted to a man. Two or three years, she decided, and thought ruefully that she could be in danger of becoming a dried-up old spinster, let alone a dried-up jillaroo.

Then it occurred to her that she still didn't know what Ben Bradshaw actually did other than work for a pastoral company, or why he should have been on his way to Campbell Downs—a huge, adjoining property, as it happened, that had been sold recently.

I don't know why I didn't think to ask more, she mused, and jumped as a knock sounded on her door.

She sat up, flicked on her lamp and pulled the bedclothes up to her throat. 'What is it?'

The door opened and Ben stood there. 'Olivia—'

'Oh, look here,' she broke in, 'this is too much! If, for no other reason than simple gratitude, you can't just leave me alone—'

'Olivia—' he advanced into the room '—if you think I've come to seduce you, you're wrong.'

'Well, what am I supposed to think?' she countered.

'I am fully dressed. I am also wet.'

She took all this in. His hair was plastered to his head and Graham's shirt and jeans were not only damp but muddy. 'So?' she said slowly.

'So seduction, I'm sorry to say, was the furthest thing from my mind.' He paused and his dark blue eyes swept over her with some irony.

Olivia released her stranglehold on the bedclothes and lowered them several inches but she tilted her chin at him with hauteur. 'What is the problem, then?'

He looked at her for a long moment with some cynical amusement clearly evident in his eyes. Then he said, 'Your roof is leaking, Miss Lockhart, ma'am. Right over my bed as it happens and, while I'm quite happy to move to another bed, I can't help wondering whether it's a good idea to let it go on leaking.'

Olivia gasped then tossed the bedclothes aside and sprang up. 'Why on earth didn't you say so sooner? Of course it's not a good idea to let it go on leaking, there are electrical wires—'

'You didn't give me the opportunity,' he murmured, and watched as she started to unbutton her pyjama top. Then he said with gentle satire, 'I think I'll leave you to dress on your own.'

'Here,' she said a few minutes later, and handed him a waterproof. She already had hers on and she crammed her felt hat on her head. 'I gather you've been out to investigate?'

'Yes. Not that I could see much. We're going to need a ladder and a tarpaulin.'

'I am. You're not climbing up the roof—'

'I'm perfectly capable of climbing up the roof, Olivia.'

'Your head. Your stitches!' she protested.

'My head is fine and I've taken the liberty of going through your first-aid kit and finding a strong bandage and a waterproof covering for my stitches.' He pointed to his temple.

'Oh. Still, I suppose I could always call Jack but he's had such a big day—he was up hours before he came to get me this morning, they all were so—'

'Lead on, Miss Lockhart,' Ben Bradshaw said firmly.

An hour later a tarpaulin was secured over the patch of the old corrugated-iron roof that was leaking and they were crawling through the roof checking the wiring.

'Seems to be all OK,' Ben said at last, swinging the torch in a wide arc.

'Yes. Yuk,' Olivia replied, and brushed a cobweb away from her face. She shuddered.

'Don't like spiders?'

'As little as you like thunderstorms. Well, I think we've done all we can. Shall we go down?'

'After you, ma'am,' he said courteously.

She climbed down the manhole into the kitchen and heaved a sigh of relief. The Aga was still alight; it served the dual purpose of a water heater as well as a stove and she took off her jacket and hat and warmed herself in front of it. Then she turned to look at Ben and had to laugh. He was wet and black but then, so was she.

'We look like a couple of drowned rats—I don't suppose Kay brought you any other clothes?'

'She did as a matter of fact. A set of pyjamas and another pair of jeans and a shirt.'

'Then I think you should change immediately—have a bath and come back and get warm. The last thing I need is for you to develop pneumonia.'

'I'm actually a lot tougher than I may look,' he murmured. 'How's this for a suggestion? Why don't we both dry off and change then I'll make us some cocoa?'

Olivia looked surprised and opened her mouth to demur but thought better of it. 'All right.'

She had a quick hot shower instead of a bath and came back to the kitchen in her pyjamas and terry towelling robe, drying her hair with a hand towel.

Ben was already there in pyjamas and her uncle's winter dressing gown and the kettle was boiling.

'That was fast work,' she commented.

He turned from the stove. 'I can work fast if necessary.'

'May I have a look at your stitches? It'll be a miracle if you didn't wet them or tear them with all that heaving and lifting you did tonight.

'Hmm,' she said a few minutes later. 'A little red around the edges. I'll put some antiseptic powder on and a new dressing but we'll have to watch them.'

He studied her downcast head as she looked through the first-aid kit, and found himself thinking that he knew of no other woman not only so capable but also so agile and athletic when it came to balancing on wet rooftops, shinning up ladders and crawling through confined spaces.

He said, 'Are you sure you didn't inflict any harm on yourself?'

'Don't think so.' She looked up and blinked at him. 'Well,' she amended, 'a couple of grazed knuckles.' She put her hands on the table and inspected them ruefully. 'But my hands were never my best asset.'

They certainly weren't soft with long painted nails like others he knew, he reflected, and paused suddenly on the thought.

'A bit disgraceful, aren't they?' she said with a chuckle, catching his suddenly narrowed look.

'Uh...no. I wasn't thinking that,' he confessed.

'What were you thinking?' she asked.

'I was thinking...that they're a good shape and I'm sure short nails are a good idea for the kind of life you lead and—that they're strong, capable hands.'

'Liar,' she said but with a twinkle in her eye. 'Are you going to make the cocoa or shall I?'

He said nothing for a moment and there was something both quizzical and enigmatic in his eyes. Then he said, 'Can you read my mind, Olivia?'

'In this instance, yes. I got the strong feeling you were thinking something quite different.'

'You're right,' he said slowly, and turned away to make the cocoa.

'Now, Ben, when I did something similar to you, you threatened to get all hot and bothered if I didn't *tell* you.'

He shrugged but said nothing until two steaming mugs were on the table in front of them. 'I was thinking—' he pulled out a chair and sat down '—that my remarks on feminine foibles were not only superior but quite unwarranted in your case and I'm only surprised you didn't take greater offence.'

She wrapped her hands around her mug and eyed him.

'You don't believe me?'

'Not entirely.'

'You're right.' He grinned. 'Well, not entirely right. I was actually thinking you're unlike most of the women of my acquaintance so it was the same thing *really*.'

'Unless you were thinking of one particular woman of your acquaintance,' she said after a little pause.

'My memory is still a bit patchy, I have to confess.'

Olivia stared at him. 'Are you *sure* you told the flying doctor this?'

'Yes. He said indiscriminate return of memory was quite usual.'

'I see. I must have been mad.'

He looked comically wary. 'Why?'

'To let you do what you did tonight, I—'

'Olivia.' He slid his hand across the table and covered hers. 'Don't worry so. I'll be OK.'

She hesitated but didn't draw her hand away. 'Your company will be worried about your plane.'

'There's not a lot that can be done at the moment.'

'No. I guess not.' She looked down at his hand still on hers then up into his eyes. 'I...I'm no further forward, Ben. Anyway, it's only a few hours since we...well...you know what I mean.'

He smiled slightly. 'I do. Because you can't make up your mind whether I'm the ultimate con man?'

A tinge of colour stained her cheeks. 'Wouldn't you have reservations if you were me?'

'Probably.' He raised his eyebrows. 'But then I'm not pressing you one way or the other.'

Olivia felt like saying that just sitting with her hand under his and in such close proximity, especially after they'd fought the elements and performed dangerous deeds together, was a form of pressure of its own. But she immediately decided that caution and discretion might serve her better.

As if he could see all this chasing through her grey eyes, Ben Bradshaw looked wry. He decided to change the subject and he took his hand away. 'Your roof needs a bit of work on it.'

Olivia sat back, not sure whether to be relieved or bereft. 'You're not wrong. In fact we need a whole new roof but it's such a large area.' She stopped and shrugged. 'I was hoping to be able to do it bit by bit but there are a lot of things that take precedence—fences, bores, pasture improvement and so on. Uncle Garth doesn't see a new roof as a priority either.'

Ben looked around the kitchen assessingly. 'That's a pity. The rest of the structure seems pretty sound.'

'It is,' Olivia said eagerly. 'They built these old brick walls to last. Do you know a lot about old buildings?'

He looked fleetingly surprised then smiled. 'I'm afraid I'm not as passionate about them as you are but then I can't boast a hundred-year association with anything. Well, I don't think I can.'

Olivia grimaced. 'Perhaps paranoia rather than passion would be more accurate but I can't seem to help it. Only…' She paused thoughtfully. 'I…no.'

'I think you should tell me,' he murmured.

'I'm sure you do,' she responded a shade tartly. 'You have a habit of insisting on knowing my innermost thoughts.'

'We are just the two of us stuck in a rising sea of water,' he observed mildly.

'Do you play cards?' she countered.

He looked amused. 'I seem to think I do but that can be a very boring way of passing the time, if that's what you had in mind.'

'It is. I'm beginning to feel as if I'm taking part in the Spanish Inquisition.'

He turned his mug around and drained his cocoa. 'On the other hand we seem to have agreed we have some sort of an effect on each other— I know.' He glinted her a wicked little look. 'We're not going to rush into anything, we're not even sure if there's anything to rush into! But we'll never know if we treat it all as a closed book. Will we?'

She looked at him frustratedly. 'It's not exactly a

two-way street, though. I know you can't help it at the moment but that's why I prefer to have a few reservations and prefer not to spill my whole soul to you, Mr Benedict Arnold.'

He narrowed his eyes. 'Let me guess, then. It's just occurred to you to wonder whether life might not be passing you by on account of your preoccupation with Wattle Creek and the hundred-year-old history of the Lockharts?'

Olivia bit her lip and pushed her fringe back with both hands.

He smiled slightly.

'That amuses you?' she queried dryly.

'No. It's the way you handle your hair. When you push your fringe aside it's, well, it's a unique little gesture that signifies something is really bothering you.'

'It needs a trim, that's all it signifies,' she said prosaically.

'Liar.' He said it softly but looked just as amused and incredulous as she had when she'd said it earlier.

Olivia coloured, looked exasperated then goaded. 'Oh, all right. It did cross my mind, that's all.'

'I think it's a very good thing that it has— No,' he drawled as she fired up to say something scathing, 'not from a self-interest point of view as you're about to accuse me of, I have no doubt, but because you have so much to offer, so much life to live here and now, it seems a shame for it to be passing you by.'

An acute feeling of annoyance gripped Olivia and her nostrils flared as her mouth hardened.

But he took the wind right out of her sails. 'You

should be lavishing all that wonderful spirit and creativity on a husband and children, my dear. Because I think you could create a richness there that would be quite something.'

Her lips parted and stayed parted until she closed her mouth and swallowed visibly. 'You…you don't know my uncle Garth by any chance?'

He raised an eyebrow. 'Why do you ask?'

'You could have taken the words right out of his mouth!'

He grimaced. 'Sorry. I had no idea what his sentiments on the subject might be but I do know how galling it can be to have people telling you what you should do with your life—'

'It didn't seem to stop you from doing just that,' she replied bitterly.

'Only in general,' he said slowly, and frowned. 'So your uncle is getting a bit restive about Lockhart heirs even by another name, Olivia?'

'He has some old-fashioned views,' she said acidly. 'If you're not barefoot, pregnant and tied to the kitchen sink by the time you're twenty-one, you're not much use to anyone in his estimation. He's convinced I'm on the shelf with only a dried-up spinsterhood in front of me.'

'Strange thinking for a bachelor,' Ben Bradshaw commented.

'Not so strange. He got left at the altar, apparently—well, almost. Thrown over for another man at least, which explains not only his bachelorhood but his cynicism on the subject of women.'

'He must surely appreciate how good you are at helping to run the station, though?'

Olivia shrugged and sighed. 'Yes, he does. But it troubles him that I should be—so footloose and fancy-free.'

'Were.'

The single word dropped into a pool of silence apart from the rain drumming on the roof.

'Say that again?' She spoke ominously at last.

'I think you know what I mean, Olivia.' His lips twisted. 'For whatever reason, we're in a position where we find ourselves fancying each other something rotten not to be too finicky about our choice of words.'

She pushed her chair back precipitously and stood up.

He remained seated, entirely unperturbed, and looked up at her attentively.

'Well, I am finicky about my choice of words,' she stated fiercely.

He raised a lazy eyebrow at her. 'Whatever words you like to choose are not going to make it go away.'

'You're wrong, you know. Your choice of words has just banished any interest I may have thought I had in you, Mr Bradshaw. Sorry, but I'm like that.'

'Why don't you go to bed, Olivia?' he suggested.

'Who…how…who the hell do you think you are?'

'The man from the moon,' he agreed wryly. 'That doesn't prevent me from making a beneficial observation. You're tired, overwrought, cross enough to indulge in a fruitless discussion about semantics—and

I'm still extremely grateful for all you've done for me.'

Olivia stood stock-still, then, to compound her overwroughtness, heard herself make a sound of kittenish frustration that she would have scorned had it come from any other woman, so she did the only thing left for her to do. She swung on her heel and marched out. To return within a moment to say merely, 'You may sleep in the other spare bedroom.'

But Ben Bradshaw, with a fading smile on his face that he hadn't allowed her to see, remained at the kitchen table for a while longer, staring at nothing in particular because he was acutely aware that his life had suddenly become very complicated. I should really walk, or swim away right now, he reflected. Why should a bump on the head change—things? How could I remember most things but not the most important thing of all?

And what is it about her that attracts you? he asked himself. She's not the most beautiful girl in the world. She's independent to a fault, practical to a degree that makes you wonder if there's anything else to her—Ah, that's it. You're something of an enigma, Livvie Lockhart. And I can't deny that I'm intrigued. How much this has to do with temporary amnesia is another matter.

He got up at last, rinsed the mugs and took himself to a fresh, dry bed.

He was awoken the next morning by Ryan and Sonia and it was an unnerving experience to open his eyes and find himself staring into two pairs of identical round brown eyes set in freckled faces just level with his own.

'Hallelujah!' He sat up groggily. 'If it isn't the heavenly twins.'

They giggled. 'We just came to see how you were.'

'How very kind of you—did you have to use flippers?'

'No, silly,' Sonia said. 'It's stopped raining. But there are some lovely puddles out there. We left our wellies outside,' she added hastily.

'Why've you changed your room?' Ryan asked interestedly as he leant against the side of the high bed.

'The roof leaked all over my other one. Is Olivia up and about?'

'She's out like a light. We looked in but we were as quiet as little mice. Weren't we, Son?'

'Yes. Think she's all right?' Sonia asked conversationally. 'It's not like Livvie to sleep late.'

Ben explained about the broken night they'd had on top of the night before.

'Well, would you like us to show you around a bit?' Ryan offered. 'Then she can really have a sleep-in.'

'How exceedingly nice of you,' Ben responded, and they giggled again.

'Have I said something funny?'

'You talk funny, that's all. You talk to us as if we're grown-up, doesn't he, Son?'

Sonia nodded vigorously.

'Well, why wouldn't I?' Ben murmured. 'You saved my life after all. Can you give me a minute to get dressed?'

* * *

Olivia drifted up through layers of sleep, opening and closing her eyes occasionally then sitting bolt upright as she realized the sun was shining. On top of this phenomenon, a glance at her bedside clock told her it was nine-thirty.

She blinked confusedly then it all came flooding back. She lay back with a heartfelt groan and wondered how on earth she was going to confront Ben Bradshaw this morning.

Consequently, she took her time dressing, in her cream and red checked shirt this morning with her usual khaki working trousers, and she made her bed and tidied her room meticulously. Then she sat down at the dressing table and trimmed her fringe. As she was tying her hair up in a loose knot she frowned. During all her activity she'd heard no sounds at all.

Sleeping in too, I guess, she mused, and braced herself to leave the sanctuary of her bedroom.

But there was no sign of him although she searched right through the house. And despite herself she couldn't help herself from starting to worry. Had he lapsed into amnesia again and gone walkabout? Had he developed blood poisoning through his stitches—why, oh, why had she allowed him to exert himself like that last night?

She had her hand on the kitchen phone to ring Jack when he strolled in through the back door.

She slammed the phone back in its cradle. 'Where the hell have you been?'

He paused then said deliberately, 'Good morning, Olivia. Yes, it is a lovely morning; still a lot of water about but—'

'You know what I mean!'

'I don't as a matter of fact.' He eyed her narrowly.

'I thought you must have lost your memory again or be having raving delusions because your stitches got infected or...or...don't you dare laugh!'

'I'm sorry.' He sobered. 'It didn't occur to me that you'd be worried. I got a visitation from Sonia and Ryan. They thought it might be a good idea to give me a little tour of the place.'

'Sonia and Ryan!'

'Uh-huh. We decided to let you sleep in.'

Her expression defied description for a long moment then she sat down at the kitchen table and said gloomily, 'Those two will give me grey hairs before long.'

'Not only you,' he said amusedly. 'I notice their father already has them.'

'So they just walked in and invited you?'

'They were staring at me from close range when I opened my eyes. I thought I was sharing heaven with two unangelic cherubs.'

Olivia tried not to but burst out laughing. She stood up, still chuckling, and went to the fridge. 'So? Did you enjoy your little tour?' She took out some eggs and bacon and a tomato.

'Well, I got down to the machinery shed and had a chat to Jack, Davo—who is pretty sure he'll have the satellite phone up and running soon—as well as the twins' father. They were of the opinion, incidentally, that by tomorrow morning, if there's no more rain, we should be able to get a four-wheel-drive vehicle out to the plane.'

Olivia placed some strips of bacon in the frying-pan and cut the tomato in half. She picked a banana out of the fruit basket and peeled it. 'What is Jack's opinion on the weather?'

'There's another low headed this way but he reckons it'll hold off for a couple of days.'

'Glory be.' She started to set the table.

'Not good news?'

'That could be all it would take to flood us right out.'

'There's still a lot of water lying about.' He pulled out a chair and sat down at the kitchen table. 'You must have some higher ground.'

'It's getting pretty overpopulated. Still, we'll do what we can do.'

'How about your neighbouring properties? I mean, could they help out temporarily?'

'Well, I think—' she turned the bacon over '—Naroo to the east would be in much the same position as we are. Campbell Downs does have some higher ground but it's just changed hands in rather sad circumstances. I—' she grimaced '—would hesitate to approach the new owners.'

He sat back and pushed his hands into his pockets. 'Why sad?' he asked with a frown.

Olivia cracked two eggs into the pan and added the tomato and banana. She turned to him and waved the long fork she had in her hand. 'It was a family concern, a bit like Wattle, but all sorts of pressures forced them to sell out to a multinational company. I believe they have beef properties in Argentina and so on.'

'You obviously don't approve.' He was still frowning.

She hesitated. 'I shouldn't be judgmental but these were people who battled and fought and went through the good times, yes, as well as the bad—I suppose what I don't approve of in principle is the impersonal nature of these giant companies and the fact that primary producers who are not giant companies—well, not many of the population realize what a tough job it is.'

'There's a saying about bookmakers—as in the betting kind—and farmers. The former never admit to winning and the latter never stop whingeing.'

Olivia turned back to the stove and basted the eggs. 'I hope you don't subscribe to that kind of trite and silly nonsense.'

'Otherwise I might find myself going breakfastless?' he hazarded with a grin.

She looked frustrated. 'Don't you agree that's how little people *understand*, though? Not that I know anything about bookmakers. By the way, if you want to make yourself useful you might make the toast.'

He got up obediently and put two slices of bread into the toaster. Then he set out knives and forks, salt and pepper, butter and handed her two plates.

A minute later they sat down to perfectly cooked bacon and eggs, fried tomato and banana.

'Mmm—' he sniffed appreciatively '—this looks wonderful.'

Olivia buttered a piece of toast. 'You haven't commented,' she remarked.

'Well, I can only comment in general.' But he ate

thoughtfully for a few moments before he said, 'Feeding this planet is becoming more and more of a task, Olivia. And that's why individuals are—battling these days.'

She looked at him with a trace of scorn. 'That's extremely general, Ben.'

'But perhaps more relevant than you may think, Olivia,' he countered with an acute little glance.

'You must admit quality and taste can suffer when things are done on a large scale. For example, take these lovely eggs you're eating right now. They're not from battery hens—their mums did actually get to range free.'

He looked wry but said, 'On the other hand, the milk millions of Australians are drinking with their tea or coffee right now is free from tuberculosis et cetera.'

'I suppose you're right,' she said with a sigh. 'But, whilst I agree that there have to be all sorts of checks and controls, I still feel quite strongly that a rural population of people who care about their land and their produce is a better way to go and that governments should see this.'

'Well spoken,' he murmured.

'But you don't agree?'

He finished his breakfast and placed his knife and fork side by side on his plate. 'I think it's becoming more complicated these days, that's all.'

Olivia clicked her tongue then stood up. 'Coffee, tea—? No, of course not. Milk or orange juice, then?'

'Orange juice, thanks,' he replied with a grin. 'I'm very relieved that you're talking to me this morning, by the way.'

She removed their plates, poured him a glass of juice, set the coffeepot on the stove and shrugged. 'I might not have been if I hadn't—got a fright about what might have happened to you.'

'Does that mean to say you look upon me as your responsibility, Olivia?' he queried idly.

'Only so far as your health goes,' she retorted.

He waited until the coffee bubbled and she returned to the table with a mug steaming aromatically, to say, 'I see you've cut your fringe.'

She blinked. 'Not all that much.'

'No,' he agreed. 'About half an inch.'

'What's it to you anyway?'

The long glance they exchanged was curiously charged, she found herself thinking, or it became so as it lengthened.

Then he said a touch dryly, 'I think you must know, Olivia.'

She moved restlessly but couldn't bring herself to look away. 'Have you remembered anything new today?'

'No,' he said.

She grimaced. 'Well, what would you like to do now?'

'What did you have in mind?'

'I'm going to clean up here, sort out your former bedroom, get someone up to fix the roof and then I'll go and see the state of play on Wattle Creek with my own eyes.' She got up and began to clear the table.

'On foot?'

'No, I'll be riding.'

'Could I come?'

She paused briefly then turned to the sink. 'That may be a bit energetic for you. How's your head?'

'I haven't had a look but I'm sure I could ride a quiet horse.'

'I'll make a decision when I've finished this.'

He watched her back as she began, vigorously, to wash up. Then he got up quietly, picked up a tea towel and started to dry the dishes.

They worked in complete silence for ten minutes, Olivia expressionlessly although she couldn't believe how unnerving it was to be so close to him as their bodies brushed accidentally a couple of times.

Or is it accidental? she wondered, the second time it happened, and shot him a grey and angry glance.

He raised an eyebrow and rather pointedly removed himself from the immediate area.

But she was still annoyed and said shortly, 'Would you mind getting the first-aid kit?'

'Roger, willco!' He strolled out of the kitchen, leaving Olivia to grind her teeth.

Nor was her mood improved when he hadn't returned by the time she'd finished all she wanted to do in the kitchen. She was just about to go in search of him when he returned with the kit, whistling softly.

'Took your time,' she commented.

'I put the damp mattress out to air and hung all the bedclothes on the line,' he replied sweetly.

'You're a housewife's dream,' she responded with some bitterness. 'No wonder you feel so sure you'd make a good husband.'

'Did I say that?'

'Don't you remember?' She stopped and stared at him.

He grinned wickedly. 'Yes. But it wasn't from that point of view that I made the comment.'

'No,' she agreed, 'it was because you actually like women and their little foibles don't drive you mad.'

'I see I shall have to guard my tongue,' he murmured. 'You have a photographic memory, Olivia.'

'No one could accuse you of that. OK, let's have a look at you.'

He sat down.

She removed the dressing and was gratified to see that the faint redness around the stitches had mostly disappeared. 'Looking good,' she murmured, and with deft fingers put a new dressing on. 'How's the bump on your head?'

He touched his fingers to the back of his head. 'Subsiding nicely, thank you.'

'And the scratches on your face are healing.' She subjected his face to a minute scrutiny which he bore with equanimity although, as their gazes locked, she could see the laughter lurking in the deep blue of his eyes.

She flushed and straightened. 'Well, it's up to you—to ride or not to ride.'

'I'd love a ride,' he said earnestly. 'I feel much in need of some decent exercise.'

'Let's go. I'll lend you a hat.'

An hour later they were saddled up, Olivia on a restive bay gelding, Ben on a black mare with white socks and wise, placid eyes.

They jogged along in silence for a while as she took in the state of the countryside. The sun was still shining although there were big white cloud domes building on the horizon. It was hot and the ground, where it wasn't covered with water, was steaming.

Olivia repositioned her broad-brimmed hat and felt the sweat trickle down her face as her shirt started to cling to her body.

She cast Ben a couple of sideways glances but he sat on the black mare with all the easy assurance of a born horseman and it was soon plain to be seen that she was responding most favourably to his light-as-silk touch on her mouth. Indeed, her eyes were losing that wise, world-weary air as she pricked up her ears and a certain spring came to her step.

And Olivia suddenly started to chuckle.

'What?' Ben enquired, drawing alongside her.

'You, that's what,' she answered, still smiling. 'Well, you and being out of the house and not soaked to the skin and being able to cast off all my earlier "mood".'

'I'm glad,' he said gravely, 'but why me?'

'I've got the feeling you're dynamite when it comes to the female of the species be they human or equine. By the look on her face, Bonnie—' she gestured to the mare '—hasn't enjoyed herself so much for years.'

'Ah. In that case, do you think we could up the pace a bit?'

'A gentle canter would be nice,' she agreed, and urged her horse forward.

They toured several paddocks, stopping once to help a calf that was bogged by means of attaching the rope

Olivia had on her saddle to it and her horse towing it out of the mire. She did the riding while Ben pushed from behind, getting himself liberally coated with mud at the same time. Then she showed him the horse paddock where he'd been found.

They dismounted and he grimaced down at the rock he'd hit his head on. 'I think I must have been already groggy from the landing. Because I still don't remember anything about this paddock.'

'I think you might have been. Otherwise you surely wouldn't have set off with no identification and no hat. But you do remember the landing?'

'I remember setting it down but that's about it. Phew! It's bloody hot, isn't it?'

'You're not wrong, and you're a mess.' She looked at Graham's jeans and patch-pocketed khaki bush shirt then grinned at him. 'But I might just have the perfect solution. Follow me.'

They mounted again and she led him to the banks of Wattle Creek. It was lined with huge old ghost gums and wattle trees that were alive with birds and the sandy bed, only a few days ago all but dry apart from some deeper holes, was now running almost to the top of its low, grassy banks.

Olivia jumped off and led her horse down to have a drink. Then she knotted his reins up and let him loose to pick the grass.

Ben did the same although he said, 'They won't go walkabout?'

'Not any horse I've trained. Now this is the best part.' She took off her hat and her boots and waded into the creek fully clothed. 'It's marvellous,' she called, sitting down in the water and scooping it over her face and hair. 'Just mind your stitches!'

'You're a genius, Olivia Lockhart, and blow my stitches!' He sank down beside her and they laughed together as the fresh, cool water ran off them although he didn't dunk his head, washing away the sweat and the mud, and the sheer act of not caring about clothes or anything was delightful.

She rested back on her hands and raised her face to the treetops that were dispensing dappled sunlight. 'This is one of my favourite spots on the whole place.' She closed her eyes.

'I can see why. It's magic.'

'Well, it's not always like this but there are a couple of holes that never dry up. And when the wild flowers come out and the wattles are in bloom it's even better.'

'An artist's paradise?' He looked around at the gnarled white trunks of the gums.

'Yep!' She opened her eyes, sat up and pushed her fringe out of her eyes.

'I'm glad,' he murmured.

'That it's an artist's paradise?'

'That too but I'm glad you didn't cut your fringe too short.'

She opened her mouth then hesitated and, in a reflexive gesture, scooped more water over her head.

He said nothing and made no move but his eyes lingered on the wet tendrils of hair framing her face then his gaze wandered down to the outline of her figure beneath the wet shirt.

She moved uncomfortably, and he looked away.

But that was no good either, she discovered. It didn't lessen the sudden tension she felt; it heightened it if anything because, unlike him, she seemed to be powerless to remove her gaze from him.

'Olivia,' he said very quietly, and she jumped as he looked back into her eyes. 'You're right; it might not be a good idea.'

She blinked and looked at her hands under the clear running water. 'You think you can read *my* mind, Ben?'

'I think to be wet and cool and in this wonderful spot is adding to the awareness of each other that we've been battling one way or another all morning. If we're to be honest.'

She looked up and detected a glint of irony in his eyes, and was moved to irony herself, she discovered. 'Honest?' She smiled unamusedly. 'If that's what you want I can honestly tell you that I could think of nothing nicer than taking off all my clothes, although I have no intention of doing it, and having a proper swim. With you.'

'That's exceedingly honest. It so happens I'm of the same mind but I'm also the one who suffers from your extreme militancy when you stop and think that you don't know me from a bar of soap.'

'You bastard,' she whispered, and jumped up and deliberately kicked water all over him. Then she swung round and started to wade to the bank.

But he was impervious to the splashing she'd given him and he caught her before she made it.

'Don't,' she warned through her teeth.

'Relax, Olivia,' he drawled. 'All I'm going to do is kiss you.'

'Oh, no, you're not!'

He held her easily in his arms and for a moment there was something dark and satanic about him. Then it was gone, although he didn't let her go. But he did say, 'After that little image you created, it's the least I can do, and the least you can get away with, Olivia Lockhart.'

CHAPTER FOUR

'I'VE changed my mind,' she shot at him.

'No, you haven't,' he murmured. 'You're feeling a bit foolish and wishing you'd never said it but look upon it like this.' He raised a wry eyebrow at her. 'It could sort things out once and for all.'

'What do you mean?'

'Well, if you don't like the way I kiss you or vice versa, we can part as friends.'

'Oh!' she groaned. 'I really don't know why I put up with you, and after all I've done for you—'

He stopped the flow of her words in a time-honoured manner. He simply started to kiss her. And he did it in a way that she should have expected but did not. He kissed her lips lightly and told her she tasted of Wattle Creek but that it was delicious.

She twisted in his arms but he bent his head lower and kissed her neck and told her that it was a particularly slender, creamy, elegant neck and that it had taken to invading his dreams.

She put her hands behind her to try to force his apart but he murmured that she had a lovely, lithe figure, and, moving his hands down to her hips, commented that he was also much attracted to her rear and he guessed that so much riding was the reason for its compact, trim jauntiness.

She gasped with a mixture of annoyance and the

effect those wandering hands were having on her equilibrium and told him, tartly, to mind his own business.

He laughed softly at her and pulled her into an almost affectionate embrace, kissed the tip of her nose and said wickedly that he wished she would tell him how.

'You...you're playing with me!' she accused suddenly.

'Not in the least,' he denied with a straight face that didn't fool her for a moment.

'Yes, you are! You're no more serious than the man in the moon! Don't tell me this is how you kiss girls you are serious about.' She bit her lip as soon as the words left her mouth and blushed brilliantly.

'Ah.' He released her but took her wrist and touched his free fingers to her lips. 'Now that—*could* be a different matter.'

'I'm sure it could!' She tossed her head. 'I'm—'

'Olivia,' he broke in, 'before you invest me with all the sins known to Adam, if I have one golden rule, it's this. I don't go around kissing unwilling girls.'

'A moment ago you told me I wasn't unwilling,' she protested, and saw the trap too late.

His lips twisted. 'But then, Miss Lockhart, it's not really for me to say, is it? Not only from the point of view of my own little rule but I'm sure your spirit of sheer independence would agree.'

'So, unless I assure you I am willing—'

'That's it in a nutshell,' he agreed.

'You must think I came down with the last shower,' she retorted bitterly.

'All right,' he replied with a sudden narrowing of

his eyes, 'here's what we could do.' He released her wrist but didn't step away. 'If you don't want to be taken seriously all you have to do is—beat whatever kind of a retreat you deem worthy of the situation. Dignified, outraged—' he looked faintly amused '—it's up to you. If you decide to stay, however, then I would deem you willing.'

Her lips parted incredulously. 'And you expect me to believe that's not still a game of some sort?'

'I'm afraid you're going to have to try me, Olivia,' he drawled. 'But may I point out that the confusion that exists between us is this—do you want to be taken seriously or not?'

She suffered, she was later to think, a stunning but quite mad seizure of the brain. Prompted, no doubt, by his sheer effrontery and because she was immensely needled to think that he was virtually saying he could take it or leave it. That he could be serious or not, in other words.

'I've never kissed a man unseriously in my life,' she murmured, and shrugged. 'Must be the way I'm built. Sorry to be such a mass of contradictions, Ben Bradshaw, but I think I'll pass.' She gazed at him ingenuously. 'Just in case *you* get more than you bargained for.'

'Now that is laying down the gauntlet, Olivia.' His blue eyes were amused but there was something else in their depths that she couldn't quite identify—or so she thought, but almost immediately found she could. A cool little challenge glinted out of them.

'It's up to you.' Her own gaze was suddenly cool and challenging.

'Never let it be said I didn't seize the moment,' he said satirically.

'Or that you're ever lost for a word,' she commented dryly.

But the air between them was suddenly taut with a different kind of tension. Gone were the games—not that she had been playing games until she'd suffered that extraordinary seizure. Yet gone also was any semblance of friendship. It was as if a kind of hostility threaded the air, woven through with a dynamic streak of naked desire.

She couldn't doubt that the way his gaze was roaming down her was peculiarly intent and intimate. It was as if her body, moulded beneath her wet clothes, was taking shape in his mind without the impediment of any clothing. And it caused her to shiver, but not with cold. It was as if there was an electric current running through her.

It amazed her that with no physical contact between them she could feel this way but that didn't prevent her from, honestly and proudly, giving as good as she got, in a manner of speaking.

Quite candidly, she returned his scrutiny. She allowed her gaze to linger on the wide line of his shoulders then travel down his tall, sleek body as she remembered that, while he might not carry an ounce of extra flesh, he'd proved himself to be both strong and agile on the roof the night before—surprisingly strong.

But of course it wasn't only his body that attracted her, she thought; he had a personality that was almost impossible to resist. It was the way he made her laugh, when he wasn't incensing her, it was... She turned off her thoughts and closed her eyes briefly.

Then, without her quite knowing why she wasn't resisting, they were holding hands and only moments later, after one searching glance, she was in his arms being kissed in a way that wasn't at all playful but very adult and extremely arousing.

It was glorious, she found, to feel him touch her breasts or her hips, it was sensational to experience the quivers of desire that ran in waves down her as they kissed deeply and their bodies pressed together—it was lovely the way he initiated moments of respite that were curiously tender.

It was unique to be able to stretch her arms above her head and have him run his hands down her body then claim her mouth as she lowered her hands to his shoulders and felt herself gathered in against the hardness and strength of him.

And she didn't resist when he pushed aside the collar of her shirt so he could kiss the base of her throat; she curved her hands around his neck and tipped her head back to give him freer access. Then she cupped his face and indicated that she desired his mouth on hers again.

He obliged until she thought she might faint from the sheer pleasure of it.

It was the horses that brought them out of it.

Bonnie suddenly tossed her head, harrumphed and wandered down to the water's edge beside them to drink noisily, causing the birds in the tree to rise skittishly then settle with much clucking.

They broke apart although Ben immediately put his hands on her waist to steady her, and kept them there.

'Oh,' Olivia said breathlessly.

'A timely interruption?' he murmured, raising a wry eyebrow.

Olivia blinked then pulled herself away and sat down in the water and scooped it over her hair and face. He sat down as well and said after a moment, 'You were right.'

'How so?' It came out a bit unsteadily.

'That I might get more than I bargained for.'

She wiped water from her eyes and squeezed out her hair.

'No comment?' he remarked.

'None that I can think of at the moment.' She stood up and waded out of the creek.

He remained seated in the water, resting back on his hands, and watched as she tried to push the water out of her khaki trousers. 'I don't think we can just leave it at that,' he said presently as she pulled her boots on.

'Well, I do,' she muttered, and looked around for her hat.

He stood up at last. 'Are you of the opinion that it speaks for itself?' he queried with a trace of amusement. 'If so, I have to agree. Mere words would be quite inadequate to describe it.'

'I'm not proposing to describe it.' She clicked her tongue and whistled softly. Her horse trotted up obediently, and Bonnie stepped into the creek and put her nose against Ben's chest and blew softly down her nostrils.

Olivia's lips twitched. 'Anyone would think she was a chaperon but if Bonnie believes it's time to go so do I,' she said wryly, and swung herself up into the saddle.

Ben ploughed through the creek followed by Bonnie, who waited patiently for him to put his boots and hat on, then accepted his weight.

They rode side by side out of the fresh, green-dappled world of the creek into the harsh sunlight and within minutes their clothes were starting to dry on their backs.

'I have to *think* about this,' Olivia said at last. 'It's no good expecting me to— I mean to say I'm not some shy virgin you can expect to be totally bowled over.'

'I'm not some shy virgin either,' he said, 'but I was pretty close to being bowled over myself.'

'I find that hard to believe.'

'I know. There's a lot you find hard to believe about me but in fact the feeling is mutual right at this moment.'

'Really? I thought I was an open book to you, Ben Bradshaw.' She tossed him a bitter little look.

He shrugged. 'That was before you kissed me in a way that, had Bonnie not intervened, could have ended up—who knows where?'

Olivia drew an unsteady breath but straightened her spine. 'If you're telling me I've passed some sort of a test—'

'I didn't say that at all,' he objected. 'But since you brought it up, did I? Pass the test, I mean?'

She clenched her teeth then decided to be honest.

'Most admirably—as you damn well know. How—I mean—what kind of a test it *was* is something I still have to decide.'

'Do enlighten me,' he invited gravely.

She shot him a grey glance loaded with irony but managed to say serenely, 'Well, we have no way of knowing whether it's a kind of stock-in-trade of yours, do we?'

'You think I might have left a trail of women languishing around the countryside? I really don't think I'm that kind of man,' he said pensively.

'I know. If anything, you think you're God's gift to women, but you don't know me very well,' she pointed out.

'As a matter of fact I knew I wanted to kiss you when you were doing your Florence Nightingale bit for the first time.'

'All right,' Olivia said unamusedly, 'let's not go into that. Let's not go into *anything* until I've had a chance to think a bit. You know, this really couldn't have come at a worse time!' She looked around frustratedly then up at the sky. 'There's so much to do, the last thing I need on my mind is the question of whether you're a charming philanderer!'

He burst out laughing. 'I'm so sorry, Miss Lockhart. I shall endeavour not to—get in your way for the next few hours.'

She cast him a sceptical look as they trotted up to the stables.

In fact she didn't see him again until that evening.

Jack decided they'd be able to get to the plane in

the Land Rover and took him off.

She was making dinner when he walked into the kitchen carrying a briefcase. It was dark, and although not raining, heavy clouds had obscured the sunset.

'You obviously found it,' she said, taking in the briefcase.

'Mmm…' He hung his borrowed hat on the stand by the door, and looked stiff and weary, she thought.

'Why don't you freshen up?' she suggested. 'Then I might shout you a beer.'

He rolled his eyes appreciatively then looked down at himself ruefully. 'The only problem is that I haven't got anything else to wear, but these clothes do feel as if they've been cast in concrete on me.'

'Wear Graham's pyjamas,' she recommended briskly, and, at the sudden little look he shot her, added, 'Don't worry, I'm in Florence Nightingale mode, I shall be able to survive you in pyjamas.'

'What a pity,' he murmured, but went away immediately, with his briefcase.

Jack poked his head around the kitchen door a moment later.

'Come in,' Olivia said warmly. 'Like a beer?'

'Love one.' He put a case that contained the satellite phone on the table. 'Davo fixed it. Found the plane,' he added, and glanced around.

'He's getting washed and changed.' Olivia handed him a stubby and poured herself a glass of wine which she sipped while she stirred the spaghetti Bolognese she was preparing.

'He's lucky to be alive and he must be a hell of a

pilot. He remembers now having to glide the plane down with no power and miss not a few obstacles in the process, like trees and rocks. Excepting for the last rock which crumpled the nose wheel.' Jack grimaced. 'Would have given him a bit of a jolt too. Then he walked six miles to the horse paddock. I guess that explains why no one heard or saw anything.'

Olivia pulled out a chair and sat down with a frown. 'Does he remember anything more about himself? I mean, why he was on his way to Campbell Downs, what he does for this pastoral company he works for? His memory is coming back in patches, apparently, which the flying doctor told him is normal, but…' She stopped and gestured frustratedly.

'I'd say he's pretty high up in it,' Jack said slowly. 'He seems to know what he's talking about in relation to stock and that kind of thing and—I get the feeling he's a pretty cool customer. There's a bit of reserve about him that may not be entirely due to his lack of memory.'

Olivia absorbed this then said, 'Well, now we're not quite so flood-bound, unless it rains tonight, surely either his company or his family will come and retrieve him tomorrow?'

Jack finished his beer and stood up. 'Got to go. As for him, I'd say they could have got him any time they liked. All they'd need is a chopper. See you in the morning, Livvie.'

Why didn't I think of that? Olivia pondered as she got up to stir the sauce again and stand the spaghetti in a pot of boiling water. She inspected the salad she'd made and put it on the table as well as a bowl of parmesan cheese. She'd made a cheesecake for dessert and she topped it artistically with fruit salad.

Then she sat down again with her wine and was deep in thought when Ben arrived, clean, brushed and wearing not Graham's pyjamas but his khaki boiler suit which she'd washed and hung out but forgotten about.

'Oh.'

'May I?' he said, and pointed to the fridge.

'Of course.'

He got himself a beer and cracked the top off it but unlike Jack, who'd drunk straight from the bottle, he took a tall glass from the dresser and poured the foaming amber liquid into it.

Then he sat down and raised the glass to her. 'Cheers.'

'Cheers. I'd forgotten about your suit.'

'So had I. But I not only feel better dressed, I feel more modest.' He took a long draught of cold beer and she watched the muscles of his throat work as it slipped down.

'Jack said you performed a minor miracle getting your plane down.'

He shrugged. 'I think luck was on my side more than anything else.'

'What will you do with it?'

'That is very problematical, Olivia. Even fully operational it would be difficult to fly it out of that paddock and although it's only a four-seater getting a low-loader or something big enough in to load it onto and haul it out is going to take some doing. But I'm bending my mind to it.'

She was silent for a time and she got up to check the spaghetti. 'Tell me more about this pastoral company and why they haven't sent a helicopter up to rescue you, Ben,' she said presently as she drained the spaghetti and poured the sauce onto it.

He grimaced. 'They probably thought I was safe enough here and they've probably loaned their helicopter out to the emergency services. I would imagine there are those much more in need of rescue than I am with all this water about.'

Olivia considered this then nodded her head in agreement. 'I guess so. Well, tuck in.' She put the steaming platter of spaghetti Bolognese on the table and sat down again but added, 'Who are they?'

'The company? You may not have heard of them, they're new in the area.'

'I'd still like to know—' She paused as the phone rang. It was her uncle calling from Tokyo.

'Uncle Garth,' she said delightedly, and for the next five minutes documented the state of Wattle Creek minutely for him, made a few notes and finally assured him that he need not dash home because if anything could be done if more rain fell she and Jack were quite capable of doing it.

But as soon as she put the phone down she looked annoyed with herself. She resumed her seat and picked up her fork. 'I forgot to tell him about you.'

'So I heard,' he said ruefully. 'What do you think he would have advised you to do?'

'Put a halter and a leg rope on you.'

He looked comically taken aback. 'You're not serious, Olivia?'

'Until he had a good chance to inspect you, probe through your background, your credit rating, the state of your teeth, et cetera—yes, I am.'

'Are you saying,' he said slowly and looking arrested as he wound some spaghetti around his fork, 'that he vets every eligible man who crosses your path?'

'Not so much that, it doesn't usually get to that stage—but he's not above subtly pointing out to me when he considers they *might* be eligible.'

'How…uncomfortable,' Ben Bradshaw remarked.

'Oh, I'm used to it,' Olivia replied blithely.

'So—are you going to?'

She leant back in her chair and surveyed him seriously. 'Put a halter on you, Ben? No. I've got the feeling it might be like trying to capture the wind, anyway.'

'Is this feeling the product of some serious thinking you've done over the last few hours?' he asked with a suddenly acute little look.

She raised an eyebrow and twirled her wineglass. 'It's just—a feeling I have. It's nothing calculated from what I know because, of course, there's so little I know. So, just—intuition perhaps, Ben?'

'I don't like the sound of that,' he murmured, and pushed his plate away. 'Thank you, by the way; that was delicious.'

'What do you mean you don't like the sound of it?' Olivia asked irritably as she got up, removed the remains of the meal and brought out the cheesecake.

'There's nothing you can do about it. Because even if you remembered every last detail of your life I still think I might…be right.'

'Well, I don't think it's wise to convict me on something as ephemeral as that, Olivia. Now, if you suffered the conviction that we wouldn't suit in bed, yes, I'd agree there was nothing more to talk about.'

She flinched inwardly but made no comment. Instead she handed him the cream courteously.

'Thank you so much,' he drawled with a glint of wicked irony, and put a large dollop onto his cheese-cake.

She put the cream bowl down with a thud and glared at him with her hands on her hips.

'Olivia,' he said softly, 'we came so close to it earlier today, and don't tell me it wasn't what you wanted as much as I did; how can we ignore it?'

As if to emphasize this, he looked her up and down critically. She'd changed into a denim skirt that swirled around her legs and a short-sleeved, silky-knit grey jumper. Her hair was in its usual loose knot with some tendrils escaping down her neck, and the kitchen light glinted through them, making them ethereally fair. The skin of her arms was also fair and smooth.

And he said suddenly, 'You're a marvel, you know. I've seen girls who live and work in the city who are more tanned than you are.'

She took a breath, sat down again and managed to say prosaically, 'I told you, I have no ambition to become a dried-up old prune. I always wear long sleeves and a hat when I'm out and about as well as sunscreen. Perhaps I'm merely vain,' she added with a twist of her lips.

'Not in the accepted sense. But if you are about this I'm glad.'

It affected her curiously because it was said rather gently. She frowned and stared at him then smiled ruefully. 'Ben, I've got the feeling you might just *be* God's gift to women; you seem to know all the right things to say and all the right buttons to push but—'

'I could say the same for you.'

She paused and felt a slow tide of colour mount to her cheeks.

'I mean to say, you were pushing a few of the right buttons yourself earlier today.' He stared at her.

The colour settled in her cheeks and refused to go away, to her considerable embarrassment. Because, unfortunately, she couldn't rid her mind of a very clear recollection of the way she'd kissed Ben Bradshaw earlier in the day.

'Could you just be God's gift to men, Olivia?' he queried. 'That was a very—sexy—encounter.'

It was her sense of humour that came to her rescue, eventually. The thought of Bonnie intervening intruded on the hot memories she was experiencing. But the subsequent thought that it might have been Ben Bonnie had sought to claim for another delightful ride in the hands of a master horseman rather than anything else caused Olivia's lips to curve then she started to chuckle.

He looked at her quizzically. 'Going to let me in on the joke?'

Olivia rose. 'I think I may be small-time compared

to you in the matter of expertise, Ben, that's all. But I'll tell you something: whether you do go around breaking hearts or not, you have a lot of style and I should feel the poorer for not having known you.' She turned to the sink.

'Just a minute, Olivia,' he said in a voice she didn't recognize—cool and abrupt.

She turned and blinked in surprise.

He stood up and pushed his chair in neatly then leant his hands on the back. 'You don't think your reserve has something to do with the fact that you may not find me as easy to push, order around and manipulate as you would like?'

She gasped.

He raised an eyebrow at her with some cynicism.

'No…'

'Then why are you going out of your way to treat me like a recalcitrant youth?'

'I am not!'

'Could have fooled me,' he drawled.

'Perhaps the boot is on the other foot,' she shot back. 'Are you having trouble pushing, ordering me around and manipulating *me*?'

'Oh, I don't think so,' he said with a faint undercurrent of sarcasm. 'Anyway, my idea of being attracted to someone doesn't involve a duel for dominance.'

'That is the worst thing you could have said to me, Ben Bradshaw,' she said through lips white with anger.

'Because it's true?' he queried with soft satire.

'Because it couldn't be further from the truth,' she stated, and strode out of the kitchen.

She went to her studio, raging inwardly, and paced around for about five minutes as she examined the turmoil of emotions surging through her.

Uppermost, she discovered, was a sense of sheer incredulity that she could have got herself into this situation with a man she barely knew. But nearly as impossible, she thought, was what he expected of her under such conditions.

The darkest thought of all, however, was how easy it would be literally to be bowled over by Ben Bradshaw.

She paused in front of one of the easels, and, with a sudden decisiveness, turned the page with the galahs over the back of the sketch book and stared at the blank, new page revealed.

Then she hooked over a stool from the table with her foot, took up a pencil and started to sketch with no clear idea of what she wanted to draw but a compulsion to not only draw but ease her feeling of being knocked right off base, and to still the insidious little whisper in her mind that was asking her just how independent and dominating she was.

It was Wattle Creek that emerged as her pencil flew. First the ghost gums with their old, gnarled and knotted trunks in some detail and birds sitting along the branches that reached out over the water. Then the creek itself and the bushes along the bank, and finally, in the creek, a horse nuzzling a man—Bonnie and Ben.

Why this scene? she asked herself painfully as she

sat back at last. But at the same time she knew she'd captured it well and that it would make a lovely card because there was a warmth that came through between horse and man.

And she knew that it was much better, from an artistic point of view, to draw a scene that had captured your imagination than to set out to put on paper or canvas something that sent no sensory messages from your mind to your fingers.

All the same, as she studied it, she knew she'd resolved nothing in this frenzy of creativity.

She chewed the end of her pencil and someone knocked on the door.

'Come in!' she called without thinking, quite sure it had to be Jack or someone from the station, and she stuck her pencil behind her ear and rose. But it was Ben.

Ben with a tray and a coffee plunger and cups on it.

She closed her mouth and stared guardedly across the room at him.

'I've come to apologize,' he said quietly, setting the tray on the table.

'I—' she glanced from him to the tray and back again '—thought you didn't drink coffee?' And winced because it sounded not only inane but feeble.

'I made myself some cocoa. It's in the jug.' He pointed. 'But I made you some of the stuff I found in the fridge. Taking great care to follow the instructions on the tin to a T,' he added. 'Given my inexperience with coffee. I'm supposed to plunge this now, I believe.' He pushed the plunger down with the palm of his hand and a serious expression.

'You're impossible, you know,' she said.

'Because I want to apologize? I should have thought that might make me the opposite,' he replied with a lurking little smile.

'No. Because you—I don't know, cut the ground from under my feet at times.'

'I thought you were going to say because I could be very nice, at times.' There was a wicked little glint in his eyes.

'I still haven't forgotten what you said.' But although she tossed her head on this statement her words seemed to lack any severity.

He poured the coffee, then the cocoa, and handed her her cup. 'I suppose I was a bit cut to the quick,' he murmured wryly. 'I mean, what you said to me was fairly damning. To be honest, I don't think I've ever been damned with such faint praise before in my life.'

'What you can remember of it,' Olivia said a shade dryly. 'It doesn't appear to have actually damned you that much,' she observed.

'Did you expect me to throw myself off the roof?' He shot her a very blue, laughing glance.

'No. But then don't expect me to be taken in either, Ben.'

He considered for a moment. 'All right. But I was—bloody annoyed at the time. Oh!' His gaze came to rest on her sketch. 'Did you just do this?'

'Yes.' It was a reluctant monosyllable she produced. Then she remembered the pencil stuck behind her ear and drew it out.

'Does that—mean anything?' he asked as he studied the sketch critically.

Olivia sipped some coffee. 'Only that sometimes artists are compulsive and it was a—moving moment in a funny way.'

'I see,' he said neutrally.

'Would you like it?' What prompted her to say it, Olivia didn't know.

'As a memento of Wattle Creek once I'm irrevocably banished from it?'

She moved restlessly and sat down on a stool at the table. He pulled the other stool up and sat beside her.

'Olivia?'

'I just thought…' She shrugged. 'Bonnie was so taken with you, that's all.'

'I can't help feeling that, despite her best intentions, I would have been better off without Bonnie's devotion—if you're going to hold that against me as well.'

Olivia grimaced and was silent.

'What was I saying?' He frowned. 'Yes. I was certainly annoyed and therefore prompted to be a bit—unkind, perhaps.'

'I'd hate to think what you'd class as *very* unkind.'

He looked at her. 'I might have touched a sore spot.'

'I don't really think so. Look, I may be independent but I've never thought I was domineering, not in that regard.'

Their gazes locked. Until he said, 'Should we call a truce?'

Her lips parted.

'I mean so that we could each get a good night's sleep, which we deserve, don't we?'

'Just that?'

'Just that,' he repeated. 'You look as if you could do with it.'

'I feel as if I could do with it. But there are still the dishes to do and so on.'

'I don't know about the "so on" but the dishes are done.'

'Again? My gratitude is boundless,' she said with a slow smile growing in her eyes.

He put his arm around her shoulders and, after a slight tensing, she relaxed and didn't pull away. 'Are we friends?' he asked lightly.

She hesitated then gave in. 'Yes. Well—'

'Don't say it,' he warned. 'I get the message anyway. Go to bed, Livvie Lockhart. You've had a big day.' He took his arm away.

She stood up after a moment. 'You keep telling me that.'

He turned to her and said humorously, 'Could be that I know what's good for you.'

Olivia was seized by the desire to run her fingers down the angles and planes of his face, and to rest her lips lightly on his. But she contained herself and said, 'Could be that you talk too much, Benedict Arnold. Goodnight. Let's hope it is a peaceful night.'

* * *

She certainly slept deeply and peacefully and awoke to a splendid dawn. Gone were the clouds of the night before and the further threat of rain and it was cool and dewy with apricot fingers of light spreading from the horizon. It enticed her out onto the veranda to watch the sun rise. And as it did and the birds woke she went barefoot down into the revitalized garden, still in her pyjamas, and picked a bunch of flowers.

Then she stood still on the edge of the lawn and stared back at the house with its old bricks, the curved veranda roof, and the creepers that grew along it. At the comfortable wicker chairs and pot plants—and thought of how much it meant to her.

But then so did all of Wattle Creek, she reflected, and turned to look towards the horizon again. She leant against the fence that surrounded the garden plot, and could see for miles. All that sunburnt country in its early morning shades of pink, sienna and that startling sandy red that so amazed people and soaked up moisture so that even only twenty-four hours after a virtual deluge it appeared dry. And in an amazingly short time would be green again.

As she drank it all in, though, and felt a surge of elation flow through her veins, she knew unerringly that to see Wattle Creek Station looking beautiful was only a fillip and she buried her face suddenly in the flowers.

Because the main source of her feeling of well-being was still asleep—most probably—but she'd woken with Ben Bradshaw on her mind and it had filled her with a sense of anticipation and renewal to think of him—and that could mean only one thing.

I've fallen in love with him, she told the flowers silently. I know I shouldn't be, I know I barely know him and all the rest but I just can't help it. I couldn't feel so good otherwise, so…happy to think that he's still here and can make me laugh, make me ache with desire, make me want to sharpen my wits on him and occasionally fighting mad at him… Just so alive. It has to be that.

And to think that only last night I was so sure it couldn't be happening to me. Or perhaps *shouldn't* be happening to me. Then he charmed me right out of it…

'Of course, what I do about it is another matter,' she said barely audibly to the rising sun.

CHAPTER FIVE

AT THE same time, Ben Bradshaw, who was not asleep but standing unseen in the shadows cast by the curtains at his veranda door, watched as Olivia turned at last from the fence and walked back across the lawn with her bunch of flowers. She was obviously deep in thought.

What is going through your head now, my beautiful Livvie Lockhart? he wondered. And immediately felt a strange little jolt. Because only two nights ago you were telling yourself she wasn't the most beautiful girl in the world? he thought dryly. How things can change. But then, you didn't expect such a passionate Livvie Lockhart, did you? You didn't really expect to enjoy kissing her to the degree that you did.

Well, he amended to himself, what you didn't expect was that she would allow it to get as serious as it got because *you* had no intention of going to those lengths, did you? And with good reason. So why the hell did you go any lengths at all? Because this girl gets to you, he answered himself—and stared into the middle distance with a frown in his eyes.

A frown that was there for several reasons, not the least being how difficult it was going to be to come clean. The sooner the better, he told himself.

'Good morning.'

Olivia looked up. She was in the wash-house sorting the laundry. It was separate from the main house, set across the lawn from the kitchen beside the water tanks, and through the open doorway the resident guinea fowl were pecking at delicacies in the grass, their grey and white spotted feathers sleek, their blue heads and red combs extremely busy.

'Good morning,' she responded, a little shyly, he thought, and narrowed his eyes. But she went on immediately with more of her usual assurance. 'Thought you were still asleep! It's an—intoxicating kind of day.'

'I see that.' He stood in the doorway and looked outside. 'So the rains didn't come again— Do you ever eat them?'

Olivia blinked and drew her mind from the sheer pleasure of his company, the little things. The way his thick dark hair lay, how blue his eyes were, how tall he was in his khaki boiler suit. 'The guinea fowl? No, of course not.'

'But they are edible. I know of a farm in Victoria that's building quite a business out of them. Their meat is not only tasty but low-cholestrol and has virtually no fat. Apparently, the French are so taken with the taste of them about eighty million birds are consumed annually. Free-range game birds are considered a gourmet's delight. And I know free-ranging is close to your heart.'

Olivia had stooped to pick up some clothes and she straightened with a quizzical expression. 'It may be but no one is eating *my* guinea fowl. I just like to have them around. You seem to know an awful lot about them,' she added curiously. 'How come?'

He paused and shrugged. 'Perhaps I have a mind packed with trivia.' He paused again and saw the fleeting little look of frustration that came and went from her eyes. 'Actually,' he said slowly, 'it's my business to know these things.'

'What do you mean?'

'Walk with me for a little while, Olivia?' he suggested.

'I—' She looked around at the piles of laundry. 'Well—'

'You did say it was a wonderful day.'

'All right. I guess the washing can wait.'

So they walked to the garden fence and, at his suggestion, sat down on the grass beneath a flowering gum. She had on her denim skirt of the night before but with a primrose blouse this morning, and a pair of brown leather sandals. She'd washed her hair and it was shiny fair, full of life and escaping from its knot in curly tendrils.

'It's so lovely after rain, isn't it?' she said, looking around. 'You tend to forget that in a few weeks it'll be dry and dusty again. OK, why did you want me to walk with you? It sounded almost ominous,' she said ruefully, hugging her knees.

He leant back on his hands and stretched out his long legs. 'I don't think you'll approve, somehow, but, you see, I'm the chief executive of the company that bought Campbell Downs.'

'What?'

'I'm afraid so. And that's what I meant about it being my business to know these things—we don't only own grazing properties.'

Olivia could only stare at him speechlessly.

'I knew you wouldn't approve,' he murmured.

'I'm stunned,' she said. 'Do you just work for them or are you a multinational millionaire?'

'I don't know about that but it is my company. I'm the chief shareholder in other words.'

'No wonder,' she breathed, 'you didn't agree with me about— How long have you known this?'

He held her grey gaze steadily. 'It has been coming back in patches, my memory, but most of this came back as soon as the plane was mentioned.'

'And you didn't tell me? How could you?' She stared at him with clear hurt in her eyes.

'There…' he paused and grimaced '…was a reason for that.'

'I'll bet,' she said stiffly. 'Was it more convenient to have me thinking you were just the son of a blacksmith, Ben Bradshaw?' She looked at him bitterly. 'In case I got too attracted to your multinational, multimillions?'

'Not at all, Olivia. I am the son of a blacksmith who married a teacher. He's dead—my mother is still alive. But although he was a raw young man from the bush he turned out, with her help, to be wise and canny and between them they started to deal in rural real estate, she inherited a run-down property, and they made a small fortune. Things have gone on from there.'

'Why haven't I ever heard of you?'

'Because we are new in this area, but you must have heard of Pascoe Lyall. It's the operating name of the company that bought Campbell.'

Olivia crossed her legs and smoothed her skirt over them. Just over the fence, the grass wasn't mown and the stalks and seed heads were waving in a gentle breeze and filling the air with their fragrance. And the honey smell from the flowering gum tips above was wafting down. But, although she automatically registered it, it brought her no comfort.

'Yes, I've heard of Pascoe Lyall.' She shrugged.

'As a matter of fact, if it had continued to rain, I was going to offer you agistment on Campbell Downs.'

'How kind of you—am I going to have to drag the reason why you couldn't have told me this as soon as you remembered it out of you, Ben?'

He raised a wry eyebrow. 'You seemed to have enough good reason to—doubt me, as it was. So, when I heard your sentiments on the subject of impersonal, giant pastoral companies, I thought I might stay mum for a while. That was one reason anyway.'

'Coward,' she said with feeling. 'Why have you told me now?'

He looked away from her and she got the feeling he was suffering a moment of indecision. Then he said, 'Olivia, I think I should not impose on you any longer. I need to get back to work anyway and there are a couple of very complicated situations I need to sort out so...' He reached through the fence and pulled out a stalk of grass to chew. 'But, with your permission, this need not be goodbye.'

'There you are!' Jack arrived beside them puffing. 'Been scouring Wattle for the two of you. Ben, Davo's had a brainwave. Instead of trying to load your plane *onto* a truck, he's come up with a winch system so we can tow it behind. We can keep the nose up, play out the chain or haul it in as we need to. What do you reckon?'

'Just might work,' Ben said thoughtfully.

'They're still predicting rain although it don't look like it at the moment, and this might be the best opportunity we'll get for a while,' Jack added with some urgency. 'And if it can be repaired here you could fly it off from our airstrip.'

'Good thinking,' Ben said and stood up. 'Like to come, Olivia?' He held his hand down to her.

She took it after a slight hesitation and stood up but said quietly, 'No, thanks. I've got plenty to do here.'

He looked into her eyes searchingly but she looked away.

He said, slowly, 'There's a helicopter coming to pick me up this afternoon—I made a call this morning. Just in case we get delayed—'

'I'll let the pilot know what's happening. Off you go!' she said brightly.

She went back to the washing but in a daze.

I can't *think*, she castigated herself once. This morning I was sure I was in love with a man I knew nothing about because I couldn't seem to help myself and it didn't appear to matter a whit whether he was a blacksmith himself, not to mention a possible philanderer.

Now I know that he's anything but—well, that he's a man of substance if nothing else I…

She rubbed her face. I what? I just don't know what to think! And two things are at the root of it—in essence he's lied to me, and I *don't* approve of vast, impersonal companies like his because I know exactly how I'd feel if I had to walk off Wattle Creek. How does that change the man himself, though? The one who made me wake up this morning with such a light, expectant heart? The man it was such a joy to behold only an hour ago?

She forced herself to keep working—it was the day of the week she not only did the laundry but also cleaned the homestead. She hung the washing up as it came out of the machine and as the sheets, towels and table linen dried, with that lovely redolence of sunlight and fresh air, she vacuumed, polished and dusted. But all the time she felt jittery and uncertain.

There was no sign of the plane-rescue crew by lunchtime, so she cut herself some sandwiches and took a tea tray to the veranda. She'd just finished eating and was pouring herself a second cup of tea when she heard a faint buzzing that grew to the distinctive whipping sound of helicopter rotors at close range.

It had 'Pascoe Lyall' written in red on its white sides and it landed just beyond the garden gate.

She could see two people in it and one didn't wait for the rotors to stop, but jumped down and ran, bent low, through the cloud of dust being whipped up. It was a girl with long hair and wearing designer jeans, high-heeled boots and a white voile blouse.

Olivia stood up and started to walk across the lawn to meet her. At the same time she took in more details of this girl: sleek and shining dark hair that fell to below her shoulders, a pair of very expensive gold and tortoiseshell sunglasses that masked her eyes but didn't hide her glossy golden skin, and a pair of full red lips.

Her figure was little short of sensational and she had an undeniable air of assurance, long red nails that matched her lips, a gold watch and a gold link bracelet, little diamond studded hoops in her ears, and a large diamond on her left hand. She also looked vaguely familiar.

They met at the garden gate.

The girl said, 'Hi! This is Wattle Creek, isn't it?'

Olivia overcame a nameless feeling of dread to agree that it was.

The girl put out her hand. 'Then you must be Olivia Lockhart—how do you do? I'm Caitlin Foster, Ben's fiancée. I've come to take him home.'

It was a moment before Olivia could make her voice work. Then she said, 'Come in. Both of you.'

By this time the pilot had arrived at the gate, a middle-aged man in a pale blue shirt and navy trousers with the insignia of Pascoe Lyall—a P and an L twined together—on his pocket beneath a pair of wings.

He introduced himself as Steve Williams then looked around a shade warily, Olivia thought, as much as she was capable of thinking rationally as a cold rage started to possess her.

'Ben's not here at the moment,' she said, and explained about the plane. 'But please come in, I'll make you some tea or whatever you'd like. They've been gone for hours so I expect they won't be much longer.'

'What a marvellous old house,' Caitlin Foster enthused.

'Thank you. Tea, coffee or something cold?' Olivia asked as she led them into the lounge when she would normally have taken them through to the kitchen. Why? she wondered. Because my pride needs propping up?

'Something cold would be *luverly*,' Caitlin said, 'but don't go to any trouble. We're so grateful for all you've done for Ben as it is. How is he? I believe he actually lost his memory for a while.'

'Only selectively,' Olivia murmured.

'Selectively?' Caitlin raised an eyebrow.

'Well, he remembered bits and pieces, and it came back in bits and pieces—quite normal, the flying doctor assured us. I'll be right back. Do sit down.'

She was back in five minutes with a jug of lemon squash and two tall glasses. 'So, how long have you been engaged to Ben, Caitlin?'

'Six months.' She had slid her sunglasses up on top of her head and revealed a pair of sparkling dark eyes. 'I keep telling him it's time we tied the knot but between our various commitments—I'm an actress and a model—we never seem to find the time.'

'Oh,' Olivia said, suddenly enlightened. 'That's where I've seen you before.'

Steve spoke. 'I believe he had to have some stitches?'

'Yes, he cut his head but it's healing well—and here he is right now…' she paused as she heard a vehicle stop outside then start up again '…so he can tell you all about it himself.'

She stood up but not before she'd noticed that oddly wary look about Steve Williams again.

She frowned then turned to the doorway as footsteps made their way down the passage. 'We're in the lounge, Ben,' she called, and added to herself, You bastard!

He came in, started to stay, 'Mission acc—' and stopped abruptly as Caitlin got up and walked straight into his arms.

'Darling! I've being going out of my mind—why didn't you ring me?'

Ben Bradshaw looked down into Caitlin's vivid face and Olivia held her breath and prayed for some sign of shock or sheer surprise, some indication that this girl came as a complete and sudden revelation to him—and immediately asked herself why. Would it be easier to forgive the fact that he was engaged if he didn't remember it?

But a moment later he said with no surprise, 'Why, Caiti, how did you persuade Steve to bring you?' And he raised his dark blue eyes to the pilot over her shoulder with a clear, pointed question in them.

Steve looked as wary as he ever had and Olivia understood even before he said apologetically and uncomfortably, 'She just wouldn't take no for an answer, boss.'

'Why should I?' Caitlin asked spiritedly, and touched her fingertips to the dressing on Ben's temple. 'Now don't be cross, darling—and don't tell me you don't remember *me*!'

'Perish the thought,' Ben murmured, and kissed her lightly on the forehead. 'Well—' he looked up and across into Olivia's eyes '—may I join the party? I'm dying of thirst.'

'I'll get another glass,' Olivia said expressionlessly.

But after she'd delivered the glass and found that Steve had taken himself back to the helicopter she said brightly, 'I'll leave you two alone; you'll have some catching up to do. Give me a call when you're ready to go.'

She went straight to her studio and with shaking fingers reached for her sketch of Ben, Bonnie and the creek. But he must have virtually followed her out of the lounge because although she'd torn it off the pad she hadn't had time to tear it up when he opened the studio door, came in and closed it behind him. And walked straight over to her to close his hands over hers then prise the sketch gently out of them.

'Go away,' she said huskily. 'But just for the record, Ben Bradshaw, when *did* you remember her? From day one? Did you ever lose your memory for more than an hour or two?'

'Olivia—yes, I did,' he said quietly.

'But you didn't even look surprised,' she countered crisply.

'I wasn't,' he agreed. 'I had in fact remembered

Caitlin, curiously enough, the night we were discussing your hands after our escapade on the roof.'

She gasped. 'How can you stand there—?'

'It was quite strange how it came back,' he persisted evenly. 'It was the difference between your capable hands and her long, always red nails that first occurred to me, then it fell into place.'

'That's no defence,' she said incredulously after a moment. 'Once you remembered you had a fiancée you—you—' She couldn't get the words out, she discovered, and was horrified to find she had tears prickling her eyelids.

'We,' he said.

'Don't do that to me again, Benedict Arnold!' she said furiously and with unmistakable emphasis.

'But it's true. Even though it started because of temporary amnesia, it affected us both. I can remember thinking, that night, after you went to bed, how complicated my life had become. Because you see, Olivia, I can't pretend to myself that I should be marrying anyone when I'm attracted to someone else, even under the influence of amnesia.'

She laughed, a choked little sound that broke off in the middle. 'That's something I may have been able to forgive you for, curiously,' she said with supreme irony, 'but not this.'

'Why?'

She blinked at him. 'Do you really need me to tell you why? In essence you lied to me, twice, not only about being engaged but who you are. And I'm damn sure you hadn't proposed to tell me about Caitlin Foster either because the last thing you expected was for her to turn up here—your pilot has been looking all hangdog ever since they landed.'

'I was about to tell you when Jack turned up this morning.'

'That would also have been too late. But what did you propose to do with her, anyway? Break the engagement until you could decide how serious you might be about me?'

'I haven't had time to decide one way or the other, Olivia. I didn't *plan* any of this any more than I planned to have to crash-land in one of your paddocks.'

She drew a breath and turned away from him abruptly.

'Nor was I aware that it meant so much to you,' he added quietly. 'You were the one who told me you weren't some virgin—'

'I know what I said.' She sniffed and turned back to him. 'What have you done with her?'

'Caiti? She's waiting with Steve— Olivia...' He paused and frowned at the suspicious moisture on her lashes.

But she took no notice and took a hanky from her pocket to blow her nose and dab at her eyes. Then she picked up the sketch he'd dropped onto the table and said quite steadily, 'Take this with you, Ben. You won't be seeing Wattle Creek again. I'll walk you to the helicopter. Is there anything—? Your briefcase. We'll get that on the way through.' And she handed him the paper and walked to the door.

'Olivia.'

Her eyes were dry but not only that as she looked

back at him over her shoulder—they were suddenly ablaze with anger. 'There is no more to say, Ben Bradshaw. Let's go.'

He studied her for a long moment and once again she thought that he might be making up his mind about something. But he said at last, 'Say goodbye to Bonnie for me. And Sonia and Ryan.'

She didn't answer, and the faintest smile twisted his lips which should have warned her but didn't.

Because he crossed the couple of feet separating them, tilted her chin with his fingers and murmured, 'As to whether it's all been said, we shall see. In the meantime, look after yourself, Livvie Lockhart. You were a wonderful nurse.' And he kissed her gently.

'So that's about it,' Olivia said to her uncle Garth four days later.

Four days during which she had futilely examined every single thing she and Ben had said to each other, every nuance, and the little thought that he couldn't, as he'd said, have planned it all. But this thought was always followed by the same one—what difference did it make? He'd admitted he'd known about Caitlin when he'd kissed her in the creek...

'What happened to the plane?'

She came back to the present with a start to see her uncle staring at her. 'Well, they flew a mechanic in and a new nose wheel and flew the plane out. More importantly, as for the floods, we didn't lose any stock although it looked touch-and-go for a while. More rain would have caused a real problem.'

They were eating dinner in the kitchen. Garth

Lockhart had arrived home that afternoon looking unusually tired but Olivia had put it down to the rigours of jet lag and having to drive himself from Mackay to Wattle Creek.

She also knew she wasn't looking her best because over the last four days she'd found it difficult to sleep and eat and not only had she conducted that futile soliloquy with herself, she'd tried to bury her anger and sorrow under a punishing workload that had seen her in the saddle for hours on end.

She'd consoled herself with the thought that at least Wattle Creek had benefited. There was not a fence hole that had escaped her eagle eye. All the stock was where it should be and the preparations for the last muster of the season before it got too hot were well in hand.

Garth Lockhart pushed his plate of roast lamb away half-eaten and Olivia said contritely, 'Sorry. I should have made a lighter meal; you must be exhausted. But it is your favourite.'

'It's not that,' he said, and looked his niece over thoughtfully. He was a thick-set man, not very tall, with sparse grey hair and a red complexion. They shared the same grey eyes, uncle and niece, but the resemblance ended there. 'What did you think of him?'

'Who?'

'Ben Bradshaw.'

Olivia hesitated and ate a portion of roast pumpkin. Then she shrugged. 'I wasn't that taken with him as a matter of fact. Then I found out who he was and was less taken.'

'He's a good stamp of a man, though. And been to all the right schools. He's also a crackerjack polo player—spent a bit of time in Argentina, I believe. That's how he got so good at polo as well as picking up the odd ranch or two there.'

'Bully for him,' Olivia murmured. 'No wonder no horse is game to throw him.' She glanced at her uncle through her lashes and frowned faintly. 'He's *also* engaged to a simply stunning girl—do you remember Caitlin Foster? She was in that TV hospital series, amongst others.'

Garth folded his hands behind his head and appeared to ruminate.

'You weren't thinking along your usual lines of eligible men to marry me off to, by any chance?' Olivia asked wryly. She frowned again. 'But you don't even know him. Do you?'

'Livvie,' her uncle said heavily, and pulled his hands away to rest his arms on the table, 'yes, I do. I've met him, at least.'

Olivia stood up and began to clear the table but she stopped abruptly. *'What?'*

'No, don't worry, I wasn't thinking of marrying you off to him,' Garth said hastily. 'Although I really don't know why you haven't found yourself a man yet, Livvie—'

'Don't start that—just don't start,' she warned through her teeth, and began to pick up plates again.

Her uncle looked at her with some surprise and growing injury in his eyes. Then he sighed and said, 'Sit down, girl. I need to talk to you.'

Olivia hesitated then did as she was bid. 'So long

as you stay off men and Ben Bradshaw in particular,' she said coolly.

'I—well, let me start at the beginning.' But he stopped, rubbed his face and didn't seem to know how to go on.

Olivia stared at him and finally said in a different voice altogether, 'Something's wrong, Uncle Garth, isn't it?' She put her hand over his. 'Please tell me,' she added gently.

'Well, I didn't only go to Tokyo, Livvie. I went to hospital and had some tests… Things don't look too good, I'm afraid. I've got to have an operation but even if it's a success—it's a heart and circulatory problem, something to do with my carotid artery, you see—I've got to take things easy for the rest of my life.'

She closed her eyes then got up and put her arms around him. 'Why—oh, why—didn't you tell me sooner?' She hugged him close then kissed the top of his head. 'But you'll pull through— How did you manage to hide it from me?' she asked with sudden guilt in her eyes as she pulled her chair round so she could sit down beside him.

He looked shamefaced and it smote her heart to think of this proud, normally pugnacious man looking like that. 'I—well, the few times I felt really off I told you—I made up stories that I'd strained my back and so on. Then, a month ago, I went to see Doc Hayden and he set up an appointment with a specialist on the Coast. I knew then that I was in trouble but I insisted on having more tests and some time to—organize things.'

'You're an old fraud,' she said softly. 'You could have killed yourself! There's nothing to organize anyway. So you'll be having this operation just as soon as it can be arranged—and there's nothing more to say!' But she flinched inwardly as the words echoed in her mind and she remembered saying them in a different context four days ago.

'I'm afraid there is, Livvie. You see, that's how I came to meet Ben Bradshaw.'

'How?' She stared at him with her lips parted.

'Livvie—' Garth moved restlessly '—we couldn't go on, not now. It's been a battle anyway, for the last few years; you know that yourself. And there's no way you could cope—'

'I— What are you saying?' Olivia whispered, going dreadfully pale.

'I went to see him. I knew Wattle would interest him because it adjoins Campbell Downs. I…it's the only thing we can do, my dear.'

But Olivia stood up and held onto the table for support. 'You obviously have no idea what kind of a man he is, Uncle Garth. But let me tell you. He mentioned not one *word* of this to me and he spent three days getting an excellent look at the place under completely false pretences!'

'Not if he lost his memory,' Garth replied reasonably, 'but I swore him to silence until I'd had a chance to discuss it with you myself.'

'I don't believe this,' she said faintly, then added with more spirit, 'Believe me, he only lost his memory very selectively!'

'What's that mean?'

'He…' she paused '…he would have known after the first day the significance of Wattle Creek. So that's why he told me things could change and all the rest! *Oh.*' She sat down and ground her teeth.

Garth Lockhart shrugged. 'Even if he did, he kept his word.'

'Well, I'm not going! Uncle Garth,' she cried, 'I know how much this place means to *you*, let alone me. There must be another way.'

'Don't you think I've done all my homework and all the sums, Livvie?' he said painfully. 'Anyway, you're too wrapped up in Wattle Creek, girl,' he added with an attempt to sound bracing. 'Do you the world of good to have a change!'

Olivia stared at him wordlessly and despite his heart problems, despite the fact that she knew he was saying what he had to say, he'd said it too often to her before not to make her blindingly angry with him for an instant.

Then she forced herself to change gear. 'I…I can't think straight.'

'I knew it was going to come as an awful shock to you but I didn't count on you meeting the man and taking a dislike to him,' Garth Lockhart said helplessly.

Olivia breathed deeply.

'But you've got your painting; remember that. And if you still want to be lumbered with an old crock like me we could find somewhere smaller. The thing is, Livvie, at least this way we've got something to sell. You know how many have had to walk off because they hung on too long.'

'Yes,' she murmured, and sat in silent thought. 'On the other hand, we would still have your expertise—'

'We don't know that.'

'Yes, we will,' she said fiercely. 'Don't even think along those lines! What is to stop me running the place with your advice?'

Garth Lockhart sat back tiredly then looked at her with sudden acuteness. 'You're worn out as it is, Livvie, and it's only been a couple of weeks.'

'That's not—' She stopped and bit her lip. And she forced herself to put the ghastly thought of losing Wattle Creek out of her mind for the time being. 'Are you on any medication, Uncle Garth? Has the operation been arranged? That's the most important thing at the moment.'

'In three days' time, I'm afraid, Livvie. They insisted I didn't put it off any longer. And I've got these pills to keep me going in the meantime. I'm supposed not to excite myself either or indulge in alcohol because of the pills, or—' he shrugged '—do anything much at all.'

She rose. 'I'm *sorry* but it…' She shook her head.

'It's not your fault, Livvie. I should have told you sooner; I just didn't know how.'

'Well, I think you should go to bed now, speaking as one who has been told she's a wonderful nurse, and don't worry about me,' she warned gently. 'I'm as tough as old boots, really. Come.'

'There's one more thing, Livvie,' he said tentatively, and she was shaken again at the difference in him.

She raised her eyes heavenwards quizzically in an attempt to amuse him.

'He's coming tomorrow.'

'Ben?'

Garth nodded.

She swallowed.

'You won't antagonize him?'

'Good heavens, no. Now, off to bed with you.'

She paced up and down her studio once she was assured her uncle was asleep. But it was hard to co-ordinate her thoughts and she found, strangely, that her uppermost feeling was one of helpless incredulity and anger that they could treat her like this.

Men, she thought bitterly. I might as well be a child, let alone a woman! How dare they? I've put as much blood, sweat and tears into this place as any-one...well, relatively—I am only twenty-five but I was mustering when I was twelve!

She sat down on a stool at last and tried to think coherently about Ben Bradshaw. But Caitlin Foster kept getting in the way. And why shouldn't she? she asked herself. We're about the same age, I imagine, but I'm sure she would make a much more glamorous and fitting wife for an international polo star, let alone millionaire. As, I'm also sure, he'll work out in due course. I don't even like polo and all the social bit that goes with it.

As she examined this thought, it brought a strangely sad little smile to her lips. As if it makes the slightest difference to how I really feel about him, she mused. Well, there's also this dreadful, deep pool of anger not only on account of Caitlin Foster but because he's going to be instrumental in turning me off Wattle Creek.

She stared at nothing for a long time, then straightened her spine and took a deep breath. We'll see about that, Mr Bradshaw.

CHAPTER SIX

SHE dressed with care the next morning after making breakfast and doing the chores.

She chose a beige hopsack-linen button-through dress with no sleeves and a collar. The slim lines of the straight dress complemented her figure and she put on a chunky red and black bangle and black patent leather shoes with little red heels.

Her uncle looked relieved when she reappeared not only dressed more formally than usual but with her hair groomed and tidy, and discreetly made up.

Eleven o'clock was the appointed hour, he'd told her, and Ben Bradshaw would be bringing an accountant with him. So she set out a silver tea tray with fine porcelain china and an iced fruit cake.

On the dot of eleven, not Steve Williams this time but Ben himself landed the Pascoe Lyall helicopter beyond the front gate. But Olivia was watching her uncle's expression and she said gently to him, 'Don't overdo things.'

He pressed her hand. 'I won't.'

Then Ben was standing in front of her and she looked up into his eyes and wondered how she could have forgotten how blue they were. 'We meet again, Ben Bradshaw,' she murmured, and put out her hand politely. 'I see your stitches have come out.'

He shook her hand. 'Yes. Good to see you, Olivia,'

he said, and turned to her uncle. 'I don't know if she's told you, sir, but your niece was extremely good to me under very difficult circumstances.'

'It was no more than I'd have done for anybody,' Olivia said with a faint smile, and turned to the other man warmly. 'But come in, please. Tea—' she stopped for a moment frustratedly '—or milk—is ready.'

Garth Lockhart looked at her bemusedly. 'What are you talking about, Livvie? When do we offer our guests milk?'

'I'm afraid I don't drink tea or coffee—Olivia has just remembered, I imagine,' Ben said humorously.

'Then you'll have a beer, man, surely! Why don't we all for that matter?'

'Because you're not supposed to be drinking at the moment, Uncle Garth,' Olivia said serenely, 'so we won't tempt you. Ben can have juice.'

'That's fine with me,' Ben said a shade ruefully but added immediately, 'By the way, this is Mark Bennett, our accountant, and he just happened to mention that he was dying for a cuppa.'

They sat in the lounge while Olivia served the tea and brought Ben a long glass of apple cider. Conversation was general then more pointed on the subject of Garth Lockhart's health. Finally, Ben suggested to Garth that Mark might like to have a look through the books so they went away to Garth's office, leaving Olivia alone to clear up.

But ten minutes later Ben appeared in the kitchen.

She glanced across at him standing tall and silent

in the doorway, then chose a tin and put the cake into it.

'So, you know the worst of me now, Olivia,' he said quietly, and walked up to the table.

'I hope so,' she murmured. 'Three shocks all on the subject of Ben Bradshaw are enough for anyone, wouldn't you say?'

He stared at her bent head as she put the lid on the tin carefully.

'How long have you known about Wattle?'

'Since last night. He only told me his health was precarious then too. But I don't know why I should have expected any different. I'm obviously just a lay figure in all this. A woman, to make matters worse.'

'He asked me, when he first came to see me, Olivia, to do all in my power not to let any of this leak until he'd had a chance to tell you himself.'

She looked up at last and her grey eyes were scornful. 'So he said. If you imagine that lets you off the hook, I don't.'

He raised a wry eyebrow. 'What would you have done in my position, Olivia?'

'A number of things,' she said after a moment's thought. 'As soon as you remembered—and don't tell me that wasn't pretty early on because I myself happen to have the clearest recollection of what you said about how things can *change*—I would, if I were you, have got myself airlifted off this place immediately and don't tell me you couldn't have arranged that. I would *not* have taken the opportunity to have a good look around under false pretences.'

'Go on,' he invited. 'I feel sure there's more.'

'There is, since you mention it.' She folded her arms and stared at him coldly. 'I certainly wouldn't have sought to *sweeten* someone who you knew very well was going to be devastated, the way you did.'

'"Sweeten",' he said reflectively. 'Is that what you think I was doing?'

'Definitely. What else should I think? Or are you going to tell me Caitlin Foster is a figment of my imagination?'

'But surely I'd have known that would do anything but "sweeten" you, once you found out?'

'Well, it makes no difference anyway,' she said shortly. 'I'm not going without a fight.'

'I don't see how you can, Olivia—'

'I am a shareholder, Ben. You may be able to buy my uncle out but I could be an entirely different matter.'

'You are,' he said with a faint smile. 'And looking very smart this morning, incidentally.'

'Don't patronize me,' she warned. 'Your credibility so far as I'm concerned is in tatters.'

'I can only repeat—I didn't plan *any* of this.'

'There's nothing to be said about the rest of it, but handing Wattle over to you is something I'm not going to take lying down.'

He paused and eyed her narrowly. 'Do you think that's wise, Olivia? Your uncle—'

'I know what you're going to say. Both you and he think you've got me hostage because of his health. But I spoke to his specialist this morning, and he believes there's every chance he'll pull through this operation. Once he feels more like his old self, it could be a different story.'

Ben said nothing but pushed his hands into the pockets of the brown twill trousers he wore with a plain white shirt.

Olivia put the cups in the sink and ignored him.

'I got the sketch framed,' he said presently.

She glanced over her shoulder and shrugged.

'Olivia, I *know* what a shock this must have been and on top of that you're probably feeling foolish about—saying the things you did, to me of all people. But that doesn't mean we can't at least have a civilized discussion.'

'Am I being uncivilized?' she murmured. 'I thought I was being quite calm and collected.'

'But literally simmering just below the surface,' he said dryly. 'Would you sit down and let me explain how unviable Wattle Creek has become?'

'No, I wouldn't!' she said through her teeth, glaring at him. 'Because I not only disapprove of all you represent commercially, I happen to be allergic to polo-playing, pin-up types—but most of all I'm allergic to liars!'

'There are two separate issues there and I'm not a polo-pinup,' he responded evenly. 'Who told you that?'

'It doesn't matter.'

'Yes, it does,' he disagreed. 'I only ever played the game as a hobby and I gave it away years ago. It was never the social side of things that appealed to me, if that's what you're objecting to, but the skills and the horsemanship.'

'You could be a ten handicapper for all I care.'

'But you were the one who brought it up, with palpable disgust,' he said coolly. 'As for the issue of why we kissed each other almost to the point of no return a few days ago—why did you, Olivia?'

'I didn't know about your fiancée at the time, remember?' she said satirically.

'And did you fancy yourself a little in love with me, Livvie Lockhart?'

'Talking of being in love,' she responded swiftly, 'I thought you were a bit in love with yourself and needed taking down a peg or two, Ben.'

'All right,' he said, and it gave her some satisfaction to see the flash of anger that came and went in his eyes. 'Put your proposition, Olivia.'

'What do you mean?'

'Well, your uncle is offering to sell me Wattle Creek—which is one entity under one title. Your shareholding—thirty per cent, I believe—is not in the actual property but in the family company that was formed to operate the station. And as such is not sufficient to block the sale.'

Why the hell didn't I think of that? Olivia asked herself bitterly. Because it never crossed my mind until last night that this could arise.

'Then my proposition is this: the least you owe me, Ben Bradshaw, is the courtesy of waiting until after the operation before you accept the offer.'

'No problem,' he said obligingly. 'I'd already decided to do so in so far as the signing of any contracts goes. But I've given your uncle an assurance that if he's of the same mind once he's up and around I will be of the same mind.'

Olivia took a sudden breath and felt the first glimmer of hope since she'd heard the news the night before.

It was as if he could see it in her eyes, though, because he said, almost gently, 'Things won't change, however.'

'We'll see.' She looked around the kitchen and fiercely willed herself not to give way to the tears that were threatening.

'There is a less painful way we could do this, Olivia.'

'Oh?' Her grey gaze jerked to his.

'I'd be perfectly happy for you and your uncle to stay on in the house. Naturally I'd have to install a manager but he could have his own cottage and there'd be no question of throwing you out before you'd made the necessary adjustments.'

'I think,' she said huskily and looked at him with unmistakable dislike, 'I might hate that more than anything.'

He returned her look dryly. 'You'd see yourself as in the position of being beholden to me—kind of thing?'

'You got it in one, Ben. But that is something I will never be.'

'On the other hand, I think I'd quite enjoy it,' he mused.

She picked up the cake tin with every intention of hurling it at him but sanity prevailed as he simply stared at her, his blue eyes and expression laden with sheer irony.

But the effort to be sane and rational told and she had to turn away to hide the tears of utter frustration that refused to be denied.

He came to stand beside her and, without a word, offered her his handkerchief.

She started to say something scathing then, with a groan, took it and wiped her eyes and blew her nose vigorously. 'I don't usually cry,' she said bitterly, 'but it was quite a shock.' Her shoulders slumped.

'I believe you. It would probably have come as more of a shock if it had come from me.'

'I wonder. Anyway, I wish you'd just go back to your fiancée,' she said bitterly. She balled his hanky up tightly.

'You know, *I* think,' he said conversationally, 'you should take the time to ponder why the thought of my fiancée incenses you so much, Olivia.'

She started to say something and saw the trap—all of which left her gasping for air like a stranded fish.

'Yes,' he agreed gravely. 'So I'll leave you to work on that little conundrum. In the meantime, I believe the operation is to be at John Flynn on the Gold Coast?'

Olivia closed her mouth and swallowed several times. 'Yes,' she said at last. 'It was a question of where to get him in at such short notice and the special facilities they require for it, and the specialist he's been seeing is based there.' She paused and frowned. 'I would have preferred Rockhampton Base Hospital; I've got friends in Rocky and it's much closer but—'

she shrugged helplessly '—the most important thing is what's best for *him.*'

'It's not a problem,' Ben said quietly. 'I've offered to fly him down—saves you driving to Rockhampton or Longreach and getting a commercial flight—and it so happens I have a house at Mermaid Beach. I don't know if you know the Coast that well, but Mermaid Beach isn't far from Tugun and John Flynn.'

'Oh, I couldn't,' Olivia said with real distress and agitation. 'I mean, thank you very much but—'

'Yes, you could,' he said casually. 'Your uncle thinks it's a great idea and it's the *least* I can do after all you did for me. You can have the house to yourself if you so desire.'

Garth Lockhart chose that moment to walk into the kitchen and it was obvious to his niece that he was a much relieved-looking man as he said, 'There you are, you two! Livvie, Ben has very kindly—'

'So he's just told me, Uncle Garth,' she said, desperately trying to inject some enthusiasm into her voice. 'I'm…I'm very grateful.'

A day later Steve Williams flew them to Coolangatta, on the southern end of the Gold Coast, where there was a company car at their disposal. And Garth Lockhart was admitted to the John Flynn hospital, named with some significance in his case, after Flynn of the Inland who had established the Inland Mission and the Royal Flying Doctor Service.

Olivia stayed with him for several hours then he

told her to go home and get some rest. The operation was scheduled for the next morning.

'I'll be back before you go under,' she promised, and kissed him.

It so happened she did know the Gold Coast, having spent many holidays on it during her university career, so it was no problem to drive to Mermaid Beach from Tugun. Steve had presented her with a key to the house although she'd seriously considered booking herself into a motel, but that would have involved giving the hospital a different contact number and possibly alerting her uncle to her state of mind.

Something that was not improved—her state of mind—on discovering that Ben Bradshaw's address was in millionaire's row at Mermaid Beach—a short stretch of absolute beachfront properties that formed some of the dearest real estate on the Coast.

She breathed exasperatedly as she turned the key in the front door. It was a two-storeyed pale grey stucco house and, as she'd known it would be from the address, the vista that greeted her from the front door was magnificent.

Champagne-coloured marble floors flowed towards huge plate-glass windows and a terrace with the beach and ocean beyond. There were ivory wooden louvres folded back at the windows, sumptuous peach couches, elegant mirrors, dark green lacquered walls and occasional tables and exquisite Persian rugs. The sun was setting behind the house and the sea was a calm, placid blue tinged with pink, and fringed with lazy white breakers.

Olivia dropped her single bag and walked to the windows, bitterly regretting that she hadn't packed a swimsuit because she could think of nothing that would have benefited her more than a surf in the sea.

Then she turned and stared around again and tried to imagine Ben Bradshaw in this environment. But what came to mind with astonishing ease was Caitlin Foster. It seemed like a natural setting for her glamour and vibrant beauty.

She bit her lip and willed herself to think along different lines. But no inspiration presented itself and she decided that she couldn't get out of spending a few nights in this mansion but that didn't mean to say she had to be impressed.

Steve had told her that there was a guest bedroom on the ground floor and she went to find it. He'd also told her that a cleaning lady came in daily and replenished the food supply in the house as and when guests were expected, and that she should please feel free to use anything she fancied. He also explained that she'd find a diagram of the security system in the kitchen.

The ground-floor guest bedroom was done out in shades of blue from chalk through to midnight and, she was pleased to discover, had not only an *en suite* bathroom but its own veranda and its own small lounge suite set in front of a concealed television set. I'll camp out here, she thought, and grimaced ruefully, because camping was not an accurate term for it. But she wouldn't have to use the rest of the house apart from the kitchen.

She made herself scrambled eggs for dinner and slept deeply and dreamlessly in the vast blue bed.

It was a long, tiring day the next day but by four o'clock in the afternoon they were able to tell her that her uncle had come through the operation well although he was in Intensive Care and they expected him to have a peaceful night.

She spoke to the specialist and he gave her the news that it would be a couple of days before they could say how successful it had been but he was cautiously optimistic. And he recommended that she go home and get a good night's rest. She also spoke briefly to her uncle but he was sedated and she wasn't sure whether he knew who she was.

So she drove back up the Pacific Highway towards Mermaid Beach at the end of another magnificent day, weather-wise, and, on a sudden impulse, stopped and bought herself a swimsuit.

The house was silent and empty and she donned her purchase, a clear yellow Lycra one-piece suit, and went for a swim.

The surf was wonderfully refreshing and invigorating and she spent about an hour in the water, catching wave after wave or just floating on her back beyond the line of breakers.

It was almost dark when she walked up the beach to where she'd left her towel, shaking and squeezing the moisture out of her hair and unaware that the man sitting patiently beside it was Ben Bradshaw until he picked it up and handed it to her.

She gasped. 'You… I mean… How long have you been here?'

'About twenty minutes.' He rose. 'Enjoy your swim?'

'I…it was marvellous,' she said disjointedly, and wound the towel around her and tucked it in above her breasts. 'But what are you doing here?'

His lips twisted. 'Come to take you out to dinner, Olivia,' he said mildly. 'That's all.'

'But you don't have to and I might not want to go,' she objected. 'In fact I ought not to go anywhere in case the hospital needs to contact me.'

He didn't answer immediately but studied her thoughtfully. They were separated by about a foot of golden sand. He was wearing jeans and a navy blue T-shirt with a white collar. She, on the other hand, was made extremely conscious beneath his slightly narrowed blue gaze of the bare expanse of her legs beneath the towel, of her wet, satiny shoulders and throat, her hair plastered to her head and sending droplets of water down her face.

But, most of all, she was achingly conscious of him and her cheeks started to burn.

'Wet again,' he said idly, and traced the path of a drop of water down her neck with one finger. 'But it has all been arranged,' he added.

She moved out of the reach of that lazy finger. 'What's been arranged?'

'I've spoken to the hospital and given them my mobile phone number in case of an emergency. I believe the news is cautiously optimistic, though?'

'Yes, but they won't know properly for a few days.'

'All the more reason for you to get some R and R, Olivia. Where would you like to go?'

'Ben—this is not necessary.' She bit her lip because it had come out sounding lame.

'On account of me being affianced, a buyer for Wattle or just an all-round cad?' he asked with soft satire.

'Since you mention it, yes,' she replied with more spirit.

He laughed quietly. 'On the other hand, that doesn't mean we couldn't have dinner in some amity. I was always all those things when I helped you put a tarpaulin on the roof, dig a calf out of the mire et cetera but we still managed to have some companionable meals together.'

'Very clever,' she retorted, 'but the difference is I didn't *know* you were all those things at the time.'

'You had the gravest doubts, however. Olivia...' he paused '...do you remember singing me to sleep one night?'

'I...well, yes but...'

'Then I think you should allow me to repay some of that devotion—to duty,' he added with a wicked little glint. 'As a nurse and a hostess, I mean. You can't be feeling a bundle of joy at the moment. In fact, I'm pretty sure you're still shell-shocked, tired and overwound and it would do you the world of good to come out for a quiet meal.'

'And I'm pretty sure you kissed the blarney stone either in this life or a former, Benedict Arnold.' She stopped frustratedly, on the point of telling him he was the last person who could ease her tensions, both personal and otherwise.

He waited for a moment then said placidly, 'Let's go, then.'

'Can I at least get changed?'

'Of course.' He possessed himself of her hand and started to stroll towards the house. 'What do you think of it?'

'Very impressive, what I've seen of it,' she said after a moment, and added with a frown, 'Is this a new strategy?'

'What do you mean?'

'This—chumminess.'

He grinned down at her as they mounted the veranda steps but only said enigmatically, 'Perhaps.'

She hesitated and looked down at his hand around hers.

'Go and change, Livvie Lockhart. Believe me, you'll feel better for a meal.' He released her hand.

She closed herself into the blue bedroom and took a shower. There was a hairdryer attached to the wall and she took her time about drying her hair to her satisfaction then went to survey the few clothes she'd brought with her but there was only one outfit that would do. A pair of slim white trousers and a ribbed, sleeveless, silky-knit top in a dusky pink.

She put on a pair of white flatties and stared at her reflection. Her hair was up as usual and she'd painted her lips barely pink. She brushed aside her fringe with her fingers, and persuaded herself to leave the sanctuary of the blue bedroom.

The main lounge was ablaze with lights, the louvres had been pulled across but tilted open at an angle so bands of dark blue night were visible through them, yet only a distorted view would be available from the beach.

There was a bottle of champagne in a silver cooler on one of the green lacquered coffee tables and Ben was lounging on a settee.

He rose as soon as she appeared and indicated the champagne with a hand.

'I… Why not?' she said a little helplessly, because she was suddenly conscious of feeling powerless. As if everything had drifted out of her control, not least the direction of this evening.

He poured two glasses and brought hers over to the peach couch she'd sunk down upon.

'Thank you,' she murmured as their fingers brushed, but he moved away immediately and sat down opposite.

'Drink it,' he said quietly. 'It'll help.'

She drank half a glass then said with a grimace, 'How did you know? That I needed help.'

He raised an eyebrow. 'Neither Florence Nightingale nor any model of a major-general was anywhere in sight.'

'I must be slipping,' she said ruefully.

'Well, you're not on your home turf either. That could account for it,' he suggested gravely.

She opened her mouth to say that, far from being on her home turf, she was also on Caitlin's turf, but remembered the pledge she'd made never to mention that name to him again.

'What?' he asked.

He had his head propped on a hand and his arm propped on the arm of the couch. His long fingers were playing with his hair and on his temple the marks of the stitches were still visible.

'This is not the kind of setting I had you figured for, somehow, Ben,' she lied, and flinched inwardly because that was as good as mentioning Caitlin's name anyway, she was sure.

But he surprised her. He looked around wryly. 'You're right. Peach couches and acres of marble are not what I'd have chosen myself. My mother is the culprit.'

Olivia's eyes widened in surprise.

'She's convinced there's a Gold Coast style, and this is it.'

'So this is her house?'

'More or less,' he agreed. 'I use it when I need it but she lives here.'

'She doesn't seem to be living here at the moment,' Olivia commented.

He smiled faintly. 'Were you hoping for another chaperon? She's still overseas as it happens. But despite all this opulence you'd like her.'

'Why? I mean, it doesn't matter one way or the other but…' She shrugged.

'You're interested in spite of yourself? I quite understand,' he said with that wicked glint again. 'Uh—she's a very strong-minded lady. She also suffers from vigorous good health although she's in her middle sixties, and when I bought the house for her she informed me that she'd lived in enough farmhouses and station homesteads to be sick of them and she was going to go in the absolute opposite direction with this one.'

Olivia smiled as she looked around again with more interest.

'Did you explore upstairs?' he asked.

'No. I decided to camp out in the blue—' She stopped and added as he looked at her wryly, 'Well, I'm more than ever glad I didn't now. I would have felt as if I was trespassing.'

'Oh, she wouldn't have minded. She's used to guests, I often put people up here for a variety of reasons, business mostly, though, and she enjoys playing hostess. Keeps her young, she says.'

Olivia drank some more champagne. 'You're lucky.'

'I know. Feeling better?'

'Yes. Thanks, but if you're serious about taking me to dinner you'd better do it soon otherwise I'll fall asleep. That's how relaxed I'm feeling at the moment, at least.'

He laughed and stood up. 'We'll walk. That should do the trick.'

So they walked up the pathway beside the beach to Broadbeach, and chose an intimate restaurant that was, he said, renowned for its pasta.

'Of course you make such a mean spaghetti Bolognese yourself, you could be a better judge than most,' he said as they sat down at a table with a red and white checked cloth and a stubby white candle. 'Mean in both senses of the word—you nearly threw it all over me.'

'It was the cream I nearly threw over you,' she said involuntarily.

'Ah—you're right. All the same, that's twice you've been tempted to throw things at me or over me.'

She opened her mouth to reply but the waiter intervened. They made their choices and he ordered a bottle of red wine.

'Did you know that a glass or two of this stuff is supposed to be good for you?' he asked, eyeing her over the rim of his glass.

'So I've read.'

'And did you know that bottling everything up is *not* supposed to be good for you, Olivia?'

She sat back and let her arms hang at her sides for a long moment. Then she said, 'There is one problem; you're the last person who could help. You are, not to put too fine a point on it, the architect of the worst of my problems.'

'I have to disagree but may I, unemotionally, tell you why?'

'Well, I'm not emotional at the moment,' she said shortly, and sipped her wine.

'Not on the surface, perhaps. However…' He paused and looked thoughtful. 'As primary producers, we are about to enter yet another era of difficulty, Olivia. Asian economies are taking a battering at the moment so our exports—live cattle, beef et cetera—are liable to take a battering for a time.'

'Yes.'

'Well, any downturn in the market at this moment, as well as any cause of loss of production, be it drought, flood or whatever, would see Wattle go into the red. And a prolonged downturn would make it impossible for it to survive as is. This is something your uncle has calculated and acknowledged.

'Capital that Wattle doesn't have at the moment is needed for more dams and bores, an injection of new strains of breeding stock and so on. It's also something he's been—trying to hide from you for a while.'

'So I gather,' she said tonelessly.

He watched her narrowly for a moment. 'There are other—forces, if you like, at work, Olivia. His health is obviously one of them but the lack of a family, other than you, is a major player, you could say.'

She sipped her wine and stared unseeingly out over the ocean. 'No heirs,' she murmured with irony, and cast him a swift, enigmatic glance.

'No heirs,' he agreed.

She pushed her fringe aside. 'I don't know what I was supposed to be—an heir factory?'

He looked at her with sudden compassion. 'No, never. And it's not so much your heirs he's regretting—they would have been too young anyway—but the lack of his own. Strong sons. Who knows? They may not have eventuated—but I think it's probably quite a common reaction to regret what may have been.'

'The other thing,' he went on when she made no response, '*is* you. He feels he owes you more than a constant battle from now on to make ends meet. And he also feels a responsibility to the people who work on the station, some of whom you would have to make redundant in the near future whereas I would be able to guarantee them their jobs.'

Olivia flinched.

'I'm sorry,' he said abruptly. 'You may also think I've chosen a bad time to say this but it could be better than for you to go on—'

'Dreaming futile dreams,' she finished for him, and thought for a bit. 'Are you getting a bargain, Ben?'

His mouth hardened. 'Not as much as I might get if you decided to hang on, Olivia.'

'I've made you angry,' she said dryly, 'but I am interested. You must have enormous resources if *you* could carry Wattle through what lies ahead.'

Their meal came at this point. Fettucine marinara for her and ravioli for him. There was a Greek salad with feta cheese and plump black olives, and herb bread. The waiter departed with many flourishes and good wishes for a healthy appetite.

Olivia picked up her fork but only curled the fettucine around it absently.

'I've hedged my bets over the years,' he said presently.

'Where does the Pascoe Lyall come in?' she asked, apropos of nothing.

'Pascoe was my mother's maiden name and Lyall was my father's first name. Eat something, Olivia.'

'I seem to have lost my appetite,' she murmured.

'No, you haven't. It's just a question of making a start and it'll do you good.'

She glinted him a less than friendly little look. 'You seem to have appointed yourself the arbiter of what I should and should not do these days, Ben.'

He raised an eyebrow at her. 'Funny you should say that because I know one thing that would do you the world of good.'

'Really? What might that be?'

'Put it like this,' he said slowly, and stared at the salad for a long moment. Then he raised his eyes to hers and they were, to her surprise, quite serious. 'After we've eaten, a walk back along the beach would be beneficial. Then if you'd like a nightcap we could have one on the terrace whilst we watched the moon—did you know it was full moon tonight?'

'No.'

'It is.' He smiled faintly. 'And then, since you've adopted the blue bedroom, we could retire to it and I could run my hands up and down your body as I did once before, and take your clothes off slowly. And we could do the thing we've been dying to do—we could make love with all the passion I know you're capable of and we could blend it with the things that make us laugh together—you could even sing to me again, Olivia.'

A tremor ran through her body that she was unable to conceal.

He said nothing but his eyes told her he hadn't missed it.

'You don't—' She moistened her lips and started again. 'You don't feel that's above and beyond the call of duty, Ben? For you, I mean?'

'I can assure you duty has nothing to do with it, Olivia.'

'It must,' she protested. 'Otherwise, how would you describe yourself, Ben? I can't quite think of it at the moment but there has to be a name for a man who is unfaithful to a woman even *before* the wedding.'

'Some would say better before than after, but…' he paused and toyed with his glass '…I'm not one of them. Therefore, there is to be no wedding. Caitlin and I have broken our engagement.'

CHAPTER SEVEN

'MADAM is not enjoying the marinara? If it is not to her liking I will replace it with *anything* of her choice,' the waiter said effusively as Olivia stared open-mouthed at Ben. 'You have only to say the word. A guest of Mr Bradshaw is our first priority.'

She closed her mouth then said hastily, 'No, thank you, it's fine.' She started to eat.

'Well, we've achieved something,' Ben remarked as the waiter left, reassured.

'I'm speechless,' Olivia responded, and continued to eat.

'I would have thought I'd earned your approval.'

'How can you say that? How...could you just do it like that? Is she...?' She stopped.

'Is she...?' he prompted.

Olivia put her fork down and drank some wine. 'Devastated, for example?' Her gaze was sardonic.

'Not really,' he replied, and finished his ravioli.

'Oh, I see. Only partially?'

He reached for his glass and stared at it absently. 'That could be the purpose of an engagement. To find out how well suited you really are, before you tie the knot.'

'I'm afraid I've thought of it a little differently—and not so long ago you could have got yourself sued for breach of promise, Ben.'

He smiled slightly.

'How can you sit there and be so calm about it?'

He raised a wry eyebrow. 'I didn't say I was calm about it.'

'But you must have loved her—why ask her to marry you otherwise? And then to break it off all because of a bump on the head! That's insane.'

'Not so insane,' he said slowly. 'But if you've had enough I feel there might be better places to have this discussion—especially if you're going to get even more hot and bothered about it.'

She breathed raggedly then looked around to see a few curious gazes directed their way. 'Let's go,' she said through her teeth. 'But I am not going to go to bed with you, Benedict Bradshaw, if for no other reason than because you appear to me to be a womanizer of the highest order.'

'Womanizer,' he mused quizzically. 'That could be the word you were looking for earlier.'

She got up and walked out.

He caught her up five minutes later as she strode along the pathway, oblivious to the delights of a full moon and its golden pathway across the sea.

'You've broken Angelo's heart, Olivia.' He stepped into place at her side.

'Blow Angelo,' she said. 'What about Caitlin's heart?'

'Essentially, that's between me and Caiti, but I don't believe I have broken her heart.'

Olivia refused to look at him and kept striding out.

He loped along beside her then stopped suddenly. 'This is it.'

Olivia looked up at the house. 'I don't want to go in.'

'That's childish, Olivia.'

'No it's not. I just—I don't know what to think.' She closed her eyes and shook her head dazedly.

He held up the long packet she hadn't noticed he was carrying. 'Angelo insisted we take the wine, since we'd had barely a glass each. Let's sit on the terrace and discuss this. You can always run away down the beach if things get too much for you.'

'Don't kid yourself that I wouldn't, Ben,' she warned.

He brought two glasses and poured the wine.

It was a still, warm night and the surf was rhythmic and soothing. As they sat in silence they saw the twinkling lights of a plane flying low and parallel to the coast on its final approach to Coolangatta Airport.

It made Olivia think of her uncle because Coolangatta was next door to Tugun.

Ben must have read her thoughts because he put his mobile phone on the table. 'Would you like to ring the hospital? I've put the number into the memory bank.'

She nodded gratefully and he got the hospital for her.

She handed the phone back to him a couple of minutes later. 'He's resting comfortably.'

'Good.' He pushed the aerial down and closed it. 'Olivia, about Caiti.'

'I thought it was between you and her.'

'I'm not planning to burden you with the intimate details but, yes, I did think I—should marry her. I never spoke a truer word, however, when I told *you* that I wasn't sure how being in love survived being married. Do you remember?'

'I...yes. It was something we agreed upon.'

'So we did. And for a variety of reasons that bump on the head and what happened whilst I had no recollection of her made me see that we wouldn't last the distance, Caiti and I.'

'Why?' Olivia asked intensely. 'You couldn't remember anything for a time, so you said, not even your name. That doesn't mean...anything!'

He cast her a quizzical little glance then put his hands behind his head and stretched his legs out. 'Perhaps not. But, for whatever reason, I found myself wondering why we kept postponing our marriage.'

Olivia moved suddenly and looked at him narrowly. 'She said... I mean...' She trailed off.

'She said something like that to you?'

'Well, yes, but—' She stopped and shrugged. 'I didn't believe it meant anything.'

'What it meant was this—we were both afraid of taking that final step. Caiti because of what she would have to give up and me because—whilst she's lovely and amusing, stunning to squire around and perhaps the kind of glamorous girl I thought I ought to be marrying, and we were good in bed—I was conscious of a lack.'

Olivia reached a little blindly for her glass. 'Poor Caiti,' she murmured.

'Only I couldn't find a name for it,' he said sombrely. 'And it wasn't a lack in her so much as in me. Because I'd tried to bury a certain cynicism on the subject of love and marriage, I'd pretended to myself that we had enough going for each other to have a marriage that was probably as good as it was going to get.'

'That is cynical,' Olivia said involuntarily.

He looked at her briefly then shrugged. 'There were other, humorous pressures.'

'Such as?'

'If you've ever felt like a prospective heir factory, my mother, whose only child I am, is positively thirsting for grandchildren. She was convinced that Caiti and I would have lovely offspring.'

Olivia stared at him. 'Well, *she* obviously had no reservations about you marrying Caitlin.'

'No, but that's because she has some quite severe reservations about me in general.' He reached for his glass.

'I don't understand.'

He gazed at the path of moonlight on the water. 'She and my father were very young when they married. Twenty-one and twenty-two; she was the older.'

He paused and grimaced. 'And that's the way she believes it should happen—not that the wife should be older but that when you get to the grand old age of *thirty-three* you're spoilt, capricious, jaded and cynical. She told me to thank my lucky stars Caiti had come along because if I hadn't found the right wife by now I most probably never would—according to what I was mistakenly looking for.'

'And you tended to believe her?'

'Yep,' he said.

'Then all I can say is—it's just as well you got a bump on the head, Ben.' Olivia shook her head and finished her wine.

'That's a change of heart.'

'Not really. I'm more than ever convinced you're a womanizer but I now see that Caitlin has had a lucky escape.'

'Well, we're agreed there.'

'Yes, but does *she*...?'

'She was actually nerving herself to tell me that we couldn't get married for another four months at least, because she'll be filming on location about a thousand miles away and will only be able to be home on the weekends.' He poured the last of the wine.

Olivia blinked.

'Are you speechless again?' he drawled.

'I...this doesn't have anything to do with me...'

He smiled. 'Dear Livvie Lockhart, you have an astonishingly short memory!'

'Why do you only call me Livvie in conjunction with Lockhart?'

'As a *non sequitur* that was almost inspired,' he said with soft satire.

'But why?' she persisted stubbornly, although her cheeks reddened.

'I like Olivia. I think it suits you and I think I shall always call you that unless I'm teasing you or I'm reminded that you're Livvie to everyone else. It will be a good way of keeping those private things between us—very private.'

'Ben,' she said helplessly, 'you don't seriously imagine that the fact that you've cast off your fiancée and admitted what amounts to your *knowing* it wasn't true love anyway recommends you to me?'

He stared at her.

'On top of,' she added precisely and with a lot more feeling, 'the shameful scam you pulled about how much of your memory was actually lost, not to mention every other thing I mistrust and dislike about you.'

There was a long silence. Then he said coolly, 'Would you rather I propositioned you differently?'

'Differently? How?' She frowned at him.

'I could offer to buy a share of Wattle Creek rather than the whole caboodle, on one condition. That you consent to be my mistress.'

She gasped and stood up abruptly. 'I would never, *ever* agree to anything like that!'

'It would solve all your problems in one go, though,' he said lazily. 'Your uncle could live out the rest of his life on a station he loves. You could do the same, surrounded by all the history of the Lockhart family that means so very much to you.' He paused and looked at her with irony. 'And it would take care of whatever it was that prompted you to kiss me so very passionately in the creek— Sit down,' he added with just a hint of menace as she looked longingly at the empty wine bottle.

'You can't order me around—'

'In the interests of my own safety, yes, I can. Don't

forget you've already thought about braining me with a cake tin. But, although I hesitate to point it out—I'm sure it will go down as another black mark against me—I am a lot stronger than you are, Olivia.'

She gasped again, but although he gave no sign of being about to leap up and overpower her she got the distinct feeling that she shouldn't put it past him.

She sank down. 'You're despicable, Ben Bradshaw.'

'I may be; I'm also the man you want, if you would allow yourself to be honest.' He shrugged. 'As I want you.'

'Want,' she said scathingly. 'Don't you think you got yourself into enough trouble the last time you tried to convince yourself that was enough?'

He chuckled suddenly but she was not to know what he was going to say because his phone rang.

It was the hospital to say that her uncle had had a sudden relapse.

'I'll take you,' he said quietly.

'No, I—'

'Olivia, don't argue.'

She didn't.

It was mid-morning the next day by the time they got back to the house at Mermaid Beach. Garth Lockhart had survived emergency surgery but the fact that they'd had to operate again was not good news.

Ben had insisted on staying with her throughout the long night, and he said, as she stood in the foyer of his mother's house looking white and exhausted, 'Bed for you, my dear. But take this first.'

'What is it?'

'A mild sleeping pill. I asked them for it.'

'Thanks. And thank you for all you've done. But I think I should stay awake in case—'

He smiled slightly and touched her cheek gently. 'I'll do that and I'll wake you if necessary. Off you go.'

The sun was setting as she swam up out of a deep sleep.

She lay still for a while as all the events of the last twenty-four hours filtered through her mind and a question came to her lips—what do you do with a man like Ben Bradshaw?

How to separate the fun side of him or the way he'd sat with her through the long dark hours of the night…getting her coffee, talking when she wanted to talk, about a wide variety of things, pushing two chairs together so she could lie down for a while…from the other side of him?

From the man who suggested you become his mistress in return for being able to stay on Wattle, she reminded herself brutally. Who lied to you by omission.

She got up at last and pulled her yellow costume on, hoping that a swim in the sea might clear her head.

He was reading on the main terrace as she came out of the house. He had his feet propped up on a table and he was wearing a pair of navy board shorts, no shirt and dark glasses.

She hesitated but he must have heard her because

he put his book down and removed the glasses to look around.

'Ah. Feeling better?'

'Yes, thank you. Any news?'

'He's resting comfortably once again—can I come too?'

Olivia sighed with relief then she blinked at him. 'Come?'

'For a swim?'

'Of course. It's going to be another lovely evening.'

'Yep!'

They stepped down onto the sand together and moments later were plunging into the water.

'Almost as good as Wattle Creek!' he called to her over the surf, then set out in a fast crawl to beyond the breakers.

She followed.

'You swim really well for a girl brought up beyond the black stump.'

They paddled in the calm water. 'My boarding-school saw to that.' She dived under the water and came up to flip onto her back. 'They also taught me how to play tennis.'

'Now that—would be interesting.'

'How so?' She moved her arms gently to keep herself afloat.

'I play a mean game of tennis myself.'

'I imagine you would. So, tennis, polo—what else do you do?'

'Oddly enough I've never been any good at golf. It doesn't suit my temperament.'

'Why not?' she asked quizzically.

He swam right up to her and his eyes were as blue as the sea beneath wet, spiky lashes. 'Trying to thrash a tiny white ball about the place for hours frustrates me unbearably.'

'What about polo balls—?

'Pucks, they're not balls.'

'Sorry, pucks, then. And tennis balls?'

'They're bigger and you can have a really good go at them and you can smash them around to relieve your feelings.'

'Are you saying you're too impatient for golf?' she queried with a smile.

'Patience is not a virtue I'm renowned for.'

She laughed, sank and came up spluttering.

'Do you think that's funny?'

'Yes—I don't know why,' she confessed. 'Well, I do; I just had this mental image of you behaving atrociously on a golf course then charming everyone witless.'

He looked injured. 'That's not a very nice thing to say, Olivia.'

'Don't tell me you don't know just how to charm people witless— Don't answer,' she said with a grin. 'I bet I can beat you back to the beach!' And she started to swim furiously.

He turned to see what she had seen behind him—a perfect breaker forming—and with his long, powerful strokes caught it as she did and they surfed marvellously all the way into the beach.

They lay side by side at the tide mark, he on his back, she propped on her elbows as they got their breath back and the water washed gently over them up to their waists.

'Aren't you tired?' she asked.

'I had a couple of hours' sleep—with my phone right beside me.'

'I suppose you're one of those people who don't need a lot of sleep either.'

He turned to look at her with a grimace. 'Is that another black mark?'

'No. I'm just trying to figure you out, Ben Bradshaw.'

'I don't think I'm that difficult to figure out. The difficulty comes from the circumstances in which we met.'

'Could I ask you a favour?'

'Be my guest.'

She hesitated.

He took the opportunity to say, 'Let me guess. No more talk of asking you to be my mistress for the moment?' He turned over, propped his chin on his hands and looked into her eyes. They were only inches apart.

And lying so close to him as the ripples came and went suddenly caused Olivia to be almost overwhelmed by sheer desire.

The skin of his shoulders and arms was sleek and golden, more tanned than she remembered. And the muscles beneath them lay taut and powerful. His back was smooth although his chest was sprinkled with dark hair, his legs long and powerful too.

And she thought that she would like nothing more than to be intensely physical with Ben Bradshaw right there and then. Because her body was developing an ache of sheer longing to be handled and pulled close, to be possessed, and a feeling of lovely anticipation grew and spread through her just at the thought of it.

'Olivia?'

She swallowed and stood up. 'Yes, please. If you wouldn't mind. I don't seem to be able to handle it too well at the moment—' She broke off and bit her lip at the utter irony of what she'd said and sent a swift prayer heavenwards that he wouldn't read her mind.

'On one condition,' he murmured, and stood up himself.

'What's that?' she asked warily.

He looked her over, from her dripping hair down to her toes and all her figure beneath the clinging yellow Lycra in between, but as she went to move awkwardly away he said gravely, although a smile touched his eyes, 'That you'll let me cook you dinner.'

'I…I didn't know you cooked,' she said lamely.

'There's a lot you don't know about me but let's not go into that—as a matter of fact, I don't, well, not that well.'

'But you just offered…*to* cook me dinner.'

'If you would help I'm sure I could manage it. Let me tell you what I had in mind.' He took her hand and started to walk towards the house. 'Prawns, rice and a salad.'

Olivia glanced at him through her lashes. 'Go on—do you have any prawns, or is that another figment of your imagination like your cooking?'

'I popped out while you were fast asleep and purchased three dozen of the finest prawns,' he told her. 'And I'm sure there's rice in the house as well as salad ingredients. I also bought a crusty brown loaf.'

'Green prawns or cooked prawns?' she enquired.

'Green—fresh off a trawler, they told me.'

'I—well, I do—know a good way of doing them.'

'I knew I could rely on you, Livvie Lockhart,' he said with infinite satisfaction.

'Did you, now? I have to tell you you're going to be the one to peel them, however, Ben,' she said seriously. 'Then they should be marinated for a while.'

'I'm yours to command.'

They went straight to the kitchen because, as Olivia suggested, they could shower and change while the prawns were marinating.

'Leave the tails on,' she instructed, 'and butterfly them.'

'How?'

She peeled a prawn and slit it down the back so that it opened out into a butterfly shape. 'That's how.'

'Hmm… OK, but it's going to take me a lot longer than you.'

'Unlike you, I have a lot of patience,' she said serenely. 'And I'm not the one who offered to cook dinner under completely false pretences. Just take your time,' she advised.

'I'm sure you can be a right tyrant, Olivia,' he commented.

She tucked her towel around her more securely and

assembled the ingredients for the marinade in his mother's pale grey, dream kitchen.

'I am good at instructing people now you come to mention it so I'll tell you how to make this. Take a bowl.' She showed him the stainless-steel bowl she'd found. 'Pour in some sesame seed oil, some soy sauce and crush in half a clove of garlic. You could also add some white wine if you were so minded but I won't bother.'

'Why not? We could drink the rest of it.'

'I seem to spend a lot of time drinking with you these days, but it's your wine.' She shrugged.

He got a bottle from the wine rack and opened it for her. 'I'll chill it before we get really decadent and have a glass or two,' he murmured, and went back to the prawns. 'Then what?'

'That's it, for the marinade. I'll do the rice now and the salad.'

'Won't the rice get cold?'

'I find it's actually better to cook rice first, in the microwave, then heat it up just before you serve it. It comes out even nicer and fluffier.'

'I could become a gourmet cook if this keeps up.'

She didn't answer and he eyed her back thoughtfully at the same time as he wondered if she knew how revealing her grey eyes were. How they'd widened when they'd been lying side by side in the water and he could have sworn the same thoughts were running through her mind as were running through his. Still, he cautioned himself, the longer I can keep this kind of friendliness up, the harder it's going to be for you to resist, Livvie Lockhart, did you but know it.

Because, for reasons you may not care to know about, I intend to have you one day, and willingly.

She turned suddenly and their gazes locked. He said nothing and neither did she until she made a curious little gesture, as if to cut the contact that seemed to be flowing between them, and reached for a knife.

'You peel, I'll butterfly them,' she murmured. 'Otherwise we will be here all night.'

Half an hour later the prawns were marinating, the salad was made, the rice done, and Olivia thankfully retreated once more to the blue bedroom.

Not that anything momentous took place, she thought, then corrected herself swiftly. Yes, it did! We looked at each other with no pretence, no dissemination and he knew how I felt just as *I* know there's an electric field around us at times that's devastatingly sensual. How long can I resist it?

But I haven't even had time to think properly about the breaking of his engagement to Caitlin, his diabolical offer to make me his mistress—I'm still unable to believe I'm about to lose Wattle Creek, really believe it, she mused. How could so much happen in the space of a week, roughly?

She threw her towel down, entered the bathroom and peeled off her costume with her mind far from what she was doing. But she finished off her shower with a needle spray of cold water that made her gasp but would, hopefully, restore some sharpness of mind to her.

And the first thing she did when she came out of the shower was ring the hospital. Prawns or no prawns, that was where she should be, she decided. But the excellent staff thought otherwise, it seemed.

'The doctor has just seen him and is much happier with his condition now, Miss Lockhart,' the ward sister told her. 'But we're keeping him sedated and will do throughout the night. There's no point in you spending another night here—get a good rest, my dear.'

'I had a rest today—'

'All the same, conserve your strength while you have the chance, there'll be quite a long convalescence for you to cope with.'

'If you're very sure?' Olivia said.

'I am.'

She put the phone down and stared at it rather helplessly. That was plan A, she reflected. Plan B? Well, the prawns at least, I guess.

'Nice,' Ben said approvingly as she walked into the lounge.

Olivia looked down at herself ruefully. She had on a long, floating dress in a cool mint cotton with cream and pink swirls on it. 'I made it myself,' she murmured.

'Ah. Another plus,' he commented, and handed her a tall glass that was almost as artistically swirled as her dress.

She took it and raised an eyebrow at him.

'A cocktail of my own concocting.'

'Not one that leaps up and bites you when you least expect it, I hope?'

He considered. 'Not really. It's mostly pineapple

juice and cream with a dash of Cointreau and crème de menthe.'

'No wonder it's so pretty.'

'Sit down, Olivia,' he invited. 'You look as if you're poised for flight.'

She glanced at him coolly and sat down on a peach couch with as much composure as she could muster. 'I rang the hospital again.' She told him what the sister had said.

'Well, that's good news—apart from the long convalescence bit.'

'Yes.'

'But he couldn't be better placed with someone like you to look after him.'

Olivia sipped some of the cocktail and found it was delicious. But she put it down on the table in front of her and brushed back her fringe. 'I don't know about that. I feel very guilty about not realizing something was seriously wrong with him. So much for my nursing skills.'

'He told me he'd done his best to hide it from you.'

'I know. I used to rub embrocation on his back and nag at him to do muscle-strengthening exercises.' She shrugged. 'I can't tell you how foolish that makes me feel.'

'I think you're being too hard on yourself, Olivia.'

She glanced up at him. He was lounging on the opposite couch and he'd changed into blue and black checked shorts and a black T-shirt. 'I think, as it happens,' she said slowly, 'that there's another reason for it.'

He looked at her narrowly. 'Such as?'

'What everyone seems to be accusing me of these days.' She picked up her glass and took another sip. 'I was so wrapped up in Wattle Creek and preserving the homestead et cetera, I was blind, figuratively, to just about anything else.'

He said nothing but she didn't miss the sudden look of compassion in his eyes. Which is tantamount to agreeing with me, she told herself, and flinched inwardly. Because the last thing she wanted was his compassion, either.

'So, I'm presented with a real dilemma,' she murmured. 'But the thing is—' she looked at him again '—I still have to pinch myself to believe any of this is real.'

'Have you been able to think about anything I said?' he queried.

'Such as your offer to buy only part of Wattle if I'd consent to be your mistress? Believe me, I need to do a lot more than pinch myself to make that seem real. Could I be right in hoping you said it in the heat of the moment?'

He laughed softly. 'As a matter of fact I was slightly annoyed at the time. Although—' there was a sudden acuteness in his eyes that she didn't miss '—it *would* solve certain things.'

It hit Olivia with almost the same force her brain seizure on the bank of the creek had—only this time it's sanity, not the opposite, she thought bitterly. But there is only one thing to do because I am never again going to put myself through the pain of…waking up to being in love with this man only to be confronted by the evidence of how unattainable he is…

Because even if he has shed his fiancée I can't exactly applaud it, and to think of me only in mistress terms—well, it speaks for itself besides being thoroughly despicable!

'Thank you,' she said quietly, 'but the answer is no. I feel quite sure we wouldn't suit.'

'Even though we can barely keep our hands off each other, Olivia?' he drawled. 'You have some strange notions.'

A flame of anger licked through her. 'Do you think so? You know, I'm reminded of something you said to me—if this isn't a duel for dominance, if this isn't something even worse such as sheer blackmail—I'm a Dutchman, Ben.'

He regarded her thoughtfully for a long moment. 'So what do you have in mind?'

She took a breath. 'The only thing I can do—give in gracefully.' She closed her eyes briefly then forced herself to open them and look directly at him. 'I won't oppose the sale of Wattle.'

He raised his eyebrows. 'That would put us on neutral territory, Olivia,' he said dryly, 'but it's a little surprising in view of what *you* once said to me.'

'I'm not interested in putting us on neutral territory,' she said tautly, and breathed raggedly as she tried to gather her thoughts. 'And what I said to you about being dragged off kicking and screaming—don't imagine I won't be screaming inside but—it's come home to me that I have been remiss and put a place before people and—there's nothing else I can do.'

'So, becoming the lover of a man you want is too high a price to pay even for Wattle Creek?'

'Simply—yes.' She opened her hands and closed them.

'Well, I admire you for that. Drink some more of your cocktail,' he suggested. 'Even if only for medicinal purposes.'

'I might choke— What do you *mean* you admire it? You were the one who suggested it!'

He shrugged and smiled a wry little smile. 'I have the feeling you'd make a very troublesome mistress, Olivia. Yes, I feel one would wonder what one had taken on! But, in point of fact, I don't run to mistresses; I'm not really that kind of man,' he murmured.

Olivia stood up carefully. 'Ben Bradshaw, if you were testing me, if you feel you have the right to test me like that—oh! I could kill you.'

'That's nothing new,' he said with a lurking little smile. 'By the way, having gone to all that trouble, should we now cook our masterpiece?'

But Olivia could only stand transfixed, as pale as paper and with her eyes huge and dark.

He sobered, stood up abruptly and came towards her.

'Don't...' she whispered.

'Don't be a fool,' he said roughly. 'What do you think I'm going to do?'

'I don't know but—'

'Look, sit down before you faint,' he ordered, then simply picked her up and sat her down and sat down beside her. 'Here.' He put the glass in her hand and guided it to her lips.

She hesitated then drank and felt the colour returning to her face.

He said, 'Would you tell me one thing at least, Olivia? It might—' he grimaced '—just rein in the Machiavellian side of my nature.'

She glanced at him suspiciously. 'What?'

'*I* am exceedingly troubled to be sitting next to you, drinking in the perfume of your skin and hair, having the feel of your body on my fingertips, the taste of your lips on mine and a host of other memories but *not* having an admission from you that things could be the same for you.'

She swallowed, moved restlessly but said nothing.

'Let's try another tack, then. What is so difficult about making such an admission?'

It was as if his words had opened up the channels of all her sensory perceptions. Their shoulders were brushing and she could feel the warmth of his body on her skin, she too could breathe the clean male tang of his skin and feel the taste of his lips on hers, the hardness of his body against her own soft slenderness, the crispness of his dark hair in her fingers...

'I...' She paused and turned to look into his eyes to find them serious for once and with his question mirrored in them. 'I...know where it would lead if I made that admission,' she said huskily. 'But for all the wrong reasons.'

'What could be so wrong about it, Olivia?' he said quietly, and, as she went to look away, put a long finger under her chin.

She closed her eyes then lifted her lashes. 'How can you not know, Ben? Only days ago you were engaged to another girl. Only—well, in the near future you'll own Wattle and I'll be gone from it—yes, it might be the sensible thing and all the rest but I'll never be able to disassociate that from you and I can't applaud the way you've broken your engagement.'

'In other words—you could never forgive me, Olivia?' He released her chin.

'No.' She sipped some more of her cocktail. 'I think I know myself well enough to know…that.'

'I see.' He sat back. 'So you're saying there could be no future for us?'

She nodded.

'And that's all I'm going to get,' he murmured wryly. 'Oh, well, you win some and lose some—shall we cook?'

The prawns were delicious.

They ate outside on the terrace and it was curiously companionable. He told her about his interests in Argentina and quite a lot about his life in general.

'Are you based at Charleville?' she asked.

'The Queensland division of the company is—we have a property there and an office—but I spend a lot of time in Brisbane, Sydney and Melbourne.'

'So where do you call home?'

He looked at her meditatively. 'Nowhere, really. I have apartments in a couple of places and this.' He gestured to the house.

'Not even the place you grew up?'

'I grew up in a lot of different places,' he said humorously. 'That's why I'm such a gregarious, eclectic character.'

'Outback properties, though?'

'Mostly,' he agreed. 'Uncle Garth said you'd been to all the right schools et cetera.'

He raised a wry eyebrow then grinned wickedly. 'That could account for me being such a polished, well-spoken, well-presented kind of bloke. As a matter of fact I even have good teeth.'

She had to laugh although something felt as if it was bleeding to death inside her.

But he seemed to be unaware of her inner turmoil although she was conscious that he was going out of his way to smooth the path of the evening for her in the charming and funny way that only he could.

They tidied up the kitchen together and when it was done she stood in the middle of it and wondered how to say goodnight.

He did it for her. 'Bed, I think, Livvie Lockhart. Goodnight—but one thing before you go.'

She looked at him. They were separated by a couple of feet, and he was leaning back against a counter with his arms folded across his black T-shirt.

She licked her lips. 'What?'

'There's only one thing for you to worry about at the moment and that's getting your uncle well again.'

'I…' she brushed back her fringe '…I think I may have learnt that lesson, Ben.'

He paused and let his blue gaze travel down her long dress and she felt herself tense inwardly, but all he said was, 'If you ever need—assistance, all you have to do is ask, Olivia.'

'Thank you,' she said very quietly, 'but I'll be fine. Goodnight.' She walked away.

But she cried herself to sleep in the blue bedroom because she knew she'd never forget Ben Bradshaw even if he was a womanizer and everything else she held against him. Because there would be so many memories to haunt her—Ben and Bonnie, the creek, this house and their swim, but also those words that would torment her: 'you win some and lose some'.

He was gone when she got up the next morning.

There was a note stuck on the fridge with a fish-shaped magnet that made no excuses or apologies for his departure but said simply that she was to avail herself of the house for as long as was necessary, and gave a number to call when she needed Steve to fly them back to Wattle Creek.

She took it off the fridge and read it through a blur of tears—there was only one personal touch to it. He'd signed himself Benedict Arnold.

She was about to screw it up and throw it in the bin when something held her back and she found herself doing the strangest thing. She raised it to her lips and kissed it gently. But then she straightened her shoulders and tore it up.

So that's that, she thought, and went to ring the hospital.

CHAPTER EIGHT

TEN days later Steve Williams was flying them back to Wattle Creek in a Pascoe Lyall fixed-wing aircraft.

Olivia watched the landscape unfold beneath them. They flew over Emerald, well named with its orchards, vineyards and cotton crops, then over the range to drier country where the colours were subtler and straggling fences and telephone wires went for miles upon miles. And finally the scrub country gave way to the Mitchell grass plains that were home to Wattle Creek Station.

Garth Lockhart, she noticed, was drinking in the landscape as well and she felt her heart contract with pity. But she'd set herself a course and it resolutely refused to encompass bitterness or regret. His doctors had been happy with the outcome of the second operation in the end and had predicted that, if he took things easily, there was a good chance of years ahead for him.

And there was a welcoming committee waiting for them on the airstrip. As Olivia saw them all lined up, she had to breathe deeply to maintain her composure, and to remind herself that at least all these familiar faces would be taken care of.

Three weeks later, the flying doctor paid one of his regular visits to Garth and drew Olivia aside afterwards.

She looked at him anxiously. 'Is there a problem?'

'No, Livvie. I just wanted to tell you you've done a great job. By my reckoning and the tests we've been doing, he's as well as he could be under the circumstances, and provided you can restrain him from leaping about the place he can live a normal life now. In other words you can relax—you look as if you could do with it too,' he added.

She breathed a sigh of relief.

'You'll still need to keep up the diet but it's worth it not only from his heart and arterial point of view, but having lost the weight he has can only do him good.'

'OK.' But as she said it brightly she felt a creeping feeling of dread.

Because, as if by mutual consent, she and her uncle hadn't talked much about the coming move from Wattle during this period of convalescence. They'd idly discussed living on the coast, not the Gold Coast but somewhere round Mackay close to the beautiful Whitsunday Passage, but that was about as far as it had got although she had discreetly started to turn out drawers and cupboards. But with this medical clearance she knew it could no longer be put off.

Something stopped her from taking the plunge, however. A couple more days of this peace and tranquillity can only benefit him, she told herself. And two then three days slid by. Then their weekly mail arrived and he came to find her with a letter in his hand and a stunned expression on his face.

She was in the kitchen lining cake tins. Christmas was only a few weeks away.

'Livvie—Livvie, sit down, girl, will you?'

She looked at him frowningly. 'Why?'

'The most amazing thing,' he said, and sat down himself. 'No, no, let me read it again in case I'm dreaming—if you had a cup of tea handy that might help.'

She shrugged and made the tea. 'OK, before I die of curiosity, spill the beans,' she said lightly and with not the slightest premonition.

Garth Lockhart stared at the letter again then said, 'Livvie, Ben Bradshaw has made us a proposition.'

She stiffened slightly.

'Instead of buying the whole of Wattle, he's offered to buy into the holding company which means in effect that we will still be shareholders but the injection of capital we need will be assured—and we won't have to leave.'

Olivia clenched her hands around her cup and winced as she spilt some tea over them. 'But…I mean, under what conditions, Uncle Garth?'

'None,' he said simply. 'I'll still have a say in the running of the place but I won't have to do any of the work. He's suggested promoting Jack to station manager and bringing him in an assistant to take a lot of the pressure off me—and you.'

For a moment she felt as if she couldn't breathe. Then she made herself say, 'But…how will you feel not having the ultimate say as you've had for so long?'

'I can work with Ben,' he assured her. 'I always

did like the stamp of a man he is. When I first went to see him, before you ever met him, I expected to have to deal with some hard-nosed, entirely profit-orientated businessman but he wasn't like that. He knew what he was talking about when it came to the country and beef production, but not only that, he was courteous and respectful. I was also expecting to be made to feel as if I was going cap in hand but he made me feel quite different.'

Olivia licked her lips. 'How so?'

'Well...' Garth paused reminiscently 'as if all my experience was valuable and of interest to him. I just didn't feel like some broken-down old codger who was about to go broke although I wasn't far from it.'

Is this what it's like to have to eat humble pie? Olivia thought. But how to deal with this? How to handle being often in contact with him again, unless...? No...

'And he's mentioned expressly that the homestead would be considered part of our shareholding. In other words, anything you want to do with it will be up to you.'

'I...can't believe this,' she said barely audibly, but one glance at Garth Lockhart revealed a new man.

And he said softly, 'Oh, Livvie, I've seen you getting around as if your heart was broken although you've tried to put such a brave front on it. I thought I knew how much Wattle meant to you— I didn't know the half of it. But you've got it back, girl!'

If only you knew, Olivia thought, and made herself swallow some tea. Knew that leaving Wattle turned out to be a mild cause of pain compared to losing Ben Bradshaw. And now this.

'When do we have to decide?' she asked.

'What's to decide?' her uncle said gaily. 'But he's coming to see us tomorrow. About lunchtime, he reckons.'

It was a baking hot day the next day, with the sky a pale, shimmering blue.

When Garth was ready to drive down to the airstrip to meet the plane, Olivia told him she still had a few things to do to get lunch ready. He took this unsuspectingly in his stride and was not to know that everything for lunch was perfected and that his niece had nothing to do at all but wait with her nerve-ends screaming.

She heard the plane fly overhead and wandered out of the kitchen because she felt unbearably claustrophobic. And she was standing under a shady gum tree when she saw a vehicle pull up at the front gate of the garden. She frowned because it wasn't the air-conditioned Land Rover her uncle had used but one of the station utilities. Only one person was in it—Ben.

She watched with her heart hammering like a tom-tom as he got out, looked around and saw her. And her limbs locked although she would have dearly loved to run away as he clicked the gate open and walked towards her.

Then he was right in front of her, all the lean, tall, vital stuff of her dreams in khaki trousers, boots and a yellow T-shirt but with his blue eyes unusually sombre.

And he took in the cool pink and grey sundress she wore with white sandals, the wisps of hair that had come down from its knot, the way her hands were clenched and a nerve that was flickering in her jaw. Then he said and put out a hand to cover hers, 'Now will you listen to me, Olivia Lockhart?'

'I...don't know what to say, Ben.'

He smiled slightly. 'Don't say anything, then, until I've explained.'

'But—'

He lifted his hand and touched her lips. 'No, it's my turn.'

'I...'

'Let's sit down,' he suggested.

She hesitated then sank down onto the grass with the skirt of her dress belled out around her. He sat beside her and leant against the trunk of the tree.

'Ben, I—'

'Just hear me out. Then you may speak.' He grimaced but went on immediately. 'I fell in love with you, Olivia. It started as an admiration then became a fascination that took possession of me in a way I hadn't believed could happen. It caused a hunger and a desire to be totally intimate with you in every way and caused me to lose all my cynicism on the subject of what the pressures of marriage could do to what I felt for you—because I know damn well that not being able to have you to live the rest of my life with would be intolerable.'

She stared at him with her lips parted and her grey eyes huge.

He grimaced again. 'What did you think I'd come to say? No, don't answer, as you often say to me. Let me go on.

'Naturally, to discover that this had happened to me when I was engaged to another woman came as something of a shock. And to realize that just about everything else about me was anathema to you, to put it mildly, came as even more of a shock.' He raised a rueful eyebrow.

'It also brought out the worst in me,' he went on. 'But when you steadfastly held to your principles I got over all the knocks to my ego and decided there had to be a way I could prove to you that, despite all the dreadful suspicions you were quite entitled to have about me, I love you, Olivia.'

Their gazes caught and held. 'I didn't plan it, I confess,' he said softly. 'I thought I had my life planned out pretty well. I thought I could work at a marriage with Caiti and the fact that she was fairly dedicated to her acting career would give us—space. And that, as I told you, it might be as good as it could get. The mere *thought* of space between you and I, on the other hand, fills me with dread. These last weeks have been a living hell, for example.'

Olivia swallowed and pushed her fringe aside.

'Could you ever accept,' he said very quietly, 'that I'm not a womanizer, just a poor fool of a man who had no idea what it was really all about until I knocked myself out in your paddock, and met you? Neither am I the kind of monster you took me for business-wise because I couldn't bear to think of you walking away from Wattle Creek, Olivia, and if you really want to we could give our children a hyphenated surname.'

She blinked and her lips curved. 'That is generous—are you asking me to marry you, Ben?'

'I am, but you were going to say something earlier?'

'Yes.' She took a breath and trembled. 'I was going to say that despite your offer I couldn't stay here because it would kill me to have to be in contact with you only on a business partnership basis. You see, losing Wattle in the end became nothing compared to…thinking that I was just a "win some, lose some" proposition for you.'

'That was what little ego I had left talking, Olivia. Plus a belated intimation that I was rushing my fences. My dear—are you sure? I have to tell you I can be diabolical at times—'

'Do you think I don't know that, Ben Bradshaw? It's just, well, I've never sung a man to sleep before—perhaps that's it,' she said helplessly, then they were laughing and in each other's arms kissing hungrily.

'Can I—can I take you somewhere?' he said.

'Right now?'

'Yes, right now.' He stood up and held his hand down to her then led her through the gate to the utility.

'I think I can guess,' she said breathlessly as he drove like the wind and they rattled and bumped over the country. 'Uncle Garth might wonder what we're doing, though.'

He brought the utility to a stop beneath the huge old ghost gums that lined Wattle Creek and looked at her with all the wicked, glinting devilry that he was capable of. 'He won't as it happens.'

Olivia got out. So did he and immediately came round to take her in his arms. 'What do you mean?' she asked.

'He knows full well that—something's on the cards, probably not this precisely but—'

'You told him!'

'I told him that I'd really like the opportunity to mend my fences with you, Olivia,' he said gravely. 'I also brought my mother along; she's dying to meet you—he's giving her a limited tour of the place in the air-conditioned comfort of the Land Rover even as we speak.'

'You are diabolical,' she breathed. 'Were you so sure I—'

'No, my darling.' His eyes changed and they were deadly serious. 'But I wasn't going to let you go without bringing up all the heavy artillery I could.'

'Ben,' she whispered shakenly, 'do I really mean—I mean…?'

But he held her so hard she could barely breathe.

'You asked me where home was, once,' he said later, when they were lying on an old rug from the utility that he'd spread on the grass beside the creek. 'It's here, within you—' he laid his hand on the region of her heart '—-and, because you and Wattle are inseparable, it will be home too.'

'That's lovely,' she said softly, 'but I won't hold you to it.'

'What do *you* mean?' He pushed himself up on one elbow and looked down at her frowningly.

'That I'll never again allow a place and bricks and mortar to mean more to me than anything else, that's all. Or, to put it in your terms, my home will be where *your* heart is.'

For a moment he looked comically put out. 'So much for grand gestures,' he said slowly, then laughed. 'Do you think I was trying to play Lord Bountiful?'

'Not at all,' she replied innocently.

'Well, I was but once again you've brought me back to earth.' He looked at her ruefully.

She sat up with a secret little smile. 'Can I tell you something?'

'Of course.'

'One morning, a few weeks ago and only a day after our first—encounter, right here…' She stopped and looked around at the dappled shade. The creek wasn't as full as it had been that day but was still running and the birds were singing and there were crickets and cicadas chorusing shrilly. Beyond the shade the landscape was shimmering in a haze of heat.

'I remember it well,' he said gravely, and sat up so that their shoulders were touching.

She glanced at him with a tinge of colour in her cheeks at what she saw in his eyes but went on steadily, 'I woke up that morning—in love.' She paused as she heard his swiftly indrawn breath. 'I told myself I shouldn't be, I barely knew you, but I did know you could be lethally charming and I very much suspected that most women would find you hard to resist. It didn't make any difference.'

'Olivia—'

She put her hand over his. 'It's my turn, Ben. Nothing I told myself altered the fact that the world had become a different place for me, a better place. My heart was light, I was filled with a sense of anticipation, I felt like a girl in love for the very first time. I went out as the sun was rising and picked myself some flowers and knew that nothing I did could change how I felt about you.'

He sighed and put his arm around her. 'Then you got one shock on top of another.'

She laid her head on his shoulder. 'I felt beat, bushed and battered, yes,' she confessed. 'And angry, deeply angry, but it didn't change. Even when I told you I couldn't see any future for us, I was still in love with you. Far too much to be able to accept anything less from you.'

'My darling Olivia,' he said bleakly, 'I—

'I'm telling you this, Ben, not to make you feel bad,' she said with a faint smile, 'but just to let you know that you *are* my Lord Bountiful, you make the very air I breathe so rarefied, it makes me giddy just to be close to you—so don't feel downcast because your grand gesture fell a little flat.'

He was speechless for a moment then they were laughing together, he exultantly, until he said, 'There's only one problem with that—I ought to take you back to lunch all proper and correct but I don't think I'm capable of it now.'

'I'd be most disappointed if you didn't kiss me first,' she murmured.

'Ah, there was a bit more to it that I had in mind.'

'Perhaps we should take our clothes off first this time?' she suggested, entirely seriously, apart from the little glint in her eye.

'Good thinking,' he replied. 'By the way I checked that Bonnie was in her stall—should she suddenly recall her chaperon duties.'

Olivia glanced around and said ruefully, 'I wish you hadn't reminded me of that. There is a pair of little people who have the unfortunate habit of turning up—anywhere.'

'You can't be referring to Sonia and Ryan!' He looked shocked.

'Strangely enough I am.'

'Then you must be a mind-reader. Steve is giving all the kids a flight over the property as it happens.'

Olivia turned to him, her eyes alight with love and laughter. 'You are diabolical, Ben Bradshaw! I doubt you had any intention of taking me back to lunch all proper and correct.'

'Well, possibly not, but you know what an impatient type of guy I am.'

'So—there's nothing for it but to humour you?' She eyed him then stood up and issued a challenge. 'Bet I can beat you in!'

'I knew, I knew you'd be like this,' he said unsteadily.

They'd frolicked in the water, splashing each other, then come together with all laughter banished as desire gripped them.

'Like what?' she asked breathlessly.

'Pale, satiny.' He held her away from him and his gaze travelled down her glistening body from her small, firm breasts, the slight swell of her belly to the triangle of darker curls at the base of it, then the sweep of her legs. 'Purely feminine under your tough jillaroo exterior—and I mean that only in a mental sense.'

'I have to tell you, Ben, that I feel exquisitely feminine when you look at me like that but also, I always knew you were something of an Adonis under your clothes.'

'You had the advantage of me, Olivia. You always did.'

'I don't know about that.' She smoothed her hands over his shoulders then down his chest and he cupped her bottom. 'But I can also remember doing something like this.' She raised her arms above her head. 'Because the way I felt when you ran your hands down me was—something else, and I had my clothes on then.'

He did it again and said, 'I may not have to tell you what it does to me.'

'Oh, Ben,' she gasped as he folded her into his arms then picked her up and carried her out of the creek to lay her on the blanket.

It was something she said several more times as he claimed her, with various shades of meaning in her voice, desire, rapture, pleading when the pleasure was almost more than she could bear and, finally, pure ecstasy.

They were quiet for a time afterwards, supremely

shaken in Olivia's case by the intensity of their love-making.

'All right?' he said at last.

'No,' she whispered.

He looked at her with concern.

She touched her fingertips to the scar on his temple. 'I'm actually better than I've ever felt in my life,' she murmured, 'just a bit stunned.'

He buried his head between her breasts for a long moment then kissed her lips. 'The feeling is mutual.'

'How are we going to...meet and greet people?'

'With extreme difficulty if you mean what I think you mean. How will we be able to tear our thoughts from us and this?' He drew his hand down her back and let it lie on her hip.

She cleared her throat and moved her body against his. 'Yes.'

'We could leave them a note,' he suggested.

She smiled but it died and it shook her even more to see an answering smile in his eyes that died just as swiftly as hers had. But he said gently after a long moment, 'How would it be if we broke the news, made some arrangements and pleaded for their indulgence? Some immediate time on our own in other words.'

'I think that would be...about as much as I could handle,' she said softly. 'I didn't know, you see...' She stopped and looked at him a little helplessly.

'Well, that's where I had the advantage of you, my Livvie Lockhart. I did know it would be like this—it couldn't have been any other way between us. And what's more, don't imagine it will ever be any different.'

Her eyes danced for a moment. 'For a non-believer you've become the opposite, Benedict Arnold.'

'I wondered if you'd ever call me that again.'

'I...well, I wondered when you signed that very impersonal note you left me at Mermaid Beach whether it might be a secret sign but then I told myself it was only wishful thinking.'

'There were times when I told myself it was wishful thinking that you'd even notice how I'd signed myself.'

Olivia breathed softly, 'I not only noticed, I kissed it—before I tore it up.'

He grimaced. 'That sounds a lot like you, Olivia.' And once again they were laughing together and gradually she felt more normal and as if she might just be able to face the world.

She told him this but added gravely, 'I could need a bit of help if I'm to be anything approaching proper and correct.'

'Anything I can do at all?' he replied promptly.

'Let me go for one thing—I don't seem to have the will to free myself.'

'You'll never know how hard this is going to be,' he said with a wicked little grin, and kissed her lingeringly. But then he did release her and, taking her hand, helped her up and led her back into the creek.

'Oh, no!' she groaned. 'This is where it all started!'

'Place your trust in wise old Wattle Creek,' he advised as they started to scoop water over themselves.

Then they found a rough old towel in the back of

the utility and dried themselves off and put their clothes on.

But he took her hand once they were dressed and she was just about to get into the utility. 'You said something about being a non-believer earlier, Olivia.'

'Yes...'

He looked down at her and the world of dappled sunlight, bird song and the chuckle of the creek receded. 'I believe in you more than anything I've believed in in my life.'

'Ben, I love you,' she replied. 'We're home where we belong.'

He raised her hand and kissed her knuckles then they looked at each other with their lips twitching. 'No,' he said.

'No,' she agreed. 'We should be strong. Think of my poor uncle and your poor mother waiting up at the house in possibly dreadful suspense.'

'I am...trying to. You know,' he said thoughtfully, 'it will give me great pleasure, incidentally, to prove my poor mother, who is not poor at all but extremely opinionated and interfering, wrong. She was so convinced I was jaded, cynical, capricious and all the rest of it.'

'Come to think of it,' Olivia said, 'it will delight me to prove to my uncle that I'm not on the shelf and a born spinster who can only paint flowers and care about a cattle station!'

'Should we hop to it, then?'

'Let's,' Olivia agreed joyfully.

OUTBACK BABY

by

Barbara Hannay

Barbara Hannay's first romance novel was published in 1999. She lives in Northern Australia, a fascinating and beautiful location which provides a rich setting for many of her books. When she's not writing, Barbara enjoys refreshing her imagination by travelling with her writer husband to explore exciting new overseas destinations, or to revisit the awe-inspiring mystery of the Australian Outback.

She loves to hear from readers and can be contacted via email at barbara@barbarahannay.com. Her website is www.barbarahannay.com

For Lucy Francesca,
who was born into our family at the time this
story was coming to life

CHAPTER ONE

WHEN Gemma heard the pounding on her front door, she knew something was desperately wrong. Startled, she hurried to answer it, hardly expecting to find her best friend on her doorstep, clutching her ten-month-old daughter to her chest as if the baby were a life-preserver.

'I need your help, Gemma. Are you terribly busy?'

Shocked by the fear in her friend's eyes, Gemma slipped a reassuring arm around her shoulders. 'Bel, you know I'm never too busy for you. Come in and tell me what's wrong.'

Isobel stepped into the flat with a shaky sigh and hefted baby Mollie higher on her hip. Her eyes darted to the pile of paperwork on Gemma's dining table. 'Oh, you *are* busy. I'm sorry.'

'Don't worry about this mess.' With a quick dismissive gesture, Gemma gathered up the designs she'd just finished and slipped them into a manila folder. For the moment she would have to put aside her own panic about deadlines and the need to dash this marketing brochure to the printers this afternoon. Isobel was obviously besieged by much more serious problems. 'How can I help?'

To Gemma's horror, Isobel's normally serene face crumpled and tears spilled onto her cheeks. 'It's Dave.'

'Dave? Has something happened in Africa?' Two months earlier, Isobel's husband Dave had been seconded by an Australian aid agency to sink wells in Somalia.

Isobel hugged Mollie even closer and rested a trembling chin on the baby's curly head. 'It's so sudden, it's terrible. He's being held hostage. I'm sure it's all some awful mistake, but rebels are involved.' She drew a deep shuddering breath, clearly trying to suppress the urge to burst into full-scale crying.

'I can't believe it,' Gemma whispered, gripping her friend's cold fingers while she gaped at her.

Surely this sort of thing didn't happen to ordinary people? Not to easygoing, cheerful Dave Jardine?

She groped for the right words and gave up the struggle. 'I'm so sorry. This is terrible. Poor Dave.' The thought of her childhood friend—the boy she'd grown up with in the bush—facing armed rebels was appalling. How could his wife bear it? She stared helplessly at Isobel's white face and whispered, 'What can we do?'

'I'm going to him,' Isobel answered with a determined lift of her chin.

'*You're* going to Africa?' Gemma pulled out another chair and sat down swiftly. This second shock was almost worse than the first. 'What can you do?' she asked at last.

'Apparently I'm the only one who can do anything,' Isobel explained with wide, frightened eyes. 'Because I'm Dave's wife, the people at the Australian Embassy think I can help. Dave's there for humanitarian reasons and they think the rebels are more likely to respond if we work on the family angle.'

'Oh, Isobel, how brave of you!!' Gemma jumped up again and hugged her. 'Lucky Dave to have such a wonderful wife.' She smiled wistfully. 'Love and the kind of marriage that you guys have—it's—it's *amazing*!' For Gemma it was beyond imagining. With a short burst of pride, she remembered that she shared responsibility for this wonderful partnership by introducing Isobel and Dave during their university days.

Her gaze dropped to the innocent baby perched happily on her mother's lap. 'You couldn't dream of taking little Mollie into a dangerous situation like that?'

'No, of course I couldn't.' Isobel sighed and pressed her lips to her daughter's chubby cheek. 'I can't bear the thought of leaving her behind, but that's where you come in, Gem. I've an enormous favour to ask.'

'Of course—I'll do anything.' Gemma did her best to ignore the nervous knot tightening in her stomach as her mind raced.

'I'm sorry I didn't ring you first to warn you, but I knew you were going to be home and...' Isobel's voice trailed away as she looked at her friend hopefully.

'Just tell me how I can help.'

'I was hoping you could mind Mollie for me.'

Gemma gulped. While she adored Mollie, she knew absolutely zilch about caring for babies. She pressed her lips tightly together before she verbalised any of the sudden doubts that swamped her. Of course she could mind a baby. Millions of women all over the world had been doing it for centuries without turning a hair. 'I'd love to have her,' she said with a bright smile.

Isobel reached out and squeezed Gemma's hand. 'I'm sorry I've dumped this on you at such short notice, but I wouldn't trust anyone else to look after my little girl. My parents are on holiday in Spain, as you know. Dave's father is too old—and it has to be someone I know well. Someone who cares about Mollie. Not a nanny I've never met. Honestly, Gem, you're my best friend and, working from home as you do, I couldn't think of anyone better.'

'I'm flattered that you trust me,' Gemma responded

warmly, but she couldn't help adding, 'You do realise, don't you, that I—I don't have much experience with babies. Actually—I don't have *any* experience with them.'

'Oh, Gemma, you've been around Mollie heaps. And you'll be amazed how it all comes so instinctively. I'm sure you're a natural!' She gave her daughter a motherly hug. 'And Mollie's really quite a good little poppet.'

'Of course,' Gemma responded quickly, not wanting to alarm her friend. 'She's a darling.' When she thought about Dave's desperate plight and Isobel's brave decision to go to Africa, Gemma knew she could hardly make a fuss about caring for one perfectly harmless and tiny human being.

Her friend's grey eyes brightened. 'Don't worry,' she said, 'I've rung Max. I'm sure he'll be happy to help you any way he can.'

'Max?' Gemma had been playing with Mollie's pink toes, but at the mention of Dave's older brother Max, her head jerked up. 'I won't need any help from *him*!'

To her annoyance, Gemma's heart began a fretful pounding.

Since she'd been six years old, Max Jardine had always managed to get under her skin. When they were teenagers, Gemma had never been able to understand why the girls in the outback town of Goodbye Creek, where she and the Jardine boys had gone to school, had scored Max a 'hunk factor' of ten. They had raved about his well-toned body and dark good looks.

'But you've seriously overlooked his personality defects,' she'd pointed out.

'What defects?' the girls had scoffed.

And Gemma had rolled her eyes in disgust. She was well-acquainted with his faults. She'd spent half her childhood on the Jardine's property, camping and canoeing or horse-riding with Dave, and Max had always been in the background, treating her like a bad smell that hung around his brother.

In the years since she'd left the outback she'd only seen Max a handful of times, but nothing had changed. He still looked on her as a lower life-form. She shook her head. 'Max Jardine would know even less than I do about caring for a baby.'

Isobel was regarding Gemma strangely. 'I didn't realise you were so touchy about Max.'

'I'm not *touchy* about him,' Gemma snapped.

Isobel's eyebrows rose. 'If you say so.'

'It's just that I fail to see how a man who spends his whole life marooned in the outback like a hermit with only cattle for company could be any use when it comes to minding Mollie.'

'Maybe you're right,' Isobel agreed cautiously. 'But let's not forget that Max *is* Dave's brother. I had to let him know what had happened.'

Gemma could hardly deny that, but it didn't help her to feel any better. 'How did he react?' she asked warily.

'Actually, I couldn't speak to him directly. There was no answer when I rang through to the property this morning, so I left a message on his answering machine. He must be out in the bush mustering or maybe fencing, so I simply explained what I was going to do.'

'And you told him I would be taking care of Mollie?'

'I said that was my plan.'

'I see.'

Gemma decided there and then that if Max Jardine knew she'd been asked to care for Mollie, she would mind this baby as expertly as a triple-certificated nanny. This wasn't just a case of helping out her best friend.

She didn't want to give Mollie's grumpy Uncle Max one tiny chance to criticise her.

Exactly why Gemma cared about Max's opinion was an issue she didn't have time to consider now. She was too busy worrying about how she could mind Mollie *and* carry on her business.

But she would find a way. She might collapse in the attempt, but she would give it her best shot.

Lifting Mollie from Isobel's arms, Gemma cuddled her close. The baby girl was soft and warm and smelt delicious. 'Tell me everything I need to know about our little darling.'

'Oh, Gem. I'm so relieved. I knew I could depend on you.' Isobel let out a relieved sigh. 'I can give you everything you'll need for Mollie. In fact, my bag's packed and I have it all in the car.'

'You mean you're heading off today?'

'It's important that I get to Dave as fast as I can. I'll get Mollie's things for you now.'

'Sure,' Gemma replied, more confidently than she felt. 'You get the baby gear and I'll make us some coffee.'

By the time she'd drunk her coffee, Gemma's mind was reeling. She had three closely written pages of detailed instructions about caring for Mollie. At the outset, Isobel had said minding a baby was simple, but Mollie came with more operating instructions than a state-of-the-art computer.

How could one little scrap require so much work? And how, she wondered, after she'd waved goodbye to Isobel, could she suddenly manage Mollie and her business? She looked at the pink and white bundle in her arms and tried to suppress a surge of alarm. She had immediate deadlines to meet and there was the constant need to drum up new clients.

Mollie's round little eyes stared solemnly up at her, reminding Gemma of an unblinking owl. Her heart melted. 'Kiddo, it's just you and me now. And we're not going to let this lick us.' She dropped a quick kiss on Mollie's curly head. Then she walked briskly back up the path to her flat, determined to tackle this task in as businesslike a fashion as possible.

A swish of tyres behind her brought her spinning around. In her driveway, a taxi was pulling up and a tall, rangy figure leapt from the passenger's seat.

Max Jardine!

How in tarnation had he got from Western Queensland to Brisbane so quickly?

'Gemma!' Max barked as he swung open her front gate and strode towards her. His piercing blue eyes were fixed on Mollie. 'Where's Isobel?'

'Hello, Max. Nice to see you, too,' Gemma replied coolly while her heart thudded. Max switched his gaze to her and he glared as ferociously as a headmaster scowling at an unmanageable pupil. Suddenly, she felt extremely self-conscious—as if her skirt was too short, her black stockings too sheer, or her platform heels too high. No matter how much decorum she'd acquired over the years, this older brother of Dave's always, always, *always* made her feel like a silly little girl. 'How did you get here so quickly?' she demanded.

'I flew. I got in early this morning from checking out the back country and found Isobel's message on the answering machine.'

Gemma remembered that she'd been told Max had invested in his own light aircraft.

'Well, Isobel's already left for Eagle Farm airport. You probably passed her.'

Max grimaced. 'So she's going ahead with this madcap scheme?'

'Yes, she's a very determined woman.' Gemma hugged Mollie a little closer. Faced by this angry maelstrom of a man, she found the baby's warmth and softness reassuring.

Cursing, Max ran impatient fingers through his dark brown hair. 'I should be the one chasing across the world after Dave.'

Gemma smacked a hand to her forehead, pantomime-style, and beamed at him. 'What a brilliant idea! Why didn't Isobel or I think of that? You're the obvious choice. You're Dave's brother. You're family but, even better, you're a man. You could spare Isobel the danger and Isobel—' Gemma felt a heady rush of excitement and relief as the next point sank in '—and Isobel could continue to care for Mollie.'

'So you don't want to look after the baby?'

'I—I didn't say that.' Her sense of relief plummeted. She and Max had hardly been talking for thirty seconds and already he'd found a way to put her down. 'Of course I'm happy to mind her, but could you really go to Africa? Do you have your passport with you?'

'Don't you think I haven't tried to go?' Max glared back at her. 'Foreign Affairs quickly knocked me back. They told me in no uncertain terms to stay out of it. Isobel is Dave's next of kin and they want the wifely touch to try to appeal on humanitarian grounds. Apparently, that's much more likely to get Dave released. I'm not happy, but I'm not going to muddy the water.'

Gemma's shoulders sagged. 'I suppose that's wise. It does sound like a touchy situation.'

Max merely grunted. He moved up the path towards

her and she found herself backing away from his determined stride. Some women had been heard to comment that now he'd reached thirty Max was even more good-looking than he'd been in his teens, but none of them had enticed him into marriage and Gemma knew why. His personality hadn't improved one jot.

'Who decided that you should be taking care of the baby?' he drawled.

She squared her shoulders. 'Her mother is absolutely certain that I am the perfect choice.'

A sudden wind gusted across the garden and Gemma ducked her head to protect Mollie, so she missed seeing his reaction. But she didn't miss the sound of her front door slamming shut. Horrified, she whirled around. *Dammit!* Now she was stranded on her own front path with a baby in her arms and Max Jardine glowering at her.

He looked in the direction of her door. 'You're not locked out, are you?'

She fumbled around in her pockets, knowing that it was useless and that her keys were still hanging on a little brass hook in her kitchen. 'Yes,' she replied through gritted teeth.

'You can't get in the back way?'

'No. I made sure I closed my back door because I was worried about my neighbour's cat and…the baby.'

For a fraction of a second, she almost thought he smiled at her. 'So it's a case of climbing through a window.'

Gemma looked at her windows. It had been windy all day and the only one she'd left open was in her bedroom.

'I can get through there in a flash,' Max offered.

She pictured him swinging his riding boots and his

long, jeans-clad legs over the sill, squeezing past the big bed that almost filled her small room—seeing the muddle of books, perfume and make-up on her bedside table and the underwear she'd left in a jumble on the end of the bed.

For some silly reason, she felt ridiculously flustered at the mere thought of Max seeing her private domain. 'It's OK,' she said quickly. 'I'll go. I—I know my way around.'

This time he was definitely smiling. His blue eyes danced as they rested first on Mollie in her arms and then on her short skirt. 'If you insist on getting in there yourself, let me at least help.' He held out his arms for Mollie.

Oh, Lord! What was worse? Did she want Max Jardine prowling around her bedroom, or Max, with Mollie in one arm, helping her up to her window and watching her skirt hike over her hips as she clambered through? Damn the man! Why did his presence always rock her so badly? This was hardly a life-threatening situation and yet she was feeling completely rattled.

'I guess you've got the longer legs. You'd better do the climbing,' she muttered ungraciously.

'OK,' he agreed easily, and in no time he had disappeared.

She saw her lace curtain snag as Max moved past it and she wondered what he thought of the ridiculously huge bed that dominated her tiny bedroom. She had taken the flat because it came fully furnished and the rent was cheap, considering how closely it was situated to the central business district. Most tenants, she assumed, would consider the king-size bed a bonus, but it was rather more than she needed.

The front door swung open.

'Miss Brown, Miss Mollie,' Max welcomed them with a deep bow.

'Thanks,' Gemma replied stiffly as she sailed past him into her flat with her head high. At the entrance to her lounge room, she paused and eyed him coolly, feeling uncomfortably more like the guest than the hostess. To right matters she added, 'I take it you've come to visit us?'

'We've got to work out what's best for this little one.'

Gemma sighed. She sensed combat ahead of her and here she was, facing the enemy without any time to construct a battle plan. The whole business of getting into the flat had set her off on the wrong foot. 'Isobel has already decided what's best for her daughter,' she told him haughtily. 'Don't forget this baby's mother is my best friend.'

'And this baby is my niece,' Max growled.

What would poor little Mollie think, if she could understand the way they were bickering over her?

Max moved away and she grimaced as he surveyed her lounge room. Its appearance had deteriorated somewhat now that Mollie's gear was piled in the middle of the carpet. Out of the corner of her eye, she noted Max's brows pull into a frown as he studied the mountain of equipment. There were numerous toys, a collapsible cot, a car seat, pram and playpen, not to mention enough clothes to dress an entire kindergarten.

His gaze also took in the piles of pamphlets and boxes Gemma had 'filed' on her sofa. Her computer and more paperwork covered the small dining table.

'There'll be much more room when I move the baby's gear into the bedroom,' she explained hastily.

Max cracked half a grin. 'Which bedroom would that be?'

'M-mine.'

'How many bedrooms do you have?'

Why her cheeks should flame at such a straightforward question was beyond her. 'Just—just the one,' she stammered.

Max stood staring at her with his hands on his hips, shaking his head as if he hadn't heard her properly. 'You're going to put all this gear in that miniature bedroom I just came through?'

'Some of it,' she mumbled.

'You'll need to buy a smaller bed.'

Gemma wouldn't give into his provocation by responding to that comment. To her further annoyance, he turned and sauntered around her compact kitchen, then back to the lounge and dining area, silently, grimly inspecting every detail. Her dwelling seemed smaller than ever with his large frame invading the space. Finally, he swivelled back to face her. And for an unnecessarily long moment, his disturbing blue eyes rested on her.

At last he spoke very quietly. 'It can't be done, Gemma. You can't take care of Mollie here in this shoebox.'

'Of course I can. Isobel has total faith in me.'

'Isobel is desperate.'

Gemma told herself she should expect a hurtful jab like this from Max and she resolved not to let him intimidate her. She matched his challenging gaze with a scornful glare. 'Isobel wasn't so desperate that she'd risk her baby's welfare. She has complete trust in my ability to care for Mollie.'

His eyes narrowed as he stared thoughtfully at the toes of his leather riding boots.

'Why don't you?' she challenged.

His head came up slowly, but he didn't speak.

'Why don't you trust me, Max?'

Before he replied, he thrust his hands deep into the pockets of his faded jeans. 'I'm sure you have good intentions, Gemma. But I keep remembering...' His Adam's apple moved up and down rapidly.

When he paused, Gemma rushed to defend herself. 'I doubt that you've noticed, but I'm not a little kid any more.'

This time his mouth curved into a relaxed smile and his amused blue gaze rested on her for an uncomfortable length of time before he spoke. 'Believe me, kiddo, I've noticed how grown-up you look these days.'

No amount of willpower could prevent Gemma's blushes. She ducked her face behind Mollie's golden curls.

'But what I'm remembering is your reaction at the hospital when Mollie was born,' he continued. 'You told us all very loudly that you were allergic to babies. You wouldn't touch her for fear she would break.'

Gemma tried valiantly to suppress a gasp of dismay. 'Newborn babies don't count,' she muttered defensively. 'Everyone's nervous about holding them. I love Mollie now.'

'But you said you were going to wait till she was old enough to—what was it? Take shopping? I think you were planning to teach her how to buy shoes and where to get the very best coffee in town.'

Stunned, Gemma stared at Max. The man had the memory of an elephant! She had only dim recollections of this conversation. How on earth did he retain such insignificant details? He must make a habit of hoarding up ammunition like this to fire when it most hurt.

'OK, I was scared of Mollie at first,' she admitted. 'I'd never been in close contact with such a tiny new baby before, but I—I've adjusted. Mollie and I get on famously now.'

At that moment, Mollie wriggled restlessly in Gemma's arms and uttered a little cry of protest. Gemma stared helplessly at the squirming baby. *Just whose side was this kid on?* She tried to jiggle Mollie on her hip. She'd seen Isobel do it many times and it always seemed to work.

'I take it,' added Max, 'you're going to *try* to play nursemaid and carry on a business as well?'

'Of course. It shouldn't be a problem.' It was the worst possible moment for Mollie to let out an ear-splitting wail, but she did. Her little face turned deep pink, her bottom lip wobbled and she sobbed desperately. Feeling totally threatened, Gemma quickly placed the baby on the floor at her feet. To her surprise, Mollie stopped crying almost immediately. She sat there quietly and began to suck her fist.

'Look at that,' Gemma beamed, feeling a whole lot better. 'I won't have to cart her around every minute of the day. I'll be able to sit her in her playpen surrounded by toys and get on with my work.'

Max's expression softened for a moment as he watched his niece, but when his gaze reached Gemma again, he scowled, shook his head and shoved his hands deeper in the pockets of his jeans. 'I'm not going to allow her to stay here, Gemma.'

'I beg your pardon?' *Not going to allow her? Could she be hearing this?* Gemma had always wondered what people meant when they described hackles rising on the backs of their necks. Now she knew.

'You heard me. I'm not going to abandon my niece.'

'*Abandon* her?' she echoed. 'How dare you insinuate that leaving her with me is the same as abandoning her?'

'Don't take it personally, Gem.'

The relaxed way Max leaned back against her kitchen bench doubled Gemma's anger.

'How on earth am I supposed to take it?'

'This is a family matter. You know the old saying about blood being thicker than water. A friend can't be expected to take on such responsibility.'

'For crying out loud, I'm more than a friend,' Gemma cried. 'I'm Mollie's godmother!' But as the words left her lips, she realised they weren't much help. This man, this enemy, this ogre—was poor Mollie's godfather.

'How on earth are *you* going to look after Mollie?' Gemma challenged before Max could respond. 'You've no women on your property and only a handful of ringers. I doubt they'll be much help.'

'I'll hire a nanny, of course. Someone with the very best training.'

She made an exaggerated show of rolling her eyes in disgust. 'If Isobel wanted a nanny for Mollie, she could have hired one herself. The poor woman doesn't know how long she's going to be away and she wants someone she knows, someone who really cares about her baby, not a stranger who happens to have official qualifications.'

Max sighed and ran long fingers through his hair as he stared at the waxed tiles on Gemma's kitchen floor. 'Isobel said she didn't want a nanny?'

'Yes,' she replied firmly.

'OK,' he said at last. With another deeper sigh, his head flicked sideways and his eyes locked onto hers. 'You and I are both Mollie's godparents, so we should make this a shared responsibility.'

CHAPTER TWO

'WHAT exactly do you mean?' Gemma asked, appalled by what Max seemed to be suggesting.

'We're both the baby's godparents. So we look after her.' His eyes revealed the briefest twinkle. *'Together.'*

She knew her mouth was gaping. 'You and me?' she gasped.

'Yeah.'

'But we can't.'

'Why not?'

'It—it's not necessary. Being a godparent is simply a gesture of intent.'

Resting his hands on the counter top, Max leaned forward. 'You can't have it both ways, Gemma. Either being Mollie's godmother is a good reason for you to take care of her, or it isn't.'

She knew she was losing ground fast. Apparently Max had been honing his skills as a bush lawyer. She ran frantic fingers through her short, dark hair. 'But it doesn't mean we're obliged to— For crying out loud, Max, that doesn't mean we have to actually do anything *parental* together.'

Max's eyes teased her. 'It's the only sensible solution. You and Mollie should come and stay on Goodbye Creek Station until Isobel returns. That way we can share the load. It's called co-operation.'

Her stomach lurched as if she were coming down in a very fast elevator. 'Co-operation, my foot!' she said at last. 'How much co-operation are *you* planning to contribute? I'm the one who'll have to make all the sacrifices. Why should *I* give up everything here to head off into the bush and stay with you?'

'Because, as I've already explained,' Max said, with exaggerated patience, 'we need to share this responsibility. That way we can both get on with our work commitments.' He pointed to the pamphlets and papers on her sofa. 'I imagine it will be much easier for you to bring your stuff to Goodbye Creek and to carry on your business from there, than for me to bring thousands of head of cattle down to this, er—cosy little suburban flat.'

He was so smug and sure of himself, Gemma wanted to thump him. She was beginning to feel cornered. 'It won't work.'

'I think it's a compromise that has distinct possibilities.'

If only she could tell him she was far too busy—booked up to organise half a dozen events—but even if she did tell such a lie, she was sure he would find a way to use it against her. Instead she glared at him. 'We'll spend the whole time fighting!'

He pretended to be shocked by her words. 'Why on earth should we do that?'

Gemma groaned. '*Maxwell T.* Jardine, I don't believe I'm hearing this. We would fight, for the simple reason that we have never agreed about anything. Haven't you noticed the only thing we have in common is that we both breathe oxygen? We can't stand each other!'

Just to prove how utterly detestable he was, Max burst out laughing.

Gemma gave in to her anger. She smashed her fist onto the counter. 'What's so funny?' she yelled.

'Oh, Gemma,' he chuckled. 'You certainly are all grown up now, aren't you?'

Choking, she gasped and spluttered. Trust Max to point out that she wasn't nearly as sophisticated and worldly wise as she liked to think she was. She had a sneaking suspicion that she might never become mature and discerning. It was her long-term ambition to become cool and detached—especially when this man was around doing his best to flummox her.

For a brief moment, Max's expression softened. Then he stepped around the counter and towards her. Gemma wished he wouldn't. When he rested his strong, warm hands on both her shoulders, her nerves were way too strained to cope.

'*Gemma Elizabeth* Brown,' he said, his voice low and gravelly.

Her eyes widened at his use of her middle name. She hadn't even realised he knew it.

'We agree on the most important thing.'

She could feel the heat of his hands as they held her. Her lungs appeared to be malfunctioning, but Max didn't notice, he just kept on talking.

'We agree that Mollie deserves very good care and, on this occasion, I think most definitely, we *do* have to do something together.' His eyes flashed as he added, 'Something *parental*. You're right, we'll probably fight like cats and dogs, but we'll manage somehow—for Mollie's sake. On our own, we'd both have major difficulties looking after the poor little kid properly, wouldn't we?'

She allowed her gaze to meet those deep blue eyes, those disturbing blue eyes, and Gemma felt less sure of her line of argument.

'Together, we stand a fair chance of success—both for Mollie and our work.'

What he proposed was unthinkable! She couldn't let

this happen. How on earth could she live with Max while he inspected her babysitting skills? She'd be a dithering mess. Holy smoke, he'd be checking up on her every minute of the day and he would soon discover she knew absolutely zero about babies.

Gemma felt as if she'd stepped aside and become a spectator of this discussion. Incredibly, she realised she was nodding, accepting Max's terms.

If only she could remember exactly when Max had turned their battle to his advantage, but she had loosened her grip on this whole scene. She'd lost sight of her counter-argument.

'I'll do my fair share,' Max added. 'I'll give Mollie her tucker or bathe her, or whatever's necessary. We can work out some sort of roster if you like.'

She passed a dazed hand across her eyes. Never in her wildest dreams had she pictured this rough-riding cattleman in a hands-on relationship with a baby. She tried to visualise him attending to Mollie, but her musings were interrupted by the telephone.

'Oh, heavens! That's probably the printers.' Gemma had almost forgotten her current project and her deadline this afternoon. 'I have to get some pamphlet designs to them before five o'clock.' She glared fiercely at Max as she hurried to the phone.

'Hello, Gemma Brown speaking.'

A woman's voice reached her. 'Gemma, Sue Easton from Over the Page. I was wondering…'

The printers were chasing her copy. Gemma reassured the woman that everything was ready and she would be at their office shortly. As she spoke, she heard Mollie begin to cry behind her and she was acutely aware of Max moving quietly in the flat.

Mollie's wails ceased abruptly and by the time

Gemma put the receiver down and turned to face Max again, she was startled to find him perched on the arm of her sofa and jogging the delighted baby on his knee.

He looked very pleased with himself. 'See? You can't manage without me, can you? I'll mind this little possum while you do whatever running around you need to this afternoon.'

'Thanks,' she replied uncertainly.

'And after that,' he said with confident assurance, 'we can plan your move to Goodbye Creek. I'll book into a pub tonight and we can head off first thing in the morning.'

As he continued to favour both Gemma and Mollie with a look of smug satisfaction, the baby's face turned red and Gemma noticed that she seemed to be concentrating very hard.

'Oh-oh.' Max's confident grin slipped. Cautiously, he lifted Mollie away from his knee.

'Has she dirtied her nappy?' asked Gemma.

'I—I think so.'

At the sight of his sudden dismay, Gemma felt an urge to grin, but she managed to keep a straight face. 'Thanks so much, Max. It would be great if you could watch Mollie for half an hour or so. I do have several errands to run—especially if I'm moving house. Let me show you where the clean nappies are...' She rummaged in the pile of things Isobel had left and produced a freshly folded nappy and a container of baby wipes and, with a deadpan expression, handed them to him. 'These are what you need.'

'You're running out on me at a moment like this?' he asked, clearly horrified. By now he was holding Mollie at arm's length.

'I'm sorry,' Gemma murmured sweetly, 'but I really

do have important deadlines to meet. You'll be fine.' She gathered up her designs and her handbag and rushed out her front door.

'He thinks he's such a hotshot babysitter, he can manage this one,' she muttered under her breath.

But she wished she didn't feel quite so guilty about deserting him.

The next day, when Max piloted their plane over the vast property that made up Goodbye Creek Station, Gemma was stunned by the unexpected flood of homesickness that swept through her. It was five years since she'd been back, but she knew the Jardine family holding almost as well as she knew the township of Goodbye Creek, where her own home had been. Her parents had owned a stock and station agency in the town. They had sold up and moved to the coast about the same time she'd gone away to university.

Now, she and Max were flying back, the plane stacked carefully with the baby's gear. Max explained that he had a well-equipped study complete with an up-to-the-minute computer and a fax machine, so Gemma only needed to bring her clothes, a box of computer disks and her paperwork.

They'd left Brisbane just as dawn broke and during the five-hour flight Mollie had alternated between napping and waking for little snacks and drinks. Gemma had kept her entertained with picture books and games of 'This little pig went to market'.

Max had chatted very politely about the weather and the scenery beneath them, but it occurred to Gemma that he was behaving more like a newly introduced acquaintance than someone who had known her for more than twenty years. But now, as heart-wrenchingly familiar red soil plains unfolded below, she felt edgy, knowing that once they landed their shared past could no longer be ignored.

Wriggling forward in her seat, she peered eagerly through the windscreen, wondering why the sight of dry, grassy paddocks and straggly stands of eucalypts should make her feel so soppy and sentimental. Way below, she could recognise the signs of spring merging into summer. Early wet season storms had brought bright green new growth and purple and yellow wild flowers were poking up through the grass.

Max's flight-path followed the course of the old creek that had given its name to the district and Gemma noted that water was already flowing down its entire length. She could make out the shallow, rocky stretch of rapids and finally the deeper section they called Big Bend.

Fringed by majestic paperbarks, this cool, shady pool had been a favourite spot for childhood picnics. At the age of ten, Gemma had rocketed in a tractor tube right through the rapids as far as the Big Bend. She'd been so proud of herself and Dave had been lavish with his praise.

'You're as good as a boy,' he'd shouted. 'You made it the whole way without squealing once. Max, isn't she great?'

But Max, of course, had merely grunted and looked bored.

As they neared the homestead, her sense of nostalgia increased.

'Nearly home,' said Max, with a contented little smile, as he worked the controls to increase their angle of descent.

First came the stockyards and the corrugated iron roofs under which hay bales would be stacked to protect them from the rain. Then she could see the smaller, original holding yard, made of old timbers weathered to a silvery grey and built in the rustic post and rail design that had been around since the pioneering days.

Gemma glanced at Mollie dozing in her little safety seat beside her. 'Has Mollie been out here before?' she asked.

'No,' admitted Max. 'This will be the first time she's set foot on Jardine soil. It's a significant moment.' He made a sweeping gesture with his arm. 'All this is her inheritance.'

'Unless you have children of your own,' Gemma said softly. 'I guess then they would all be shareholders.'

He turned and their eyes met. His blue gaze held a disquieting mixture of uncertainty and bitterness. 'Yeah,' he said, and then jerked his head back to the front. 'There's always that possibility.'

They swooped a little lower and the familiar sight of the muddy dam dotted with black ducks and the rusty metal skeleton of the old windmill standing sentry nearby made her feel ridiculously emotional. She blinked her eyes to clear the misted view. In her imagination, she could hear the squeak and clank of the old windmill as it slowly pumped water to the drinking troughs.

Within seconds she was exclaiming. 'Max, my goodness! You've installed a satellite dish.'

'Got to keep up with technology.'

Their plane continued its descent and he nodded to their right, past the machinery sheds and workshops. 'I've put in some new windmills, too. That one over there has a solar panel and an electric pump.'

'Is it better than the old one?' she asked, doubtfully eyeing the shiny modern equipment.

'Too right. Before, it was always a case of no breeze, no water. Now we can get a constant flow if we need it.'

But the biggest surprise came as they made the final dip towards the airstrip, when Gemma saw the homestead, which for as long as she could remember had been a comfortable but shabby timber home with peeling paint and vine-covered wrap-around verandahs.

'Wow!' Her breath exhaled slowly as she absorbed the changes. Max's home was now a showplace. 'What have you done to the house?' she asked.

He was concentrating on making an initial swoop over the strip to clear the ground of horses and birds before attempting a landing. 'Painted it,' he muttered tersely as he swung the plane around to double back for the approach.

Below them, skittish horses cantered out of their way and a flock of cockatoos, feeding on grass seed, lifted their wings to disperse like so many pieces of white paper caught in a wind gust. The plane plunged lower and finally touched down on the gravel runway.

'What a difference,' Gemma exclaimed, still staring at Max's house, amazed by the transformation. The homestead's timber walls were now painted a pretty powder blue, the iron roof was a clean, crisp silver and all the trims and the lattice on the verandahs were gleaming white.

As they taxied down the short airstrip, Max shot her a cautious glance. 'You like it?'

'It's beautiful, Max. I had no idea the old place could look so lovely.' She was startled to see an unexpected red tinge creep along his cheekbones. 'Who did the job for you?'

'Did it myself,' he muttered. 'During the dry season, of course.'

Another shock.

As the plane came to a standstill, Gemma assimilated this news and sat quietly, thinking about the lonely weeks Max must have spent on the task. The life of an outback cattleman was solitary and hard and the men who survived it were tough, complex creatures. And they didn't come much more complicated than Max, she thought with a wry grimace. 'It's fantastic,' she told him with genuine warmth. 'You've done an amazing job.'

He looked embarrassed and she realised he was probably more used to her scorn than her praise. She allowed herself a private smile as she thought about that. They were probably both much more comfortable fighting than co-operating.

An old utility truck had been left at the end of the runway and Gemma and Max were kept busy for the next ten minutes, transferring Mollie and the gear into the vehicle. Even though it was only a few hundred metres to the homestead, there was too much to lug such a distance.

It was late morning. The sun was already high overhead and very hot and so, by the time they reached the kitchen, a cool drink was the first priority. Gemma found Mollie's little feeding cup, while Max swung his fridge door open and grabbed a jug of iced water.

Just before he closed the fridge, he paused to survey its contents and frowned. 'I might have to stock up on a few things from town,' he commented before filling a glass and handing it to Gemma. 'I'm afraid I wasn't expecting you and I haven't got the kind of fancy things that women like for breakfast. I'm still a steak and eggs man myself.'

Gemma's eyes widened. 'How do you know what women like for breakfast?' The question was out before she really thought through what she was saying. She'd always pictured Max as a crusty bachelor living the life of a lonely recluse in the back of beyond.

Max went very still and she cringed with sudden shame as she recognised just how rude and downright stupid her query sounded. How on earth could she retract her words?

Before any bright ideas struck, he spun around, and the glance he sent her way was tinged with wry amusement.

Had she left her brains in Brisbane? Of course this man would have attracted and entertained women. He was quite well off and had the kind of rugged and rangy masculinity that swarms of women hunted down. Unlike her, they'd be willing to overlook his gruffness.

She knew by the heat in her cheeks that her embarrassment was obvious, but she was also just as sure Max wouldn't miss an opportunity to make her suffer further for her foolishness.

'Now let me see.' He cocked his head to the ceiling as if considering her question. 'How is it that I know so much about women's breakfast habits?'

His eyes narrowed as if he was giving this matter his undivided attention. 'I think I probably picked up some pointers—like women's belief in the importance of orange juice—from all those television advertisements.'

Totally flustered and unable to think of an appropriate retort, Gemma concentrated very carefully on holding Mollie's cup at just the right angle for her to drink easily.

'But it beats me if I can remember just how I uncovered the mysterious feminine desire to dine first thing in the morning on low-fat yoghurt and muesli. That really has me stumped.' Relaxing back in a wooden kitchen chair, he joined his hands behind his head with elbows pointing to the ceiling. 'I guess I found out about European women's predilection for coffee and croissants from some foreign movie.'

'For heaven's sake,' Gemma growled at him. 'Good luck to any long-suffering woman who's had breakfast with you. The poor thing would need a ton of luck and a truckload of tolerance to put up with your chauvinism.'

He took a deep swig of iced water and chuckled. 'I'd say you're probably right.' Setting the glass back on the table, he grinned at her. 'You'll be able to find out tomorrow morning, won't you?'

'I think I could do without your early-morning charm,' she sniffed. 'And Mollie and I will have soft boiled eggs and toast soldiers for our breakfast.'

She turned away from his mocking grin and made a fuss of Mollie. But it was difficult to stop her mind from dwelling on the unexplored area of this conversation—the particular circumstances that led to a woman sharing breakfast with Max.

They didn't bear thinking about.

And yet, in spite of her efforts to ignore such offensive details, an unbidden picture planted itself firmly in Gemma's mind. A vision of a lamp-lit bedroom—with cool, white sheets—and Max's brown, muscle-packed back encircled by softly rounded, pale and feminine arms. A night of intimacy…

She felt an unpleasant wave of panic.

Would Max Jardine be charming in the company of other women?

Surely not.

'Do you have any bananas?' she asked, in a desperate bid to change the subject and to rid herself of these extremely unsettling thoughts. 'I—I could mash one for Mollie's lunch while you set up her cot.'

His eyes surveyed the kitchen. 'No bananas, I'm afraid. You might have to give her some of the tinned stuff we brought with us. I'll take a run into town first thing tomorrow morning. We should make up a shopping list.'

Gemma was so grateful they were no longer talking about Max's women that she spent the afternoon being particularly obliging and co-operative. Max made cold roast beef sandwiches for their lunch and they ate them at a table on the side verandah and washed them down with huge mugs of strong tea while Mollie played with her blocks on the floor nearby. Out in the paddocks the white cockatoos screeched raucous greetings as they returned to the grass seed to feed.

Then, after lunch, as Max had never bothered with a housekeeper, together they dusted and vacuumed spare rooms for her and Mollie's use. They set up Mollie's folding cot and her other equipment in a bedroom on the cool side of the house, with doors opening onto the verandah.

Gemma's bedroom was right next door. She had stayed in it before—a pretty room, very feminine, with pink and white curtains and a white candlewick bedspread on the old-fashioned iron bed. The bed-ends were decorated with shiny brass knobs and pretty pieces of porcelain painted with rosebuds.

She was startled to see a silver-framed photo of Dave and herself on the mahogany dressing table. It had been taken five years ago—in the days before Dave met Isobel—when Gemma was eighteen and she and Dave had still been 'going together'. Their liaison had been a casual arrangement that they'd drifted into as they grew older. She'd come back from university for his twenty-first birthday.

In the photo, they were dancing. Dave, dressed in a formal dinner suit, was laughing, and she was smiling at the camera and looking very pleased with herself in a pale blue evening gown with thin straps, a fitted bodice and a softly floating, long skirt. There were tiny white flowers dotted through her dark brown hair. At the time, she'd thought she looked very romantic.

Now she shuddered as a painful memory forced itself on her.

The night of Dave's party had ended with a shameful and embarrassing incident. A scene she had worked desperately hard to forget over the years. Surely Max had wanted to forget it, too? At the time he had been as upset as she was about what happened.

Shaking, she turned to him now. 'Why didn't you throw this old photo away?'

Max set down her suitcase, straightened and frowned in its direction. An unreadable emotion flashed in his eyes and his mouth tightened. After a moment, he said with a shrug, 'Didn't cross my mind.'

Rigid with tension, it took Gemma a moment or two to take in his words. Then relief flooded her. He must have forgotten what had happened that night! Either that or the incident that had caused her so much grief over the years had never really bothered him. Gemma forced herself to shrug as nonchalantly as he had. 'Fair enough,' she said.

She knew she should be relieved, but it took some time for her to feel calm again and to convince herself that she was happy with his detached reaction.

By evening, they had worked out how to barricade off the section of the verandah adjacent to the study, so that

Mollie could have a safe area to crawl and play while Gemma worked. Gemma had unpacked her clothes and had showered to wash off the dust from her journey. She'd bathed the baby girl in the old claw-foot tub in the main bathroom and fed her mashed vegetables. Max had ambled down to one of the ringers' huts to discuss station matters and explain about his visitors.

When he returned, he fixed a simple supper of steaks and salad while Gemma gave Mollie her bottle and settled her for sleep.

Everything went like clockwork. Gemma couldn't believe how obliging Mollie was and how conciliatory Max had been. She was beginning to feel calm and confident and even optimistic about the whole venture. Surely this mood wouldn't last?

They ate together, and their steaks were followed by a simple, no-frills dessert of chocolate chip ice cream and tinned apricots. Then coffee. They chatted about people they both knew from around the district and Max was a surprisingly entertaining host—slipping humorous anecdotes and juicy titbits of gossip into the conversation.

As he drained the last of his coffee, he put his cup down and leaned back in his chair. 'I should have offered you a nightcap. Would you like a liqueur or brandy?'

She shook her head. 'No, thank you. I'm quite tired, but you have one.'

'Not tonight.' He looked at her thoughtfully. 'You haven't told me anything about the trip you made to England after university.'

'I didn't think you'd be interested,' she answered stiffly.

His eyebrows rose the tiniest fraction. 'I don't need a

travelogue, but I'd like to know whether you found what you were looking for.'

The coffee cup in Gemma's hand rattled against its saucer. 'I went to London for two years' work experience.'

After a little, Max said, 'I suspected you were running away.'

He'd dropped the charm and reverted to Big Brother mode and Gemma's sense of relaxation was falling away at breakneck speed. She should have known the truce had been too good to last. 'What would I have been running away from?'

He frowned. 'You and Dave were so close for so many years. Everyone in the district thought of you as a couple.'

'Yes, but I'm sure everyone knew it wasn't serious.' She was stunned to think that Max might have thought she'd been pining after Dave. 'Heavens, Max, Dave and I just sort of hung out together out of habit. I mean—being with him was always fun and sweet and everything, but when we parted it was quite painless and definitely for the best.' She added quietly, 'There was something missing in our relationship.'

Heat leapt into her cheeks. She didn't add that there had seemed to be something missing in every relationship she'd attempted. Gemma had a dreadful suspicion that there was something missing in her own personality. She feared she just wasn't suited to romance. No matter how handsome and charming and eager to please her the young men she'd met had been, none of then had ever once made her feel giddily, genuinely in love. Not the kind of love she was hoping to find.

'You thought you would find that missing *some-*

thing...in London?' Max's eyes were lit with a puzzling intensity.

Blue fire.

The way their gaze locked onto hers robbed her breath. This man of all people shouldn't be asking her such questions.

'No, I wasn't hoping for that,' she said at last, and prayed that he couldn't guess she was lying through her teeth.

'No suave English gentleman swept you off your feet?'

It was time to finish this conversation. Gemma didn't like it at all. She especially didn't like the way her heart began beat so frantically when Max looked at her.

Unless she put an end to this now, she might end up admitting to him that although she'd met plenty of nice young men, none of them had captured her heart. And the very last thing Gemma wanted was for him to continue this line of questioning and uncover her embarrassing secret.

None of her family or friends knew the truth about her love life. Or rather her lack of a love life. Gemma was quite certain that she was the only twenty-three-year-old female outside a nunnery who was still a virgin.

She lifted her chin to what she hoped was a challenging angle. 'There were several men,' she told him. 'But, Max, you're not *my* big brother. I'm not giving you an itemised account and you don't need to keep watch over me. It's none of your business how many men I've met or—or how many affairs I've had.' Pushing back her chair, she jumped to her feet. 'I haven't asked you one tiny question about your breakfast companions.'

He stood also and looked down at her from his menacing height. 'What would you like to know?' he asked while a poorly suppressed grin tugged at the corners of his mouth.

'I have absolutely no interest in your philanderings.' She spun on her heel and began to stomp away from the table. Then she stopped abruptly, remembering her manners. 'I'll help you clear the table and tidy the kitchen,' she mumbled.

'Thank you, Gemma,' he replied with a studied politeness that annoyed her.

In silence they worked, Max gathering up the plates and cutlery, Gemma collecting the cups, place mats and serviettes. Together they walked into the kitchen and set their things down at the sink. They both reached for the tap at the same time. Their hands connected.

As if she'd been burnt, Gemma snatched her hand away from the contact, but Max's reaction was just as quick and he caught her fingers in his strong grasp.

His thumb stroked her skin once, twice...and she felt her blood stirring in response. Her hand trembled.

She wanted to pull away, but she was too fascinated by her body's astonishing reaction. Never had she felt so unsettled, so fired up by a man's simple touch. She didn't dare look at Max. She stood by the sink, mesmerised by the sight of her slim white hand in his large, suntanned grip. She could see little hairs on the back of his hand, bleached to gold by the sun. A faint trace of the fresh, lemon-scented soap he'd used in the shower still clung to his skin and his work-roughened thumb continued to move slowly over her hand, making her feel shivery and breathless.

'Gem.' His gruff voice barely reached her over the savage drumbeat in her ears.

She couldn't move, couldn't speak.

'Gemma,' he said again, and his other hand reached

under her chin, forcing her head up until their eyes met. Max was looking as startled as she felt. His breathing sounded just as hectic.

When his fingers began to trace ever so gently the outline of her face, she could feel her skin flame at his touch.

'Gemma Brown,' he whispered, 'whether you like it or not, I'm going to keep watching you…just like I always have.'

And the moment was spoiled. Gemma was embarrassingly disappointed.

'For Pete's sake!' she exclaimed, wrenching her hand out of his grasp and pulling right away from him. She was fearfully angry with him and she wasn't quite sure why. 'You are not my brother, my bodyguard or my guardian angel!' For a dreadful moment she thought she might burst into tears. 'Go paint some more walls. Get a life, Max, and leave me to get on with mine!'

This time she didn't care about good manners. Gemma rushed out of the kitchen and left him with the dirty dishes.

CHAPTER THREE

THE grimy dishes were still sitting on the counter top waiting to be washed when Gemma walked into the kitchen the next morning. Added to last night's pile were an extra-greasy frying pan, a mug and more plates—things Max must have used for his breakfast before he headed off at sunrise.

'Who does he think he is?' she asked Mollie as she surveyed the dreary mess. Mollie merely whimpered and rubbed her face against Gemma's shoulder. She'd been restless during the night and still seemed rather fragile this morning. Having slept very fitfully, Gemma wasn't feeling too chipper either. In their own separate ways, both Max and Mollie Jardine had kept her tossing and turning for hours.

She set Mollie down on the floor while she hunted through Max's cupboards for a saucepan to boil their eggs, but Mollie began to cry almost as soon as Gemma walked away from her.

'Aren't you going to let me do anything this morning?' Gemma sighed. She tried to cheer the baby up with clucking noises while she set about making their breakfast.

After popping two eggs into a pot of water, she slid bread into the toaster and boiled the kettle for a mug of tea for herself. The phone rang. Gemma glanced at Mollie, who was still making miserable little whimpers and she deliberated whether she should let the answering machine deal with the call. Then, having second thoughts, she handed the baby a saucepan lid, hoping it would keep her happy while she dashed to the phone.

The call was from Brisbane—the printers were wanting to clarify some final details about the pamphlet—so Gemma was glad she'd answered. But when she returned to the kitchen, her heart sank.

Max stood in the middle of the room, with his hands on his hips, staring in dismay at Mollie, who was howling loudly and banging the saucepan lid on the floor in time to her wails.

She dashed into the room and swept the baby into her arms. 'Why didn't you pick her up?' she challenged Max, deciding to attack him before he could begin to accuse her of neglect.

But he clearly didn't react well to being scolded. His eyes narrowed. 'Where were you?' he asked.

'Where was *I*?' She knew she sounded shrewish, but was too frazzled to care. 'After pacing the floorboards all night, trying to calm your niece, I was answering an important business call. Where were *you*?'

'I've had one or two things to attend to,' he snapped. 'I need to talk to my men—delegate more jobs now that I have other responsibilities.'

'Who are you trying to kid?' Gemma cut in. 'You wouldn't recognise a responsibility if it was formally introduced to you. Who rocked Mollie back to sleep when she wouldn't settle last night? Me! Who waltzed off this morning without a care in the world and left the kitchen covered in grease? You did!'

'I'm sorry you had a bad night,' he replied with annoying composure, 'but calm down, Gemma.' He reached over and lifted the miserable Mollie from her arms. 'I had every intention of doing the dishes—same as I always do them—at lunchtime.'

'Lunchtime?'

Gemma might have launched into another tirade, but she noticed that Max's nose had begun to twitch. Was he feeling angry or just very guilty? Neither of the above, she realised with dismay as the acrid smell of smoke reached her.

'It seems you've burnt the toast,' he said quietly.

Black smoke billowed from the corner of the kitchen and Max, with Mollie on one hip, lunged across the room, switched the toaster off and flung its doors open.

Wasn't it just typical of this man? Gemma thought as she watched him. He could buy himself a smart little plane, a satellite dish and a fancy computer and still not have progressed to a pop-up toaster.

On the stove, the eggs were boiling so rapidly they rattled against the saucepan. 'Oh, blast! They'll be hard-boiled!' she wailed. This was definitely *not* her morning.

She snatched the saucepan from the stove, thumped it into the sink, then whirled around to glare at Max. He was nuzzling Mollie's tummy with his nose and making her laugh.

Laugh! Out loud!

Proper chuckles!

Gemma could feel her bottom lip drooping into a pout. How dared Mollie be so sweet and responsive to Max when she was the one who'd lost all the sleep? She sagged against the kitchen bench and, with a self-pitying sigh, folded her arms across her chest.

Max glanced at her. 'I'll take her out to see the puppies and give you some space to have another go at cooking breakfast,' he suggested.

She drew in a deep breath and nodded. Some peace and quiet, some space...that was what she needed...

And yet she felt strangely abandoned watching Max

take Mollie outside—as if they belonged together and she was the outsider. He carried her so easily, without any sense of awkwardness. He would make a good father… She found herself wondering how many of Max's breakfast companions had been hoping to marry him, to have him father their children.

Groaning at the stupid direction of her thoughts, Gemma picked up the blackened pieces of toast and, with grimly compressed lips, tossed them into the bin before setting out to remake breakfast.

By the time Max and Mollie returned, she had set the little table on the verandah and her breakfast and Mollie's were ready. She had decided against eggs after all and had made Mollie some porridge, settling for tea and toast for herself. And she'd assumed Max might want some more to eat so had made extra for him.

'Thanks,' he said as he settled Mollie on his lap and proceeded to feed her milky porridge with a tiny spoon.

'We could do with a high chair. It would make mealtimes much easier,' Gemma commented as Max intercepted Mollie's plump little hand before she could dunk it into the porridge bowl.

'I'll add it to my shopping list, but I'm not sure if Goodbye Creek runs to high chairs.'

'So you're going into town this morning?'

He nodded. 'Want to come?'

Gemma hesitated and took a sip of tea, shocked by her ready willingness to accept his offer. The idea of going to town with Max seemed more appealing than she could have thought possible. Her mind ran ahead of her, wondering what she might wear.

He was looking at her thoughtfully. 'Of course, you might appreciate some time to set up your office. I could take Mollie with me and get her out of your hair for the morning, while you get your business sorted out. It's a hot day for travelling and seeing you've had a rough night…'

Gemma placed her mug carefully back on the table. What on earth was wrong with her? Max Jardine was offering to get out of her way. She should be celebrating. This time yesterday she would have *paid* him to stay away.

His suggestion that she take the morning to reorganise her business was so brimming with common sense that she couldn't refuse without looking foolish. So why on earth did it make her feel downright miserable? Her tiredness had to be the answer—plus the fact that she had already grown so attached to Mollie that she hated to be parted from her.

'A morning to myself would be great,' she told Max brightly. 'You finish your toast and I'll go clean up Mollie and make up an extra bottle for you to take.'

'Better give me some extra clothes for her, too,' Max said as she stood to go. 'We might be some time.'

They were gone for most of the day. Many, many times Gemma went to the front verandah to peer down the dirt track, searching for the cloud of red dust on the horizon that would tell her the truck was returning. She hadn't the courage to tell Max that there wasn't much work on her books at present. He already had a low enough opinion of her without adding fuel to his fire.

But by ten o'clock in the morning she'd finished her work and she spent the rest of the day roaming restlessly around the house.

After lunch, she washed and dried all the dishes, vowing that she would have to change some of Max's bachelor habits. Then she set a sprinkler on the front lawn and picked some flowers from the old rambling garden that Max's grandmother had established many, many years ago. Exotic-smelling white gardenias, roses in two shades of pink and some yellow crucifix orchids.

After arranging the flowers in a crystal vase on the hall table, she piled a blue bowl with tangy bush lemons and set it on the kitchen dresser, then brought in Mollie's washing from the line, folded it and put it away.

By mid-afternoon, Gemma wondered if she should start thinking about the evening meal, but decided to wait and see what Max had bought.

At about four, a trail of dust signalled their return at last. Trying not to hurry, she made her way through the house to greet them, unable to disguise her pleasure when they pulled up near the kitchen door.

Max grinned at her as he swung his long frame down from the driver's seat and her heart gave a silly little lurch. He held a finger to his lips. 'Mollie's asleep,' he whispered. 'I'll try to get her out without disturbing her.'

Expertly, he unbuckled Mollie's car seat and lifted her gently out of the truck. In his strong arms, the baby girl looked comfortable and safe and Gemma's throat constricted painfully. The combined effect of Max's surprisingly tender manner as he handled his little niece and the way his usually grim gaze softened when he looked at her lying asleep in his arms upset her.

He hunched one broad shoulder forward to accommodate the little head covered in damp curls and the thoughtful gesture touched her deeply. But Gemma didn't want her emotions to be touched—such reactions were out of order and made her distinctly uncomfortable.

She felt better when she set about the businesslike task of unloading groceries and carting them through to the kitchen.

'How was town?' she asked when Max joined her.

'Same as always.' He shrugged. 'Mollie caused quite a stir.'

'I guess babies are a bit of a rarity out this way.'

He nodded and continued the unloading without further comment. He brought in a rather battered-looking high chair, which he proudly announced he'd found in the secondhand shop, and then he carried through an Esky full of cold goods and began to load the freezer with more tubs of chocolate chip ice cream and packets of frozen corn cobs and peas.

At last he looked up. 'Get plenty of work done while we were away?'

'Oh,' Gemma replied, with a vague wave of her hand, 'yes—heaps.'

'Mollie's been awake for most of the day. So many people wanted to make a fuss of her. I'd say she needs a good sleep now.'

'I guess so,' Gemma agreed. With a plastic scoop, she transferred sugar from a huge hessian bag into an old-fashioned metal canister. 'Would you like some afternoon tea?'

He glanced at his watch. 'I should mosey on down to the ringers' place and have something there. I need to know if Chad and Dingo were able to fix the pump on the five-mile bore.'

With that, he reached for the Akubra hat hanging on a nail near the back door and was gone.

Gemma clamped the lid down tight on the sugar canister, lugged the bag into the pantry, then sat down at the kitchen table and propped up her chin with her hand. She stayed there staring at the door where Max had disappeared. The clock on the wall ticked loudly.

Running her fingers through her short hair, she let out

a long sigh. A gloomy sense of depression settled on her, like a thick, suffocating fog.

Just why she felt so low was a puzzle.

She knew she should be delighted with how well this whole babysitting business was progressing. Instead of snarling at her and constantly annoying her, Max was keeping his criticisms to a minimum and, for the most part, he was being polite. If she overlooked the matter of the washing up, he was going out of his way to be co-operative. And instead of hanging around and making her nervous all day long, he was giving her space. He much preferred the company of his ringers to hers.

Was she imagining it, she wondered, or was he actually avoiding her?

Why should it matter?

The blast of a car horn sounded outside. A visitor. Gemma jumped to her feet and hurried down the hallway to find a dusty sedan pulling up at the front of the homestead. The driver's door swung open and a woman with a mass of bright red hair emerged. As Gemma watched, she opened the back of her car and, when she leaned in to retrieve something, the denim of her jeans stretched sinfully over well-rounded buttocks.

Gemma's eyebrows rose. Their visitor was wearing a sheer white blouse through which her lacy bra was clearly visible. It was tucked into the tightest jeans she'd ever seen.

'Yoo-hoo! Maxie!' the woman called as she straightened again. In one hand she was holding what looked like a casserole dish wrapped in a tea towel. She slammed her car door shut and began to sashay on very high heels towards the stairs.

Was this one of the breakfast ladies?

Gemma found herself studying the woman very carefully. Her age, she guessed, would be just the other side of thirty, and there was really only one word to describe her figure—curvaceous. On a highway, such curves would come with a sign warning danger. Except, Gemma noted grimly, these curves came in all the right places—exactly where men were supposed to want them.

Lucky Max.

When she saw Gemma standing on the verandah, the visitor paused.

'Hi,' Gemma called.

'Hello,' came the cautious reply. It was very clear to Gemma that the woman was shocked to see her there. She stood staring, her eyes popping and her carefully painted mouth wide open.

After an uncomfortable stretch of silence, Gemma asked, 'Are you looking for Max?'

'Yes… I am…' The visitor tossed her mane of gleaming red hair, like an animal preparing for a battle.

Gemma pointed to the dirt track leading away from the homestead and towards the ringers' huts. 'He's down there.'

'With Dingo?'

She nodded. 'I'm sure you're welcome to go on over, if you want to see him.' Coming down the steps, she held out her hand. 'Or perhaps I can help you?'

A petulant frown marred the woman's otherwise pretty features. 'I don't know,' she muttered. 'You see, I was expecting…' She fiddled with the tea towel that covered the container she was holding. Her fingernails were very long and painted to match her hair. 'I thought…' Then, with an embarrassed shrug, she shoved the covered dish towards Gemma. 'Here, you might as well take this. It's a casserole. I didn't know there was a woman here, though. You see, I thought Max was trying to look after the little baby on his own and I figured he might need a hand.'

Gemma offered the woman her sweetest smile. 'How kind of you, but I don't know if I should accept this meal. That's why I'm here. To help Max out. We're caring for Mollie together.'

'I wonder why Max didn't mention you.'

Gemma shrugged. She'd been wondering the same thing.

'You're not from round these parts, are you?'

'Not any more, but I grew up out here. I'm Gemma Brown. An old friend of…of the family and I'm the baby's godmother.' She extended her hand.

It was accepted reluctantly. 'Sharon Foster. I own Sharon's Hair Affair, the beauty salon in town. Max dropped by this morning.'

'Nice to meet you, Sharon. He just…dropped by…did he?'

'He was tickled pink to show off the kid.'

Gemma struggled to imagine Max in a beauty salon, surrounded by women all fussing over Mollie. 'Can I offer you a cup of tea or coffee, or a cold drink?'

Sharon shook her head and she gave Gemma the distinct impression that she'd choke on anything she gave her. 'No. I'll be right, thanks.'

'And you're sure you don't want to see Max ?'

There was a long moment of hesitation during which Gemma was subjected to a lengthy scrutiny. Eventually Sharon made up her mind. 'No. No, I won't bother him. Look, you might as well keep the casserole. There's only enough for two.'

'Thank you.'

'It's beef stroganoff.' Sharon looked smug. 'I know it's Max's favourite.'

'Really?' Gemma murmured with teeth clenched in a grimacing smile. 'You're so thoughtful. I'm sure he'll just gobble it up. What a pity you can't wait to see him after coming so far out of your way.' She knew the drive from town took at least an hour. Now this woman faced the long, dusty drive back.

'Yeah, well… Might see you some time,' Sharon said uncertainly and without the slightest effort at sincerity. She turned and tottered back to the car. Her departure was accompanied by a slamming of doors and a roaring acceleration down the track.

As Gemma walked back into the house, trying not to think about other times Max and Sharon Foster had shared beef stroganoff, she heard the unmistakable sounds of Mollie waking. She hurried to attend to her and had just finished changing her nappy when the phone rang. Balancing Mollie on her hip, she dashed to answer it.

'Hello, Goodbye Creek Station.'

'Er…hello,' replied a woman's voice. 'Do I have the right number? Is that the Jardines' place?'

'Yes.'

'*Max* Jardine's?'

'Yes, that's right. Were you wanting to speak to Max?'

'Oh…er, yes, please.'

'I'm sorry. He isn't in at the moment. Can I take a message.'

'Excuse me, but who is this?'

'Gemma Brown. I'm…a…I'm looking after Max's niece.'

'Oh! *Oh...*I see. I didn't realise he'd hired a nanny.' The feminine voice was mellow and sophisticated.

Gemma resisted the urge to let out a loud, exasperated sigh. 'He didn't actually hire me. I'm a close family friend—Mollie's godmother.'

'I see,' the caller said again, with less enthusiasm.

'Can I be of any help?'

'Uh...this is just a social call, really. I met little Mollie in town this morning. Max dropped past my surgery to say hello.'

'He took Mollie to a doctor's surgery?' Alarmed, Gemma took another look at the baby in her arms. She seemed healthy enough. 'Was there something wrong with her? Max didn't mention any problems.'

'Oh, no. It wasn't a professional visit. We're just...' The caller paused to indulge in a self-conscious little laugh. 'Max and I are just good friends. And he was so excited about his little niece, he just had to show her to me.'

'I'm sorry, I didn't catch your name.'

'I'm Helena Roberts-Jones, the local GP.'

The hairdresser, the doctor... With a nasty blaze of anger, Gemma wondered how many more of Max's women she would have to deal with.

'I'll tell Max you called,' she said in saccharine tones. 'It's good to know there's medical help nearby if we need it—especially with a baby in the house.'

'Thank you,' came the subdued reply. 'Goodbye, Gemma. Perhaps we'll meet up some time?'

'That would be nice.'

'Oh, one more thing,' Helena Roberts-Jones purred. 'Could you do me a tiny favour?'

'I—I guess so.'

'Could you please check with Max if he needs me to order him a dinner suit for the Mungulla Ball?'

'Sure. With pleasure,' muttered Gemma.

She dropped the receiver in its cradle and, with teeth clamped together, made her way to the kitchen, to find Mollie a drink. 'Who'll be next, Moll?' she asked the innocent baby in her arms. 'The local schoolmarm?' Luckily, Mollie wasn't perturbed by her godmother's tension. She simply chuckled and played with the gold chain at Gemma's neck.

With Sharon's casserole safely deposited in a slow oven, Gemma wandered through to the large and comfortable lounge room and settled on the softly carpeted floor to play with Mollie and try to forget about Max's harem. Not that she really cared how many of the local females he courted, she told herself.

But she did object to being thrust into the role of his social secretary.

Nevertheless, she was surprised and a little taken aback by the interest of these women. Yesterday, when the little issue of breakfast had arisen, Gemma had decided Max was teasing her. But now she wasn't quite so sure. In spite of the comments various women had made from time to time about his looks, she'd never really thought of him as a ladies' man. Surely he was too stern and aloof?

For the next half-hour, Gemma lolled on the lounge room carpet and built towers out of blocks for Mollie to knock over. And she played peek-a-boo using a huge velvet cushion. Each time she reappeared from behind the soft blue cushion, the baby squealed with delight.

'Someone's having fun,' came a deeply masculine voice.

Gemma lowered the cushion to find two dusty riding boots in front of her. She looked up.

'Boo,' grinned Max.

'Good evening,' she replied primly. She didn't enjoy finding herself kneeling at Max Jardine's feet. She struggled to stand.

'Don't let me spoil the fun,' he said. 'Stay there. I'm going to crack open a beer. Would you like a drink?'

About to snap back with a negative reply, Gemma thought better of it. Her nerves were feeling distinctly frazzled. 'Yes, I'll have a beer, too.'

'Right you are.'

When he returned with two long glasses of icy cold beer, she left the floor and sat on one of the chintz-covered armchairs. Max relaxed into a deep chair opposite her and stretched his long legs in front of him. Mollie crawled over to him and patted his leg happily. He lifted her with one hand onto his knee. She crowed with delight.

Gemma hunted for something to say. She wanted to let off steam about Max's callers, but decided this was an occasion when she should put into practice her intentions to stay calm and collected. If she made a fuss, Max might think she cared about his women for the wrong reasons. 'Is the bore fixed?' she asked.

'Yes. Chad and Dingo are handy blokes to have around.' He took a long, thirsty swig of beer. 'You can meet them tomorrow night. They always come up here on Friday nights. I cook a roast and we have a few beers. Nothing flash, of course. As you know, social life in the bush is fairly quiet.'

Gemma felt her plans to be calm and uncritical flying out of the window. *'Quiet?'* she repeated. 'You surprise me, Max. From what I can see, your social life seems rather lively.'

'It does?'

'I mean if we start with the Breakfast Club…'

Max straightened and almost dropped Mollie off his knee. 'I beg your pardon?'

'Your lady friends. Your *breakfast* companions.'

'Gemma, what the hell are you talking about?'

'How about I start with Sharon Foster? Helena Roberts-Jones?'

He stared at her, obviously taken aback. Then he set Mollie back on the floor and downed his beer in one long gulp. 'Have you been spying on me or something?'

She shot him a searing look. 'I don't need to go searching for your women, Max. I've been beating them off with a stick all afternoon.'

'The hell you have. What do you mean?'

'There have been phone calls, casseroles, visitors in see-through blouses and skin-tight jeans.'

He had the grace to frown and look confused as if she were talking in a foreign language. 'What on earth are you raving on about?'

'Ever since you came home from town there's been an endless stream of women callers.'

'Really?'

'Definitely. You and Mollie sure made a big impression this morning.'

'I must admit, I couldn't believe the way everyone carried on.'

'Well, you tried hard enough to get their attention… calling in at the beauty salon…dropping in on the lady doctor… I guess we'll hear from the school teacher next.'

At that very moment, the phone on the little side table rang.

'It'll be for you,' Gemma growled.

Max looked at the telephone as if it were a venomous snake about to bite him. Gingerly, he lifted the receiver. 'Jardine speaking.'

As he listened to his caller, a red flush flared in his cheeks. 'Susan? What a…surprise.' His hand fiddled with the collar of his shirt, as if it was too tight. 'A *nice* surprise, of course.' He turned, so that he was no longer facing Gemma. 'That's very thoughtful of you, Susan. *Tonight?* Well, actually, I think…'

Gemma picked up Mollie and, with a grim little smile, quietly left the room.

CHAPTER FOUR

FROM outside the lounge room, Gemma could still hear Max's low coaxing tones as he murmured into the phone. He seemed to be placating his caller's ruffled feathers. But, not wanting to eavesdrop on his conversation with Susan—the schoolmarm or librarian, or whoever she was—Gemma shut the elegant French doors which separated the lounge and dining areas.

She decided to do justice to Sharon Foster's meal by setting the table in the formal dining room, so she carried Mollie and her high chair through from the kitchen. In the linen cupboard, she found a delicate white lace tablecloth, which she spread over the polished timber table. As a centrepiece, Gemma set the vase of flowers she'd arranged earlier in the afternoon and two silver candlesticks holding slim, pale blue candles.

After a moment's hesitation, she approached the magnificent English oak sideboard and discovered a set of very good quality silverware and an exquisite blue and white Wedgwood dinner service.

'It's a pity to have all this going to waste,' she told Mollie.

She finished setting the table, lit the candles and stepped back to observe her work with a critical eye. The overall effect was surprisingly pretty.

By the time Max sauntered through the French doors, Mollie was halfway through her meal. He and Susan had had a jolly long phone call, Gemma thought grumpily.

'You'll be happy to know that Susan isn't a school

teacher,' he announced, before nonchalantly shoving his hands in the pockets of his jeans and rocking back on his heels. 'She's the post mistress.'

Blast him! It was only because she knew the quality of the tableware that Gemma resisted the temptation to bang something. She squared her shoulders and eyed him with as much haughty disdain as she could muster. 'I don't care if the entire Australian women's basketball team are interested in you. They can phone you—or drop by—as often as they like. Just as long as I don't have to keep taking their calls.'

'I'm sorry you've had to deal with this.' His attention was caught by the dimmed lights and the table. He eyed the candles with deep suspicion. 'Are we—am *I* expecting company?'

Gemma suppressed a smile. 'No, but we have something special for dinner, so I thought I should make an effort. Can you finish feeding Mollie while I fetch our food?'

'Sure.'

As she moved away, Max called after her. 'You might be interested to know that I put a call through to the embassy in Somalia as well. I managed to speak to Isobel.'

Poor Isobel! Guiltily, Gemma turned back. 'That's wonderful. How is she? Has she seen Dave?' How could she have become so caught up in her own grumbles about Max that, for a moment, she'd almost forgotten about her friends' horrendous situation?

'Actually, she sounded very tired and depressed. She's only just arrived in Somalia, so she hasn't been able to see Dave yet. There's a certain amount of red tape to get through first.' His mouth twisted into a half-hearted smile. 'I did my best to cheer her up.'

Gemma stepped towards him and rested her hand on his arm. He was standing with a spoonful of Mollie's dinner in one hand and her bowl in the other. At Gemma's touch, he froze. 'I'm sure she loved hearing from you. Don't worry about Dave,' she said gently. 'I have every faith that he will be OK.'

'Yeah, of course.' He nodded before continuing to spoon food into Mollie's waiting mouth with the precision of an expert.

'How did Isobel take the news about our decision to share minding Mollie?'

'Her initial reaction was stunned disbelief.'

'I'll bet it was. She knows I—I—well, she knows you and I aren't soul mates.'

Max grunted. 'Once she got over the first shock, she seemed to warm to the idea. And the Embassy have given Isobel an e-mail address, so we'll be able to keep her posted about how Mollie's doing and she'll keep us up to date as well.'

'That's great.'

When she returned from the kitchen with two plates of Sharon's beef stroganoff and a rusk for Mollie to chew on, Max sniffed appreciatively. 'Smells good.'

'You should enjoy this. It's a very special treat.'

'It is?'

She smiled sweetly. 'You don't recognise this tasty dish?'

Lifting a tentative forkful of the beef and mushroom mixture, he tasted it, chewed carefully and swallowed. He looked puzzled. 'I'm not totally familiar with the flavour. It's rather fancier than my usual meals.'

'Oh? Surely Sharon's not mistaken? She assured me this was your favourite.'

Max seemed to choke a little and reached for his water glass. 'My favourite?'

'Yes,' Gemma replied with a devilish sense of satisfaction. 'Sharon Foster cooked this for us with her own two hands—well, if I'm honest, it wasn't meant for *us* exactly—I'm sure she didn't plan for me to be enjoying her culinary efforts.'

He chewed thoughtfully. 'She's a good cook, isn't she? This is very tasty.'

Gemma wasn't going to give him satisfaction by admitting anything of the sort. 'After poor Sharon drove all the way out here this afternoon, I thought the least I could do was go to the trouble of setting the table nicely with candles and flowers. I've tried to reproduce the evening just how she would have wanted it for you.'

'Gemma,' Max asked, not trying to hide the glitter of scepticism in his eyes, 'are you being catty?'

Her cheeks grew uncomfortably warm. Trust Max to try to turn this situation against her. She took another mouthful of beef to give herself time to think of an answer.

He watched her obvious discomfort. 'I think I detect a little of the green-eyed monster.'

'Why on earth would I be jealous?' she exploded. 'That's utter nonsense, Max.'

'I'm relieved to hear it.'

Her hands clenched tightly in her lap. *Damn him!* How on earth could Max even begin to think that she was jealous of his women? Why, she was downright sorry for them. Wasting their feelings on a grumpy recluse like him. If the poor deluded souls were hoping to trap him into marriage, they had Gemma's heartfelt sympathy.

She glared at him. 'Isn't it enough that you have

Sharon, Helena *and* Susan all panting after you? Surely you don't expect me to go weak-kneed as well?'

He frowned and Gemma was forced to lower her own eyes, so that she didn't have to meet his piercing gaze. To her intense dismay, when he looked at her like that, she felt goose bumps forming on her arms. Surely he wasn't remembering that long ago time? A time that she'd rather forget.

His voice cut into her thoughts. 'So I'm safe from your affection. That's a weight off my mind.'

She wasn't looking at him, but she could tell by the sudden wariness in his tone that he was as uncomfortable talking about such matters as she was.

'You're very safe, Max. As far as I'm concerned, you've about as much sex appeal as toenail clippings!' She refused to look up.

'Oh, well,' he said with an exaggerated sigh. 'I guess three women out of four is not a bad score for a bloke from the bush.' Suddenly, the tension left his voice. 'Seriously, Gemma, it's not really all that surprising that Mollie's stirred up all this feminine interest.'

Her head shot up again. 'Only you could blame a stampede of women to your door on a helpless baby.' She glanced at Mollie innocently chewing on her rusk and rubbing moist crumbs all over her chubby, little face. 'You should be ashamed of yourself,' she cried. 'This *feminine interest* has nothing to do with Mollie.'

He smiled slowly. 'I must admit I didn't think about any repercussions when I headed for town. I just wanted to show off Dave's little daughter, but I should have gone to Helena first. She would have been able to warn me.'

'Warn you?'

'About the effects of a bachelor and a baby on women.

Apparently most women find it a pretty heady combination.'

'Oh?'

'Yeah. Didn't you know? A fellow with a baby is a real chick magnet.'

'*Chick* magnet?'

'That's what Helena told me.'

'That doesn't sound like the scientific terminology you'd expect from a doctor.'

'I wasn't visiting Helena for medical advice. She and I—'

'I know, I know,' Gemma cut in coldly. 'You're just good friends.'

'That's exactly right.' He shrugged and held out his hands, palms up, as if pleading innocence. 'Anyway, it seems that lots of females happen to find a single bloke with a baby kind of…irresistible, although you've remained quite untouched.'

Her chair scraped loudly against the polished timber floor as she jumped to her feet. 'That's because I've been overexposed to the single bloke in question. I'm sure the dear doctor would classify me as a hardened case.'

She made a fuss of wiping Mollie's face and forced a hard edge of sarcasm into her voice. 'It's just as well some of us are immune to your fatal charms, Mr Jardine. Half the women in the district have started behaving foolishly—throwing themselves all over you.' For a shocking moment she hesitated as an unwanted memory taunted her again. Her eyes caught his and she blushed before hurrying on. 'We—we can't let the entire Australian outback come to a grinding halt.'

Lifting Mollie out of the high chair, she dropped a light kiss on her head. 'I'm going to fix this little girl's bottle.'

At the dining room doorway she turned to face Max, still sitting at the table, a bemused expression on his face. 'By the way, I mustn't forget to give you a message from your *very* good friend, Dr Roberts-Jones. She must have been so busy imparting all that helpful information, she forgot to ask you if you need to hire a formal dinner suit for the Mungulla Ball. You are to let her know if you want one.'

She dashed away without waiting to hear his answer.

The next day, Gemma was spared an overdose of Max's company. He was busy with station matters all morning and he charged in at lunchtime with instructions for roasting the large piece of beef he'd extracted from the cold room the night before.

'The ringers will start dropping by around sunset, but they won't expect to eat straight away. Make sure there are plenty of potatoes,' he called as he raced off, leaving the fly-screen door to bang behind him and without so much as a passing glance at the pile of dirty dishes in the sink.

Scant minutes later, he dashed back and popped his head through the door again. 'Oh, and there's a Pommy Jackaroo joining us tonight. He's been working on Mungulla, but he's shown a flair for horse work, so I'm using him here for a few weeks.' His eyes darted to the sink and he hesitated, then sent her the grin of naughty schoolboy, who hadn't done his homework. 'Mind if I skip sink duty just this once?'

When he looked at her like that, Gemma felt a weird little pain in her chest. 'I hope you have a very good excuse.'

'This Pom and I are pretty busy trying to break in some extra horses. We're going to need more mounts this season because after the rain there's so much feed on the ground. It'll be dangerous using motorbikes for cattle work.'

Giving an exaggerated sigh, she held out her hands. 'If I get dishpan hands, you can pay for my next manicure.'

He touched one of her hands with his rough fingers and winked. 'If I speak to her extra nicely, Sharon might give you a slap-up manicure for free.' Then he dashed away again before she could reply.

At a quarter to six, shortly before sunset, Gemma heard Max's footsteps re-enter the house and head for the bathroom. She checked the oven. Assuming that the men would want to sit and enjoy a few beers before they ate, everything was coming along nicely. She'd added carrots, pumpkin and onions as well as the mandatory potatoes to the baking tray and she'd unearthed a deep-dish apple pie from the depths of the freezer.

For the occasion, she'd set the dining table again with the good china and silver and she'd dressed Mollie in a pretty little pink and white dress. Gemma had thought about dressing up, but understood enough about outback ways to know that this evening would be a casual affair. Nevertheless, she'd exchanged her usual cotton sundress for a pair of tailored white jeans and a sleeveless red silk shirt.

She was rather looking forward to the evening ahead. In the past she had enjoyed similar times, when she'd sat on the verandah, watching the sun go down and the stars come out, and listened to background drone of cicadas while the men swapped jokes and yarns about the bush. The men in the outback were always great storytellers. If the jokes became a bit rough, they would apologise to her, but they never made her feel unwelcome.

'The roast smells great.' Max came into the kitchen, with his hair wet from the shower and slicked back. He was still buttoning his light-blue cotton shirt and hadn't yet tucked it into his jeans. He smelled clean and spicy—the kind of smell that made Gemma's feeble brain think about getting closer.

Horrified by her reaction, she turned and took several steps clear away from him.

'Hey,' he said, watching her walk, 'you look…you…look… Do you think you should be wearing jeans like that when there'll be so many fellows around?'

'What's wrong with my jeans?'

'Well there's nothing *wrong* with them, exactly. That's the problem. They're just right. They look terrific. But you'll give these blokes ideas.'

'What kind of ideas?' she asked, pretending innocence.

'They might think you're—available.'

Feeling emboldened by his apparent discomfort, Gemma folded her arms and cocked her head to one side as she eyed him steadily. 'I had no idea I was *un*available.'

Max scratched his exposed chest and looked at her with a puzzled frown.

'What have you told them about me?' she persisted.

'Nothing. Absolutely nothing. Well—' He fiddled with one of his shirt buttons and Gemma wished he would hurry and get the shirt done up. She didn't need to see that broad, brown chest and those sleek, sculpted muscles. He cleared his throat. 'I've told them—just in case they got the wrong idea, you see—I've explained that you and I are not an item.'

'I—I'm very glad they understand that,' she muttered

while she hunted noisily through the saucepan cupboard to find a pot for boiling beans.

'But, unfortunately, they didn't really believe me.'

She found a suitable pot and thumped it down on the counter top. 'Well, what would they expect, Max? You have so many women who *are*—items. I suppose they've seen me about the place and leapt to a very logical conclusion.'

'Gemma, I think you might have been getting the wrong idea about me. I'm no lady-killer.'

Slowly and deliberately, he tucked the shirt tails into his jeans and Gemma swung her glance to the floor. It unnerved her to see him doing intimate things like that. The movements emphasised his manliness—the pleasing angle his body made as it tapered from his shoulders through to his hips—and it made her forget his problem personality. If she didn't rein in her thoughts right now, she might be lining up with Susan, Sharon and Helena.

'I never suspected that you *killed* ladies, ' she hissed, waving the saucepan at him.

'You're deliberately misunderstanding me.'

'I'm deliberately telling you to get out of here. Go play host while I—'

'While you play Cinderella? No way.' He stepped closer and grabbed her hand as it gripped the saucepan handle. 'We're partners, remember? I don't want you stuck in the kitchen like a meek little servant.'

If she were honest, it wasn't a role she fancied, either.

'Let's take Mollie and go out on the verandah and relax with a well-earned drink.'

When she followed Max outside, Gemma was relieved to find that the ringers, Chad and Dingo and a young apprentice they called Squirt, were just arriving. They all had a distinctly scrubbed-up look about them and reeked of after-shave, and they looked a little shy and awkward while Max made the introductions and handed round beer stubbies in polystyrene holders.

Gemma was contemplating breaking the ice with a question about their day, when another man appeared around the corner of the homestead and made his way onto the verandah. She knew at once that he must be the Pommy Jackaroo.

As he approached, his body silhouetted against the setting sun, he seemed to her to be every inch an Englishman. She watched him come closer and she could see that his skin had been burnt a ruddy brown in the outback, but his neat, light-brown hair, grey-blue eyes and dignified bearing marked him as coming from the same mould as many of the nicer young men she had met in London.

Max introduced the newcomer to Gemma as Simon Fox and he watched warily as the young man returned her greeting. Gemma couldn't help noting the way Max's eyes darkened while Simon's lit with appreciation as they exchanged a firm handshake. She was impressed when the young Englishman took the trouble to show polite attention to Mollie, who was sitting on Gemma's lap, blissfully sucking her toes.

Once Simon had accepted a beer and lowered his length into a low-slung squatter's chair, the conversation soon settled into a leisurely discussion of the importance of a good stock horse. Gemma listened with interest to the men's thoughts about the comparable benefits of motorbikes over horses for station work.

'There are plenty of places where a good stock horse will beat a motorbike hands down any day,' affirmed Dingo. 'For starters, there are far too many hills and gullies to the north of here for a motorbike and you'll always need a good horse for mustering and yard work.'

For a moment Gemma stopped listening as she thought about her own experiences in the bush and the excitement of a good muster. The smell of dust and the thrill of thundering hooves as her horse tore over the red soil plains. The heart-stopping danger as she watched the men catch and throw bullocks. And then there was the intense satisfaction of being part of a fast-paced, energetic team during yard work, when they branded, ear-tagged and vaccinated each beast inside a minute.

All through her high school years, when the wet season finished and the mustering began, Gemma had never missed the chance to join the team on Goodbye Creek station.

'You can't beat a horse for walking cattle and holding them,' she heard Chad drawl, before taking a deep thirsty swig at his beer.

She turned to Simon. 'And I understand you're something of an expert with horses?'

'I seem to have a bit of a knack,' he agreed modestly.

They exchanged friendly smiles.

'He's not too bad for a Pommy Jackaroo,' chipped in Dingo with a sly grin.

'Have you been in Australia very long?'

'Eighteen months. And that's too long, as far as my family are concerned,' he explained with a laugh.

'I guess they're missing you.'

'My father thinks I've done enough adventuring around the antipodes and it's time to come home and be of some use to the family.'

'They're farmers?' Gemma asked with genuine interest. Out of the corner of her eye, she sensed Max shifting restlessly on his chair.

'How's that roast?' he asked suddenly. ' You'll need to get the beans on by now, won't you?'

Lord, the man was a spoilsport! Gemma felt her anger flaring. For the first time since she'd arrived at Goodbye Creek someone was treating her like a human being and she was having a normal conversation that had nothing to do with babies, hormones or other people's love lives. She was tempted to tell Max to check his own roast, like he did every other Friday night when she wasn't there, but the men were all looking at her with an expectant air.

If she gave their boss a piece of her mind, she knew they would either be shocked to the soles of their riding boots, or they would assume she and Max had an 'understanding'—and that, married or not, she was his 'missus'.

That was the last thing she wanted them to think, so she rose and meekly handed Mollie over while she went to the kitchen to check the meal.

The roast was fine, the beans boiled beautifully and the rest of the evening went without a hitch. And after they had eaten and were replete with good food and fine wine, everyone moved back to the verandah. Gemma felt completely relaxed for the first time since she'd arrived at Goodbye Creek. Jokes and yarns were swapped, accompanied by the occasional slapping at a mosquito or the clink of glasses as they downed a nightcap.

After the men eventually left, she checked on Mollie and came back into the kitchen to find Max up to his elbows in hot sudsy water, tackling the washing-up straight away, rather than leaving it till the next day. Surprised, she took up a tea towel and quietly worked beside him.

She found it safer to look at the view through the

window over the sink than to watch his strong hands gleaming with soapy water, or his muscular arms with shirt sleeves rolled back. Outside, the moon was hanging high in the sky like a shiny saucepan lid. Bathed in its light, the paddocks looked pale and silvery. From down near the creek, she could hear a lone curlew calling.

She found herself thinking again about how much she loved the bush and how, at one time, ages ago, she had never expected to leave it. Now, the bush still felt like home—as if she belonged. And yet, any day soon, she hoped to hear from Isobel that Dave was safe and then they would be coming back for Mollie. Handing Mollie back to her mother meant returning to Brisbane.

Leaving the bush.

And Max.

'How long are you going to spend drying that one plate?'

His voice penetrated her cloud of thoughts and Gemma realised she'd been standing in a daze for ages and there was no more room on the dish rack. Hastily, she dumped the plate she'd polished bone dry and grabbed another.

Max shook his head in mock exasperation then picked up the baking dish and scratched at a blackened patch with the steel wool pad. 'Thanks for tonight,' he said. 'It's nice for a change to have the little feminine touches that I kind of gloss over, like flowers on the table, red wine, gravy…and apple pie.'

She smiled at him, and thought how different he looked when he wasn't frowning at her. She was beginning to understand why some women were attracted to Max. Well, lots of women, she had to admit. There were odd moments when he let his charm shine through—even for her.

And those charming moments had been getting to her recently, so that she'd found herself thinking about them when he was away during the day. She'd even thought about what it would be like when he really turned on the charm. The effect would probably be quite stunning.

Heart-stopping.

She wondered why he hadn't married. There didn't seem to be a shortage of volunteers for the job. Now that Dave was carving a different career path for himself, Max could do with someone to help him run the household as well as the property. When she thought about the amount of renovating he'd done in recent years, she realised that he'd been working extremely hard.

Surely it was a too much for one man to manage on his own?

She stood side by side with him, drying several more plates, and realised that a week ago she would never have dreamed of connecting Max and marriage.

'You and the Pommy Jackaroo seemed to hit it off,' he said, after they'd worked together some time. His blue eyes met hers, glanced away and met again, before he went back to scrubbing fiercely at the bottom of the blackened baking dish.

'Yes. He's a nice young fellow, isn't he?'

'"A nice young fellow,"' Max scoffed. 'You sound like somebody's grandmother.' He shot her a sceptical grimace. 'You two seemed to be cooking up something when he was in the kitchen helping you with dessert.'

She should have known that her eagle-eyed overseer wouldn't miss a trick. 'Actually,' she said quickly, deciding not to beat around the bush, 'Simon has asked me to go with him to the Mungulla Ball.'

Max's scrubbing movements stilled. 'The sneaky devil.' He let the baking dish slide beneath the suds as he rose to his full height and stared down at her. 'And you explained why you couldn't oblige, didn't you?'

Gemma lifted her chin. 'I certainly did not.'

'You didn't?' He let out a mirthless huff. 'For heaven's sake, Gemma, you'll have to explain to him first thing tomorrow that you can't go.'

'No way!' she cried defensively. ' I really want to go to that ball. It's for Ruth and Tom Neville's tenth wedding anniversary. You're going with Helena, aren't you?'

'She spoke to me about it weeks ago. I accepted before—before I knew about Dave—otherwise I would have—'

For several heartbeats, Gemma waited for him to finish the sentence, but it seemed he'd changed his mind. He was concentrating on rinsing the baking dish with fresh, hot water.

After the silence went on too long, she answered back. 'Well, Simon couldn't speak to me about it weeks ago. We only met tonight.'

'Exactly. That's my point. You hardly know the man.'

Gemma shook her damp tea towel at him. 'Max, can I remind once again that you are not *my* big brother? You don't have to worry about me. I really don't need you to vet my dates.'

'What about your other responsibilities? What about Mollie?'

'For Pete's sake!' For the second time tonight she felt like Cinderella. This time she was fighting for her right to go to the ball. 'Don't try to use Mollie as an excuse, Max. You know as well as I do that babies and children go to balls out here. You, Dave and I cut our teeth on outback balls. The Nevilles will have plenty of rooms set aside for the little ones to sleep in.'

Max eased his weight back against the sink with his hands folded across his chest and eyed her thoughtfully.

'I'm going, Max,' she challenged, stepping forward and jabbing a finger into his hard chest. 'And, what's more, I'm going to have the time of my life.'

He clasped her fingers in a hand that was warm and damp from washing up.

Something drastic happened to Gemma's ability to breathe. Max was holding her hand against his chest and, Lord help her, she was thinking how interesting it would be if he kept on hauling her closer.

His eyes were so very blue when they were this close. 'You've always been a mouthy little shrimp,' he said while his thumb massaged her fingers, her hand, her wrist. 'Have you any idea how you look when you're all fired up like that?'

His question hung in the silent room.

'No,' she whispered breathlessly.

Had she risen on tiptoes? Or was Max leaning closer? They seemed to be almost touching. What an incredible mouth he had. So sexy. 'How do I look, Max?'

'Definitely kissable,' he said in a voice that sounded half trapped in his throat.

Heaven help her! It was what she wanted him to say and what he mustn't say. His lips were on her forehead. She could feel them caressing her with their soft, warm pressure. His arms were coming round her and they felt sensational and she knew that any minute now his lips would seek hers.

But—but this was all wrong!

This was *Max!*

She knew that she couldn't let him kiss her!

Just in time, she struggled out of his embrace and

staggered backwards across the kitchen, her breathing ragged, painful, panting.

Max stood, still as a rock, with his back to the sink and his arms hanging empty at his sides. He regarded her with a steady, unsmiling gaze.

'You mustn't kiss me, Max.'

'No?'

Desperately, she shook her head.

'You're saving yourself for the Pommy Jackaroo?'

She didn't know what else to say, couldn't think how else to answer. 'I guess I am.'

At that, his face hardened into a blank mask. 'Then I wish you good luck.' He nodded curtly. 'And goodnight, Gemma.'

'Goodnight,' she echoed as he strode slowly out of the room.

Her shoulders sagged as she sank onto a kitchen chair. So close. She'd almost let Max kiss her.

But Gemma knew for certain that to kiss Max Jardine was to book a passage on the *Titanic*. She must make sure that he never tried to kiss her again.

CHAPTER FIVE

'I'M AFRAID I don't stock much formal wear.' Jessie Block, the stout and rather worried-looking owner of Goodbye Creek's one and only dress shop, shook her head gloomily. 'And I've almost nothing in your size, Gemma.'

With eyes the colour of faded denim, she studied Gemma and frowned.

'I'm too small?'

'Too small and too young,' sighed Jessie. 'All the young people get their clothes when they go to the city, or they have them sent out.'

'I haven't time to have anything sent out.'

It was already Wednesday, just a few days before the ball, but it was the first day Max had been free to babysit so that Gemma could escape into town to find something to wear. She'd known that at this late stage the chances of finding something suitable in a tiny outpost like Goodbye Creek were almost nil. She stared at the racks of Jessie's frocks and suppressed a grimace. They were mostly florals and prints in fabrics, styles and sizes suitable for the most conservative and matronly of souls.

She would just have to stick to the basic black that she'd thrown into her bag at the last minute. It had served her faithfully many times in the past and, while it was no longer the height of fashion and it definitely wasn't a ball gown, it would do at a pinch.

Jessie was rummaging around, shuffling coat hangers and desperately pulling out the most unlikely offerings.

'I'm sorry,' she said, as Gemma shook her head at a lime-green and feathered concoction. 'I really don't think I'm going to be able to help you.'

'That's OK,' Gemma reassured her. 'It was a stab in the dark thinking I might find something at this late stage.'

'What a pity.'

'Thanks for going to so much trouble.' Gemma slipped the strap of her bag back over her shoulder and turned to leave the shop.

'Wait a minute!' Jessie exclaimed. 'I've just remembered something. It's right at the back because it's never been suitable—' She darted excitedly to a rack at the back of the shop and hunted through a row of tired and outdated-looking clothes covered with plastic film. 'I'm sure it's still here,' she muttered.

But Gemma had resigned herself to wearing her black and she had no faith whatever in anything Jessie might unearth. 'Please, don't go to any more bother.'

'It's no bother,' came the predictable reply.

Gemma hovered near the doorway. Already she was thinking about what else she wanted to buy while she was in town. More formula for Mollie, a new toothbrush, some fresh oranges…

'Eureka!' shrieked Jessie. She charged back to Gemma, reverently holding a dusty plastic bag in front of her as if she were offering the Holy Grail. 'I'm sure it's your size,' she beamed.

As Jessie peeled away the plastic cover, Gemma eyed the garment dubiously. There seemed to be nothing of it. It looked more like a bundle of spangled cobwebs than a dress.

'It looks much better on,' urged Jessie.

It would need to.

'You'll try it?'

'Is it my size?'

Jessie nodded enthusiastically and led the way to the curtained cubicle at the back of the shop. 'Sing out if you need a hand,' she called as she drew the curtain closed.

Gemma was no longer in the mood for trying on clothes. Her eagerness had faded soon after she saw what was available. She was sure this dress would be no more suitable than the others. But, to please Jessie, she wriggled out of the trouser suit she'd worn into town and reached for the coat hanger.

The dress was so soft and shapeless Gemma took a few minutes to work out the front from the back and how exactly to put it on. Eventually, she slipped the cobweb-fine garment over her head. One arm slid into a slim, fitted sleeve while the other stayed bare as the dress slid over her breasts, past her waist and hips to skim her ankles. She took a deep breath and looked in the mirror.

And took another, sharper breath—more like a gasp.

'How are you going, dear?' Jessie called through the curtain.

'I'm almost ready,' Gemma replied. She needed a moment to examine the dress without Jessie fussing around her. She had to get used to the idea that this garment suited her. Suited her? It was amazing. When Cinderella's fairy godmother had waved her wand, she couldn't have achieved a more magical transformation.

The off-one-shoulder gown was soft and clinging and fitted her perfectly. Silvery blue, it looked as if it had been spun out of moonshine—and the sparkle it put into Gemma's light-blue eyes was quite amazing. She reached up and fluffed her short dark hair and, as she moved, she noticed long slits up each side of the skirt. 'Good, it will be suitable for dancing,' she said softly.

'What's that, dear?'

Time to put Jessie out of her misery. Drawing back the curtain, Gemma did an excited little spin. She was feeling great! 'What do you think?'

'Oh, my dear! Oh, Gemma! I knew it would be perfect!' Jessie circled around her, sighing with delight. 'You'll blow Max away with this!'

'Do you think so?'

'Oh, yes, love.'

Something nasty, like an electric shock zapped through Gemma. She clapped her hand to her mouth and wished with everything she had that she could take back this silly conversation. 'It's not what Max thinks that counts,' she hastily corrected. 'I'm not going to the ball with Max.'

Her words echoed over and over in her head. *I'm not going to the ball with Max.* And her sense of happiness and excitement drifted away, heading straight for the ground like dying autumn leaves.

Gemma covered her face with her hands and gave a little shake. This was so silly. She'd known all along she wasn't going with Max. So why had she been thinking about him when she first saw her reflection in the mirror?

'I'm going to the ball with Simon Fox,' she explained, looking Jessie squarely in the eye.

'Oh?' Jessie looked puzzled. 'Is he from around these parts, dear?'

'Yes.' Gemma laughed. 'Surely you've heard about the Pommy Jackaroo?'

'Oh, yes. Of course.' Jessie looked exceedingly embarrassed. 'I'm sorry. I just thought with you staying out at the Jardines' place to look after the baby and all—'

'Max is taking Dr Roberts-Jones.'

'Oh, I see.'

Gemma was startled by how forlorn Jessie looked. 'But I'm still going to buy this dress, Jessie. How much is it?'

The shopkeeper named a ridiculously cheap price. 'It's old stock,' she explained. 'And I'll never be able to sell it to anyone else.'

Once Gemma was back into her street clothes and the dress was paid for and carefully wrapped in lavender tissue paper, she found it easier to shrug off her sense of depression. Lately, she'd been letting herself get tied up in knots about Max. At night, she kept dreaming about him and the way he'd told her she looked kissable. What she had to remind herself, in the broad, bright light of day, was that Max had a string of women he told things like that.

And he would be taking one of them to the ball.

Besides, she might as well be positive. There was a very good chance that Simon Fox would find her kissable, too, and that was preferable any day to being kissed by Max Jardine.

But although Gemma gave an outward appearance of calm over the next few days, by the time Saturday, the day of the ball, arrived, she was as keyed up as a teenager on her first date.

Simon, Max, Mollie and Gemma had arranged to travel together to Mungulla and meet Helena there. All their party clothes were packed carefully into one suit pack, while in the back of the four-wheel drive they loaded tents and swags for sleeping plus Mollie's folding cot.

Gemma knew from past experience that many revellers would stay up and party all night, progressing straight from dancing and drinking to the recovery breakfast in the morning. But she was most definitely planning to pitch a tent down by the creek and catch a few hours' rest before breakfast and the long, dusty drive home the next day.

On the journey, Gemma stayed in the back of the cabin with Mollie, while the men sat in front, but she was determined not to be left out of the conversation. She wanted to get to know her partner better before she found herself dancing in his arms all evening, and besides, there was so much to discuss about London.

Simon knew most of the pubs and restaurants she had frequented while she lived there and they had also seen many of the same shows. Their discussion warmed up as they threw around names like Notting Hill Gate and Richmond Park and Simon grew quite animated. As they chatted, Max sat in grim, jaw-clenched silence, gripping the steering wheel with whitened knuckles.

His moodiness reminded Gemma of the Max of old, the Max who'd looked down on her girlhood friendship with Dave, and it made her more determined than ever to find Simon utterly fascinating.

They turned off the bitumen highway and rattled over the gravel road that led into Mungulla station, past pale, grassy paddocks dotted with skinny gum trees and sleek, grey-coated Brahman cattle.

Simon turned back to Gemma. 'What a pity we didn't cross paths while you were in London. I could have taken you down to our farm in Devon.'

'Devon!' she exclaimed. 'I *loved* Devon. It would be wonderful to—'

Crunch! At that moment, the vehicle swerved and hit an enormous pothole. Gemma was thrown against the door. Mollie woke up and began to cry and Simon, who had only just managed to hold himself upright, turned smartly to the front again.

Gemma glanced suspiciously at Max's stiff back and her eyes caught his narrowed gaze in the rear vision mirror. She had the distinct impression that he'd hit that pothole in a deliberate attempt to stop their conversation. But if he thought he could prevent her from spending an enjoyable evening with Simon, he was going to be disappointed.

The sun was slipping low towards the distant rim of blue hills by the time they reached Mungulla. Many people had arrived ahead of them and their vehicles were parked in the shade of the huge paperbarks lining the crest of the bank that ran down to the creek. Trestle tables and chairs were set out on the stretch of lawn in front of the long, low homestead and in one corner a timber floor had been constructed for dancing. The African Tulip trees that framed the lawn were strung with lights.

'This is going to look absolutely gorgeous once it's properly dark,' Gemma said as she took in all the preparations.

They climbed out of the car and stretched their cramped legs.

Simon touched Gemma's arm and asked in his usual gentlemanly manner, 'Can I help you with Mollie's things?'

'She'll be right, mate,' cut in Max. He wrenched open the back door of his vehicle and tossed Simon a folded canvas tent. His actions were so rough that the Englishman grunted as he caught the heavy bundle. 'Do us a favour and set this up somewhere,' Max ordered. 'I'll look after the rest.'

He gathered up Mollie's equipment and headed for

the homestead. Gemma hurried after him, Mollie in her arms. 'I hope you're not going to spoil this evening by being rude to Simon,' she hissed through gritted teeth.

'Wouldn't dream of it,' he replied.

'Huh!' Gemma huffed. 'You almost winded him when you flung that heavy tent in his stomach.'

Max stopped in his tracks and stared at Gemma. With his spare hand, he pushed his broad-brimmed hat back and scratched his head. 'For crying out loud, Gemma. The man's out here to be toughened up. Of course he can catch a tent without flinching. How on earth do you think he manages to stay on a bucking horse or throw a bullock?'

Gemma's upper lip curled. 'I'm not talking about Simon's strength or lack of it. I'm talking about *your* behaviour. You just remember to mind your manners.'

'There's nothing wrong with my manners.'

'Let's hope not. I'd appreciate it if you were nice to my partner this evening. That way we'll all be able to have a pleasant time.'

He grunted. 'You'll be very sweet to Helena, of course.'

'Of course.'

Their hostess Ruth Neville greeted them with excited hugs and showed them where to set up Mollie's cot. By the time that was organised, the sun was almost set and guests, dressed in their finery, were starting to drift out of the homestead and out of the tents to gather on the lawn.

'Better get into our party clobber,' Max said. 'Let's hope the Pommy Jackaroo has the tent up. Do you want to get changed first?'

'No. You two fellows will be faster than me,' Gemma replied quickly.

While the men changed, she sat on the cool creek bank and tried to concentrate on the tranquillity of the bush and the creek below, but, to her annoyance, her imagination kept intruding, seriously disturbing her quest for peace and inner calm. No matter how hard she tried, she couldn't eliminate the pictures of Max that kept flashing through her mind. She tried to focus on Simon, her neat and personable partner.

Instead, Gemma found tempting visions taunting her… Visions of Max, only metres away, dressing inside the tent. She could picture his strong brown back and tightly toned buttocks as he shed his jeans and work shirt… The play of muscles in his chest as he raised his arms to haul a clean shirt over his head…the sideways jerking movement of his neck as he did up the tiny button at his collar and knotted his tie.

She had never seen Max do any of these things, so it was entirely disconcerting that her imagination could present such clear and detailed pictures.

'All done, Gemma. Your turn.'

The men emerged from the tent. Two handsome fellows looking their dashing best in sleek dark suits with gleaming white shirts and elegant black bow ties. Gemma smiled at Simon and tried to stifle any sense of comparison. Who cared if Max was taller, darker, broader-shouldered or had bluer eyes and a fuller, sexier mouth?

Simon was nice-looking, charming and polite—the kind of gentleman her mother had told her to look out for—the perfect partner for such an enchanting evening.

'You both look absolutely splendid,' she told them as she scrambled to her feet, and she sent Simon another encouraging smile.

'Don't take too long,' Max urged. 'We're getting thirsty.'

'I don't mind waiting for Gemma if you want to go ahead, Max,' Simon offered.

'No,' came the abrupt reply, accompanied by a frown. 'We may as well all go up together.'

As she slipped into the tent, Gemma grinned back at them. 'I don't have any problem zips, so I won't need any help with changing.'

'We weren't getting our hopes up,' Max drawled in reply.

Without a full-length mirror, Gemma had to hope that her dress was straight. The men had left a small lantern burning in a corner of the tent, and as darkness was encroaching very swiftly she needed its light to help her apply make-up while she peered into the minuscule mirror of her compact.

Given the limitations of her situation, she found complicated make-up difficult, but she was determined to make her appearance more dramatic than her usual casual look. Quickly she applied eye-shadow, mascara, a dusting of blush on her cheeks and lipstick. There wasn't much more she could do with her short, dark hair than run a little styling mousse through it with her fingers, so that it separated into feathery wisps.

Finally, she was satisfied and she slipped out of the tent. 'Hope I haven't taken too long.'

The men had been standing with their backs to her, looking at something on the far side of the creek. As she called to them they turned simultaneously and she felt self-conscious standing there before them in her new, dramatic, softly clinging gown.

Simon grinned broadly. 'My goodness,' he breathed. 'You look absolutely gorgeous.'

Max gave a very good impression of someone who had been shot by a stun gun. The shocked expression on his face sent Gemma's heart thumping and her knees to water. She reached for one of the tent's guy ropes to steady herself.

To her relief, he seemed to recover in a moment or two, but he walked towards her, smiling a strange, sadly lopsided little smile. 'We're waiting for Gemma Brown. Have you seen her?'

Gemma felt dizzy when he looked at her like that. She wondered how on earth he expected her to answer. 'She ran away with a gypsy,' she whispered and, blinking back silly tears, she dashed past Max to Simon.

Looping her arm through the Englishman's, she beamed up at him. 'Let's party, Mr Fox!'

'At once, Miss Brown!'

The trio crossed the stretch of paddock between the creek and the homestead and joined the revellers. A tall, willowy woman with auburn hair drawn back into a neat chignon separated from one of the groups and seemed to glide towards them, her pale, slender arms extended to Max.

Helena Roberts-Jones.

Dressed in an elegant cream chiffon gown and draped in pearls. Her attire toned perfectly with her titian colouring. 'Max, darling.'

'Helena.'

They embraced with a gentle, refined hug.

'So glad you were able to get away at last.'

'Yes,' Helena replied. 'I sent up a very demanding prayer—more of an order, really. No babies are allowed to be born tonight. No one's allowed to get appendicitis—or any other kind of illness, for that matter.'

'I'm sure no one would dare,' Max reassured her.

With a hand at her elbow, he turned her to meet Gemma and Simon.

'Oh,' Helena said when she was introduced to Gemma. 'So you're the young lady I spoke to on the phone—the nanny who's been staying with Max.' Her eyes widened. 'You sounded younger on the phone.'

'She usually *looks* much younger, too,' Max commented dryly.

'Oh, well,' shrugged Helena with a self-conscious little laugh, 'it's amazing what can be done with make-up.'

Gemma didn't appreciate Helena's attempt at a snub, but she had to admit that Max's partner was beautiful and exceedingly elegant. How good Helena and Max look together, she thought with an unexpected pang of dismay.

But this was not jealousy! She couldn't possibly be jealous. She didn't care what kind of women Max dated. It was wonderful that he and Helena were perfect for each other. They looked like people in an advertisement for something expensive—an exclusive restaurant, perhaps. He was the ruggedly handsome, worldly wise man and she his beautiful, steady, capable wife.

A girl approached their group with a tray of champagne cocktails and they all took a slim glass flute and toasted each other. Soon people from other groups, mainly friends from neighbouring properties, joined their little circle and more introductions were made. Several people who had known Gemma when she was growing up in the district greeted her as an old friend. A silver platter of delicious savouries came their way.

Night fell swiftly and completely while Gemma and Simon discussed stock horses with a cattleman who had travelled all the way from Julia Creek. The lights in the trees and the floodlights for the dance area came on, creating dazzling spots of colour and intimate shadowy areas around the garden.

An old friend Gemma had known since schooldays claimed her, and by the time she glanced back to where Max and Helena had been standing, they had disappeared.

After a time, Simon walked towards her. 'Would you like to dance?'

She looked across to the makeshift dance floor. Only a few couples were gyrating to taped music. She preferred to dance on a crowded floor.

'Apparently the band should be here by now,' Simon explained. 'I think Max has gone down the track a bit to see if they made it across the creek.'

'Helena went with him?' Gemma couldn't help asking.

'I'm not sure.' Simon took her hand and led her to the dance floor.

He held her companionably close without any tasteless groping and he moved smoothly in time to the music, guiding her expertly around the floor. Gemma couldn't help admiring Simon. He was one of those rare gems—a capable, resilient worker in the bush and a socially adept gentleman. She wished she felt more excited to be with him.

After the first bracket of songs finished, they stood together on the dance floor waiting for someone to change the tape. 'You're looking very beautiful tonight, Gemma. The belle of the ball, I'm sure.'

'Thank you.' She accepted his praise with a slight bow of her head and wished that his opinion meant more to her.

When the music started up again, there was a little

cheer from the crowd on the dance floor. It was a slow romantic number and once more Simon took her in his arms.

'Do you mind being labelled the Pommy Jackaroo?' she asked.

He laughed. 'I was a bit taken aback at first, but I know now that it's used with grudging respect. It means I may be a bit wet behind the ears—'

'But you're still a likeable sort of bloke.'

He looked into her eyes, as if searching for an answer to a question he hadn't asked. 'Something like that.' After a few more laps around the floor, he asked, 'I understand you grew up in these parts?'

'Yes, that's right.'

'But you don't talk about it much.'

Gemma grimaced. 'Everyone around here knows my life story. You can't keep any secrets in the outback.'

He smiled. 'I've discovered that.'

They swirled past another dancing couple.

'So you already know all about me?'

He looked a trifle embarrassed and slowed his pace till they were merely shuffling together. 'I know that everyone in the district expected you to pair up with Max's kid brother Dave, but you didn't. And now you're back here with his daughter.'

'My goodness,' Gemma groaned. 'When you put it like that it sounds highly suspect, doesn't it?'

She quickly explained that she and Dave had never been serious and told him about Dave and Isobel in Africa, and she was startled by the relief that shone in Simon's eyes when he heard her version of the situation. His hand at her waist tightened its hold and Gemma drew in her breath to keep her body from touching his. She stared sadly at the star-studded sky over his shoulder and knew with a terrible certainty that tonight wasn't going to be the dazzling evening she had hoped for.

The setting had all the right ingredients. Above them arched the huge outback sky, like an enormous dome lined with black velvet and studded with diamonds. Every so often, the familiar, heartwarming call of black cockatoos came floating up from the trees along the creek. All around them happy, hard-working people were enjoying one of the rare opportunities life in the bush afforded to dress up to the nines, kick up one's heels and have a good time.

This should be a night to remember. She wanted so much to enjoy herself with Simon.

But she had run slap bang into her same old, same old problem…

It didn't seen to matter how many likeable and charming men she met. When they got interested in her and their ideas turned to romance, she wanted to back off.

The bracket of songs finished, and Gemma opted for another drink. Simon fetched it for her and they went to join a group sitting at a table near the sunken fish pond. A little fountain played in the middle of the pond, its soft splashing sounds making a comforting backdrop. But Simon sat close beside her with an arm draped over her shoulders and several times, as they chatted, she found him looking at her, an intense spark burning in his eyes.

She set her glass down on the table. 'I'd like to go and check on Mollie,' she murmured, and, stood quickly. She hurried away before he could reply. Across the lawn she sped, holding her dress away from the dew-covered grass.

In the bedroom off the side verandah, Mollie was sleeping like an angel, but Gemma stayed watching over her for some time. There was a soft night-light in the room and she could see the little golden head, the thick dark lashes lying against her soft cheeks, one pink starfish hand resting on top of the patchwork quilt and the other cuddling a tiny pink rabbit. What a darling little girl she was.

It occurred to Gemma that she was doing rather a good job of looking after Isobel and Dave's baby—and she was enjoying it, too. That was totally unexpected. She leaned across the cot and whispered a prayer for the safety of little Mollie's parents and she wondered if she would ever have a baby of her own. Not if she continued to run away from every man who ever looked twice at her, she thought with a sigh.

A mirror on the opposite wall caught her attention. She saw the reflection of her lovely gown and couldn't help admiring its colour—the pale, silvery blue of moonlight. As she stared at the mirror she saw a dark shape move behind her on the verandah. But there was no sound and she reasoned that it must have been a shrub being blown by the wind.

But a second later she was gripping the railing of Mollie's cot with a shaking hand.

Images of a shadowy figure…a pale, blue dress and…a darkened verandah…dropped into her mind as if somebody was slipping slides into a projector.

Déjà vu.

It had happened before.

This scene, these images… A party on a night like this…a dress this colour…

And the photograph Max still kept on the dressing table in her room.

CHAPTER SIX

GEMMA slid her arms along the cot's wooden railing until her fingers interlaced. She lowered her burning face to rest on her hands. Every detail of the memory of that night replayed once more in her mind. Piece by relentless piece.

Five years earlier, when she was eighteen, she had come home from university for Dave's twenty-first birthday party. The Jardines had invited nearly everyone in the district to a huge celebration at the Goodbye Creek homestead.

That evening Gemma had had the time of her life in her lovely new dress—her first formal evening gown—pale blue with tiny straps, a figure-hugging bodice and a dreamy, floating skirt.

It had been a hot night, but she had danced and danced in her new silver sandals and drunk rather too much champagne. She'd stood by Dave as he'd cut his birthday cake and, in front of all the guests, he had kissed her. This had been greeted by a rousing chorus of cheers and loud cat-calls. And, while his father had made a speech, Dave had flung a possessive arm around her shoulders.

By midnight, after she'd given every second dance to Dave and divided up the others between the eager young men from the district, Gemma had been exhausted and just a little dizzy. When the band had finally stopped for a well-earned break, she had been relieved that her dancing partner, the head stockman from Acacia Downs, was happy to rejoin his mates around the beer keg. Gemma had dashed away to hunt down some cool lemonade and a quiet spot to catch her breath.

She had found just what she needed at one end of the verandah, an old rattan lounge chair lined with ancient patchworked cushions and screened from the party by a vine-covered lattice. Gratefully she'd collapsed into it, flinging one leg over the chair's arm while she sipped her icy lemonade and not caring one jot that it was an unladylike pose. Hot and sticky, she had tried to fan herself with her hand.

'Oh, boy,' she murmured softly. 'What a great party.'

She wondered where Dave had got to, but wasn't too worried. There were so many people about; he could be anywhere. The ice clinked as she drained the lemonade and she placed the glass on the wooden floor beside her. Releasing a deep sigh of satisfaction, she slipped off her sandals and wriggled her aching feet. Already she was feeling much better.

A soft sound behind her brought her curling around in the chair to peer into the shadows.

Someone was there. A man, leaning against the verandah railing and, like her, enjoying a moment of peace. She was sure she recognised the familiar silhouette.

'Dave?'

The answer reached her soft and low from the shadows. 'Hi, Gemma.'

In a flash, she was out of the chair and closing the distance between them. Standing high on her bare toes, she threw her arms around his neck and dropped a carefree, happy little kiss on his lips.

Of course, he kissed her back.

And she knew at that moment this man wasn't Dave.

She should have pulled away! Of course she should have. Especially when the dreadful truth dawned.

The man she was kissing was Max.

But a part of her, some dreadful, shameless part of her, didn't care! From the moment Max's mouth landed hotly on hers Gemma couldn't help herself. His kiss was so exciting, so intensely arousing, all she worried about was that he might stop.

She felt as if she'd stepped through a door straight into womanhood. She didn't know if it was the champagne or the hot night, the moonlight, or a taste of midnight madness, but in a heartbeat she and Max were exchanging kisses more breathtaking than anything she'd experienced before. Kissing Dave had been nice, but now something seriously sexy was happening.

She had no idea tasting and touching could drive her so wild. His mouth was hot and demanding as his tongue sought hers, making ripple after ripple of shocking, heated pleasure flood through her. For the first time in her life she knew why people made so much fuss about making love.

At first she looped her hands around his neck, but soon they were straying restlessly through his thick hair and across his shoulders, and, under her seeking fingers, she could feel the roll and flex of his hard muscles as he tugged her closer.

Then his hands began to move. Her skin sizzled as slowly, lazily, he made teasing trails from her waist, up her sides to her breasts. Cascades of sensation streamed through her and she heard a soft moan drifting from her lips.

Next moment she was pushing her breasts into the willing heat of his hands, wishing she could tear away the filmy fabric of her gown. It didn't matter that this man usually regarded her with disdain. Right now, she didn't want anything between her skin and his daring touch. An astonishing, warm and pulsing hunger fanned through her. And she realised that she wanted to give herself to him. Wanted him to possess her completely.

Willed him to take her.

'Oh, please, please,' she whispered.

He gave a gruff cry of protest, but still held her close, burying his face in her neck.

Having no experience and very little skill, Gemma responded purely by instinct, urging him with her body to understand her need. This astonishing need she'd never felt before. Boldly, she pressed herself into him, standing on tiptoe to nudge his lower body with hers, thrusting her swelling breasts against him, taking his face between her hands and covering his mouth and jaw with more eager, hungry kisses. 'Please make love to me.'

'Oh, God.' Max went very still. His harsh breaths as he dragged air into his lungs were the only indication he hadn't turned to stone. 'I'm so sorry, Gemma.'

At the sound of his voice the spell was broken—shattered into a thousand accusations.

Shaking, Gemma backed away from him, her hands tightly clasped at the neckline of her dress.

In stunned disbelief at what she'd done, she watched as Max raised an arm and drew it across his forehead, as if trying to clear his brain of what had just happened.

She was dazed, numb with shock, unable to speak.

How could she have done all that? With Max?

He was still in darkness, so she couldn't see the expression on his face, but she could see the slump in his shoulders, and the way his head hung low. She could tell that he was as horrified as she was by what they'd just shared.

The tears came as she edged further away from him. Her vision blurred so that his dark form swam against the night sky. *How on earth had it happened?* She'd been in darkened corners with Dave before now and she'd never behaved like that.

Dave had never been like that!

This knowledge was too awful to bear. It sent her scurrying down the verandah, without stopping for her sandals. She ran into her bedroom and stayed in the silent house for the rest of the night, while the party continued outside.

When Dave came looking for her, Gemma pretended to be asleep. She wanted to tell him what had happened, to say that it was a mistake, that she was sorry. But the admission was too terrible. The words remained locked in her throat.

So instead of unburdening her guilt when Dave stood in her doorway, she closed her eyes and made her breathing regular and deep. After some time, she heard his footsteps echo as they moved away down the verandah and into the warm night.

She would never speak about what had happened to anyone.

The next morning Dave expressed puzzlement over her early departure from the party and she told him she'd had a headache from too much champagne. After that little lie, there was no way she could try to explain what had really happened. In the daylight, it seemed even harder to understand how she could ever have allowed herself to behave like that.

And, of course, she could never bring herself to speak to Max about it.

For the next few days, he was away on some remote part of the property. 'Checking boundaries,' someone told her.

Two days later, just before she returned to the city, a slightly nervous Dave asked her if they could 'have a bit of a chat' and the outcome was his suggestion that perhaps he and Gemma shouldn't feel too committed to each other just because they'd been friends since forever.

Her guilty heart reacted wildly. *Had Max spoken to Dave?*

But he seemed to be thinking on a different tangent. 'I know everyone around here has always expected that one day we'd be a couple, but, hell, Gemma, I'm sorry, but I think we maybe need some space—a chance to meet a few more people.'

Once she got over the shock of Dave's suggestion, Gemma adjusted to it rather quickly.

Dave continued, 'You see, we're only young, and I'm not sure we've got everything happening the way it's supposed to for people who eventually get hitched. Maybe we never will.'

She looked hard at him then, and realised that a part of her had always known she and Dave could never be more than friends. 'I know what you mean,' she whispered, and her cheeks flamed as she remembered the shameful way she'd behaved in Max's arms.

'You're sure you understand?' he asked, his sense of relief making his eyes shine.

'There's supposed to be more than friendship—something a bit more—cataclysmic.'

'Cata-what?' Dave sounded puzzled, but then he grinned ruefully. 'You mean fireworks, the earth moving—that sort of thing?'

Suddenly embarrassed, Gemma simply nodded.

Dave leaned over and brushed her cheek affectionately with his knuckles. 'We've been the very best of mates, Gem. I'm sure we always will be.'

She was surprised how easily she'd got used to the idea of parting with Dave but, although she'd learned a thing or two about 'chemistry' on the night of the party, she couldn't let herself think that this willingness to separate from one brother had anything to do with how she felt about the other.

Max returned to the homestead the afternoon before she was to go back to Brisbane and he tried, just once, to speak to her.

She was taking a final walk along the tree-shaded track by the creek and had stopped to sit on a flat granite boulder to watch electric-blue dragonflies chase each other across the sunlit water. The sound of a twig snapping alerted her that someone was coming, and when she looked up she saw Max's tall figure striding towards her through the trees.

Alarmed, she jumped to her feet, and was poised for flight when his voice reached her.

'Gemma!'

Her face flamed with embarrassment and she felt sick.

'Gemma,' he called again, his long strides bringing him very close now. 'We need to talk.'

She didn't want to speak to him, couldn't bear to discuss that kiss. Talking about it would only make everything they had done all too shamefully real. The horrid truth, that she had offered herself in a wild fit of passion to Max, of all people, was terrifying. She couldn't deal with it.

She wouldn't let him near.

Running away felt foolish, but Gemma had to flee that

scene. Like a hunted rabbit she darted off, not following the track, but ducking and diving through the undergrowth. To her relief, Max didn't follow her. She imagined it was beneath his dignity to scramble after her through the scratchy acacia scrub and lantana.

By the time she reached the homestead, breathless and panting, she'd decided that the only way she could ever face the rest of her life was to behave as if the incident had never happened.

She'd done her best to keep that memory locked away ever since. In her mind she'd pictured herself forcing the regrettable interlude into an ugly little padlocked box, and whenever it tried to haunt her she would visualise the lid snapping tight and the fat key turning in the lock, holding the horrible memory inside. And for long stretches of time it had worked. She'd been able to forget about the kiss and get on with her life. But every so often the memory caught her by surprise.

Like tonight…when once more she wore a dress of pale, pale blue and knew that, behind her, a man waited in the dark.

Gemma raised her head and the shadowy shape on the verandah behind her moved. She watched the reflection in the mirror and saw Max step forward until he was framed by the doorway. A wall light outside made his dark hair shine, but cast shadows lower on his face. Hardly daring to breathe, she remained very still with her back to him.

'Everything OK?' he asked softly, coming closer. He stopped just behind her, looking over her shoulder at the sleeping baby girl.

She turned, ever so slightly, in his direction. 'She's sleeping like an angel,' she whispered.

He was so close she could feel his warmth at her back, the stirring of his breath against her hair when he murmured, 'She's cute, isn't she?'

His hand touched her bare shoulder and she jumped.

'Come outside,' he said close to her ear.

Knowing she couldn't spend the rest of the evening watching a baby sleep, she followed him—after a slight hesitation. As she did, she sent up a frantic prayer that, after all these years, Max had forgotten that terrible incident.

On the verandah again, he paused, and she was so nervous she rushed to speak, to fill in the moments that must follow with safe, harmless chatter. 'Did you find the band?'

'Yes.' He cocked his head in the direction of the party. 'They're a group of townies and so they're not used to driving in the bush. They tried to take that bend just before the creek far too quickly and their van ended up in a ditch.'

'Goodness—was anyone hurt?'

'No, they were very lucky. The singer has a sprained wrist, but Helena's attending to it.'

'Poor Helena. She hasn't been able to keep her night free of medical duties after all.'

'She's used to it.'

'Will they still play for the dancing?'

'Sure. They're setting up now.'

'Great,' she said, extra brightly. She stepped quickly away from him. 'Then let's go. We'd better find our partners and dance the night away with them.'

'Hold it, Gemma.' His hand reached out and caught hers.

Just like that—her fingers were linked with his. Such

a flimsy trap and yet, for the life of her, she couldn't pull away. 'What—do you want?' The words felt squeezed from her throat.

'I want to tell you how lovely you look tonight.'

The moon, spilling through the shubbery, illuminated his face and Gemma saw a startling tenderness that made her want to weep.

'Thank you,' she whispered.

'Are you enjoying yourself?'

'Of course. I'm having the time of my life. It's a wonderful party.'

He gave her a look that said he didn't believe her, but he grinned anyway and said, 'Glad you're having a good time. It would be a pity to waste this stunning dress.' He touched her skin, just above the sloping neckline of her gown, and she was sure her heart stilled.

In the burning silence, he whispered, 'You've grown up, Gem.'

Tears welled in her throat, making it hard to reply. 'What—what did you expect?'

'Oh, I expected something quite spectacular.' The skin around his eyes creased as he smiled.

This conversation was dangerous, but she was mesmerised by his voice, deep, yet rough around the edges, as if his throat felt as choked as hers. She couldn't drag herself away, despite the embarrassing memories still hot in her thoughts.

As if sensing her confusion, Max took both her hands in his and pulled her towards him. 'Now that you're so grown-up, I think it's time we talked about a little matter that we should have discussed long ago—five years ago.'

'No, Max, no!' She hated the sudden note of panic in her voice.

'The night of Dave's twenty-first.'

'Don't do this,' she pleaded, trying to pull her hands from his.

This was exactly what mustn't happen. Remembering was one thing, but she couldn't talk about that night now any more easily than she could then. It was much better to go on pretending they'd both forgotten.

The light in his eyes dimmed. 'You're frightened?'

She gave a tiny nod and looked away, unable to meet the directness of his gaze. 'It's not worth dredging up the past, Max.'

'You don't want to hear my apology?'

'*Your* apology?' *He thought he was to blame?* Through brimming tears, she dragged her eyes back to meet his.

'Hell, Gemma, don't sound so surprised. I knew exactly who was in my arms that night, but you thought it was Dave. I deceived you and I've had to live with the weight of that deception all these years. I cheated you *and* my brother.'

'Oh, Max.' She couldn't stop the tears from flowing and she lunged forward. His strong arms come round her and she sank against him, burying her face in his chest.

'Damn it,' he murmured as he stroked the back of her neck. 'I've been worried sick that you'd been traumatised by this whole business.'

The full-blown remorse she heard in his voice shocked her. On that night all those years ago, when her sense of guilt had coiled through her like a hissing, striking serpent, she hadn't stopped to consider that Max might be feeling guilty. She had always been quite certain that she was the evil one. She was the sinner.

Far worse than Eve in the Garden of Eden.

The biblical Eve had simply held out a piece of fruit

to Adam, but Gemma had hurled herself into Max's arms, rubbed her body all over him and pleaded with him to make love to her.

Oh, Lord.

And now he was claiming the guilt. When all along she'd known it was Max she was kissing…

In the distant garden, a guitarist from the band twanged a few notes and she could hear the singer clearing his throat into the mike. 'One, two, three, testing…testing…'

As these ordinary, familiar sounds reached her from the party, from the ordinary, familiar world beyond the verandah, Gemma felt she was emerging from a dream. It was as if everything that had happened in her life so far had been leading her to this point and as if her entire future might well be shaped by her next move.

It was time to be honest with Max.

She knew that if she were as adult as Max assumed her to be she would let him off the hook. Any mature woman in her situation would admit that she'd known exactly which brother she was kissing that night, and then she might even let him know that she was quite interested in kissing him again and see what he had to say about that.

That was probably what most well-adjusted women would do.

Or she could play the part of the outraged virgin, grudgingly accepting his apology while struggling out of his arms.

That would be childish and deceitful but, then again, she'd practised being a coward for five years now.

Or there was one other way…

CHAPTER SEVEN

LIFTING her face from his dampened shirt front, Gemma swiped at her tears and sniffed. 'For heaven's sake, Max,' she began in a shaky, high-pitched voice. 'Don't torture yourself with a guilt trip about some little old kiss that happened five years ago. That's ancient history. I haven't been worrying about it. I haven't given it a moment's thought.'

'You haven't?' He looked so disbelieving she found it hard to meet his gaze. His hand reached out and with his fingertips he touched her wet cheek. 'If that's so, why all these tears?' His attempt at a laugh fell short of the mark. 'And why do I look like I've spilled drink all down my shirt?'

'I'm sorry about that,' she said, seeing the damage her tears and her mascara had done. 'I'll get something to mop you up.' She turned, about to dash away, but he grabbed her arm and swung her back.

'Hey, not so fast, Gemma Brown.'

And she wished, oh, how she wished that she wasn't back so close to him again. Any minute now she would be doing a repeat performance—reaching up on her tip-toes, throwing her arms around Max Jardine's neck and kissing him till morning. Her stomach flipped at the thought.

She forced the tremors out of her voice. 'You had something else you wanted to say?'

His sad and thoughtful expression as his gaze rested on her made her feel he understood more about what she hadn't been saying than what she'd actually said. Eventually, he broke the silence. 'So that was just some little old kiss, was it?'

Her palms were sweating and, instinctively, she rubbed them down her thighs, but when his gaze lingered there, she hastily clasped her hands in front of her. 'I'm surprised that a man who has, at the very least, *three* women currently panting after him, would give one little kiss a second thought.'

He emitted a strange little grunt, and a moment later his hands were gripping her shoulders, holding her squarely in front of him. His eyes glinted fiercely. 'What if I *have* thought about that night—more than once or twice? What if I think we should try to lay this ghost?' His head dipped closer and she felt dizzy with longing. 'How about we try that little old kiss again, Gemma, and you can show me that I'm forgiven?'

Gemma's heartbeats thundered in her ears. Her weak and foolish body wanted to be in Max's arms again and to experience that passionate mouth locked with hers! But she couldn't bear to make a fool of herself again. 'There—there's nothing to forgive,' she stammered.

'That's not what your tears tell me.' His lips lowered to kiss her bare shoulder and, in spite of her caution, Gemma arched her neck sideways, offering an inviting path for him to follow all the way to her mouth. Already her senses anticipated the moment when his lips reached hers.

'I'm so glad you've grown up, Gemma,' he murmured, his breath hot against her skin. 'You smell wonderful. Feel so womanly, so soft.'

Oh, Lord. His mouth was too close. She needed him.

'Five years is a long time between kisses,' he whispered.

And at that moment she discovered just how immature and unsophisticated she still was. While her body yearned to be seduced, her mind succumbed to panic.

'Max, wait a minute.' Pushing against his chest with both hands, she broke his hold and stepped back. 'This is—this is all wrong!'

His hands rose in a gesture of helplessness. 'It feels all wrong to you?'

One part of her wanted to admit that being in his arms felt every kind of wonderful, but instead she rattled off a string of desperate excuses. 'It doesn't matter how it feels. I know it's wrong. You don't love me.' Her voice broke a little to make that admission, but she hurried on. 'I'm sorry if you got the wrong impression about me five years ago. I'm not free and easy with my—with my—'

Her eyes fixed on his exquisite mouth and for a breathless moment she couldn't continue, couldn't remember exactly what she was protesting about. She struggled to focus on the world beyond this verandah—the guests in the garden, the sleeping baby nearby. 'The point is—I came out here at your insistence to look after Mollie, not to be your—your mistress.'

'Mistress?' he repeated, his brows frowning low over amused eyes.

'Yes.'

'Your imagination's running away on you, Gemma. There's a hell of a jump from one little kiss to…everything a mistress has to offer.'

Oh, Lord! And didn't she know it? It was a jump she'd never made. Fierce blushes burned in her cheeks. His words embarrassed her, angered her, *hurt* her! Smouldering, Gemma drew further away, wrenching her shoulders back and pointing in the direction of the party.

'That's exactly why you should get back out there to Helena.'

He remained standing before her in silence, as if he needed time to adjust to what she was saying.

'How can you kiss me when Helena's waiting?'

'That's a very good question.' Max watched her face carefully. 'Think about it.'

But she couldn't think about it. Not when her brain was seized by mind-numbing confusion. 'And Simon will be dreadfully worried about me. Any minute now he'll turn up here looking for me. How can you think about kissing me again? This is just as bad as last time. Don't forget I came to this ball at the invitation of another man.'

'Huh,' muttered Max. 'Of course, we wouldn't want His British Highness to find you in a compromising clinch.'

'Certainly not!' she hissed. 'And if you're any sort of a man—any sort of *gentleman*—you wouldn't have tried this a second time!'

He let out a loud, weary sigh. 'You're so right. You'd better get back to the party.'

'I intend to.'

As she turned to go, he called, 'So, Gemma, have we sorted things out?'

She looked back at him over her shoulder as he stood there with an arm outstretched, and it took all her will power not to run back and have him hold her again.

'You're fine about—about everything?'

'Absolutely everything, Max.'

She turned quickly again before the stupid tears threatened and she hurried down the steps into the garden. Never had she felt so confused—bewildered by her own feelings and by Max's behaviour. How could he want to dally with her and exchange a few kisses when he had Helena waiting nearby?

Think about it, he'd said. But what conclusion could she come to other than the fact that Max could kiss any number of women at the drop of a hat? Did he fancy himself as some kind of outback Don Juan?

Grateful for the subdued lighting in the garden, she dabbed at her wet face with a handkerchief and, as she threaded her way through the laughing guests, she vowed to find the Pommy Jackaroo and be very, very nice to him for the rest of the evening.

The band, eager to make up for lost time, played loudly and energetically into the early hours of the morning. Their singer, thanks to Helena's expert attention, seemed to have recovered from his ordeal and crooned seductively while nursing his arm in a sling.

Gemma danced with Simon, or sat with him and listened to his stories about adjusting to the life in the outback, and, once or twice, she allowed him to kiss her. They were very nice kisses. Like Simon himself. Skilful, practised, not too demanding—and yet hinting that he would be keen to demand a great deal more if she showed the right response.

When Gemma couldn't dredge up the appropriate response, she felt very depressed. Her partner remained charming and polite. But as the evening wore on, pretending to be even vaguely interested in him became more and more difficult.

And there were only so many times she could check on Mollie as an excuse to get away.

When she wasn't dancing, Gemma tried desperately to avoid watching Helena in Max's arms as they glided elegantly around the dance floor, but she didn't miss the touching moments of intimacy the other couple shared. She saw how Helena dropped her head onto Max's broad shoulder as they danced and the way she smiled up into his eyes as if she adored him. And she noted the possessive way Max held her close, his hand cradling her sleek hip. *The two-timing rat!*

As Gemma sat watching the dancers and twisting the stem of her champagne flute between anxious fingers, she reflected guiltily on her feeble response to Simon's romantic efforts. It was the same pattern all over again. The same sense of something missing that had dogged all her relationships with men.

She caught sight of Max's rugged profile dipping courteously towards Helena as she whispered something in his ear.

And suddenly Gemma was shaking, feeling ill, as a terrible realisation flooded her thoughts. She tried to hold back the knowledge that pounded in her head. *My dilemma is Max's fault. I've been in love with him for five years.*

Damn his sexy eyes!

Every man she'd met, since that night five years ago, had only been able to offer a pale shadow of what Max had given her. His kisses and caresses had stirred and aroused her beyond her wildest imaginings. Dave had simply been the first in a series of young men who had found a disappointing response when they'd tried to kiss Gemma.

And it was all because of Max.

He had given her a taste of a different kind of loving.

And, by doing so when he had no real interest in her except as someone to tease and spar with, he had wrecked her chances of happiness.

From beneath wet lashes, she stole another surreptitious glance at Max and Helena. They had stopped dancing and were laughing over a joke told by their host, Tom Neville. Helena's arm was draped casually around Max's neck and she nestled her beautifully groomed head against him. When she laughed, she buried her face in his chest.

Gemma dragged her gaze elsewhere, before she made a fool of herself by crying openly. It was so painful to finally accept the fact that after she'd tasted Max's brand of lovemaking *she* had never been satisfied with anyone else.

But if she wanted him now, she would have to take her place in the line-up beside a string of other women.

By one a.m., Gemma couldn't take any more. She was too emotionally drained to keep pretending enjoyment and too exhausted to dance another step, so she flopped back into another chair and smiled apologetically at Simon. 'I'm absolutely pooped,' she told him. 'And I know Mollie is going to wake at the crack of dawn, so I'm going to call it a night.'

He jumped to his feet. 'I'll walk you down to the tent.'

'Thank you.' An expectant gleam in his eyes made her hesitate. 'Um—don't rush, Simon. I'll make one final check on Mollie first.'

Feeling foolish, she dashed towards the homestead again. To her left, she could see a couple of teenagers emerging from the darkness at the edge of the lawn, the boy swaggered slightly and the girl was trying to look super-cool as she combed tousled hair with her fingers. They seemed to take a little fumble in the shadows in their stride. Was she the only person who remained scarred for life by that kind of experience?

'Gemma.'

As she reached the foot of the stairs, Max's voice

called from behind. She hesitated, not sure if she could face him again, but eventually she turned around.

He was alone. Tall, dark, handsome in his debonair tuxedo, and alone. In the moonlight, his hair looked soft and exceedingly touchable. Gemma clenched her fists as if to ward off his spellbinding impact.

'Are you going back to the tent now?' he asked.

'Yes,' she replied coldly. *Did he have to check on her every move?* She couldn't help snapping back with, 'What's it to you?'

Max cleared his throat. 'My things are in the tent,' he said, glaring at her as if she were planning a string of shocking crimes. 'Could you toss my swag and my clothes out before you and, er—the Pommy Jackaroo—I'm sorry, you and *Simon* settle in there?'

Highly embarrassed, she let her eyes dart away.

'I presume you two want the tent to yourselves,' Max drawled. His words were accompanied by a loud yawn, as if he found the whole subject tedious.

'N-no,' she stammered. 'Don't worry about that.'

'Don't worry about what, exactly?'

Gemma was sure he was being deliberately obtuse. 'We—Simon and I won't need the tent.'

'I beg your pardon?'

'We're not looking for privacy.'

'You won't be needing the tent to yourselves?'

She huffed out an angry sigh. 'You're not hard of hearing, Max. You heard me the first time.' Looking up at the cloudless night sky, she added, 'It's a beautiful night. We can sleep under the stars in our swags.' She forced a face-splitting smile his way. 'And leave the tent for you and Helena.'

To her surprise, his confident gaze dropped and, with his hands in his pockets, he shuffled his shiny black dress shoes in the dewy grass. 'Helena's been offered a comfortable bed up in the homestead.' He looked up again and grinned at her, a surprisingly shy grin. 'You know how highly respected doctors are in the bush. Her hostess can't let her rough it with the common folk.'

'Of course,' Gemma responded, and a silly little laugh escaped as she tried to cover her highly unsuitable sense of relief. 'I'm sure the poor darling's exhausted and needs her—her rest.' She hesitated. 'In that case, I guess we three can all share the tent.'

He looked startled by her suggestion. His throat worked. 'No, you're right. It's a clear night. I'd prefer to sleep under the stars myself.'

She followed his gaze up to the heavens. The silhouette of a huge bird, probably a tawny owl, was winging its way to the east, with the Southern Cross as its backdrop. Her comment came spontaneously. 'I love these big outback skies.'

'Yeah? I guess you'll miss them when you go back?' He looked unusually ill-at-ease, as if this was a question he hadn't meant to ask.

'Definitely.' She nodded and wrapped her arms around herself, wishing he would leave her.

Standing here with him again—alone—she felt far too vulnerable. She dropped her gaze, afraid that if he looked into her eyes he would discover the bitter home truths she'd had to face up to this evening.

She didn't want him to guess the awesome power he had over her.

For another thirty seconds she hovered on the bottom step, embarrassed and lost for words, and then she turned abruptly and hurried up the steps that led to Mollie's room.

'Just throw my things out of the tent anyway,' Max

called after her. 'I might see this party through till dawn yet… And, Gemma?'

At the top of the steps she paused, but there was no way she could look back. She stood with her back rigid, but her ears were straining to catch his words.

His voice drifted up to her, low and gentle as a lullaby. 'Sleep tight.'

When she told Simon that she wanted to sleep outside, he was a little surprised and, she suspected, disappointed.

'That's what everyone does,' she replied with what she hoped passed for wide-eyed innocence. 'We get changed in the tents and use them for storage, but why waste a wonderful night stuck under canvas when you could be out here?' She flung her arms wide to take in the warm night, the silver-speckled sky, the creek bank and the bush beyond.

Simon scratched his head as he surveyed the scene. Other visitors were settling for the night. Some dark humps suggested people already asleep under the stars. In other areas people were sitting on their swags still chatting and laughing quietly. Further along the bank a group had lit a small camp fire and were gathered in a circle, spinning more yarns and tossing back more drinks. But from one or two tents nearby she could hear rustling, suppressed giggles and sultry murmurs. There was no doubting what was happening in there.

Simon stepped towards Gemma and said in a quiet voice, 'I had something a little cosier in mind.'

With her hands clasped in front of her, Gemma turned to face him. 'Not this time, Simon. But thank you for a lovely evening. I've thoroughly enjoyed myself.'

His face tightened. 'Do you really mean that?'

'Of course I do. I've never had a more charming or attentive escort. And there's absolutely no doubt that you can out-dance Aussie blokes.'

He was silent and she knew that he'd hoped to be more than her dancing partner. She saw a little flash of hurt in his eyes and, because she could offer him no comfort, she hurried into the tent to change before dragging her swag out onto the grass.

When she finally settled for sleep, Gemma was grateful for her emotional and physical exhaustion. To her surprise, she slept soundly and the next morning, although she was still very tired, she woke out of habit around dawn to find Max lying only a few metres away, curled on his side. She felt a familiar pain in her chest as she stole a secretive look at him sleeping there, his mouth open just a little, so she could hear the soft hush of his breathing. Simon was on the other side—sound asleep on his back with one hand flung over his eyes.

As quietly as she could, Gemma scrambled out of the swag and made her way down the bracken-covered bank to the creek where she planned to wash her face. White mist trailed softly over the surface of the water like a bridal veil. Early mornings were her favourite time in the bush. She perched at the water's edge, enjoying the almost spiritual silence broken every so often by the occasional lilting songs of magpies or the cheeky chatter of budgerigars and honeyeaters.

Dipping her hands into the chill, clear creek, she splashed her face. *Oh, Lord*, she thought as the refreshing water hit her cheeks. *I love it out here.* She tipped her head back and stared at the criss-cross of leafy green branches above her. Through them she could see patches of sky. Although it was early morning, the heavens were already bright blue—blue as Max's eyes.

I don't want to go back to Brisbane.

The thought bounced into her mind and wouldn't budge. The longer she sat there, the more she was sure of it. Ever since she'd come back, her heart had been remembering and absorbing the things she loved most about the bush and now it ached for this tough, uncivilised country. And this yearning had nothing to do with a certain tough, uncivilised cattleman.

She whispered a wish that she could stay.

So many times in her teens she'd paddled a canoe down this creek, sliding silently under the willow-like branches close to the dank, brown banks. Behind the curtain of green lace, she'd stayed in the shaded, totally private world for hours, watching till a water rat came slinking out of its home beneath the tangled roots of a paperbark. She would throw leaves and sticks onto the water, knowing such movements would bring black bream darting out from beneath logs to snap at the surface in the hope of finding a juicy insect. Sometimes a long-necked tortoise would poke its little head out of the water and stare at her with yellow eyes.

All her life she had known and loved this creek, this district. It was in her blood and the thought of leaving it again brought a pain like a heavy fist gripping tightly in her chest. The first time she'd left had been important. She'd needed to discover the world beyond this little corner of the outback. But now she'd been away and seen what the rest of the world had to offer, and suddenly she knew with absolute certainty this was where she wanted to be.

It made no sense, of course. Her work belonged in the city and she needed to get back there as soon as she could.

And, even more importantly, she needed to forget

about Max. Hanging around would only make things far worse—rub salt in the freshly opened wound.

With a sad sigh, Gemma turned away from the creek and, after slipping into the tent to tidy herself, she hurried up to the homestead, knowing there was every chance that Mollie would be awake by now. In the garden, there were several others up and about already and some stalwart party animals, who had obviously stayed up all night and were flopped in chairs in one corner, looking a touch the worse for wear. Their host was lighting the barbecue in preparation for the recovery breakfast and he gave Gemma a good-natured wave as she passed.

Mollie was wide awake when Gemma entered her room. Wide awake and beaming with a big surprise.

'Good heavens!' Gemma cried as she dashed towards the cot. 'Mollie, you clever little muffin! You're standing up!'

The baby gurgled at her, obviously very proud of herself as she stood, clinging to the cot railing and peering over the top. Gemma hugged her and smothered her with kisses. 'You clever, clever little girl. Fancy standing up all by yourself. Oh, what will Mummy and Daddy think? And Uncle Max?'

This news was too good to keep to herself. Gemma ran to the doorway. How weird that she should feel so madly excited! She had to fetch Max. 'Stay there, darling. Don't move!' she called to Mollie before racing along the verandah and flying across the lawn, down to the creek bank.

'Max! Max!' she called, but when her cries were met by groans from sleeping forms in nearby swags, she knelt beside him and shook his shoulder, whispering, 'Max! Wake up! Come and take a look at Mollie!'

'What's wrong?' Max shot out of the swag and shoved aside the tumble of hair in his eyes. 'Gemma! What is it?' Wearing nothing but jeans, he looked as wild and ready for action as a Hollywood hero.

'It's all right, Max.' Gemma touched his arm, but when he looked down at her hand on his skin, she drew back again. 'Mollie's standing up!'

He frowned as he took in her news. Then his jaw dropped. 'She is?' His face creased into a grin. 'That's fantastic!'

'Come and see for yourself.'

She tugged at his elbow.

Together they raced back to the homestead. Max took the steps two at a time and reached Mollie before Gemma but, to her relief, the baby was still performing her clever act, standing with her little hands clutching the rail and crowing proudly as she bobbed up and down on unsteady legs.

'What a little champion!' he laughed, skipping around the cot and looking proud as punch as if somehow he'd achieved this small miracle himself. He grinned smugly at Gemma. 'If she's true blue Jardine stock, we'll be watching her standing up today and riding a pony to-morrow.'

Gemma laughed. 'Give the poor girl a break.'

'No fear,' responded Max. 'We'll have her running to meet her parents.'

'Is everything all right?'

A cool voice in the doorway brought them swinging around. Helena, looking pale without her make-up, but ultra-elegant in a classically tailored white silk dressing gown, leaned against the door post and peered in at them uncertainly. 'There seemed to be a commotion.' Her eyes darted suspiciously from Max's half-dressed state to Gemma and back again.

'Just a little celebration,' Max explained. He stepped aside and made a deep bow, sweeping one arm in Mollie's direction like a ring master in a circus announcing the star act. 'Mollie Jardine has joined the rest of the human race. Drum roll, please. May I present one small lady, who is now *standing upright*!'

Helena looked at Max as if she suspected he'd lost his marbles. 'From all the panic, I thought at the very least she'd developed measles. It's been going around. How old is she, anyway?'

Max beamed back at her and announced in the same grandiose manner, 'A mere *ten months*!'

Rolling her eyes to the ceiling, Helena muttered tersely, 'What's all the fuss? It's about time. Some babies are already walking at this age.'

Gemma found herself watching this little exchange with interest. From the way Max's face closed up, she could tell that he was miffed by Helena's snub and Helena was clearly much less impressed by his interest in Mollie than she had seemed when she'd telephoned after his trip to town. Had there been a lover's tiff?

'I'd say our clever little girl needs rescuing,' she said quickly, stepping forward and lifting Mollie out of the cot. 'She's learned to pull herself up, but I don't think she knows how to let go again yet, and she definitely needs a nappy change.'

'And you need to go back to the tent and get properly dressed,' Helena told Max, taking in the details of his exposed muscles and unshaven jaw with a puzzling, displeased frown.

As Helena turned away and drifted back down the verandah, Gemma set about changing Mollie. Then she took her down to the roomy Mungulla kitchen to fix her some breakfast.

By the time she emerged into the garden to join in the adults' breakfast, guests were making their selections from the mountain of food spread beside the barbecue. Crispy homemade sausages shared pride of place beside fried eggs, onions, tomatoes and mushrooms as well as baskets of freshly baked damper and a choice of bush honey, golden syrup or mango jam to spread on it. And, of course, there was plenty of good strong billy tea to wash it down.

Max had already piled his plate and offered to take Mollie while he ate picnic-style under one of the shady wattles. As he sat cross-legged, the baby happily practised her new standing skills, one hand gripping his jeans tightly. In her other chubby fist she clutched a wedge of his damper, which she was allowing a cheeky magpie to peck at.

Helena, looking immaculate in a neatly pressed white linen shirt and slacks, moved next to Gemma and Simon as they loaded their plates.

'You slept well?' she asked them solicitously.

Gemma's eyes flicked to her right to meet Helena's steady gaze. 'Not so well as you did, I'm sure. The ground was rather lumpy.'

'It was a warm night,' Helena responded. 'Must have been a little close in the tent.'

Gemma concentrated hard on spearing a juicy sausage. Helena's unexpected concern made her edgy.

'Oh, we weren't in the tent,' Simon hastily intervened. He shook his head. 'I can't understand why Australians love to abandon perfectly good tents to sleep out in the open.'

Helena's impeccable eyebrows rose as she stared at Gemma. 'So you and Max were outside, then?'

'And Simon, of course,' Gemma added.

'One big happy family,' Simon elaborated dryly.

'Oh, I see. The three of you.' Helena seemed extraordinarily delighted by this news and her reaction puzzled Gemma some more. What on earth did the other woman think had been happening down in the tents?

When they all settled to eat their breakfast, Helena seemed much more relaxed and prepared to take a renewed interest in Mollie's feats, but there was a tangible air of tension between Max and Simon.

It seemed to Gemma, as she munched on her tasty sausage, that the men had been involved in some kind of argument while she'd been giving Mollie her breakfast. Last week they'd carried on as if they were great mates—the best horse-breaking team in the state—and now they could barely speak to each other.

And the situation hadn't improved by the time they'd finished eating, thanked their hosts and made their farewells before rattling back along the track from Mungulla to Goodbye Creek. It was a solemn and silent journey. Perhaps they were just tired, Gemma decided, but the tension was still there. Nobody seemed interested in talking.

Occasionally, when another car passed in the opposite direction, Max would raise a finger or two, or perhaps his entire hand from the steering wheel.

Gemma whispered to Simon, 'That's known as the *outback salute*. Watch how many fingers he raises and you'll be able to gauge how well he knows the other driver.'

But Max glared at her so fiercely that she and Simon

exchanged guilty looks and reverted to uncomfortable silence.

As if in sympathy with their bleak mood, storm clouds gathered ahead of them like huge black and purple bruises. But while weather would usually be a subject of intense discussion for people who worked the land, they all stared through the dusty windscreen at the threatening storm but no one commented. They were wrapped in their own grim thoughts.

The skies opened before they reached home, turning the dirt road to slippery red mud in a matter of minutes. They dropped Simon off at the ringers' hut and after a muttered, businesslike exchange between the jackaroo and Max, they drove on to the homestead. When they clambered out of the car, Max tried to protect Mollie by holding her inside his shirt, but the heavy rain poured straight through the fine cotton.

'I'll dry her off quickly,' Gemma offered when they hurried inside. In no time, she had fetched a thick, fluffy towel and rubbed Mollie warm and dry. She changed her into fresh clean clothes.

Max stepped into the room. His gaze took in Gemma's wet hair and saturated T-shirt and skirt. The temperature had dropped with the rain and she was shivering slightly. 'You need a warm shower,' he said softly.

'I do indeed.' She looked down and was embarrassed to discover how thoroughly transparent her white shirt was now that it was wet. 'I look like Sharon Foster.'

His face broke into a slow, sexy smile. 'Not a chance, Gemma.'

She bit her lip. Of course her curves were nowhere near as magnificent as Sharon's.

'Off you go,' he urged. 'I'll keep an eye on Mollie.'

When she emerged from her shower, dressed in jeans

and a red gingham shirt with her hair towelled dry into a cap of wispy curls, Gemma found Max with Mollie on his lap, sitting at the computer in his study. He looked up at her and his face was flooded with joy. 'There's an e-mail message from Isobel. She and Dave are on their way home.' His mouth curved into an enormous grin.

She'd never seen him look like that. Excited, relieved. He looked even happier than he had this morning over Mollie's accomplishments.

His enthusiasm was infectious. 'That's wonderful!' she cried. 'Mollie, Mummy and Daddy are coming home!' She turned back to Max. 'I take it Dave's OK?'

'As far as I can tell he's fine. Isobel hasn't given too many details. Have a look at her message for yourself.'

Over his bare shoulder, Gemma peered at the computer screen.

Hi Max and Gem,

Great news, guys. Dave has been released. I actually got to touch him and hold him this morning. You've absolutely no idea how happy I am. We're flying out tomorrow! And we'll be with you guys the day after.

Can't wait to get home to see our little Cuddlepie.

We owe you two so much. Please give Mollie heaps of hugs and kisses and, hey, hug each other, too. You're both angels.

Much love,

Bel, who is heading off to buy Dave some shaving gear. My face is scratched to bits already!

'I'm so happy for them,' she breathed.

Max reached for her hand and gave it a gentle

squeeze. 'I've given Mollie her hug.'

She stared at him, her heart jumping. *Oh, and now you'd like yours?* she tried to ask, but no words would emerge.

It should have been so easy to step towards him and give him a swift friendly hug. Except Gemma knew that, from her point of view, the minute she put her arms around Max all thoughts of friendship would fly out the window.

So instead of offering a casual reply, she stood there tongue-tied and pretended she didn't know what he was implying.

The expectant light in Max's eyes died. He dropped her hand. 'You should be extra pleased. This means your ordeal's over, Gemma. In a couple of days you'll be free to go back to Brisbane.'

CHAPTER EIGHT

DISAPPOINTMENT spiked Gemma's chest. Only a short time ago she would have been glad to escape, but now, even if she ignored the confusing jumble of feelings she had for Max, the thought of leaving Goodbye Creek so soon filled her with despair.

How awful to feel a sense of destiny and connection to this place when, in reality, she didn't belong here any more than Simon, the Pommy Jackaroo.

Max was watching her thoughtfully. 'That's what you want, isn't it? To get back to Brisbane as fast as you can?'

She had to press her fingers into the top of his desk to stop their tremble. 'Actually—I—I've been thinking I might be able to drum up a bit of work out here.'

He shook his head as if he hadn't heard her correctly. 'Station work?' he asked cautiously.

'No, something along the lines of what I do in the city—events co-ordination, promotions—that sort of thing.'

The idea, that had been sitting in the back of Gemma's head for days now, was so vague and nebulous she felt silly speaking about it.

Max popped Mollie on the floor and she crawled off eagerly to investigate the sand-filled door stopper. He straightened slowly and frowned at Gemma. 'What on earth are you going to find out here that you could promote to the public? Fresh air?'

'I've been thinking about the township,' she said hesitantly. 'When I was shopping the other day, I was shocked by how badly Goodbye Creek's gone downhill in the past few years. So many people have left and no newcomers have replaced them. Max, it's practically a ghost town.'

He picked up a pen on his desk and rolled it between thumb and fingers. 'You have heard about the rural recession, haven't you?'

'Of course. I know lots of people, including my own family, have headed for the city in droves, but it seems such a pity. There are still folks who have lived out here all their lives and who want to go on staying here. This town is where they belong. And the people on the properties—like you—all need towns for decent supplies. The cities on the coast are too far away.'

'What exactly do you have in mind?'

'I haven't thought it through properly yet.' She turned away to avoid his scrutiny. It was too hard to think when she could see those piercing blue eyes fixed on her. 'But there must be a way to attract people back to Goodbye Creek.'

'Tourists?'

'They would be a start,' she said carefully. 'And if the tourists brought in money to boost the economy, more people would want to stay here. The first settlers came to the district because there was gold in the creek. Perhaps I could do some research into those times.' As she spoke, Gemma could feel her enthusiasm gaining momentum. 'There must have been bushrangers. They're colourful characters. I'm sure I could come up with some great ideas to generate fresh interest. '

Max leaned forward and placed the pen carefully on the varnished timber surface. He rested his elbow on the desk, dropped his head and kneaded the bridge of his nose. Finally he looked up at her. 'I can't believe you're serious about this.'

His rejection of her idea was so genuine, so complete, it struck her like a physical blow. The old rage she'd felt towards Max so many times in the past surged through her, but she sensed that if she threw a tantrum now she might as well kiss her fledgling project goodbye.

'Max, give me a break. I respect your understanding of the cattle industry. I'll admit you can brand and muster cattle, yard them and sell them as well as anyone—better than most. But you don't know the first thing about my line of work.'

'Fill me in.'

'What's the use?' she fired back, hands on hips. 'You would only take extraordinary delight in pointing out the error of my ways. Forget, it, Max. I should never have mentioned my idea. I said it's still in the very early stages.'

He hitched himself out of the chair and stood before her, feet planted wide apart and shoulders back, his face a grim challenge. 'Does your interest in staying out here have anything to do with a young gentleman from England?'

Whoosh! Gemma exhaled air with the speed of a punctured tyre. She gaped at Max. His question had caught her totally unprepared. Did he really care if she had a special interest in Simon, or was he simply playing his favourite game—finding ways to annoy her and boss her around?

She folded her arms across her chest and tapped a foot as her mind whirred in a frantic effort to come up with a suitable answer. Blast him! Why should she lay her cards on the table when she had absolutely no idea what games he was playing in *his* private life?

She would leave Max guessing. 'What does my interest in Simon have to do with you?'

His face tightened. 'I happen to be his current employer.'

'Surely that doesn't give you the right to know about his—um—personal affairs.'

'But I happen to have information that could make you change your mind about staying.'

Gemma swallowed hard, totally unsure where this conversation was heading. 'How do you mean?'

'If you are planning to hang around in the hope of seeing more of our Pommy Jackaroo, you could be sadly disappointed.'

'Why?'

'He won't be here. He's heading off tomorrow to take part of the herd to my new holding up near Wild River and he'll be gone for at least three weeks.'

'Wild River!' Her anger had been simmering. Now it boiled over. Gemma could see in a flash that Max was deliberately sending Simon north to get him away from her. He'd probably given the jackaroo his marching orders before breakfast this morning. No doubt it had brought on the tension between them.

She wasn't in love with the Englishman, but that didn't matter. What mattered was that Max was interfering in her life. Acting out the nosy big brother role just as he always had.

'Why the blazes are you sending him way up there?' she shouted.

'The Wild River property needs restocking and I can't get road trains in. It's too remote.'

'But why send Simon? Why not one of the ringers?'

The question seemed to annoy him, and he scowled at her. Some emotion she couldn't read burned in his eyes. 'He'll take Squirt with him and a couple of contract musterers.'

'It's a rotten thing to do, Max.'

His mouth tightened into a grim line and his voice grew very quiet. 'So you do care for him?'

'I thought Simon was here to work with the horses. I thought he was some kind of expert,' she snapped back, knowing she had deliberately avoided answering his question.

Max looked a little flushed around the neck, but his eyes were hard as flint. 'He's a good rider. That means he'll make a good drover. And anyway, he's out here to see the countryside.' Impatience sharpened his voice. 'I'm giving him an excellent opportunity to see some more of it.'

'Sure. The most desolate and toughest territory possible.'

'It's going to be tough, but it'll be character-building.'

Her chin jutted defiantly. 'Simon doesn't need *you* to build his character. His character is quite fine already.' Her anger sent her marching across the room. She came to a halt in front of the window and stood with her back to him. When she spoke, she tossed the words over her shoulder. 'But there's someone else around here who definitely needs his character improved.'

Glaring through the window, she could see that the rain had stopped. The leaves of a hibiscus bush looked shiny and washed clean and its large scarlet flowers were heavy and drooping. The warm and musty smell of dampened earth came to her on a soft breeze. Behind her, she could hear Max's fingers drumming. A threatening, ominous beat. He was angry with her.

Too bad. She was angry with him. He had interfered in her life, scolded her and bossed her one too many times. What was sauce for the goose was most definitely sauce for the gander. She wasn't about to apologise.

But life was so unfair!

If only she could turn off her feelings. Max was the last man in the world she wanted to fall in love with, and yet it was hard to be in the same room with him without making a detailed, lingering study of the way he carried himself confidently and proudly, of the easy, untapped strength in his movements and the distracting attractiveness of his smile. And after last night it was impossible to stop her mind from revisiting old memories of his sensuous mouth, his slow, teasing hands, his devastating kisses.

Slowly she picked up Mollie's favourite toy—a stacking set of bright plastic rings—and she took it to her. 'I'm sure you're tired of pounding that doorstop,' she said to the baby girl. Without looking at Max again, she crouched down beside Mollie and began to play with her, but as she made herself comfortable on the carpet her eye was caught by the title of a book on the shelf beside her. *The Golden Years*. It was a history of gold mining in Queensland.

Curious, she picked it up and glanced cautiously at Max. 'This could have the kind of information I need.'

He was still leaning against the desk as if lost in thought and he frowned again. 'So you really meant it—about researching the district and wanting to revitalise the town single-handed?'

'I'm not so dewy-eyed that I think I can do it totally on my own.'

'But you want to stay on—after Dave and Isobel collect Mollie?'

'I don't know, Max. Perhaps it is a silly idea.'

'Now that you know Mr Fox won't be here.'

'For heaven's sake, no! Leave Simon out of it. If I had more time, or if I'd started earlier, I might have been able to find out how viable my ideas are. But as things stand, I really only have tomorrow to check things out. I can't do much in one day.'

'You could at least put out a few feelers.'

His reply startled her. 'You think it's worth it?'

'I wouldn't have a clue, Gemma. But if you've only got this afternoon and tomorrow, then you may as well make the most of the time left.'

He walked across to the bookshelf and crouched down, running a tanned finger along the spines as he scanned the titles. 'There are a few more history books here that might be useful.' Pulling a thick book from the shelf, he handed it to her. 'How about we make ourselves a sandwich lunch and then we can both spend a quiet Sunday afternoon doing a spot of research?'

Gemma got up off her knees, clutching the two books to her chest. 'You mean it, Max?'

'No. I was only joking. I'd much rather do my accounts.' He relieved her of one of the books and began to thumb through it idly. 'Of course I mean it. There's not much point in your going to town tomorrow with high-flying ideas and no facts to back them up. That's like firing blanks. You need some decent ammunition.'

They spent the most unexpectedly pleasant afternoon. Gemma had to keep pinching herself. There was no fighting, no tension between them, just a calm sense of something that felt remarkably like companionship. Outside, the rain started falling softly again, its pattering on the tin roof providing a soothing lullaby. Mollie ate her lunch and drank her milk and curled up on a cushion on the floor for an afternoon nap.

On the carpet nearby, Gemma sprawled on her side, slowly munching corned beef and tomato sauce sandwiches while she read the history books and took notes.

Max kicked off his boots and lounged in an old leather armchair also reading, his feet, in thick socks, crossed at the ankles. When he found something he thought might be of interest, he read it aloud to Gemma. They discussed its relevance and sometimes she took notes.

'I think you'll want this,' he said, sitting up straighter. 'There *was* a well-known bushranger in the district.'

'Really? I hope he has an interesting name—like Thunderbolt.'

'How does Captain Firelight sound? That's what he was known as, but I'm afraid his real name was Frederick Flagg.'

Gemma rolled onto her back, propping herself up with her elbows. 'Captain Firelight sounds OK. Yeah. It sounds good. What did he do?'

Max scanned the page. 'He was attracted here by the gold—obviously. He was the usual bush larrikin—bailed up the stage coaches when they were heading back to the coast full of gold.' He read half a page further, then looked up at her and beamed. 'Freddie Firelight was in the bar at the local pub when the troopers tried to snaffle him, but, because he'd shouted drinks for the entire bar, all the locals wanted to protect him. In a final bid for freedom, he jumped out a side window and the troopers fired shots after him. The bullets went right through the pub's wall.'

'Wow!' laughed Gemma. 'Did he get away?'

'No. Eventually they ran him down.'

'If only those bullet holes were still in the old pub

wall,' she sighed, but then she looked up at Max, her eyes bright with growing excitement. 'If we could reproduce a few authentic touches, I could convince a city TV crew that it would be worth covering a story like that.'

From his chair on the other side of the room, Max grinned at her. 'You look so pretty when you get all excited like that. Your eyes light up and you—you just glow.'

His words shocked her. And she saw a softness in his eyes that did crazy things to her chest. She could feel her heart beginning to pound hysterically and her face growing bright and hot.

Don't get fired up, she warned herself. *He just dropped a casual comment. Doesn't mean anything. Not a thing.*

But she was feeling very confused. This afternoon Max had been acting as if he'd been through some kind of metamorphosis. Like a toad turning into a prince. Converting from big brother mode to friendship—perhaps a close friendship. No lectures. No reprimands or scowls. Instead he'd showered her with warm and friendly smiles. Making her feel respected and liked.

And now this compliment…

Confused and blushing, not daring to allow herself even a shred of hope that he suddenly cared for her, Gemma glanced at her watch. 'Goodness, look at the time,' she blustered. 'We've let Mollie sleep for far too long and now we'll never get her back to sleep tonight.'

'Better wake her.' Max padded across the room in his navy blue socks and stood beside her, looking down at Mollie. 'You think she looks like a Jardine?'

Still feeling flustered by Max, Gemma pretended to study the sleeping baby carefully. Washed in late-afternoon sunlight, Mollie's golden curls, long lashes, and plump, dimpled face looked totally angelic. 'She's far too pretty to look anything like you or Dave,' she teased. 'I'm sure she must take after Isobel's side of the family. Wait a minute,' she added with an impish grin as Mollie frowned in her sleep. 'Look at that frown. Now that's a definite Jardine feature.'

'Cheeky minx.' He cuffed a feather-light brush to the side of her head and for a moment afterwards his hand lingered, as if he wanted to test the texture of her dark hair, rolling it softly between fingers and thumb.

And when his hand stayed there, just that shade too long, the impulse to lean her head into the curve of his palm was overpowering. Gemma closed her eyes as she pictured what might happen next. With just one tiny movement she could turn ever so slightly and rub her cheek against him—an innocent enough movement, like a cat wanting to be stroked.

And then she could kiss his fondling fingers…

But, of course, she didn't have the courage.

Would never have the nerve to do any such thing.

Instead, Gemma bent forward, away from his touch, and gave the sleeping baby a gentle shake. 'Time to wake up, little girl,' she murmured.

Behind her, Max straightened, yawned and stretched his arms high, as if he hadn't noticed the tension that zinged between them only seconds before. 'It's stopped raining,' he commented. 'I'll take her for a walk. I need to have a quick look around the place and check up on what the men have been up to while we've been away.'

On the floor, Mollie stirred and rolled over at top speed, her little eyes wide, instantly awake and alert, ready for action.

'Oh,' groaned Gemma. 'Wouldn't you just love to be able to wake up that easily.'

'You don't seem to have too much trouble. You were up with the birds this morning,' Max responded quickly.

Gemma shrugged the comment away. She was in no mood to expand on her own habits of sleeping and waking. Right now, she was quite certain that talking casually to Max about practices even vaguely associated with bedrooms would send her into an absolute dithering mess.

'I'll get her a clean nappy,' she muttered. After she'd returned, and had watched him change the baby with the speed of an expert, she said to him, 'While you're gone, I'll have a think about what I can cook for dinner.'

'Right you are,' agreed Max, and he sat a delighted Mollie high on his shoulders and headed out of the room, whistling 'Molly Malone' slightly off-key.

After they left, Gemma felt more confused than ever. Did she sense a slight shift in the way Max regarded her? Was it her imagination running away again? Perhaps he was still playing the big brother role. Or was he? The way he looked at her this afternoon. So sad sometimes. As if there was so much more he wanted to say. As if he was holding something back.

'You're dreaming, Gemma Brown,' she told herself. 'Concentrate on food.'

Needing a distraction, she decided to try to cook something different. Max was a surprisingly good cook, but he tended to produce rather conservative meals. Time to spice up the menu, Gemma told herself as she surveyed the pantry shelves. There was a tin of red kidney beans and another of tomato soup. She knew there was some minced beef in the fridge and capsicums growing in the vegetable garden, so she could make chilli con carne, if only Max kept chilli powder.

But his supply of herbs and spices was severely limited.

'No wonder this man is so set in his ways,' she grumbled to herself as an exhaustive search of the pantry proved fruitless. 'He doesn't have enough spice in his diet.' Setting the ingredients on the kitchen counter top, she went into the garden, wondering if an extra red capsicum could make up for the lack of chilli.

She left the house and crossed the wet grass to Max's vegetable garden and the smell of damp soil filled her nostrils. Rejuvenated by the storm and sparkling with rain drops, the plants looked fresh and thriving. But although the rain had stopped for now, the grey sky seemed to press low towards the earth like a heavy, wet blanket. The air closed around her, warm and oppressive. In the distance, thunder still rumbled, threatening another storm.

Gemma walked slowly between the dripping rows of tomatoes, lettuce, capsicums and carrots, enjoying the distillation of scents that hovered around her—the sharp tang of tomato leaves as she brushed past, the sweet crush of garlic chives beneath her feet and the earthy warmth of damp soil.

She bent to pick a beautiful, shiny red capsicum and noticed a fat grasshopper munching on a lettuce in the row behind. Lunging forward, she swiped at it and almost lost her balance. But as she dipped and swayed for a moment, she saw a little bush that had been hidden from view before.

It was covered with tiny red chillies.

'Excellent!' she cried triumphantly. And, as they were very small, she picked five. Now, when she hurried back to the kitchen, she was satisfied that she would be able to give Max a meal to remember.

Everything was simmering nicely and Gemma was boiling water for rice to accompany the meal when she heard the creak of the screen door opening. She turned, to see Simon stepping inside.

'That smells wonderful,' the Englishman said, drawing in a deep breath.

Tucking a wing of hair behind her ear, Gemma smiled at him. 'Hi, Simon.' She wondered if he had come to say goodbye. 'Would you like to join us for dinner?'

He rolled his eyes and laughed wryly. 'Thanks. But I wouldn't dare.'

She frowned. 'For heaven's sake, what do you mean?'

'Not worth upsetting the boss.'

'Good grief, why should that upset him? You're not letting Max intimidate you, are you?'

He folded his arms across his chest and his grey eyes regarded her steadily. ' I don't think it's worth rousing his temper. I'd prefer to restrict any wrestling I have to do to cattle.'

'Wrestling?' Gemma stopped stirring and rested the wooden spoon across the top of the saucepan. 'Are things that bad between you and Max?'

He shrugged. 'I think everything will be fine once I'm out of the way.'

'What on earth have you done to get in his bad books?'

His face twisted into a grim smile. 'Gemma, how can you ask?'

Fine hairs lifted on the back of her neck. 'I—I don't understand,' she replied, annoyed by the way her voice cracked.

'No, I don't think you do.' He looked down at the

wide brimmed hat in his hand and fiddled with the brim. 'Sometimes it's like that.' He sighed. 'People can't see what's right in front of their noses.'

'Simon, please!' Gemma shook her head at him. 'What are you trying to say?'

His mouth tilted into a bemused, wistful smile. 'It's not for me to say much at all, Gemma.' He touched her cheek briefly. 'Except goodbye and good luck. I'm actually looking forward to seeing the country up north—the big crocodiles and all the bird life in the Gulf. But I'll be heading home after I finish this trip to Wild River.' He moved back to the doorway. 'Perhaps I could offer just one tiny spot of advice.'

Flustered, Gemma took up the wooden spoon again and gave the meal some unnecessary pokes. She shot a sideways glance to Simon. 'I'm listening.'

'I think you're searching for your own special slice of happiness.'

She frowned at him. 'Isn't everyone?'

'Sure. But some find it closer to home than others.'

Then he turned swiftly and was gone, out through the door into the purple twilight, before she could recover enough to say goodbye.

Suddenly she felt overwhelmed, as if her emotions had been stirred as thoroughly as the chilli con carne. Gemma's eyes filled with tears. Surely Simon wasn't implying that Max could make her happy?

How could that be?

A tear rolled down her nose and was in danger of dropping into the cooking pot. She wiped it with the back of her hand. How could she be happy with a man who already had Helena, Sharon and Susan and heaven knows who else? Being part of a harem was definitely not Gemma's idea of happiness.

She sniffed away another tear that threatened to fall. What puzzled her was how Simon could possibly guess her feelings for Max. It had only been last night that she'd discovered these emotions for herself. Surely her feelings didn't show?

She covered her face with her hands. If Simon had read her heart, could Max also tell how she felt? Was her face a dead give-away?

Max's whistle just outside jolted her out of her musings. Gemma grabbed a tea towel and scrubbed at her tear streaked face only seconds before the flyscreen door swung open.

His dark hair had been whipped by the wind, so that some fell over his forehead. His cheeks and eyes were glowing. With Mollie in his arms, he looked incredibly happy—wonderful.

Oh, heaven, what could she do about this? She loved this man. And she could no longer tell whether it had happened last night, this afternoon, or perhaps a long time ago, but at some point in time her instinctive need for his physical embrace had expanded into a stronger need for so much more.

She had a sneaking feeling she was *properly* in love. *The real thing.* Wanting the give and take of day to day living, yearning to share his burdens. The kind of loving that led to a lasting commitment.

A lifetime together.

She shook her head and threw back her shoulders. Enough of such nonsense. She had no chance of a lifelong love with Max Jardine. She had more chance of waking in the morning to discover he'd turned into a frog!

He grinned at her. 'Mollie and I have quacked at the ducks on the dam,' he announced with a chuckle. 'And we've let the chickens out for their green pick. The dogs have been fed and—' He sniffed and looked eagerly towards the cooking pot. 'I'm famished. What's for—' Stopping mid-sentence, he stared hard at Gemma. 'What's the matter?'

She gulped. 'Nothing. I'm fine.'

'You don't look fine. You look all blotchy and red eyed, like you've been—' His eyes narrowed. 'Gemma, I saw the Pommy Jackaroo moseying over this way before. Has he been upsetting you?'

'No,' she answered hastily. 'Certainly not.'

His jaw clenched. 'And now you're heartbroken—because he's going away.'

'No, of course not. It's—it's the chillies. They made my eyes water when I cut them up.'

He frowned. 'Chillies?'

'Yes. Our dinner. Chilli con carne,' she announced proudly. 'Have you had it before?'

He eyed the cooking pot again and asked with a teasing grin, 'What is it with women and foreign tucker? First we had Sharon's beef stroganoff and now you've got this chilli con carne?'

Tossing the wooden spoon back into the pot, she glared at him, hands on hips. The last thing Gemma needed this evening was to be compared with Sharon Foster. She had absolutely no desire to be reminded that Max had a string of women. 'A varied diet is essential to a healthy body and mind and eating corned beef or steak six nights a week and roast beef on the seventh hardly amounts to variety.'

For a moment his face set into stubborn, defensive lines and Gemma expected an argument, but, to her surprise, Max dipped his head respectfully. 'I beg your pardon, Gemma. I'm sure your chilli dish is delicious. Is there time to give Mollie a quick bath before you serve up?'

'Of course,' she muttered.

And she banged things around in the kitchen as she heated Mollie's dinner and set the table for their meal. There would be no extra fuss tonight—plain thick white china and battered old cutlery and eating at the scrubbed pine kitchen table.

By the time she had things ready, Max had come back with Mollie smelling sweetly of baby powder and looking shining clean and more cherubic than ever in a fresh white nightie. Gemma couldn't help picturing him with a baby of his own, bringing her up in this home that he'd worked hard to make nice and on this land he'd worked hard to tame. It wouldn't be an easy life. His children would have to learn to work hard too and to entertain themselves. And to take the lean years with the good.

But it could be quite, quite wonderful.

She took a deep breath as he sat Mollie in her high chair in front of her bowl of beef broth and mashed vegetables. Gemma set two loaded plates on the table and took her place beside Mollie. 'Don't wait for me,' she said as she spooned some vegetables into the baby's mouth.

'Thanks. I am feeling rather peckish.'

Out of the corner of her eye, she saw Max dip his fork and take a hungry, man-sized helping of food. Then she heard his gasp and the clatter of his fork as he dropped it. Gemma watched, horrified, as he jumped to his feet, spluttering with his hand clutched to his throat. Then he dashed across the room to the sink, grabbed a glass from the dish drainer, filled it with water and gulped it down. This action was followed by another glass of water.

'Max! What's the matter?'

'Bloody hell! What the heck did you put in that?' he wheezed. 'It's lethal.'

Gemma stood and nervously crossed the kitchen. 'Are you all right?'

'I'm not sure,' he said, filling the glass for the third time.

'Perhaps those chillies were hotter than I realised.'

'Where'd you get them from?'

'Your garden.'

'*My* garden? I don't grow chillies.'

'Yes, you do.' She looked away from his glare. 'Perhaps the seeds were dropped by birds.'

'Did you taste this stuff while you were making it?'

'No. I've made it lots of times before, but I must admit I usually use dried chilli powder.' What she couldn't admit was she'd been so busy thinking about *him* that she hadn't really focused on the meal. She'd been working on automatic pilot, her mind in the clouds.

He shook his head. 'I defy any man to eat that stuff.'

Her fragile emotions, already strained to the limit, threatened to give way. 'Perhaps I could pick the chillies out?'

Max shook his head. 'Don't bother. I guess I'll have to make some more corned beef sandwiches.'

'Or get Sharon to make you a decent meal,' Gemma couldn't help shouting at him. Her lower lip trembled. 'I don't suppose *she* ever makes mistakes.'

'Don't be childish.'

Gemma closed her eyes to hold back the tears. Here she was once again, feeling immature and useless. Why did she always make a fool of herself around this man?

It seemed that although she was twenty-three he would probably never think of her as anything but an annoying, half-witted kid. No wonder he always adopted the big brother role with her.

At least he seemed to recover from his gastronomic ordeal fairly quickly. Gemma kept her mouth tightly shut as she removed the plates of food and fed Mollie while Max made a pile of sandwiches.

She was relieved that he didn't continue to tease or lecture her.

'Well, Mollie,' he said, handing her a crust to munch on, 'two more sleeps and your mum and dad will be home.'

'I suppose she remembers them,' Gemma commented.

Max's eyes widened. 'I hadn't even thought about that. Surely she won't have forgotten her mother? It hasn't been that long.'

'How do you feel about handing her back?'

He didn't answer straight away, but just sat there staring at Mollie, his jaw propped on an upturned palm. 'I can't wait for both of you to leave,' he said at last. 'You know what a reclusive old bachelor I am. It's time I had this place to myself again. It's been overrun with females.'

She wondered if he was bluffing, trying to cover how he really felt. But after tonight's effort, perhaps he meant it.

'I guess you're hoping I don't have too much success in town tomorrow,' she said. 'You won't be happy if the locals are enthusiastic about the ''Welcome to Goodbye Creek'' festival I'm planning.'

He took a long sip of tea and, when he set the mug down, his eyes held hers. 'I'll reserve my judgement till we see what tomorrow brings.'

She dropped her gaze and paid careful attention to the geometric pattern of the blue and white tablecloth. 'If people want me to go ahead with the project, I'll find somewhere to stay in town. I wouldn't want to be a bother to you.' She felt braver after she'd said that, as if she could almost believe it.

'That's fine,' he said softly.

Again, stupid tears threatened. She jumped up and began to clear the table, hoping all the time that Max might reach over and touch her, tell her he was joking and he didn't want her to go. But he didn't move and didn't speak. He simply sat staring at Mollie. Looking sad.

CHAPTER NINE

GEMMA'S day in town didn't go quite the way she'd planned.

Mid-afternoon found her slouched in a corner of the waiting room of the Goodbye Creek Police Station, hot, hungry, completely frustrated and more than a little embarrassed.

Last night's disaster with the chillies paled to insignificance beside today's effort. At least Max hadn't been there to make matters worse.

'Gemma, what's happened?'

Oh, cripes! Gemma swivelled around to find Max shoving his shoulder against the glass doors of the waiting room and dashing towards her with Mollie in his arms. He almost skidded to a halt.

'Are you all right?' He looked breathless and anxious and her heart developed a strange version of a quickstep as she jumped to her feet.

'I'm OK, Max.'

Panting, he stared at her. 'You're sure?'

'Sure I'm sure. I'm just being held for questioning.'

'What in the blazes is going on?'

'They're talking to the publican, Mick Laver, now.' She chewed her lip. 'How did you know I was here?'

As soon as he'd established that she was in one piece, Max switched from simply staring at Gemma to skewering her with his very best, no-holds-barred glare. With his free hand, he raked his hair wildly. 'I had a phone call from Susan.'

'The *post mistress*? What did she tell you?'

'She left a message to say there'd been a shooting at the pub and that the police had carted you and Mick Laver away.'

'Oh, I see.' *Good one, Susan*, Gemma muttered to herself. She could have done without the helpful intervention of another of Max's women. 'I'm sorry you had to find out like that.'

'What the hell's been happening, Gemma? Who's been shot?'

'No one's been shot.'

'No?' He was breathing deeply, as if he'd run all the miles into town, but any concern he'd shown when he'd arrived seemed to be churning into anger.

Wincing at the sight of him returning to full scowl mode, Gemma twisted her hands together nervously and struggled to find a way to calm him. 'It's a pity you've been dragged into this. But there's nothing to worry about.'

'All I want is an explanation! You come into town today to discuss a little business and the next thing I know you're heading for jail!'

'It's not that bad,' she said, trying to sound much calmer than she felt. 'Here, let me take Mollie. You look like you're about to drop her.'

Max seemed to have to drag his attention back to the baby in his arms, as if he'd forgotten her existence. 'Er—thanks,' he said, looking and sounding hassled.

'If you'll come and sit here, I'll explain what happened.'

He handed the baby to Gemma and their eyes met. She gulped. *Good grief! He looked angry enough to start hurling furniture around.* 'Don't worry,' she hastened to reassure him. 'Nobody's been hurt. It's all a storm in a teacup.'

He seemed reluctant to sit, as if he would prefer to pace the room like a caged tiger, but when Gemma returned to her seat and waited for him he eventually joined her, although he kept his hands on his thighs, clenching and unclenching them restlessly.

Mollie sneezed and Gemma searched for a tissue.

'I got the impression you'd been shot,' he snapped.

'If I'd been shot,' she told him testily, 'they would have taken me to the medical centre, not the police station.'

'I've already been there.' He jumped to his feet again and spun on his heel, striding to the far wall and back.

She concentrated very hard on wiping the baby's nose.

From the far side of the room he fumed, 'I'm waiting for a decent explanation, Gemma.'

Here he was again—acting like her big brother, or, worse still, her sergeant major. 'I'm beginning to wish I had an *indecent* explanation,' she snapped. 'If I'd done something sordid you could really have an excuse to sound off, but all I was doing was trying to help your struggling old town.'

For just a second his grim mask slipped. 'Something *sordid*, Gem? Let's not get melodramatic.'

Gemma groaned. 'If anyone is indulging in melodrama, it's you, Max. Now do you want to hear what happened, or do you want to make a spectacle of yourself?'

He looked at her sharply. 'I imagine you've created a big enough spectacle for both of us.' He approached her once more and took a seat again. In a more controlled voice he asked, 'For the last time, what happened?'

'Not a lot really,' she told him with a shaky attempt

at a smile. 'My plans started out well. I told Mick Laver at the pub about my background in promotions and my idea for a ''Welcome to Goodbye Creek'' festival and he was mad keen on the idea.' Wrapping her arms around Mollie, she held the baby closer. 'I explained to him how I wanted to promote the town and how important the pub used to be in the gold rush days. And he was totally fired up! So I went on to tell him about the shoot-out between Captain Firelight and the troopers and he was furious that he'd renovated the place and puttied up the original bullet holes. And that's when he had his brainwave.'

Max shook his head. 'Mick's famous for having bright ideas that backfire.'

'You might have warned me.'

He didn't reply to that—just waited for her to continue.

'Well, he had a ripper of an idea today. He decided to shoot some fresh bullet holes.'

'What? Through the pub wall?' Max asked incredulously.

Gemma nodded. 'Spot on. Before I could stop him, he whipped out the rifle he keeps under the counter near the till, and—Kapow! Kapow! Goodbye Creek pub has two new holes in its wall.'

'Of all the hare-brained schemes…' Max whistled through his teeth.

'I had no idea he would get so carried away,' Gemma added defensively.

'You obviously got him over-excited. What did you do? Suggest there'd be unlimited publicity, crowds of tourists clamouring for drinks at his pub? Tell him Goodbye Creek will be a boom town again?'

'*I* got him excited?' Gemma shouted in frustration. 'That's rich! You can't blame his actions on me.'

He shook his head. 'You should have taken things more slowly and you certainly shouldn't have put yourself at risk like that when—when I—when your main responsibility is Mollie.'

She sprang to her feet. 'We're supposed to be sharing the care of Mollie and I'm sure I've held up my part of the bargain. I only asked for one day.'

'Yeah. I let you out of my sight for *one* day and you end up in all this mess.'

There was only so much of this Gemma could take. 'Max, do you know what your problem is?' In her arms, Mollie coughed and let out a little whimper. Gemma forgot she was about to accuse Max of egomania and shot him a worried glance. 'Do you think she's getting a cold? She did get soaked through in that storm yesterday.'

He frowned and looked a touch shamefaced. 'I don't know,' he muttered. 'I think she might have been coughing a bit earlier in the day, but she's been eating well.' He touched Mollie's plump little knee. 'Don't you dare get sick on us now, possum. Your mum and dad arrive home tomorrow and we want you firing on all cylinders.' He glanced at Gemma again. 'If there's no real problem here, why all the fuss? Why are you still being held ?'

Gemma shrugged and rolled her eyes. 'There's a police inspector in town and he made the local sergeant extra nervous. When they heard the shots, they both came bursting into the pub with their pistols drawn.'

'Sounds like everybody's been over-reacting,' Max replied.

'Especially you!' Gemma retorted, but at that moment Mollie whimpered and gave another little cough and

suddenly she was more worried about the baby than Max. 'Perhaps you'd better take Mollie home again. I'll be back as soon as I can.'

Max studied Mollie, and on cue she offered him one of her sunshiny smiles. 'She doesn't look too bad,' he said. 'I'd like to speak to Dan Kelly first, just to know there won't be any problems.'

'Max, won't you ever learn to trust me to sort out my own life?'

What a dangerous question! Gemma was glad that before he could answer a door in the opposite wall opened and a uniformed man and Mick Laver, the publican, came out.

The policeman nodded at Max. 'She's free to go,' he said straight away. 'We've sorted out this scallywag and don't plan to press any charges.'

About time! thought Gemma, just a little miffed that the sergeant was talking about her to Max as if she were a minor. She'd wasted the best part of the afternoon sweating it out in this grimy, boring waiting room and she hadn't made it even halfway through the list of things she'd hoped to achieve today.

But Max was shaking the sergeant's hand, smiling and thanking him as if the man had done him a good turn. He turned to Gemma. 'Let's go. Do you want to bring Mollie home with you? Your vehicle has the proper seat for her.'

Gemma frowned. 'I'd been hoping to stay in town a bit longer. There are still a lot of people I need to talk to.'

Sergeant Kelly squinted at her while he pushed his police cap to the back of his head and scratched his grey curly hair. 'You'll be making sure the little baby travels in the regulation safety seat, won't you, Miss Brown?'

Gemma smiled sweetly at him. 'Of course, sergeant.' She could argue this one with Max when they got outside.

Mollie coughed again and the cough had a raspy edge to it. Gemma felt faint stirrings of alarm. 'I'll come now,' she decided quickly. 'The Goodbye Creek Festival is not as important as our little girl.'

As she rattled through the bush on the trip home, Gemma toyed with the notion that Max had been so angry because he cared about her. It was a comforting thought—but not something she could dwell on. She was growing more worried about Mollie. Her coughs were getting worse and she seemed fretful—quite unlike her usually sunny self. The very last thing she wanted was for Isobel and Dave to come home, eager to see their little daughter, and to find her sick. Until now the babysitting project had gone so well!

Clutching the steering wheel, Gemma felt Mollie's forehead with her free hand. She didn't feel hot. Surely that was a good sign? Suddenly, she felt totally inadequate again. Caring for a healthy baby was one thing, but what did she do if Mollie got sick?

When they returned home, Max's reaction, as soon as he heard Mollie's worsening cough, was to ring Helena at the medical centre straight away, but she was out on an urgent call.

'I guess we'll just have to keep her comfortable,' suggested Gemma. 'Do you have any eucalyptus oil? We could rub her chest with it.'

Max fetched the oil, while Gemma changed Mollie into her nightgown. Together they stared down at the baby lying on the change table, looking so frighteningly quiet as Gemma rubbed her little chest. Although she didn't look ill, there was none of her usual bounce, no chuckles when Gemma gave her ribs a tickle.

Together they fed her, rocked her and put her to bed and, to their dismay, Mollie went to sleep quickly, as if she were quite exhausted. They looked at each other, their eyes wide with despair.

'Now what do we do?' Gemma asked Max, as he stood at the end of the cot with a clean nappy draped over one shoulder and Mollie's empty bottle in his hand. 'Watch over her?'

'Perhaps all she needs is a good night's sleep,' he suggested. But he looked wretched with worry. 'We should get ourselves something to eat and then we can check on her again.'

They ate a scratch meal in the kitchen. In silence. Instead of chatting eagerly about Isobel and Dave's arrival in the morning, they both avoided the subject, just as they avoided any further discussion of her disastrous day in town. Gemma was concentrating on Mollie, willing her to get better quickly. Halfway through the meal, Max got up and turned the radio on, as if he needed to be distracted from his own thoughts, and they continued eating while listening to a summary of a cricket test match between England and Australia, but neither took much notice of the score.

While Gemma dished out their second course of cheese and crackers with the fresh grapes she'd bought in town, Max went back to Mollie's room to check her again. He returned looking sombre and sat down heavily. 'She's still asleep, but I'm afraid the coughing hasn't stopped.'

He looked so miserable that Gemma felt the urge to cheer him up. The radio wasn't helping. The cricket broadcast had finished and a symphony orchestra had begun to play something sad and slow. 'We mustn't sit here being morbid,' she cajoled. 'Surely we can do something to lift our spirits—but I'm hopeless at telling jokes. I can never remember the punch line. Um—perhaps we could try a game of I Spy?'

His eyes widened. 'I Spy?' Putting down the cheese knife, Max propped his chin in one hand and frowned, as if giving the matter careful thought. Finally he favoured her with a slow grin and his eyes danced with tolerant amusement. 'And what exactly do you spy, Gemma?'

Feeling very tense, and just a little ridiculous, she began self-consciously to recite the childish chant. 'I spy with my little eye—' She paused and looked around the kitchen, hunting for something interesting. 'Something beginning with *s*.'

'Spider?' he suggested quickly.

'Where?' Gemma jumped out of her chair and scanned the room frantically. Spiders were the one form of wildlife she hated. But she it didn't take her long to realise that she'd been tricked. 'Play fair, Max,' she warned as she sat down again. 'There aren't any spiders.'

'OK.' He grinned. 'I'll try again. Something beginning with *s*.' He glanced at the dresser and a photograph taken of his grandfather during the war. 'Could it be soldier?'

Her fist thumped the table top. 'You must be a mind-reader.'

'Didn't you know I read minds as a sideline?' As he said this, Max rose to his feet slowly and moved around the corner of the table to her. His eyes were no longer smiling, but fixed steadily on hers. He reached for her hand. 'How about you, Gem? Can you read minds? Tell me what I am thinking about.'

Instinctively, she knew that he wanted to kiss her, but for the life of her she couldn't answer him. Her chest swelled with a rush of emotion as she allowed him to pull her out of her chair. They stood together, their gazes locked, their eyes asking silent questions.

And offering silent answers.

He cradled her close. Then lowered his face. She felt his delicious mouth moving over hers, warm and seeking, teasing her lips apart, felt his stubbled jaw graze her cheek and felt his strong hands holding her body against him.

And this time Gemma didn't panic.

She nestled closer, needing the reassurance and compassion of his arms. Understanding his anxiety about Mollie, she wanted to offer him her comfort in return.

This was a very different kiss from the one they had shared five years earlier. This time there was no urgent, desperate passion. This time Max was offering her a gift of tenderness and Gemma could feel his caring and warmth seeping into her. She had no idea kissing a man could feel so sweet—so right—like a blessing. She knew in her heart that it was good. Was meant to be.

They kissed and kissed some more, his mouth moving slowly, slowly over hers, tasting her, delving to explore her inner secrets. Sending her dizzy. Their bodies pressed closer, without haste, but showing each other, in every way they knew, that they yearned for an even closer intimacy.

A happy tear seeped from under her eyelashes and Max kissed it away. 'Little Gem,' he murmured, 'thank you for trying to cheer me up. You've no idea—'

The sound of slow hand-clapping startled them. Clap…clap…clap.

Gemma jerked her head sideways to discover Helena Roberts-Jones, leaning against the kitchen doorway. Her eyes were wide with embarrassment and a disconcerted smile twisted her mouth, distorting her usually attractive appearance. 'Well, my goodness,' she remarked, lowering her hands to her hips. 'How touching. How deeply touching.'

Stunned, Gemma stood ramrod-still, waiting for Max to release her, to say something, but he seemed as stupefied as she felt. She was aware of how moist and rosy her lips must look, but resisted the impulse to wipe her mouth with the back of her hand. It was too late to remove any evidence.

Finally Max dropped his hands to his sides and cleared his throat. 'Ah—Helena. I've been trying to reach you.'

'So I noticed.'

'No, seriously.' He stepped towards her. 'We're worried about Mollie.'

'You don't say?'

Guiltily, Gemma stood beside the kitchen table watching Max, not daring to speak.

'You can't have been too worried,' Helena told him frostily. 'I've been knocking on the front door for some time, but there was no answer, so I let myself in. If I'd been one or two minutes later, I might have really embarrassed us all.'

From Mollie's bedroom nearby came a little wail and a cough.

'That's the baby,' said Max.

'Oh, I'd never have guessed.' Helena rolled her eyes.

Max glared at her. 'Can't you be professional about this?'

She glared back. 'I was being *mega* professional, Max. I got a message that you were trying to contact me about a medical problem so, as I've been over at the Pearsons', because all four of their kids are down with the measles and the littlest one is really sick, I thought I'd call in here on my way home.'

'Thanks, Helena. We really appreciate it. I mean it. And we *are* really concerned about Mollie.'

Helena's face settled back into its mask of professional composure. 'What's the matter with her?'

'She's coughing a lot.'

'And she's listless,' Gemma added. 'But I don't think she has a fever.'

'I'd better take a look at her,' Helena said in her businesslike, matter-of-fact manner. She picked up her bag from the floor and moved towards the bedroom. Max followed. Mollie was still crying.

'Can I make you some coffee?' Gemma called after them.

'Thanks,' Helena replied grimly, and Gemma gathered up the dirty plates and cutlery from the table and carried them to the sink.

Surely Mollie couldn't have measles? There'd been a dreadful epidemic the year before. She remembered reading in the papers that children had died. Gemma's lower teeth nervously nibbled her upper lip as she switched on the kettle and spooned coffee into three mugs, placing them on a tray along with a little milk jug and sugar basin. As she poured steaming water into the mugs, her mind was completely taken up with her concern for Mollie. The Pearson children lived on the neighbouring property.

She hunted in the pantry for a packet of biscuits and wondered if Helena needed something more substantial to eat. But she found it difficult to concentrate on practicalities when her mind was focused on picturing the doctor in the bedroom examining Mollie. *What had she discovered?*

And, as well as her fear, she also had Max's kiss to think about. But that was something beautiful and precious that she must tuck away safely for now. Later she would think about it, savour it. Wonder about it. But even now, while she worried about Mollie and squirmed with embarrassment at the way Helena had caught them 'in the act', the impact of the kiss stayed with her, giving her an underlying sense of promise—like a talisman.

Finding the biscuits at last, she piled them onto a plate and carried the loaded tray through to the lounge room. Helena and Max were coming down the hall from Mollie's room, talking softly. They looked up when they saw Gemma.

'What's the verdict?' she asked nervously.

Helena tucked a stethoscope into her bag. 'I don't think there's too much to worry about,' she said. 'No measles symptoms at this stage. Her throat looks rather red, but I hesitate to prescribe antibiotics. Max and I have given her some baby painkiller. That might make her feel more comfortable.'

'Otherwise we continue as we have,' Max added, with a reassuring wink for Gemma.

Helena nodded. 'And keep in touch with me if you have more concerns.'

'I must say I'm relieved that it doesn't seem serious!' Gemma placed the tray carefully on the coffee table. 'This parenting business is nerve-racking.'

As she eased herself onto a sofa, Helena shot her a wry smirk. 'Parents are the bane of my life.'

'You look tired, Helena.' Max handed her a mug of coffee. Gemma noticed that he added milk and one sugar. He knew exactly how Helena took her coffee.

'It goes with the territory.'

'You've chosen a hard life as a rural doctor in outback Queensland,' Gemma suggested with as much sympathy as she could muster.

Taking a deep draught of her coffee, Helena shrugged. 'You're lucky to be going back to the city in a day or two.' She swung a sultry glance Max's way. 'Nobody out here has it easy. Look at our dear boy, Max. He has to be a Jack-of-all-trades. Cattlemen have to be able to do everything with little or no help—one minute they're fixing a broken-down motorbike in the middle of nowhere and next they're spaying heifers.' Her affectionate smile as she looked at him transformed her face.

Gemma felt her own smile growing a little stiff. 'You're both heroes.'

'We certainly are.' Sarcasm underscored Helena's voice as she put her coffee cup back on the tray. She pushed herself to her feet. 'But if I'm going to stay heroic I'd better make tracks.'

Max stepped forward gallantly. 'I'll see you out.'

'Thanks.' She scooped up her doctor's bag with one hand and looped her free arm through his. 'Bye, Gemma,' she called over her shoulder. 'Don't worry too much about that little baby. But I've given Max strict instructions to call me if he's at all concerned.'

Gemma offered an ineffectual wave to their retreating backs. The two walked with their heads leaning together, talking earnestly. For Gemma, it was like being back at the ball. Once again, she was struck by how good this couple looked together. Both were tall and handsome, strong characters—confident of their place in the world—*at ease with their sexuality.* They would make an excellent partnership. A perfect match.

What was a little kiss beside all that?

She stared down at her coffee. The mug was half full, but her stomach churned at the thought of drinking any more. Fifteen minutes earlier, in Max's arms, she'd been on cloud nine. Her heart had been full to bursting with happiness and—and what she'd thought was love. Max had held her so tenderly, kissed her so intimately, murmured her name…

Now, she'd come to her senses. She'd come hurtling back to earth with an almighty, heartbreaking thud. And the truth was as sharp and clear as an outback winter's morning. All that had happened this evening was that she'd joined the ranks as one of Max Jardine's women.

CHAPTER TEN

GEMMA hurried through the washing-up, while her mind boiled. She wanted to have everything done and to be out of the kitchen before Max returned. *No, she didn't!*

What if he acted indifferently, as if their kiss had never happened? *What if he wanted to continue where they'd left off?*

Her head spun. Her eyes burned.

Not for a moment did she question whether she loved Max. But when it came to his feelings for her, the questions were endless.

And they began with…what about…Helena? Sharon? Susan?

Did he kiss them as tenderly, as lovingly as he'd kissed her? Surely not.

Her mind seemed like a candy floss machine, going round and round, spinning out questions like pieces of sugary floss, only to have them dissolve as soon as she tried to catch hold of the answers.

By the time she'd washed the few dishes and wiped down the bench tops, Max had not returned. Gemma blacked out images of the two of them saying farewell outside by concentrating her thoughts on Mollie. The baby was the only member of the Jardine family she should worry about tonight. She turned out the light in the kitchen and hurried down the hall to her bedroom. By opening the French doors between hers and Mollie's rooms, she would have more chance of hearing her. And as she hastily prepared for sleep she prayed for a peaceful night and that she would find Mollie much better in the morning.

She woke with a fright, sitting bolt upright in bed, clutching the sheet and trembling in the dark with an unknown fear. Then it came to her. The horrible noise that had been haunting her dreams. A hoarse, brassy cough followed by a harsh, high-pitched wheezing sound. And then little cries.

Mollie!!

She leapt out of bed and dashed to the cot. Mollie sounded much worse. Gemma's heart crashed crazily against her ribs as she lifted the little form in its white cotton nightdress out of the cot and clasped the baby to her. Up close, the coughing and wheezing sounded horrifying. 'Oh, little girl,' Gemma whispered. 'What's happened to you? Oh, Lord! What are we going to do?'

Without a moment's hesitation, she rushed with Mollie in her arms down the hall to Max's room. He was already awake and swinging his long legs from beneath the sheets. Shuttered moonlight striped the room, showing up the deep distress in his face.

'She's worse?' was his immediate question.

Sick with fear, Gemma nodded. 'She sounds terrible, Max. I think she's having trouble breathing.'

'God, no.'

For a moment they both stood in petrified silence, listening to the dreadful barking and wheezing noises coming from Mollie.

'I'll ring Helena,' Max said immediately.

'I'll rub some more eucalyptus oil on her. It's all I can think of to do.' *Oh, Isobel,* Gemma thought as she hurried back to Mollie's room. *I'm so sorry. I've tried to take care of your little girl. Oh, God! I can't bear this!*

Mollie gave a little whimper.

'There, there, sweetheart,' Gemma crooned as she changed the baby's nappy and rubbed her chest. 'You'll be all right. The doctor will tell us what to do.'

She heard Max's step on the floorboards behind her.

'No luck,' he muttered with a curse. 'I can't get an answer. I rang Helena's home number and the medical centre. Nobody's answering. I don't know what the hell's going on.'

'What are we going to do?' Gemma's question emerged as a terrified whisper.

Max took a deep, agonised breath and groaned. He looked away and crossed his arms over his bare chest. 'I haven't got a damn clue,' he muttered harshly. 'I'll just have to keep trying to get through to someone.'

'Perhaps we could ring one of the women on another property? Someone who's had children.'

Max grunted his disapproval. 'We don't want old wives' tales. We want proper medical attention.' He spun on his bare heel. 'And it's no use jumping in a vehicle and rushing into town if Helena's not there. She's the only doctor for two hundred kilometres. I'm going to keep on that darn phone until I get some answers.'

With her heart thumping in terror, Gemma watched him race back to the telephone in the kitchen, his retreating back, brown and sleek above long blue and white striped pyjama pants. He pinned so much faith on Helena. *Only Helena had the answers!* She pressed her lips to Mollie's soft cheek. 'There's got to be some other way to get help,' she whispered.

Mollie seemed less distressed in her arms, so Gemma

walked her up and down the darkened hallway. The only light came from patches of lamplight spilling through bedroom doorways. As she walked, up and down, up and down, she crooned soft songs—snippets of pop tunes, nursery rhymes, lullabies—whatever soothing bits and pieces came into her head. She had no idea what the baby thought of them, but they helped, just a little, to make Gemma feel calmer.

But the coughing and the nasty, frightening wheezing sound continued.

Gemma passed the door to the study. The curtains weren't drawn in that room and the moonlight sent its blue light tumbling through the window and across the carpet. Hoping a glimpse of the outside world and the serene bush might give her some kind of comfort, she moved into the room and crossed to the window, her bare feet cushioned by the velvet-soft carpet.

But, outside, the darkened clumps of trees and the vista of paddocks painted in pale moonshine seemed remote—unfriendly and unhelpful. She turned away quickly before useless tears could form. Now was not a time to give in to her fears. She had to be strong for Mollie. With her back to the window, she faced the rows and rows of books on the opposite wall. And they seemed to be staring back at her, voicing silent accusations.

'I wonder,' she whispered to Mollie and stepped forward. 'This library is old and extensive. I wonder if there would be such a thing as a book on baby care.' Spurred by a burst of fresh hope, she snapped on the light and squinted at the sudden brightness.

While clucking soothing noises to Mollie, her eyes hungrily raced along the titles, searching, searching… There were countless books on animal husbandry and farm management, international markets and economics, action-adventure novels and spy thrillers—the kind of collection she would expect a man like Max to have. This was useless. How could she expect him to have a book on baby care?

Deeply disappointed, she sank into Max's leather armchair, hoping against hope that any minute now he would come racing back with good news. She saw his computer sitting on the desk and thought of the last happy e-mail they'd received from Isobel. Good heavens! It was after midnight. Isobel and Dave were arriving later this very day. And to find Mollie like *this*!

She jumped to her feet again. Where was Max? She couldn't bear being alone with Mollie any longer.

As she raised her hand to flick off the light switch, she saw it. A shabby old book with a peeling paper dust jacket shoved sideways on top of some others. The word 'baby' in the title caught her eye. 'Please, please,' she whispered as she pulled the book out from where it was tightly wedged. She read the title. *Caring for your baby. The first three years.*

Trembling and anxious, Gemma lowered herself back into the armchair. She settled Mollie over one shoulder and, with a frenzied sense of desperation, read down the list of contents. There was a section on illnesses. Thank heavens!

Max burst into the room, his eyes wild and despairing. 'I finally got through to the medical centre! There's been a bad smash on the highway. Helena was called out there, of course. Now she's riding in the ambulance trying to stabilise someone in a critical condition while they travel to Mt Isa hospital.'

'She won't be able to help us?'

Max shook his head and slammed one balled fist into

the other. 'I can't believe this! Who'd live in the bush? What a disaster!' He stepped closer and uncurled his hand to cup Mollie's head. 'How's our little one?'

Gemma didn't need to answer. Mollie's distress was all too evident. She sighed. 'I'm afraid she's much the same. It's awful, Max.' She held out the book. 'But I've found this old book on childcare. I'm hoping I might find something in here to help.'

With a hopeless kind of gesture, he scowled. 'I wouldn't hold out too much hope. That looks like it came out of the Ark. It must have been Mum's or perhaps even my grandmother's. I'm going to get back on that phone and try the Flying Doctors. There's got to be someone, *somewhere* who can help us.'

This time Gemma didn't watch him go, she was too busy reading. In spite of his doubts about the book, she wanted desperately to find something helpful. She quickly reached the section on coughs and colds. Running her finger down the page, she scanned the text, looking for a description that fitted Mollie's terrible dry, barking cough and wheeze. And then she found it.

Croup. Gemma read through the section again. Yes, that had to be it. The symptoms sounded exactly like Mollie's. Feeling elated, sick and scared, she read on. The book stated, of course, to call your doctor immediately if you thought your child had croup. She felt her stomach contract. 'What else? What else?' she whispered desperately. There was a paragraph or two about cold steam humidifiers. She and Max had as much chance of finding one of them as finding the doctor in a hurry. Finally, at the bottom of the article, was a last-ditch suggestion.

Take your baby into the bathroom, close the door and run hot water in the bathtub or run a hot shower.

The heat will steam up the room. The moist air should rapidly improve the baby's breathing.

Right! Gemma jumped to her feet. This was something she could do. And it sounded safe enough, no matter what was actually wrong with Mollie. She charged out of the room and down the hall to the bathroom.

Eager for as much steam as possible, she wrapped Mollie carefully in a towel and laid her on the bath mat while she turned on the taps in both the shower and the bath. Then she sat on the floor with her back to the white tiled wall and nursed Mollie, while the bathroom began to fill up with steam.

And that was where Max found them twenty minutes later.

He banged loudly on the door. 'Gemma, are you in there?'

'Yes,' she called. 'Come in.'

He flung the door open and charged in, then came to an abrupt halt. Through the steam, he peered at her. 'I finally got through to someone at Flying Doctor Base,' he began, but stopped and dropped to his knees beside her. 'How's Mollie?'

'She's heaps better,' Gemma told him. 'She's gone to sleep and she's breathing easily again. It's amazing the way the steam's helped. Like a miracle.'

'Wow,' he replied, the word drawn out on a long sigh. He swivelled so that his back was against the wall and he slid his length down until he sat next to her. Just for a moment, he dropped his head sideways to rest on hers. 'I eventually got through to a nursing sister at the base who suggested doing exactly this. She said it should work if it wasn't a really serious case of croup.'

'I'd hate to see a serious case.' Gemma felt his head lift away again and she turned to look at him. His blue eyes were only inches from her and his body and hers were touching at the shoulders; the rest of his bare torso was a whisker's distance. She became conscious of her tongue running slowly over her lips.

'Thank goodness it worked. Thanks so much, Gem. You did all this on your own while I rushed around like a demented, headless chook.'

'I'm just so glad it worked,' she replied drowsily, her eyes mesmerised by the steamy sheen forming on his skin.

He took a deep breath and looked down at Mollie lying asleep in her arms. Her little chest rose and fell in its usual regular rhythm and her breathing seemed soft and even. Lowering his head, Max dropped a light kiss on the downy head. 'Don't frighten me like that, ever again,' he told the sleeping Mollie. Then his eyes met Gemma's.

His expression was so intense Gemma felt tiny pin-pricks of tension break out on her arms and her back—all over her body. His Adam's apple moved up and down and he attempted a very wobbly smile. 'Do you think—?' he began, then cleared his throat. 'Is there any chance—?' His hand came up to touch her hair, damp from the steam-filled room.

Slowly he traced the outline of her face, the soft curve of her cheek, the rounded, perky chin. His thumb rubbed her lower lip. He seemed suddenly shy. Gemma knew that he was thinking about another kiss. She was absolutely certain she wanted to kiss him back. What was stopping him?

'Why don't you just say it, Max?'

'Say what?'

'Whatever it is you're trying so hard to get out.'

His hand rested lightly against her cheek. 'Later,' he whispered, and looked again at the sleeping Mollie. 'Now's not the right time.'

But Gemma thought this was a perfect time for getting closer to Max. She turned her face to his and lifted her lips. Every cell in her body screamed out for him to kiss her.

And, to her infinite relief, he did. Holding the sides of her face in his big hands, he kissed her deeply, daringly. With his tongue and his lips Max showed her exactly what had been left unsaid moments before and Gemma almost dropped Mollie, her body felt so limp and melting.

Between kisses, she gasped, 'I see what you mean.'

'What's that?' he asked, kissing her neck, her eyelids, her shoulder.

'Now isn't a good time. I'm either going to drop Mollie or squash her.'

'Here, let me take her.' Max lifted the sleeping baby gently out of Gemma's arms and slowly stood up. 'Do you think it would be OK to put her back to bed now?'

'Yes. I guess so.' Gemma replied, feeling lonely without his arms around her. 'She hasn't coughed for quite some time.'

He cocked his head towards the shower. 'I'd say we're about to run out of hot water anyhow. You turn off the taps and I'll take Mollie through to her room.'

In a daze of awakened desire, Gemma turned off the taps, hung up the bath towels and switched off the bathroom light. She padded down the hall to Mollie's room, but it was empty. Her room was empty, too. Puzzled, she stepped back into the hall and made her way down the passage to Max's bedroom.

He was lying on his huge bed with Mollie cradled in the crook of one arm and he sent Gemma a tummy-flipping grin as he patted the mattress on the other side of the baby. 'I've decided we should keep her with us for the rest of the night.'

'With—with *us*? You mean *me, too*? Here with you? And her?'

'I do.' He smiled. 'You have any objections?'

'Ah—I—I don't suppose so. I mean, I haven't—' Gemma gulped and stood shyly at the end of his bed, keeping her eyes lowered, unable to return his gaze. But looking downwards merely showed her the state of her nightdress. After half an hour in a steamy bathroom, the fine, pale pink cotton clung to her every curve. Self-consciously, she lifted her arms and crossed them over her chest, then took two steps forward.

Every part of her wanted to be there on the bed with Max. If he made love to her the way he kissed her, she was quite sure there could be nothing more beautiful in the whole world—but vestiges of the old fear clung. He knew so much and she knew so little… Then again, she reasoned, Max could hardly hope to ravish her if Mollie was there with them…

Hesitantly, she lowered herself onto the mattress and the three of them lay on the wide, king-sized bed with its crisp, clean, white sheets—Max and Gemma with little Mollie sleeping soundly and peacefully between them. The tiny warm body close to hers was very reassuring.

She felt his hand touch her shoulder. He began to

massage it slowly. 'Relax, Gemma. You're exhausted. You need to sleep.'

She rolled over and stared at him, wondering if she'd heard him correctly. Up close, against the pillow, he looked divine. 'You want to go to *sleep*?'

'It's what most people do at this time of night, especially when they've been through what we've just experienced and have a sick baby to care for.'

'Oh,' Gemma said softly, not sure if she was relieved or disappointed. 'Of course.'

'Did you think I was going to use innocent little Mollie as bait to lure you into my bed and then have my wicked way with you?'

'No, not really,' she lied.

He leaned closer and murmured in her ear, his voice rumbling and shockingly sexy, 'I'm sure I can find a much better way to tempt you to sleep with me, Gemma.'

She was sure he could, too. He'd put in a pretty good effort in the bathroom when he'd kissed the living daylights out of her. Just remembering sent her nerves a-tingle. But what she should get off her chest now, she decided, as she lay only a short distance from him, was a confession about how inexperienced she was in these bedroom matters.

'Max,' she said, lying stiffly, not looking at him and pulling the sheet up to her chin. She stared at the delicate blue ceiling, groping for the right words. But the perfect words wouldn't come, so there was nothing for it but to head straight to the heart of the matter. 'Do—do you know much about virgins?'

His silent response was no help at all. Gemma still couldn't bring herself to look at him. She didn't want to read his reaction to her admission. All too often in the past those blue eyes had dismissed her or mocked her.

'Did you hear me?' she asked a crack in the ceiling.

'I heard you, Gem, but I hardly know how to answer.' She sensed rather than saw him turn his head in her direction. 'Is this question intended to launch a discussion about my personal life, or a general chat about today's society, or is it perhaps scientific? Are you wanting a biological definition of virginity?'

A hot blush crept up her neck and into her cheeks. 'It—it's purely a social issue,' she said, her eyes still avoiding contact with his. 'I mean, these days, apparently many girls lose their virginity at an early age.'

'Yes,' he replied cautiously.

'But that's only *many*, Max. There is still a large group of perfectly normal, healthy and well-adjusted young women who—'

'Why on earth are we talking about this subject now, at this time of night?'

Couldn't he guess?

Perhaps not, she thought with alarm, when she remembered how she'd behaved every time Max had kissed her.

Out of the corner of her eye, she admired the play of muscles in his back as he reached over and switched off the lamp on the bedside table. Then, in the dark, she felt the mattress give as he leaned over Mollie towards her. His warm, sensuous lips brushed hers and then pressed her eyelids closed. 'Stop fretting and go to sleep, Gemma.' He kissed her mouth again—an undemanding, affectionate, goodnight kiss.

She felt amazingly relaxed, considering she was in a man's bed for the first time in her life.

'Just count yourself lucky this little angel is lying between us,' he murmured, dropping more kisses onto her bare shoulder. 'I promise you won't escape me so easily next time.'

Next time?

It was a thought that should have kept her wide awake, but as Gemma lay there, cuddled close to Mollie, with Max's dark shape nearby, a feeling of peace and a sense of rightness settled over her, and she yawned, blissfully happy. Through the dark, she whispered to him, 'So you don't mind, Max?'

'Mind what?' he mumbled sleepily.

'That I haven't…ever…' She couldn't bring herself to finish the sentence, but Max didn't help. He remained completely silent. Gemma figured the penny had dropped. He was probably shocked that the girl who'd acted like a brazen hussy in his arms at the age of eighteen was trying to claim she was still a virgin five years later.

She felt compelled to try to explain. 'Actually, the reason I've never—um—never made love has something to do with you.'

Abruptly, he rolled onto to his side and propped himself on one elbow. Through the dark, she could feel his eyes staring fiercely at her. 'Then you'd better tell me.'

'You kissed me a long time ago—that night of Dave's party, when I was eighteen.'

'Yes,' he said quietly and she could hear the tension in his voice.

'You spoiled me for any other man, Max.'

'Oh, God,' she heard him moan, and he flopped back onto the bed and lay staring at the ceiling, his hands clasped beneath his head.

He sounded so upset; she wished desperately that she'd never started this ridiculous conversation. They were both exhausted. She should have taken his advice and gone to sleep. Now her clumsy admission had completely spoiled the happy contentment of a few moments ago. The last thing a man like Max would want to discuss with a woman in his bed would be the details of her inexperience with men.

As if to prove her right, he rose swiftly from the bed and headed straight for the door opening onto the verandah.

'Where are you going?'

'I've got to do some thinking,' he replied gruffly. 'And I can't do it lying in bed next to you.' Then he disappeared into the night.

CHAPTER ELEVEN

TEARS streamed down Gemma's face as she lay wretchedly awake beside the soundly sleeping baby. She wanted so badly to go after Max. If only she hadn't been so desperate to off-load her confession! She'd made everything between them so much more complicated.

Complicated? She'd ruined everything!

A few hours ago, Max had been kissing her as if he thought the world was about to end! 'Just count yourself lucky this little angel is lying between us,' he'd said. 'I promise you won't escape me so easily next time.'

But then she'd made a first-class fool of herself—blaming Max for her virginity—burdening him with her hang-ups—and now there would be no next time. Tomorrow, as soon as Mollie was safely handed over to Isobel and Dave, he would bundle her onto a plane and get her out of the district as fast as he could.

Lord! When would she ever learn to play it cool? If she hadn't shot her mouth off, Max would be sleeping peacefully beside her now instead of prowling angrily through the dim, dark depths of the house.

It wasn't until the grim, grey dawn light began to creep into the room that the tears and her exhaustion took their toll and she drifted miserably off to sleep...

She woke late to find bright sunshine spinning through the slats in the timber louvers and striping the honey-toned floorboards of Max's bedroom. Yawning and stretching, she rolled over. *Mollie was gone!* Frantically, she pushed herself onto her elbows as the events of the night came back to her. With them came a new rush of fear that had her bounding out of the bed.

Where was Mollie? Was she sick again?

'Max!' she called as she raced frantically through the house. She stopped briefly in her own room to haul on shorts and a T-shirt, wondering all the time what had happened. There was no one in Mollie's room, the lounge room was empty and so was the kitchen. She stopped for a moment, clutching the back of a kitchen chair, a little out of breath and on the brink of panic.

Calm down, she ordered herself. *You managed during a crisis last night and you'll manage again.* And as her breathing steadied, so did her thoughts. *Surely Max would have woken her if there had been an emergency?* She stood frowning as she considered where to look next. Then she heard sounds coming from the verandah.

Totally unexpected sounds—like a man and a baby laughing!

Curious, Gemma stepped through the doorway onto the verandah and saw them.

Max was squatting and Mollie stood beside him, her little feet firmly gripping the bare timber floor and one chubby hand on his knee to hold her balance. She was laughing and squealing with delight as the cutest little blue heeler puppy rolled and played in a pool of sunshine at her feet.

'For heaven's sake,' Gemma cried, hurrying towards them. 'Look at her! Who would have thought she would recover like this?'

Max scooped the gurgling Mollie in one hand and the puppy in the other as he jumped to his feet. 'Gemma.' His eyes held hers and the anxiety she saw in them made the breath catch in her throat. 'I looked in earlier and found Mollie wide awake, but you were still snoring.'

'Thanks for getting her. I slept like a log,' she lied. 'What about you?'

'I was fine,' he replied unhelpfully.

He didn't look as if his night had been 'fine', Gemma thought, noting signs of exhaustion and tension in the grim set of his face and the dark smudges beneath his eyes. 'I can't believe how well Mollie looks,' she said, dropping an impulsive kiss on the baby's cheek.

'The sister at the base told me it can be like that with babies. One minute they look like they're on their last legs and the next they're up and running as if nothing was ever the matter.' He chuckled as Mollie tried to clutch the puppy's ear. 'I wonder if her parents will let her have a puppy?'

'Knowing how crazy Dave was about dogs when he was a boy, I'm sure there's a very good chance.' Gemma scratched the puppy's forehead.

So this is how it's going to be, she thought. *We both pretend those kisses last night didn't happen.*

Some things never change.

'I guess Isobel and Dave will be here shortly after lunch,' she said in the most businesslike tone she could muster. 'I'd better get their room ready.' She turned to go.

'Steady on,' intervened Max. He let the puppy scamper away to join his brothers and sisters. 'You're not doing anything of the sort until you've had breakfast.'

'I guess I *am* rather hungry,' she admitted. 'Have you eaten?'

'No, not yet.' He raised a questioning eyebrow. 'We'll break with tradition this morning and eat together?'

'Good idea,' Gemma replied, almost enjoying the thought. But a memory of the day she'd arrived and their embarrassing discussion about women's breakfasts spoiled the short burst of pleasure.

Other women had eaten breakfast with Max. But what had happened beforehand? They certainly wouldn't have given him a blow-by-blow in-depth account of their inadequacies as a lover.

'Orange juice?' Max directed his question at Gemma as he helped Mollie into her high chair.

'I guess so,' she muttered. 'I'll get it.' She filled two glasses while Max fetched a packet of baby cereal from the pantry.

'Can you look after Mollie while I cook us something? What would you like? Do you fancy bacon and eggs?'

'Thank you. It's probably what I need.'

He must have heard the wintry edge in her tone, because he swung round and stared at her hard. 'Is something the matter?'

Oh, help me! Gemma thought, feeling suddenly much worse than she had last night. *Everything's the matter! I'm in love with you and I feel terrible instead of happy. And I've made you mad with me and I don't know what to do about it!*

With hasty, nervous movements, she began to spoon Mollie's cereal into a bowl. 'Of course there's nothing the matter. Everything's just hunky-dory.'

Max stood still in the middle of the kitchen and his brow creased momentarily as he scoured tense fingers back and forth through his hair. He looked as if he wanted to say something, but must have thought better of it and turned instead to the stove.

She stirred milk into Mollie's cereal and began to feed it to her while Max fiddled with a frying pan. In spite of her misery, Gemma tormented herself by watching his every move. She couldn't help admiring the easy roll of his wrists as he cracked eggs and slipped them into the sizzling pan. Couldn't help loving the way his thick, dark hair ended in a straight line just above his collar. And as for the way his backside neatly filled his jeans—that was nothing short of a work of art.

'Keep your mind on the job. You're getting cereal all over Mollie's face.' Max scowled when he caught her staring at him.

Gemma blushed as she dabbed away the blobs on Mollie's cheeks. 'I'm sorry,' she muttered. 'I got caught up in my thoughts.'

With an egg flip, he transferred the crispy bacon strips and sunny eggs from the pan to their plates, then set them on the table. As he sat opposite Gemma, he looked at her with a slight frown. 'Dare I ask what kind of thoughts you're having?'

Blushing again, she picked up her glass of orange juice. She had been thinking about the impossible—about making love with Max, of how he would look *out* of those jeans. Best to steer clear away from that subject. 'I was thinking it's kind of a relief that after we came out here more or less hating each other and fighting like we have since we were kids, that we've made a measure of progress. We—we've ended up—less antagonistic.'

Max placed a forkful of bacon back on his plate. 'I've *never* hated you, Gemma.'

The glass slipped in her hand and she quickly placed it back on the table before she spilled juice everywhere. 'But Max—'

'I know you always thought I did,' he continued. 'And in the end, I decided that perhaps it was best if you went on thinking that I didn't care about you.'

'But—but when we were young?'

'And you idolised Dave? Back then I was always jealous of Dave.' Max's gaze dropped to the plate of food in front of him and he toyed with his fork.

'You were *jealous*?' Gemma squeaked.

When he looked up again, she was startled by the intense emotion his eyes revealed. 'Even when you were a skinny little kid, Gem, your perky smile and bright eyes fascinated me. But my kid brother was the funny one—the one who made you laugh. You thought everything he did was so jolly admirable and adventurous.'

She reached a trembling hand to touch his arm where it rested on the table. 'But I was frightened of you, Max. You were always scowling at Dave and me.'

'That's because I was fairly young, too, and I didn't know how to handle my emotions.'

She let out a long, astonished breath and wondered if her poor heart could possibly bear the knowledge that Max hadn't hated her for all these years. 'All this time.'

But what good was knowing this now? Maybe she and Max weren't fighting any more, but an unbridgeable gulf of tension and doubt stretched between them.

'Anyhow,' he added gruffly, as if he regretted his admission, 'I've slaved over a hot stove, so we'd better eat and get on with preparing everything for our visitors.'

All morning, as together they tidied the house and made up a spare bed, getting ready for Isobel and Dave's return, Gemma felt as tense as tightly strained fencing wire. Max was polite and friendly, but the sexy teasing, the come-to-me-baby light in his eye that had thrilled her last night, had vanished.

When Isobel and Dave arrived, she was happy to stop thinking about herself and become absorbed in the excitement of the joyful parents reuniting with their daughter. She and Max grinned happily as they listened to their exclamations of surprise over how Mollie had grown in just two weeks and how she could stand all by herself.

But Gemma still found it incredibly difficult to drag her eyes away from Max. She was watching all the time for his expression to soften. But the Max of old, the reserved and frowning big brother was back.

At least he sat beside her on the lounge, while they explained as gently as they could about Mollie's croup. The parents accepted this news with remarkable calm. Gemma decided that, after dealing with armed rebels, croup probably seemed like a very minor drama.

Then Isobel and Dave told them the astonishing news that they'd heard radio coverage in Brisbane of the fiasco in the Goodbye Creek pub.

'I told you we'd attract media attention,' Gemma crowed triumphantly to Max. 'You watch. This is just the start of something big for Goodbye Creek.' But her excitement at the news was tarnished by his bored response.

'It's just a flash in the pan. Nothing will come of it.'

And of course they listened attentively to Dave as he expanded on his ordeal in Somalia. He was a good storyteller and the details of his capture and imprisonment were both alarming and fascinating, but with Max sitting some distance away, his fists firmly clenched on his knees, Gemma's thoughts kept straying. She kept thinking about the way he'd kissed her and held her last night—before everything had gone wrong.

When Dave finished, Isobel leaned forward in her chair and stared at them both shrewdly. 'I'm so grateful to you guys for everything you've done for Mollie,' she said. 'But I must confess, I'm also rather disappointed. I had high hopes that I would come out here and you would have some good news for us.'

'We've shown you how close Mollie is to walking,' Gemma replied quickly.

'Yes, but I'm not talking about Mollie. I'm talking about you two. You've been living together for almost two weeks and—and—' She shook her head and fixed them with an exasperated glare. 'You're still as wary of each other as opponents in a boxing ring.'

Gemma and Max exchanged self-conscious glances.

Dave jumped up and crossed the room to give Max a hearty slap on the shoulder. 'Cheer up, big bro. Isobel tries to matchmake wherever she goes. Gemma, don't worry, we'll take you back to the civilised coast with us and we'll leave this old grouch to his Brahman bulls and his bush.'

Max stood to return his brother's back slap. 'I can always rely on my family to understand me.'

Gemma's lips stretched into a very flat smile.

Straight after dinner, a jet-lagged Isobel and Dave took Mollie off to their room. The baby's cot had been moved in there, so the little family were alone together at last.

And, once again, Gemma and Max were alone in the kitchen. Max scowled at the pile of dirty dishes. 'My next investment will be an automatic dishwasher.'

'Great idea,' Gemma muttered. 'Although once we've all gone…' Her voice trailed away, and abruptly she turned to the sink, flicked on the tap and began rinsing dinner plates.

Max put the milk jug back in the fridge. 'It seems strange not having to worry about whether Mollie has settled for the night.'

She swivelled around to look at him. 'I know what you mean. I've become quite used to thinking like a mother.'

As he recrossed the room to return the salt and pepper shakers to their spot beside the stove, he commented, 'You've been absolutely fantastic with Mollie. The perfect little mother.'

His gentle words touched her. 'I really enjoyed looking after her. And I know you did, too, Max. You were so sweet with her.' She gathered up cutlery to be washed. 'You'll make a wonderful father.'

She hadn't really expected a response, but Max was silent for so long that eventually she glanced over her shoulder towards him. He was standing rock-still in the middle of the kitchen, his shoulders hunched with tension and his hands thrust firmly in the pockets of his jeans. He looked so wretched her heart jogged a crazy little war dance in her chest.

'Max, what's the matter?' she whispered.

'Gemma, I'm so sorry.'

'Sorry?' Snatching a kitchen towel, she hastily dried her hands.

He expelled his breath on a long sigh. 'I'm sorry I frightened you so badly all those years ago. You know—the night when you thought you were kissing Dave.'

An agonising lump wedged in Gemma's throat. She tried to talk, but nothing would come out.

'Ever since then, I've had a dreadful feeling that I really messed you up,' he went on, his mouth contorted by emotion. 'And now I know the truth, I can't forgive myself.'

Gemma shook her head and tried to get rid of the pain in her throat by swallowing. Behind her, she clutched the edge of the sink. 'Please,' she managed at last. 'Please, don't torment yourself. I'm the one who should apologise.'

'For Pete's sake, you were only a kid.'

'But you didn't frighten me.'

'Of course I did,' he stormed. 'I tricked you and scared you witless. You ran away. You wouldn't talk to me—couldn't bear to face me. You even got out of the country—and—now you tell me— For crying out loud, Gemma. I can't bear to think how I've hurt you.'

She raised a shaking hand to her mouth. The remorse in his voice shocked her. And his pain was her fault. She'd let him carry so much guilt—had never let him off the hook by admitting to her share of deception. 'You've got it all wrong!' On unsteady legs, she took a step towards him. Her eyes and throat stung. 'You didn't trick me or frighten me.'

'What's that?'

'You didn't trick me.'

He stared at her, his throat moving rapidly and his eyes disbelieving.

'I knew all along that I wasn't kissing Dave.' Gemma couldn't stand the pain she saw in his face. She stepped closer and took his hand. Touching him again made her feel stronger. 'Please believe me. I'm sorry I didn't tell you ages ago, but I've always been so embarrassed by the way I behaved that night.'

'But you said I've spoiled you for other men.'

'Oh, Max, that's not because I was traumatised. It's because I've never found any other man who can make me feel the way you did.' Bravely, she lifted his hand and pressed her lips to his palm. 'Your kisses were too—too wonderful, you see. You made me feel so full of *wanting* you.' She heard the sharp intake of his breath. 'I've never been able to dredge up that kind of wanting for anyone else.'

In his eyes, as he looked down at her, she saw a savage battle between hope and disbelief. Hardly knowing where she found her courage, Gemma stood on tiptoes and kissed his shadowy jaw. 'No one can kiss the way you do, Max. And all I want is for you to kiss me like that again.'

While her heart thumped crazily, she waited for his response.

'Struth,' he whispered at last. His hands reached for her hips and grasped them firmly. 'You mean there's nothing to keep us apart?'

'Nothing I can think of.'

She could sense the dreadful tension leaving him. 'And you'd like another kiss?' Already he was teasing her again. His mouth was curving into his beautiful, slow smile and his hands were moving possessively over her bottom.

Gemma's pulses throbbed. 'I could do with another of your kisses right now.'

'I'll see what I can manage.' He glanced around the kitchen with its dirty dishes. 'Let's find somewhere more romantic. Come outside,' he said softly.

She didn't know if she could bear to wait till they travelled the short distance, but without another word he swept her effortlessly into his arms and carried her out onto the verandah. Setting her down, he looked around them. 'Now where out here were we exactly on that night?'

And for Gemma it suddenly seemed as natural as saying 'hello' to lead him across the weathered timber floor to the railing in the shadows. With a little laugh, she pushed him against a wooden post. 'You were about here.' She stood close in front of him. 'And I think I was about—'

'You hurled yourself into my arms.'

'Like this?' She threw her arms around his neck and

their eager mouths and bodies surged together. For Gemma, it was like coming home to be back in Max's arms, having his sexy lips reaching her mouth.

It was a kiss of pure seduction, starting slow and lazy and becoming bolder and more intimate until she felt fabulously dizzy and drowning.

Bursting with longing.

All she wanted was to give herself up to the wild fever his touch aroused. 'I want you so, so much,' she whispered.

'I love you, Gemma Brown.'

Oh!

For a stunned moment they stared at each other.

Gemma's heart pounded even harder than ever and her eyes welled with tears. She didn't want to cry. 'You—you do? You—*love—me?*' No, she mustn't cry. This was the happiest moment in her life. Or it would be if his understanding of love matched hers. 'What—what exactly do you mean when you talk of love, Max? Don't you also love Helena?'

'Helena?' His hands dropped to his hips and his head tipped to one side. Gemma took a cautious step away from him. In the dim light she could see that he was staring at her with an annoying, puzzled look in his eyes.

'You can't pretend you don't know what I mean.'

He shook his head. 'No, no. There's nothing between us. Please believe me.' He held out his arms to her in a gesture of innocence. 'When I first met Helena eighteen months ago, I guess something could possibly have developed, but it didn't. We've been exactly what I told you—good friends.'

'You seem so perfect together.'

He frowned. 'I don't see how you make that out. Helena's almost finished her two-year contract out here—

doing her stint of country service. She can't wait to get back to the city in a few months' time. Life stuck out on an outback property wouldn't suit her at all. No, I've been a handy social escort for her and she's been a pleasant companion. But that's all it's been. Helena's an impressive woman and a competent doctor, but she's not the woman I need.'

He reached for her and hauled her towards him again, one hand cradling the nape of her neck. 'She's not you, Gem. It's you and I who are perfect together.'

Gemma wondered if her heart would actually explode. It seemed to swell so hugely in her chest. 'It seems too good to be true.'

'It's the absolute truth.'

She felt his hand under her chin, turning her face to look at him again. 'Gemma,' he said softly, with a strange little growl in his voice, 'you're the only woman I love and you're the only woman I want to share my life with.' He pulled her hard against him and she could feel his heart pounding away, just like hers.

He buried his face in her hair and his hands moved impatiently down her back and up again, as if he needed to know and touch every part of her at once. 'God, I need you, Gem. And I need you here. I need you to stay out here and love me and grow old with me. Is there any chance you could manage that?'

'Any chance?' How could so many wonderful, impossible dreams be handed to her in an instant? With a choked cry, Gemma slipped her hands round his waist and rested her head against his shoulder. 'There's a very, *very* good chance,' she whispered.

She pulled back slightly, so that she could look up into his face. 'Max, are you really asking me to—to—*marry* you?'

'Yes,' he told her with a shy smile. 'Please marry me, Gemma.'

'Oh, my goodness! Don't let me go. My legs have gone all shaky.'

He bent quickly and scooped her up in his arms again. 'Better?' he asked.

She grinned. 'Much better, thanks.'

His lips teased and tasted hers. 'So when can I expect an answer?'

'You know the answer, don't you?'

Crossing to the stairs, Max sat on the top step and settled Gemma on his lap. 'I know I claimed to be a mind-reader last night, but tonight I'd kind of like to hear you tell me what you're thinking. My guess might be wrong.'

'Actually,' she told him, relishing the feel of his tightly stretched denim beneath her, 'I happen to be madly in love with you.' She kissed him full on the mouth with a fresh burst of daring that both surprised and thrilled her. When she paused for breath, she added excitedly, 'I thought there was no chance you'd fall in love with me and I've been so sick at the thought of going back to Brisbane to live miserably ever after.'

Hardly believing how happy she felt, she dropped her head onto his shoulder again. It was a wonderful place to be. His smooth, tanned neck was temptingly close and she couldn't resist more flirtatious kisses and nibbles.

'So what's your answer?' he murmured huskily. 'Do you want to get married and stay here in the outback with me?'

'You bet I do, Max. I love this place. Try stopping me from living here.' With a laugh, she added, 'Think of all the breakfasts we can share from now on. Here in the homestead kitchen, or perhaps down by the creek, or out on mustering camps.'

He chuckled and she raised her lips to his. Groaning softly, Max took her mouth in a kiss so sexy she felt shivery and melting, totally electrified. Her mind threw up wild ideas, and, turning in his lap, she straddled him so they could be much, much closer.

Above them, the blue-black sky was spotted with stars, like the roof of a medieval cathedral. From the horse paddock nearby came the occasional soft clip-clop of hooves and, from further away, the soft call of a curlew. And floating all around them on the summer's night air wafted the sweet heady scent of the starry white jasmine that climbed latticework on either side of the steps.

Happiness zinged through Gemma and only one thought marred the moment and brought her stomach bunching into knots. 'Max?'

'Yes, sweetheart?' He nuzzled her neck.

'You're sure you don't mind?'

'Mind what?'

'That I'm so inexperienced.'

He relaxed his close hold on her, but kept his hands on her arms, rubbing them gently. 'Would this question be a sequel to that serious little discussion you started last night about modern social trends?'

'Yes.' Gemma looked straight into his eyes, trying to read his expression.

He kissed the tip of her nose. 'You're trying to tell me that I'll be your first lover?'

'Yes. Do you mind?

'Do I *mind?*' Locking his arms around her once more, he hugged her tight. 'Oh, Gemma, how could you ask such a question? Why, darling, I feel incredibly honoured to know that I'm going to be your first and only lover.' He kissed her forehead. 'Honestly, I'm a very privileged man.'

Deliriously happy, she trailed her lips over the underside of his jaw, and scattered more cheeky little kisses up and down his neck. 'I knew I was right to wait for you,' she murmured.

His lips caressed hers. 'We've both been waiting a long time to be together.' He nipped her soft lower lip between his teeth. 'Are you interested in making up for lost time?'

Gemma's smile widened as his lips moved slowly down her throat towards her breast. 'I'm very, very interested,' she whispered, and she opened her arms to her man—the one man in the world she wanted.

[illegible] his hands [illegible] her buttocks, [illegible] into a [illegible] position.

[illegible] she trailed her lips over the under- side of his [illegible] and scattered [illegible] kisses up and down his neck. "I knew I was right to wait for you," she murmured.

His [illegible]. "We're [illegible] meant to be together." He slipped her [illegible] between his teeth. [illegible] interested in making up for lost time.

Gemma's [illegible] as his lips moved down her throat towards her breast. "For now," she [illegible] "this [illegible]," and she opened her arms to her [illegible]—the one that [illegible] she wanted.

WEDDING AT WAVERLEY CREEK

by

Jessica Hart

Jessica Hart was born in West Africa, and has suffered from itchy feet ever since, travelling and working around the world in a wide variety of interesting but very lowly jobs, all of which have provided inspiration on which to draw when it comes to the settings and plots of her stories. Now she lives a rather more settled existence in York, where she has been able to pursue her interest in history, although she still yearns sometimes for wider horizons. If you'd like to know more about Jessica, visit her website www.jessicahart.co.uk.

CHAPTER ONE

ELLIE parked the ute in the shade of the gum tree and got out. She was stiff after the long drive, and she paused for a moment with her hand on the door, her eyes on the homestead before her.

Bushman's Creek. Jack's home.

It was over three years since she had seen him, but his image shimmered in the heat as clearly as if he stood before her as he had then, vibrant with reckless energy, smiling that smile that made the breath clog in her throat, brown eyes alight with laughter.

Ellie sighed. She had tried so hard to forget Jack. She had reminded herself a million times that Jack was simply an old friend, someone who thought of her—if he thought of her at all—as no more than the kid sister he had never had.

She had tortured herself by remembering every one of his girlfriends, all of whom had been pretty and lively and about as different from her as they could possibly be. She had even stayed away for three long years in the hope that his memory would fade, but none of it had done any good. All she had wanted was to see him again.

And now she was back.

She had thought it would be safe enough. Jack, her mother had said vaguely, was away. No risk of running into him and getting sucked back into that cycle of hopeless longing. Ellie remembered the confidence with which she had set off that morning, and smiled wryly to herself. She should have known better. Jack might not be here, but the memory of him lurked wherever she looked, almost as disturbing and exciting as Jack himself.

Making a determined effort to push his image aside, Ellie banged the door shut with unnecessary force and headed across the dusty yard to the homestead. She wasn't here because of Jack. She was here to find out exactly what her wayward elder sister was doing, and why she was staying with Jack's brother, Gray.

'Ellie!' Far from seeming guilty or defensive, as Ellie had half expected, Lizzy was delighted to see her. 'I can't tell you how much I've been longing for someone to gossip with,' she confided when the excitement of their first meeting for three years was over and they were sitting at the worn kitchen table. 'It's been so *boring* with no one to talk to all day.'

At least that gave Ellie the opening she needed. 'Lizzy, what are you doing here?' she asked. 'Mum told me you'd broken off your engagement and moved in with Gray...what on earth's going on?'

'Oh, trust Mum to get the wrong end of the stick!' Lizzy rolled her eyes. 'I *have* broken off my engagement, but of course I haven't moved in with Gray! We decided we weren't suited a long time ago. No, I'm just holding the fort until Clare gets back.'

'Clare? Who's Clare?'

'Gray's wife. Didn't Mum tell you about the wedding?'

Ellie shook her head in confusion. 'Do you think you could start again at the beginning?'

'It's perfectly simple.' Lizzy poured boiling water into the teapot and turned to set it on the table. 'Gray married an English girl called Clare a couple of months ago. I wish you could have been here, Ellie. It was a lovely wedding.'

She sighed nostalgically as she pulled out a chair and sat down. 'They're in England at the moment, having a long-overdue honeymoon. I was at a loose end anyway, and it suited me to get away from Perth for a while and help out here,' she explained as she poured the tea into two mugs. 'But I'll be hot-footing it home as soon as they get back, so you can tell Mum to stop worrying!'

Ellie took the mug her sister held out automatically. 'Gray's not here?' she said, as if she had only just realised what Lizzy had said. 'Do you mean you're here on your own?'

'Oh, no,' said Lizzy casually. 'Jack's here.'

Ellie's heart jerked painfully, the way it always did whenever Jack's name was mentioned, and she put the mug down with a hand that was not quite steady.

'Jack?' she said, horribly conscious of the tight, high note in her voice. What was it about the mere thought of Jack that made it hard to breathe normally? She cleared her throat. 'I thought Mum said that he was away.'

'He was. He travelled around the States and South America for a while, but he came home about a month ago. I'm surprised Mum hasn't heard.'

Ellie didn't reply. Green eyes oddly unfocused, she was gazing out of the window. Beyond the verandah, the great ghost gums hung over the creek, their branches outlined in crystalline detail against the blue glare of the outback sky, but Ellie didn't see them. Jack's face shimmered in front of her eyes, and all at once she was intensely conscious of the wooden chair beneath her thighs, of the colour of the mug and the smell of the tea and the beat of her own heart.

Jack. The world was more vivid just knowing that he was near.

'How…how is he?' she asked, trying desperately to sound casual.

'Well…' Lizzy hesitated, and at the sound of steps outside an expression that was almost relief flitted across her face. 'You can see for yourself,' she said. 'This'll be Jack now.'

There was a clatter as the screen door leading out to the verandah banged shut, and without quite realising what she was doing Ellie rose to her feet, clutching the back of her chair for support as she faced the door.

Jack was brushing the dust off his hat as he came into the kitchen. 'Lizzy, have you—' He broke off as he realised that Lizzy wasn't alone, and looked enquiringly.

Every time Ellie prayed that the magic would be broken, and every time it was the same. All Jack had to do was walk into the room and the air evaporated from her lungs, leaving her breathless and giddy and intensely conscious of the blood singing along her veins.

Every time she prayed that he would be less attractive than she had remembered, but he never was. He was always exactly the same. The same long, lean body, the same dark blond hair, the same brown eyes starred with laughter lines. The same puzzled look as he searched his memory for why she looked vaguely familiar.

He hadn't carried *her* image in his heart since they had last met, Ellie thought sadly. She was used to not being remembered. It wasn't that she was plain. She was just unremarkable, just ordinary. Ordinary brown hair, ordinary eyes, a quiet, ordinary face.

'Hello, Jack.'

Her fingers dug into the back of the chair, she forced herself to sound casual. It was always like this, pretending to be politely pleased to be meeting an old friend, terrified that someone would guess how she felt. Sometimes Ellie marvelled that no one ever had. Couldn't they all *see* what he did to her just by standing there? Couldn't they hear her heart thudding against her ribs?

Jack's face cleared in belated recognition. 'Ellie!' he said, smiling as he gave her a brotherly hug. 'I didn't recognise you there for a moment. You've grown up!'

She had grown up a long time ago, but Jack hadn't noticed. He would always be vaguely surprised to discover that she wasn't still running around in dungarees with her hair in bunches, Ellie thought with an edge of bitterness. She would only ever be Lizzy's little sister, too young to play, too young to dance, too young to kiss.

'It's good to see you again,' he went on with a final squeeze of her shoulders. 'I haven't seen you for ages.'

'Three and a half years,' said Ellie, then cursed herself for sounding as if she had been keeping count. 'About,' she added lamely. Her knees felt weak from his touch, and she sank back down onto her chair.

Jack laid his hat on the table, and it seemed to Ellie that a faint shadow crossed his face. 'What have you been doing with yourself all that time?' he asked.

Loving you. Trying to forget you. 'Oh, you know... working, travelling, that kind of thing.'

She watched him covertly as he pulled out a chair and sat down opposite, and saw with something of a shock that he wasn't quite the same after all. For the first time since she had known him, he looked tired. The vibrant, restless energy had gone. There was a strained look now in the eyes that had used to glint with daredevil charm, and the long, curling mouth had hardened into a bleak line.

A cold feeling settled in the pit of Ellie's stomach as she looked at him. What's happened? she wanted to cry, but Jack was forcing a smile, asking her where she had been travelling.

'In the States, mostly,' she said, still distracted by the change in Jack's expression. 'I was a nanny for a bit, and then I got a job on a ranch in Wyoming. I loved it there.'

'I don't know why you didn't just stay at home,' commented Lizzy, eyeing her younger sister with resigned affection. 'I can't believe that you spent three years in the States and didn't go to New York once!'

'I don't like cities.' Ellie wondered why she always felt so defensive about it. 'I'm not like you, Lizzy. I'm a country girl.'

'There's nothing wrong with that,' said Jack, smiling slightly as he looked from one sister to the other.

It was hard to believe that they were related. Lizzy was blond and bubbly with bright blue eyes and an indefinable air of style, overshadowing, as always, her quiet sister. Both girls wore jeans, but there the resemblance ended. Lizzy's jeans were beautifully cut, and she wore with them a fine white shirt more suitable to shopping or a casual alfresco lunch than an outback cattle station.

Ellie, on the other hand, looked ready to help out down at the cattle yards. Her jeans were serviceable, the blue shirt worn with use, and the hair waving softly around her face had been cut to demand as little attention as possible.

Aware of how dull she always appeared compared to vibrant Lizzy, Ellie hurried to change the subject.

'Lizzy's been telling me that Gray's married,' she said a little breathlessly. 'I'm sorry I missed the wedding.'

'So am I,' said Jack, and she looked at him in surprise. She couldn't imagine Jack not being at his own brother's wedding.

'You weren't here?'

He shook his head.

'Why, what were you doing?'

There was an odd little pause. Jack glanced at Lizzy, then opened his mouth to speak, but before he could answer a crackle broke the suddenly tense silence, followed, incredibly, by the sound of babbling.

Ellie, who had just lifted her mug, froze with it halfway to her lips and stared around her in puzzlement. It was so unlikely a sound to hear in the bachelors' kitchen at Bushman's Creek that she couldn't help wondering if she had imagined it. 'Did you hear that?' she asked hesitantly. 'It sounded almost like a baby!'

Lizzy and Jack grinned. 'It is a baby,' said Lizzy, pointing at a baby alarm plugged in on the worktop to show where the noise was coming from. 'That's Alice.'

Ellie put down the mug so abruptly that tea slopped over onto the table, but she didn't notice. She was staring at her sister as all sorts of wild possibilities chased themselves through her mind. 'You've got a *baby*?' she said, very carefully, and Lizzy laughed at her expression.

'Don't worry, she's not mine—although I wish she was! She's so gorgeous!'

'You don't say that when you're trying to feed her,' said Jack, and even in the midst of her amazement Ellie couldn't help the familiar twist of envy as she saw the affectionate look that passed between him and her sister. Lizzy and Jack were the same age, and they had always been very good friends.

'Where did this baby come from?' she asked blankly. 'Surely she's not Gray's?'

She was looking at Lizzy, who was shaking her head, and so was quite unprepared for what came next.

'She's mine,' said Jack.

A clock somewhere ticked into the long, long silence

that followed. Very slowly, Ellie's eyes moved from her sister to Jack.

He didn't say what I thought he said, she told herself frantically. He's joking. Staring at him, green eyes dark and blank with shock, she willed his face to break into a teasing grin, hoping against hope that he would laugh and tell her that of course he wasn't serious, of course he didn't have a baby.

Having a baby would mean that he had found someone he truly loved and had settled down, and why would he do that? He was careless, carefree Jack, who always had a different girl in tow, who had always enjoyed life far too much to saddle himself with the responsibility of a wife and child.

No! she wanted to shout. Tell me it's not true!

But Jack only looked back at her with a twisted smile. 'It was a surprise to me, too,' he said.

It was the news Ellie had dreaded as long as she had known that she was in love with Jack. She hadn't been able to do anything about the fact that he didn't love her, but loving him had been bearable because his affairs were never serious, because it had been obvious that Jack simply wasn't the type to settle down.

Except that now he had.

Ellie felt as if an iron hand had gripped her round her throat, and she was submerged in a great, rolling wave of despair mingled with sheer rage at her own stupidity. How many times had she let herself believe that Jack would never commit himself to one woman? All those nights, all those *years* wasted, dreaming that he would look at her one day and the scales would fall from his eyes, that he would realise then that she was the only woman he could ever truly love!

How could she have pinned so many hopes on such a

fantasy? Of *course* Jack was going to find someone special in the end. Of course it wasn't going to be her.

Jack and Lizzy were both looking at her expectantly. She had to say something, but her tongue was so unwieldy in her mouth that she had trouble getting the words out. 'I…didn't realise…you were…married, too,' she managed at last. Her voice sounded as if it was coming from a long way away.

Sadness flickered across Jack's face. 'I'm not.'

'But…' Totally confused by now, Ellie looked dumbly at the baby alarm, which was still emitting the sound of incomprehensible baby conversation. Had she misheard after all?

Lizzy put a hand on Jack's arm. 'Do you want me to explain?' she asked gently.

'No, it's all right.' Jack mustered a reassuring smile. 'I'll do it. I'm going to have to get used to telling people how I suddenly acquired a daughter.'

Turning back to Ellie, he drew a deep breath. 'Pippa—Alice's mother—came to Bushman's Creek as a cook, nearly two years ago now. She was an English girl, travelling around Australia, but as soon as she arrived it was as if she'd always belonged here. I fell in love with her the moment I laid eyes on her.

'She was…' Jack's voice cracked slightly, and he paused for a moment. 'She was the kind of person who lights up a room when they walk into it,' he went on at last.

Like you, thought Ellie.

'I'd never felt like that about anybody before,' said Jack, unaware of her mental interruption. 'I suddenly realised what love was all about. It was the same for Pippa. We had three wonderful months together, and then…'

Ellie swallowed. 'Then what?'

'Then we blew it.' Jack smiled tiredly. 'We had one of those stupid little arguments about nothing, and somehow it got out of control. Before either of us quite knew what had happened Pippa had packed her bags and gone back to England, saying she never wanted to see me again.'

He sighed, and although he looked at Ellie it was obvious that he was seeing the girl he had loved and lost. 'I should have stopped her getting on that plane, but I was too angry, and too pig-headed, and too bloody *stupid* to go after her straight away,' he said with sudden bitterness. 'I told myself Pippa was too emotional and dramatic for the outback, and that I'd soon get over her.

'The only trouble was that I didn't. I spent a year missing her and pretending that I wasn't. I tried everything I could to forget her, but nothing worked. There were memories of her wherever I looked, and in the end I thought it would be easier if I went away for a while. I spent a little while in the States, and then went on to South America. I thought that would be a place where there would be no associations to remind me of Pippa, but it was no good, and in the end I just gave up.'

The way she had done, thought Ellie, remembering her own desperate attempts to dislodge Jack from her mind. She understood more than he realised. She knew exactly what it was like to realise that there was no point in struggling any longer and that she might as well accept that Jack was the only man she was ever going to love.

'I got on a plane to London,' he told her, his voice slowing as he reached the most painful part of his story. 'I knew I could contact Pippa through her sister, so I went there first. I'd planned exactly what I was going to say. I was going to tell Pippa just how much I loved her.

I was going to beg her to marry me and come back to Bushman's Creek. I was going to promise to make her happy.'

Ellie listened numbly. Every word was like another layer of ice closing around her heart. She wanted to close her eyes and cover her ears, but she couldn't look away from the anguish in Jack's expression as he stopped to draw a steadying breath.

'I was too late,' he said, his voice empty of all expression. 'When I finally got to Clare's flat, there was no one there.' He looked away, his gaze resting blindly on the kettle, a muscle working in his jaw the only clue to the suppressed emotion inside him. 'A neighbour told me that Pippa had died not long after her baby had been born, and that her sister had taken the baby to be with its father in Australia.'

'Oh, Jack…' said Ellie helplessly. The despair she had felt when she had learnt that Jack was a father seemed so trivial compared with what he had gone through, and she ached with pity for him and the girl he had loved.

'That was the first I knew about Alice,' he said, as if the words were being torn from him. 'I couldn't take it in at first. All I knew was that Pippa was dead and that I hadn't been able to tell her how much I loved her.'

'Clare is Pippa's sister.' Seeing that Jack was struggling, Lizzy continued for him. 'Before Pippa died, she made Clare promise to bring Alice out to Australia so that she could grow up with Jack at Bushman's Creek.'

Ellie listened, but her attention was focused on Jack. His face was so bleak that she ached to comfort him, but there was nothing she could do and nothing she could say that would help.

'Clare kept her promise,' Lizzy was saying, 'but of

course by the time she got here Jack had gone. She and Gray looked after Alice together until he came home.'

'And now I *am* home,' said Jack. 'Gray and Clare have got their own life to lead, and I've got a daughter to look after.' He looked seriously at Ellie. 'I don't know what I'd have done when Clare left if it hadn't been for Lizzy.'

'You'd have learnt to change nappies even quicker than you have done!' Lizzy replied. 'And talking of changing nappies…'

She cocked an eye at the baby alarm, from where Alice's chattering had changed to a distinctly imperious shout, and Jack pushed back his chair with a rueful smile.

'I seem to be getting plenty of practice anyway,' he said. He glanced at Ellie. 'Do you want to come and meet my daughter?'

Ellie heard herself say that she would like that, and somehow managed to get to her feet. To her own surprise, her legs were quite steady as she followed Jack along the corridor.

Jack pushed open the door, and at the sight of him a baby with wisps of blond hair and a pair of cheeky brown eyes exactly like her father's broke into a beaming smile. She had hauled herself to her feet and was clutching the bars of the cot, her chubby little legs bouncing unsteadily up and down as she struggled valiantly to keep herself upright.

'Dada!' she shouted.

Jack swung her out of the cot, his big hands holding her securely up in the air, and the way he smiled lovingly up at his daughter before bringing her down to his face for a kiss made something ache deep inside Ellie. There was absolutely no doubt who held first place in Jack's heart now.

'This is Alice,' he said proudly, then sniffed cautiously

at her nappy. 'But I think I'd better change her before I introduce you properly!'

Ellie perched on an old toy box and watched as he laid Alice down on a table that had clearly been set up for just this purpose and unbuttoned her Babygro. It was obvious that the whole business of looking after a baby was new to him, but the tenderness and care with which he changed Alice's nappy were all the more moving for being so ham-fisted.

Watching Jack's harassed attempts to remove the dirty nappy, set a clean one in place and prevent Alice from rolling away to play with her toes, it seemed to Ellie that he had never been closer, nor, perversely, so out of reach. It was hard to imagine the old Jack changing a nappy, but now that the faint air of glamour which had clung to him in the past had been dulled by the preoccupations of fatherhood, he was no more likely to notice her than he had been before, when he had been the life and soul of the party.

Less, Ellie amended to herself. Jack's womanising days might be done, but he clearly had no thought for anything other than Alice and his bittersweet memories of Pippa. The faint hope that it would be her turn one day had gone. She would just have to accept that all she could ever be to Jack now was a friend.

And friends helped when they were needed.

Getting to her feet, Ellie wordlessly removed the dirty nappy from Jack's hapless grasp, disposed of it, and deftly fastened the clean one into place when he stood gratefully back.

'How do you make it look so easy?' he demanded as he wrestled with the poppers on the Babygro.

Ellie laughed. 'I've had lots of practice. Unlike Lizzy, I've always been a hands-on aunt, and I looked after several babies when I was a nanny in the States. There was a time when I could change nappies in my sleep.'

'I feel as if I'm doing that now,' Jack admitted ruefully. 'Only not as efficiently as you!'

He let Alice grab hold of his fingers and pulled her into a sitting position. 'I had no idea how exhausting it is to look after a baby,' he went on, looking over Alice's small blond head at Ellie. 'I think I had a vague idea you had to give them a bottle occasionally but otherwise they spent most of their time sleeping.

'I know better now, don't I?' he said to Alice, who burbled happily back at him. Finding her father conveniently at hand, she let go of his fingers and clutched at his shirt instead, using him as support to pull herself to her feet with a triumphant yell.

'I don't think I've ever been as tired as I've been this last month.' Jack's hands were ready to catch Alice the moment she lost her balance. 'I've had a crash course in fathering—and it's not even as if I've been able to spend all day with her. Lizzy's been the one who's really been looking after her.'

'Well, it looks as if you're doing a good job,' said Ellie. 'I never thought I'd see you change a nappy!'

'I know.' Jack grimaced. 'If you'd asked me two months ago if I wanted kids, I'd have said, No way! But the moment Clare put Alice in my arms it felt absolutely right.' He smoothed Alice's soft blond hair in a gesture of such tenderness that Ellie felt tears sting her eyes. 'Right, but scary. I've never been responsible for anyone before. She's so small and dependent. I'm terrified I won't be able to look after properly.'

'Of course you will,' said Ellie stoutly. 'Look at her! She's absolutely gorgeous!'

As if understanding, Alice looked over her shoulder at

Ellie and gave her a wide smile that showed off her four little teeth. 'Do you want to hold her?' offered Jack, scooping her up, and Ellie held out her arms.

'I'd love to,' she admitted.

Alice was a warm, solid weight, and Ellie cuddled her, loving her sweet baby smell. 'I love babies,' she confessed, and laughed as Alice explored her face with inquisitive little fingers. 'How old is she?'

'Ten months.' Jack's expression was suddenly sad. 'I've missed a lot of her life so far.'

'You're making up for it now, Jack,' said Ellie gently. 'She's happy and healthy and secure. You can't do more for her than that.'

'If she is, it's mostly due to Clare.' Jack wasn't ready to be reassured. 'She spent all her time with Alice, and I worry that I can't do the same. But with Gray away, I can't run the station and look after a baby. Lizzy's been fantastic, but I can't ask her to stay much longer. I know she's got plans to launch out into a business of her own, and she must be starting to think about going back to Perth soon.'

'I'm sure she'll stay until Clare gets back. It doesn't sound as if that'll be too long.'

'I know, but it's not fair to rely on Clare. She's done so much for Alice already, and she and Gray deserve some time on their own.' Jack picked up one of the toys Alice had thrown out of her cot and turned it absently between his fingers. 'I've been thinking about it a lot, and I've decided that Alice and I need to make a fresh start in a place of our own.'

Ellie rested her cheek against Alice's downy head. She could see that the idea made sense. 'Are you thinking of buying another property?'

'The old Murray place is up for sale,' he told her. 'Len

Murray died a couple of months ago, and his daughter isn't interested in the station. A lot of land to the north and east is being sold separately, but Waverley would still be a fair-sized property. It might be just what I'm looking for.'

'But, Jack, Len Murray was a virtual recluse,' Ellie protested, lifting her head in concern. 'I remember the last time Dad went over there, he said Len hadn't done any work on the station for fifteen years and everything was in a terrible state—and that was nearly five years ago. Things won't have improved since then.'

'It's worth a look,' said Jack stubbornly. 'Waverley Creek wouldn't be more than—what?—half an hour in a plane from here. I don't want to take Alice too far from Clare, and I can't think of anywhere else as convenient that's likely to come up for sale. I'm going to look at it tomorrow.'

He glanced at Ellie, who had settled Alice instinctively on her hip and was regarding him with a faint frown. 'Why don't you come with me?'

'Me?' she echoed in astonishment.

'You know more about running a station than most people,' Jack pointed out. 'You were always out mending fences and catching bulls when Lizzy was painting her nails and dreaming of the bright lights.'

'Yes, well, it turns out that Lizzy's experience is more useful than mine when it comes to getting a job,' sighed Ellie.

'Not to me,' said Jack. 'Much as I love Lizzy, I don't think she'd be much use when it comes to buying a cattle station. You'd know what you were looking at, and I could really do with a sensible opinion.'

He looked at her with a coaxing smile that crumbled

all her defences at a stroke. 'Come with me,' he pleaded. 'You could stop me doing something stupid!'

It wasn't fair of him to smile at her like that, thought Ellie, hugging Alice to her as if to ward off the force of his charm. If she were sensible, she would tell him she was busy. She would accept that Jack was never going to love her and she would go away and make herself forget him. She absolutely *wouldn't* torture herself by spending time with him and letting herself be sucked back into the old, terrible spiral of secret longing.

But could she really resist the prospect of a day by his side? Ellie asked herself honestly. So what if it was only because she could drive a truck and lasso a calf and talk knowledgeably about branding and breeding programmes? For the first time in all those long, hopeless years of dreaming she had a chance to be alone with Jack and know that he wanted her to be there.

So how sensible was she?

'Go on,' said Jack. 'You'll enjoy it.'

And Ellie succumbed to temptation, as she had known all along that she would.

'All right,' she said. 'I'd love to come.'

CHAPTER TWO

'WELL, what do you think?'

Ellie hesitated. There were a couple of chairs on the Waverley verandah, but, like everything else in the homestead, they were so old and rickety that she and Jack had elected to sit at the top of the verandah steps instead.

She thought of the homestead they had just finished inspecting, each room more depressingly grimy than the last, of the overgrown yards, broken fences and dilapidated sheds. 'It would be…a challenge,' she said at last.

Jack couldn't help grinning at the careful tact of her reply. 'You think I'm mad to even consider it, don't you, Ellie?'

'No,' she said surprisingly. 'This must have been a really nice property once, and it could be again—but it would take an awful lot of work.'

'I don't mind that. You don't have time to think when you're working.'

Ellie nodded, her eyes on the broken windmill. 'Sometimes it's easier that way,' she agreed.

The understanding in her voice made Jack glance at her curiously. It had been good to have her with him today. He had asked her to come on a whim, and had been surprised at how pleased he had been when she agreed.

Of course, he had always been fond of Ellie. He and Gray had grown up with Lizzy and Kevin, but Ellie had been much younger, a quiet little girl overshadowed by her boisterous brother and sister, only allowed to tag along on sufferance. Lizzy and Kevin had complained loudly about having to look after her, but he and Gray had never had a little sister, and, although they would have died rather than admit it at the time, they had found Ellie's open adoration rather appealing.

Now he found his gaze resting on her profile as she looked out at the ruined yards, lost in her own thoughts, and he wondered why she had ever needed to lose herself in work. For the first time it occurred to Jack how little he actually knew her. Ellie had always been a listener, not a talker. Even as a little girl, she could be relied upon to applaud his successes, admire his plans and sympathise with his woes, but she had never told him any of her own.

But then, thought Jack, he had never asked.

Suddenly he became aware that Ellie had turned her head and was looking at him, a question in her clear green eyes. 'Sorry,' he said, recollecting himself hurriedly. 'What did you say?'

'I just asked what *you* thought about Waverley.'

'I think I'd like to see a bit more before I make up my mind,' said Jack on impulse. He got to his feet, brushing the dust off his jeans. 'Shall we explore? I saw some saddles in one of the sheds, and those horses looked as if they could do with a ride.'

He set off with his long, easy stride towards the paddock, where a group of horses grazed in the sparse shade, their tails twitching against the flies. Ellie followed meekly, as she had done so often in the past.

'Do you think we should?' she asked dubiously when she caught up with Jack at the ramshackle fence.

'Why not?' he asked, and produced a piercing whistle that made the horses lift their heads and stare at them suspiciously.

'Well, it's not your property,' Ellie pointed out with a dry look. 'We ought to ask someone before we just waltz off with their horses.'

'There's no one to ask,' said Jack reasonably. 'And anyway, we're not taking the horses, we're just borrowing them for a while.'

He whistled again, and this time the horses succumbed to curiosity and came cantering over to inspect them. They shoved their heads over the fence, and Jack had to raise his voice over the sound of their whickered greetings.

'Who's going to mind? If I were the seller, I'd be more than happy to let anyone thinking seriously about taking this place off my hands do whatever they wanted, and if I were the horses, I'd be glad of the exercise!'

Seeing that Ellie was still looking unconvinced, he patted the neck of a big bay with a white blaze down its nose. 'What do you say, old fella? Do you want to show us Waverley Creek?'

The horse tossed its head up and down and snorted. 'There you are!' said Jack virtuously. 'He's dying to get out.'

It was typical of Jack that he could even get horses to do exactly what he wanted, thought Ellie, resigned, but she couldn't help laughing, and went off with him quite willingly to find the tack.

The horses didn't prove quite as eager to be ridden as Jack had so confidently predicted, but, like him, Ellie had been riding since she could walk, and she was more than capable of bringing her mount under control. After trying a few initial tricks, the horses settled down, and they headed quietly enough along the homestead creek, with only the occasional half-hearted buck or skittish sidestep to spoil the peace.

They picked their way through the trees that clustered along the banks of the creek. During the wet season it would be full, with an angry torrent, but it was long months since they had had any rain and the last of the water had collected in deep green pools. It was very still. Beyond the fractured shade, the heat shimmered over the red earth, wavering in the glare of the sun.

Ellie was very conscious of Jack riding beside her. He sat easily on the big bay, holding it in check with one hand while the other rested casually on his thigh. Oblivious to the birds that protested at their approach, wheeling and squawking in indignant crowds before settling back into the branches above their heads in huffy silence, he was assessing the land with narrowed brown eyes. Jack might have been the life and soul of every party in the district, but that didn't mean he didn't know just as much about what it took to run a successful cattle station as the other, less social graziers.

Content to let Jack worry about yields and crops and acreages, Ellie breathed in the scent of dust and hot, dry leaves, and gave herself up to the pleasure of being with him. Last night, lying alone in the bed she had slept in since she was a child, she had given herself a severe talking-to. It was time to stop dreaming. Jack was grieving for Pippa, and had more than enough to worry about adjusting to fatherhood. He wasn't ready to think about love again, and he might never be.

She couldn't stop loving him, but she could stop dreaming she would ever be more to him than a friend, and right now, riding beneath the trees in the hot hush of afternoon, with Jack close beside her, friendship was enough for Ellie. She felt alert and alive in a way she hadn't for three long years. She could smell the drifting fragrance of eucalyptus in the air, mingled with the scent of red dust and horse and the leather on her hands. She could hear the horses' hooves, the jingle of the bit, the galahs squabbling in the treetops.

Most of all, she could see Jack, outlined in heart-wrenching clarity against the trees on the far side of the creek. It was as if only now she could let herself believe that he was really there, and her senses tingled with awareness of every tiny detail about him: his fingers around the reins, the glint of hairs at his wrist, the slanting shadow cast by the brim of his hat.

Turning his head, Jack saw her smile and he lifted his brows. 'You look happy,' he commented.

A faint flush stole up Ellie's cheeks. 'I'm just glad to be home again,' she said, and, afraid that the expression in her eyes would betray her, she looked around her at the quiet creek.

'I missed all this so much when I was away. I was homesick for three years,' she confessed with a shame-faced smile. 'Sometimes I'd close my eyes and wish that I was home, somewhere just like this, and every time when I opened them again and found that I wasn't, I wanted to cry.'

Ellie stopped, aware that she had said more than she had meant to, but Jack didn't appear to have guessed that he had always been there in her dream. When she glanced at him, she found that he was watching her, a faint frown between his brows.

'Why didn't you come home if you missed it that badly?' he asked her, vaguely disturbed by how much he hated the idea of Ellie being miserable and alone.

'I thought about it lots of times, but I knew that if I did I'd just end up having to get a job in the city, like Lizzy, and that wouldn't have been any better. I only ever wanted to be in the outback.'

With you, she added mentally, knowing that she could never tell Jack that.

'But couldn't you have gone home? It's not as if you wouldn't be a useful person to have around,' said Jack, puzzled. 'There must have been lots for you to do on the station.'

'I could have done, but Mum and Dad retired last year. They're still living on the station, but there isn't a lot of room in their new house, and although I can always stay in the homestead with Kevin and Sue, I don't think it's fair on them to have me hanging around permanently. It's fine to come back for a visit, but it's their home now, not mine.'

Concerned, Jack turned in his saddle to study her. 'So what are you going to do?'

'I'm not quite sure.' Ellie shrugged slightly and tried to laugh. 'Ideally, I'd find a job here, but Mathison isn't exactly full of career opportunities. It would be different if I could do something useful, like fly a helicopter, but I can't.' She sighed. 'I could be a station hand or a housekeeper, I suppose, but those kind of jobs are only ever seasonal, and I'd never be able to call anywhere home.'

Jack was frowning. 'It's not fair on you. I know Lizzy couldn't wait to head for the city, but it's different for you. Couldn't you and Kevin have run the station together?'

'Not once Kevin married Sue. Sue's great, and she's always really welcoming, but it's their property and they need to get on and run it their way.'

'I still don't think it's fair,' said Jack stubbornly, and she smiled faintly.

'It's just the way things are, Jack. I don't think it ever occurred to Dad that Lizzy and I wouldn't marry nice local boys and end up on their properties!'

Jack ran a mental eye over all the eligible men in the district. He could think of a few who could do with a capable wife like Ellie, although none who would be good enough for her. 'Perhaps it'll still happen,' he said, even though the thought gave him a strangely hollow feeling.

Ellie kept her eyes fixed between the horse's ears and smiled a brief, mechanical smile. 'Perhaps,' she said.

They rode in silence for a while, until they came to a place where the water had collected in a deep pool between the rocks and the trees leant over to admire their reflections in its still surface.

'Let's stop here,' said Jack.

He tied the horses up in the shade while Ellie sat on a rock worn smooth and red with time. Taking off her hat, she ran her fingers through her wavy brown hair and leant back on her hands with a sigh of contentment. Sheltered from the outback glare, the waterhole seemed to her a peaceful, almost magical place, but the tranquil atmosphere appeared lost on Jack.

He prowled restlessly around the water's edge, lobbing in an occasional stone to gauge its depth. 'I could teach Alice to swim here,' he said as he hunkered down to test the temperature of the water with his hand. 'It reminds me of the waterhole at home. We used to swim there all the time when we were kids.'

'I remember,' said Ellie. 'I used to love our visits to Bushman's Creek.'

'We had some good times, didn't we?' Jack straightened, his nostalgic smile fading. 'I want Alice to grow up with those kind of memories,' he said seriously.

'She will, Jack.'

'What if she's lonely?' The worried look was back in Jack's eyes as he came to sit next to Ellie on her rock.

'You had Lizzy and Kevin, and I had Gray, but Alice won't have anyone to play with in the same way.'

Leaning forward, he rested his arms on his thighs, holding his hat loosely between his knees as he gazed abstractedly across the water. 'Waverley Creek's got a lot of problems, but it feels like the right station for me,' he said. 'I'm just not sure if it's the right place for Alice.'

Ellie was very conscious of his nearness, and of the fact that Jack was quite unaware of hers. It meant nothing to him that her thigh was barely inches away from his, or that by leaning very slightly together their shoulders would touch. He was preoccupied with more important matters, like his daughter's future.

'The right place for Alice is wherever you are, Jack,' she told him, wishing the same could be true for her.

'Even if it means growing up on her own?'

Ellie's eyes rested on the dust between the rocks, where she was tracing a pattern with the heel of her boot. 'You might meet someone else,' she made herself suggest. 'You could have more children.'

'I don't want to meet anyone else.' Jack's voice was flat and final. 'What Pippa and I had was special. How could I expect to find a love like that again?'

'Maybe you'll find a different kind of love,' said Ellie, without lifting her gaze from the dust at her feet, and she sensed rather than saw Jack's involuntary recoil at the very idea.

'Easy for you to say,' he said harshly. 'You've never been in love.'

'Yes, I have.'

Jack was taken aback at the edge to the quiet voice, and he turned his head to look at Ellie curiously. She sounded almost bitter, he thought. Surely she was too young to sound like that?

He did a quick calculation in his head and realised with something of a shock that she must be at least twenty-five. Plenty old enough to learn about disappointment and regret and heartache. It just seemed odd to think of little Ellie in love, Jack decided. She had always been such a tomboy.

She still was. He thought of how she had looked when he had picked her up this morning. She had been waiting for him at the airstrip, perched on the bonnet of an old ute, looking trim and practical in jeans and an old blue shirt. No bag, no sunglasses, no lipstick, no fuss, Jack had noted with approval. Just a hat in her hand, and she was ready to go. Good old Ellie; she was always the same.

He glanced at her affectionately, but she was looking away, and he found himself studying her averted face with amusement that faded into a dawning sense of puzzlement.

Had Ellie always had such smooth honey-coloured skin? And where had that delicate bone structure come from? Jack felt oddly unsettled. It was like running up to someone you knew, only to discover at the last moment that they were a stranger after all. This was the same Ellie who had jumped off the ute to greet him, but suddenly she didn't look like a tomboy at all.

Jack's eyes drifted down to her mouth and he frowned. No, not at all.

'I didn't know,' he said slowly, wondering when she had changed, and why he had never noticed before.

'Why should you?' Ellie spoke lightly, but she kept her face averted.

What kind of man would Ellie fall in love with? thought Jack. What kind of man had stirred the passion banked beneath her quiet surface? Whoever it was, he had changed her from a tomboy into someone disturbingly unfamiliar. Was it the same man who had caused the bitterness in her voice?

'Was it someone you met in the States?' he couldn't help asking.

At first he thought that Ellie wasn't going to answer, but then she shook her head. 'No,' she said in a low voice. 'I went to the States to forget him.'

'And did you?'

Ellie turned slowly until she was looking straight at him, and Jack found himself noticing as if for the first time that her eyes were a beautiful colour, somewhere between grey and green, and very clear.

'No,' she said at last. 'I tried to, but I couldn't.'

'He must be someone special.' There was an odd note in Jack's voice. He was intrigued by the idea of Ellie being in love, but it left him feeling peculiarly ruffled at the same time.

Ellie dropped her eyes, a faint smile just touching the corners of her mouth. 'He is.'

'So, is that why you've come home?' demanded Jack, unable to account for the harshness in his tone. 'To try and work things out with him?'

Her smile faded. 'There's nothing *to* work out. He's not in love with me, and I know that he never will be. It's just a dream, and I've accepted that, but it doesn't stop me loving him. I didn't come home expecting anything to happen,' she told him, almost as if she needed to reassure him. 'I just thought it would be easier being in the same place, that's all.'

'Poor Ellie.' Jack reached over and squeezed her hand. '*You* need to find someone different, too.'

'I know.' To her horror, Ellie felt tears sting her eyes, and she blinked fiercely as she tugged her hand away.

Jack's sympathy was harder to bear than anything else. His clasp was warm and comforting, but it wasn't comfort she wanted from him. 'But you were right; it isn't that easy.'

'No,' he agreed soberly. 'At least you understand how I feel about Pippa. I can't imagine loving anyone else the way I loved her. I know it sounds corny, but it's as if I found the other half of me, and now I've lost it again.'

When Ellie stole a glance at him, he was staring down at the ground beneath his feet, his expression very bleak. 'No one else can take Pippa's place,' he went on after a moment. 'Anyone I met now would have to accept only ever being second best, and I could never ask anyone to do that.'

Ellie's heart twisted at his words, but she knew exactly how he felt. She had tried so hard to fall in love with other men, but deep down she had always known that it would be hopeless. No matter how nice or attractive or charming they were, they would never match up to Jack. Only he would do.

'Yes, I do understand,' she said quietly.

Jack looked up at that, his eyes dark and brown and sad, and his smile rather twisted. 'It looks like we're in the same boat,' he said.

'At least you've got memories.' I've only ever had dreams, Ellie added bitterly to herself. She hadn't lost what Jack had, but she had never known the joy of being loved by him either. 'And you've got Alice.'

'Yes, I've got Alice.' Jack sighed and got restlessly to his feet once more. 'And it's because of Alice that I need to forget about how I feel and think seriously about meeting someone else and getting married. If I don't, she's going to grow up with a succession of housekeepers. She needs a mother, not someone who'll stay for a few weeks or a few months and then get bored or tired of the conditions and go to work somewhere easier.'

'It doesn't have to be like that, does it?'

'No,' he agreed, 'but it probably would be. You know how hard it is to get good, reliable people to stay in the outback. Anyone with any sense would take one look at the homestead back there and head straight back to the town.'

Hunching his shoulders, Jack frowned across the creek. 'I don't think buying Waverley Creek is going to work, Ellie. It's a fine station—or it could be—but perhaps it would be better for Alice if we stayed at Bushman's Creek after all.'

'But you don't want to do that,' Ellie objected, and he sighed as he ran his hand through his hair in a gesture of weariness.

'No, I don't. Quite apart from anything else, it wouldn't be fair on Gray and Clare. But my only alternative is to find myself a wife…and where am I going to find someone who'd be prepared to take on me and Alice and Pippa's ghost?'

He was standing with his back to Ellie, arguing with himself more than with her, and she looked at him with a peculiar mixture of pain and pleasure. The back of his head was utterly familiar to her, and she let her eyes travel longingly from his broad shoulders to the lean hips and down the long legs.

It was wonderful just to be near him. All that time in the States, when she had longed to see him again, and now here he was, and she had to face what she had known all along, that he would never love her the way she loved him. She had dreaded the time that Jack would fall in love, and it hurt just as she had feared that it would...but could she bear to go away again and not see him for another three years?

No, thought Ellie, I can't. Anything would be better than that.

She drew a deep breath. 'What about here?' she asked, before she had a chance to lose her nerve.

'Here?' Jack glanced over his shoulder at Ellie, sitting defensively straight on her rock. She was braced against his scorn, but his expression was half-abstracted, half-puzzled, and he was clearly wondering if he had heard her properly.

'You could marry me,' she heard her voice saying.

Jack swung round at that, to stare blankly at her. 'Marry *you*?' he echoed.

He sounded so incredulous that Ellie flinched. For a moment she was tempted to pretend that she was only joking, but a still, clear voice inside her told her that this would be her only chance. She had got this far, so she might as well see it through, and if Jack laughed or recoiled in disgust, well, at least she would have tried.

'You want someone to live permanently at Waverley Creek and help you look after Alice,' she said, amazed at her own calm control. 'I want to stay permanently in the outback. The conditions here won't bother me, and I'm not likely to get bored like other girls you might get from an agency.'

Jack eyed her uncertainly. His smile had faltered as he realised with a shock that she was quite serious. 'Ellie,' he said rather helplessly, 'I can't marry you.'

'Why not?'

'Because...' Thrown by the directness of the question, Jack raked his fingers through his hair. Surely it was obvious? 'Because...'

'Because you don't love me? I know that.'

'I think I was trying to say because you don't love *me.*'

'Then we're in the same boat,' said Ellie, 'just like you said.'

'But, Ellie, why would you want to marry a man you don't love?' asked Jack, still struggling to come to terms with her extraordinary suggestion.

It was Ellie's turn to get to her feet. Unable to sit still any longer, she went to stand by the edge of the water-hole, where she could look into his face without crowding him. 'I want to stay in the outback,' she told him simply.

Jack's brown eyes narrowed. 'To be near this man you're so in love with?'

'Partly,' she said carefully. 'Partly because I want to belong somewhere. I don't want to have to go to work in the city and just come back for occasional visits. I want a home of my own here, a place I could have a stake in. If I married you, I could help you build up Waverley into a great station again.'

Jack wasn't looking convinced, and she hurried on before he had a chance to turn her down flat.

'Think about it, Jack. A marriage of convenience might not be what either of us wanted, but it could work. I know how you feel about Pippa. You wouldn't have to pretend with me, and I…I wouldn't expect anything from you that you couldn't give.' Ellie tried a smile. 'You'd get stability for Alice, and a free housekeeper on a permanent basis!'

'And what would you get?' asked Jack slowly.

'Security,' she said. 'I haven't got any money, Jack. There's no way I could afford to buy and run a station of my own, and I haven't got any other skills to make a place for myself. The only way I could stay in the outback is to get a job where I'd be completely dependent on someone else…or to marry.'

It seemed so bizarre to be standing at the creek edge, calmly discussing marriage with little Ellie Walker, that Jack shook his head slightly to shake off the feeling of unreality. She had to be desperately unhappy to even think of such an idea, he realised in concern.

'Ellie,' he said, taking her hand, 'you're young. Too young to tie yourself to a man you don't love. You'll meet someone else eventually.'

'I won't, Jack,' she said, and her gaze was very steady. 'There's only ever going to be one man for me.'

'You seem very sure that he doesn't love you,' said Jack, picking his words with care. He let go of her hand. 'What if he changes his mind?'

'He's not going to do that.' Ellie smiled a little sadly. 'I've wasted enough of my life hoping that one day he'd notice me and fall in love with me, but I think it's time I faced reality.'

Her eyes slid away from his, and she turned her head slightly so that Jack shouldn't read the truth in her face.

'I've accepted that it's not going to happen the way I wanted,' she said, 'but I know, too, that I'll never be happy away from him. At least if I married you I'd be able to be near him.' Her voice cracked and she stopped abruptly, afraid that she had already revealed too much.

Jack's eyes rested curiously on her averted face. 'Who is it, Ellie?' he asked, wanting to know but unsurprised when she only shook her head.

'I can't tell you.'

'You don't think that if we got married I'd have a right to know?'

'No.' She still wouldn't look at him. 'It wouldn't make any difference.'

'But it's someone you'd see if you lived with me here?' he persisted.

'Sometimes, yes,' she said cagily.

'It would be easier to make a fresh start,' said Jack gently. 'Being married to me, seeing him but not being able to be with him…that would be very hard.'

'Not as hard as not seeing him at all,' said Ellie. 'I'd have a home, somewhere to belong, and I'd know that I wouldn't have to go away again. I'd have Alice and a chance to share in Waverley. I think it would be enough.'

Jack rubbed a hand over his face and tried to think clearly. 'I don't know, Ellie. It's a crazy idea.'

He stared into the water and thought irrelevantly that it was almost exactly the colour of Ellie's eyes, very green in the sunlight but shading into grey in the shadows, just as her eyes had darkened with unhappiness. Marrying Ellie…it *was* a crazy idea. He couldn't believe that he was even thinking about it.

But he was.

There was no denying that marriage would solve a lot of his problems, and although it would never have occurred to him to think about Ellie before, in many ways she would be ideal. She was practical and sensible, someone you could rely on not to make a fuss or complain or panic when things when wrong.

She would be good for Alice, too. Jack remembered how calmly she had changed Alice's nappy, how she had cuddled her, the easy way she had settled her on her hip. Ellie knew how to deal with babies, and she knew how to deal with cattle.

She wasn't anything like Pippa, of course, but perhaps that would make it easier. Ellie understood exactly how he felt about Pippa, so he wouldn't have to pretend to be in love with her, the way he might have to with someone else. Jack didn't think he could bear to do that.

With Ellie, he would never have to pretend. He could say what he felt, be the way he wanted, and know that she would always accept him, and make no demands on him in return. Yes, she would be an easy person to live with. She wasn't Pippa, but she was a friend. There might be worse marriages.

He stood gazing into the water for so long that Ellie began to lose her nerve. She must have been mad to even suggest it, she thought in panic, and her cheeks burned as the full enormity of what she had done sank in.

Things would never be the same between her and Jack again. He was bound to guess that she was grasping at any chance to be with him. He would feel awkward and embarrassed and would avoid her whenever he could, and she might as well have stayed in the States for all she would see of him.

Why hadn't she thought before she opened her mouth? Ellie asked herself miserably. There was no way Jack would ever marry her. She should have left things the way they were and accepted that she would only ever be a friend. Now he was standing there trying to think of a kind way to tell her that she was the last person he would ever consider marrying.

'Look, forget I mentioned it,' she blurted out at last, unable to bear the silence any longer. 'It was just a silly idea.'

'No, it's not silly,' said Jack to her surprise, and he turned back to face her. 'It's not silly at all.'

Ellie swallowed. 'But?' she asked, hearing the hesitation in his voice.

'But we both need time to think about what getting

married would mean. Marriage is a big step, and we don't want to rush into anything we might both regret.'

'So what are you suggesting?' Ellie's voice was calm, but inside she was trembling wildly at the realisation that he hadn't turned her down flat after all.

'That we wait until after the Wet,' said Jack. 'I'm going to put in an offer to buy Waverley Creek, but it's going to need a lot of work over the next two or three months just to make the homestead habitable. If you stay at home with Kevin and Sue, you could come over and help me.'

He hesitated. 'It seems stupid to say that we need to get to know each other better when we've always known each other, but it might give us a chance to get used to the idea of being married—and a chance to change our minds if we don't think it would work after all. We could spend the wet season working on the homestead together, and then if we both still think it's a good idea, we could get engaged then. Does that sound fair to you?'

'Yes,' said Ellie, hardly daring to believe that Jack was really considering marrying her. 'It sounds very fair.'

In a daze, she picked up her hat and followed Jack over to where the horses waited patiently, twitching their tails against the flies. She let him untie them and took the reins he handed her with the same sense of glorious disbelief.

'I don't think we should tell anyone what we talked about today,' said Jack as he settled his own hat on his head. 'Not even Lizzy.'

'Definitely not Lizzy,' Ellie agreed quickly. Lizzy would be appalled if she knew that her sister was prepared to marry a man who didn't love her, and she would do everything in her power to dissuade her. 'What will you tell her?' she asked, worried that Lizzy would somehow guess what they had discussed anyway.

'Just that we had a good time.' Jack watched her swing herself easily onto the horse and smiled. 'It's true, too. I did.'

He *had* had a good time, he realised with a sense of surprise. Ellie was a very restful person to be with. Somehow she made things seem not only possible, but simple.

The future was suddenly looking much brighter than he would have believed possible when he had left Bushman's Creek that morning, weighed down by worries about Alice and what to do for the best. Now he had not only made a decision about buying Waverley Creek, but Ellie had come up with an amazing solution to the problem of how to care for his daughter.

Jack was conscious of a rush of gratitude. The marriage idea might not work out—he couldn't help thinking that Ellie would change her mind when she thought about it—but at least he was thinking positively about the future now, and for the first time since he had learnt of Pippa's death it seemed less bleak and less lonely. That was due to Ellie.

'I'm glad you came with me today, Ellie,' he said seriously.

Ellie looked down into his warm brown eyes, and her heart melted at the thought that if she married him she would be able to look into them every day.

'So am I,' she said.

CHAPTER THREE

'THERE!' Ellie stood back to admire her handiwork. 'That's the window finished in here.'

She smiled down at Alice, who was having a lovely time banging an old brush around inside an empty paint tin, and gestured at the window with her own paintbrush. 'What do you think, Alice?'

Alice looked up at the sound of her own name, and her face split into an adorably mischievous grin that showed off her two bottom teeth. She was the most sociable baby Ellie had ever met, and loved to talk, chattering away in her own incomprehensible language whenever anyone spoke to her. She jabbered approvingly in reply to Ellie now, and thumped her brush against the wooden floorboards as if for added emphasis.

'That means that she thinks it looks great,' said Jack's voice from behind her, and Ellie swung round.

He was leaning casually against the doorframe in a paint-splattered shirt, wiping his hands with a rag and watching her and his small daughter with amusement. Ellie's heart turned over. The two of them had been working together on the homestead at Waverley Creek for the last couple of months, but her insides still jerked themselves into a ridiculous knot whenever she caught sight of him unexpectedly.

Alice shouted with delight as she spotted her father, and she threw the paintbrush and can aside to crawl eagerly across the floorboards and clutch at the bottom of his jeans. Jack let her clamber unsteadily to her feet, using his legs as a support, before he swung her up into his arms and tossed her high in the air, shrieking with excitement.

Ellie couldn't help laughing. She loved seeing Jack and Alice together. They so obviously adored each other that it was impossible to resent the fact that there was no room in Jack's heart for anyone other than his baby daughter.

'What's she saying now?' she teased him.

Jack caught Alice in his big hands and bent his head towards hers, nodding solemnly as he pretended to understand her excited babble. 'She wants to know why you're still working,' he announced.

'I just wanted to finish the window,' Ellie explained. She put her brush into a jar of turpentine and hunted around for a rag to clean the worst of the paint from her hands. 'How are you getting on in the kitchen?'

'I've finished. Come and see.'

'Oh, Jack, it looks wonderful!' Ellie exclaimed a few moments later as she stood in the middle of the kitchen. It was hard to believe that it was the same room they had inspected with such dismay two months ago. Then, it had been dingy and depressing, encrusted with dust and dirt. Now, with everything scrubbed clean and freshly painted, it had been transformed into a bright, welcoming room.

'It looks a lot better, doesn't it?'

Pleased with her reaction, Jack stood Alice on the worktop and held her hands so that she could balance on her wobbly little legs.

'Gah, gah, boo, *ma*!' she cried, thrilled.

'You're quite right as usual, Alice,' said Jack seriously. 'It *is* time for a beer!'

Ellie laughed, but stole a glance at her watch. 'I could start the window in Alice's bedroom,' she began.

'Oh, no, you couldn't,' he said firmly. 'You've been

working all day, and you've done enough. Here,' he went on, sweeping Alice up and depositing her in Ellie's arms. 'You take Alice and stop arguing. I'll find the beers.'

Ellie was pleasantly weary, and not that sorry to be bullied into carrying Alice out onto the verandah and sitting down for a while. The furniture that had been left in the homestead when Jack bought it had been so old and dirty that Jack had thrown the whole lot away, but he had brought over a couple of canvas chairs and a folding table, where they sat and had lunch or a beer when they had finished work for the day, and Ellie was looking forward to taking the weight off her feet.

She set Alice on the wooden floor and gave her a toy from the bag that Jack had brought with him that morning. He liked to have Alice with him whenever he could, and since he had been spending as much time as possible at Waverley Creek Ellie had got to know his small daughter, and was well on her way to being as besotted by her as Jack himself.

For Ellie, the last two months had been a magical time. It had been wonderful to be home, to be doing something useful, and although cleaning the homestead had been hot, back-breaking work, she had enjoyed seeing the old house come back to life before her eyes.

And then, of course, there was Jack. Ellie didn't care how hard she worked as long as she could sit with him on the verandah here at the end of the day and talk.

They were friends, better friends than they had been before, but still just friends, and she had accepted long ago that Jack wasn't looking for any more than that. Kevin and Sue had begun to raise their eyebrows and comment on the amount of time she and Jack were spending together, but although they had camped overnight in the homestead once or twice, so that they could get more work done, he had treated her exactly as he would a sister.

Jack had never mentioned the idea of marriage again, and Ellie was reluctant to raise the subject in case he had changed his mind. She couldn't bear to think about what would happen if he had. It would mean no more days at Waverley Creek, no more Alice, with her naughty brown eyes and gorgeous smile, no more Jack.

Ellie closed her mind to the very thought. Refusing to consider the future, she was content to be with Jack while she could, storing up memories of sitting alone with him in the dark, of seeing him smile and knowing that there was no one else for miles and miles around.

'Here you are.'

She started as Jack appeared with beers in polystyrene beakers to keep them cold. He handed her one, then squatted down to offer Alice a drink in her special cup. She cast her toy aside and took the cup instantly, her little hands clutching the two handles as she guzzled noisily, her lids with their absurdly long lashes drooping contentedly.

Jack watched her for a moment with a faint smile, then straightened to lean against the verandah rail, facing Ellie. 'Here's to you, Ellie,' he said, raising his beer to her. 'Thank you.'

She glanced up at him in surprise. 'For what?'

'For everything,' he said seriously. 'Do you think I haven't noticed how hard you've worked over the last two months?'

He looked around at the scrubbed verandah and the freshly painted windows. 'This is going to be a nice house when it's finished. If it wasn't for you, I wouldn't be here at all. I certainly wouldn't be able to think about moving in yet.'

Ellie put down her beer and looked at him in consternation. 'You're not thinking about moving in already?'

'We've just got Alice's room to finish,' Jack pointed out. 'The others can wait until we've got more time. It may not be very grand, but at least the house is liveable now. I don't see why we shouldn't move in as soon as possible.'

We? thought Ellie. Did that mean Jack and Alice, or was she included too?

All at once the golden afternoon seemed to dim. Jack was getting impatient, and that meant things were going to change. For better, for worse... Whatever happened, this magical time when she hadn't needed to think about the future was about to end.

Restlessly, Ellie got to her feet. 'I didn't realise you were thinking of moving so soon,' she said.

'Gray and Clare have been back over a month now,' said Jack. 'They're both wonderful with Alice, and there's no denying things are easier with Clare there, but...' He hesitated. 'Well, the fact is that it's harder than I thought it would be. They're so in love, just like Pippa and I were. Sometimes it hurts to see them.'

He turned round to lean his arms on the verandah rail, and his brown gaze rested unseeingly on the distant horizon. 'It's not that they spend their time kissing and cuddling, far from it. It's just the way I see them look at each other, the way they seem to belong together.'

Ellie leant next to him on the rail. 'I can understand that it must be difficult for you,' she said quietly. 'Clare and Pippa were sisters, weren't they? Does she remind you of Pippa?'

'Sometimes,' said Jack. 'She doesn't look anything like Pippa, but every now and then she says something, or turns her head in a certain way, and then it's as if Pippa's standing right in front of me again.'

His mouth twisted painfully. 'You know, a lot of the time I can make myself believe that things are just the way they were before, that Pippa's back in England, just waiting for me to go and apologise for that stupid argument we had. But when I see Clare use the same kind of mannerisms, it brings it all home somehow. Clare wouldn't be here if it wasn't for Pippa, and Pippa is dead.'

'Oh, Jack,' said Ellie helplessly, and when Jack looked into her warm green eyes he felt ashamed for upsetting her.

'Don't look like that, Ellie,' he said, putting his hand over hers, as if she was the one who needed comforting rather than him. 'It's not that bad most of the time. It's not fair of me to complain. It sounds as if I resent Gray's marriage, and I don't at all. I'm really glad that he's found Clare, and that the two of them are so happy together. I just think it would be easier if Alice and I lived here, that's all.'

Alice and I, Ellie noted dully. No one else. 'I see,' she said.

Jack read disapproval into her comment. 'Obviously I won't bring Alice over until everything's ready for her,' he tried to reassure her, 'but I hope it won't be too long now—thanks to you and all the work you've been doing here.'

Ellie mustered a smile. 'I'm glad I could help.'

'You've certainly done that. I could never have done it without you,' said Jack sincerely. He looked out at the land with satisfaction. 'Only another week or so, and this will be home.' Glancing at Ellie with a sudden, boyish smile, he admitted, 'I can't wait!'

She kept her eyes on the dusty track that shimmered off into the distance. 'So you move to Waverley. What happens then, Jack?'

'A lot more work.' Jack sounded as if he relished the prospect.

'And with Alice?'

'That's up to you, Ellie.' He turned slightly to look at her as she leant on the rail beside him. 'It's hard to believe that it's only a couple of months since we first came to Waverley. Do you remember that day?'

The memory of it was engrained on her heart. 'Of course,' she said, not looking at him.

'I've been thinking a lot about that conversation we had down at the creek,' said Jack.

Ellie's mouth was very dry. 'And?'

'And I think that marrying you would be a very good thing—for me,' he said slowly. 'It would be good for Alice, too. I'm just not sure it would be so good for you.'

'Isn't that for me to decide?'

'I don't want you to do anything you might regret,' he told her, choosing his words with care, and he smiled slightly. 'You're a useful person to have around, Ellie. You would solve all my domestic problems, but all I can offer in return is a lot of hard work bringing up a baby and getting this station back onto its feet.'

'And the chance to stay where I belong and do what I love doing,' she pointed out. 'It seems a fair exchange to me.'

Jack shook his head. 'You deserve more than that.' He paused. 'You said that you wanted security, and I *can* give you that. As my wife you'd be entitled to a half-share in Waverley, and if you wanted to leave I'd have to buy you out. You wouldn't need to worry about money again.'

Ellie straightened in consternation. 'I didn't mean financial security, Jack,' she protested. 'I just want to be somewhere I could stay. There's no need for you to give me anything.'

'I don't think you realise quite what it's going to mean to me to have you here,' he said, regarding her with a quizzical air. 'It's all very well to talk about employing people to help, but the more I thought about living at Waverley, the more I realised that I couldn't do it without you. A financial stake in the station is the least you deserve! Quite apart from anything else, think of all the money you're going to save me in wages for housekeepers and cooks and nannies!'

Ellie didn't smile back. 'I wish you wouldn't do it, Jack,' she said, hugging her arms together as if to ward off his generosity. 'It makes me uncomfortable just to think about it.'

'Then don't think about it,' said Jack. 'You just need to know that it's there, and you might as well get used to the idea because it's one of my conditions. If you won't accept it, I won't marry you.'

There was a note of finality in his voice that gave Ellie pause, and she eyed him uncertainly. She hated the idea of benefiting financially from marriage when all she had ever wanted was to be with Jack, but he was so stubborn that she wouldn't put it past him to do exactly what he said and refuse to marry her unless she agreed.

Jack read her expression without difficulty. 'Don't be so proud,' he said with a touch of exasperation. 'It's not as if I'm buying you.'

'That's what it feels like,' she said a little bitterly.

'Ellie, be sensible,' he said more gently. 'If we were getting married under normal circumstances, you wouldn't think twice about sharing in all my worldly goods, would you?'

Ellie kept her face carefully expressionless. 'But they're not normal circumstances, are they, Jack?'

'No,' he agreed. 'I think we should treat our marriage as a proper partnership. We won't be a normal husband and wife, but we can be partners, and to do that we need to have equal shares in Waverley.'

'All right,' said Ellie after a moment. There was obviously no point in arguing further, and anyway, it wasn't as if she would ever want to sell her share. She would only ever own half of Waverley on paper.

'Thank you,' she added, uncomfortably aware that she had sounded more than a little ungracious for someone who had just been promised half a cattle station.

'I do have one other condition,' said Jack.

She eyed him warily. 'What's that?'

'That if you ever want out of the marriage, you'll tell me. You may not feel now that there's any hope for you with this man that you're in love with,' he went on quickly, as she opened her mouth to protest, 'but things might change. I don't want you to feel trapped, Ellie, or that you've lost your chance at happiness. You have to promise me that if you *do* ever feel like that, you'll say. I'll let you go without any hard feelings.'

Of course he would. Ellie turned her face away and fought down the hurt twisting in her guts. She knew that Jack was trying to be kind. He couldn't know that every time he made it clear that he didn't love her, her heart cracked a little more.

'It's only fair,' he urged her when she didn't say anything, and Ellie swallowed.

It wasn't as if she didn't know how Jack felt. If she didn't like the fact that he wasn't in love with her and wasn't even going to pretend that he was, she should back out now. There was no point in expecting something from him that he couldn't give.

'It's only fair if you'll tell me, too,' she said, marvelling at how cool and unconcerned she sounded. 'We'll be partners, just like you said, not a real husband and wife. If there ever comes a time when you fall in love again, I hope you'll let me know.'

Forcing herself to meet his eyes, Ellie went on, 'We should make it part of our agreement that if either of us wants to end our marriage, the other won't contest it.'

Jack considered the matter, although she was sure that she had seen a flicker of relief in his eyes. 'If that's what you want,' he said at last, and then he held out his hand. 'Shall we shake on it?'

After the tiniest of hesitations, Ellie put her hand into his and felt his fingers close around hers. The touch of his flesh sent a throb of response through her, warming her blood and tingling just beneath her skin.

The effect was so disturbing that she made to draw her hand away, but Jack kept a firm hold of it. 'Now that we've agreed on all that, perhaps we can agree on the most important thing,' he said, with a smile that made her heart thud with painful intensity against her ribs. 'Will you marry me, Ellie?'

How odd, thought Ellie. She had imagined this scene so many times, but she didn't feel at all as she had always expected. Irrelevantly, she found herself remembering her grandmother's favourite saying: Don't wish too hard for what you want, or you will surely get it.

All she had ever wanted was to marry Jack, and now here he was, asking her to do just that, and all she could feel was a faint, poignant sadness that life never turned out quite the way you expected it to. In her dreams, Jack wanted to marry her because he loved her the way she desperately loved him, but this was real life, and she couldn't help wishing that he wanted her as a wife and not as a friend, as a lover instead of a useful person to have around.

He was waiting for her to answer. Ellie looked into his warm brown eyes with their lurking smile and felt her sudden doubts dissolve in a familiar clench of longing. So what if it wasn't perfect, the way she had dreamt it would be? At least she would be with him. It would be enough.

She took a steadying breath. 'Yes,' she said, 'I will.'

Jack hadn't missed her hesitation, and his clasp tightened. 'Are you sure?' he asked, only half teasing.

'I'm sure.'

'Good,' said Jack, his smile fading slowly as he looked down into Ellie's face. Her brown hair was pushed anyhow behind her ears and there was a smudge of paint on her cheek, but the grey-green eyes were clear and true.

His gaze dropped to her mouth, and without warning he found himself wondering what it would be like to kiss her. She had just said that she would marry him. Wouldn't it be the most natural thing in the world to kiss her?

What was he thinking of? Jack caught himself up guiltily. It might be natural to kiss under normal circumstances, but the circumstances weren't normal. This was Ellie, the closest thing he had to a kid sister. Ellie, who was in love with another man and who had made it clear that their marriage would be a purely businesslike arrangement.

And that was what he wanted too, Jack reminded himself. Marrying Ellie would only work if they could stay friends, and the best way to do that was not to complicate matters by kissing her.

On the other hand, they *were* going to get married. He could hardly just shake her hand again, could he?

'Good,' he said again, and bent his head to kiss her cheek instead. It was a nice, safe compromise, he thought, although he was very aware of the smooth warmth of her skin, of how close his lips were to hers.

Instinctively, Ellie closed her eyes as the faint roughness of his skin grazed tantalisingly against hers and she felt his mouth brush the edge of her lips. It was nothing, just a brief, brotherly kiss, but it was enough to make the ground drop away beneath her feet, sending her heart lurching into her throat and leaving her giddy and aching with awareness.

And then Jack was straightening, dropping her hand, stepping away from her almost abruptly, as if even that brief physical contact had been too much for him. Convinced that even that most fleeting of kisses had reminded him bitterly of Pippa, Ellie flinched inwardly. She couldn't bear to look at him in case she saw the effort he must be making to disguise how he felt having to kiss her when he was still so in love with Alice's mother.

Hugging her arms together, she avoided Jack's eye and stood tensely by the verandah rail, watching Alice, who was happily oblivious to the sacrifices her father was making for her sake. Mug clutched in one fat little hand, she was stuffing a much-battered soft toy into her mouth with the other and talking rather indistinctly to herself.

'Well.' Jack picked up his beer and then put it down again. He felt ridiculously awkward, and he eyed Ellie uneasily. It was just as well he had only tried a peck on the cheek. There was obviously only one man she wanted to kiss her, and clearly it wasn't him.

'Well,' he said again, hating the forced heartiness in his voice, 'when shall we get married?'

'As soon as we can organise it.' Ellie strove to sound natural but couldn't quite carry it off. 'Unless you'd rather wait?' she added with stilted politeness.

Jack shook his head. 'Let's get it over and done with as soon as possible.'

He had spoken without thinking, but when he glanced down at Ellie he surprised an expression in her eyes that made him wish he had chosen his words more carefully, and he winced inwardly at his lack of tact. Their marriage might be a matter of convenience for both of them, but there had been no need to make it quite so obvious that he was dreading the wedding.

'I guess you'd rather have a quiet wedding?' he said, to break the constrained silence.

'I would, but I'm afraid we'll never get away with it.' A little colour had come back into Ellie's cheeks, and she was able to look at him almost naturally. 'You know what Mum and Lizzy are like. They'd never forgive me if we didn't have a proper wedding, and if we just go off by ourselves they'll wonder why.'

She hesitated. 'I don't want them to know why we're getting married. They'd be terribly upset if they knew the truth. Lizzy's going to be difficult enough to convince as it is. She knows how you feel about Pippa and I think she'd do everything she could to dissuade me from this if she thought we weren't going to have a genuine marriage.'

'You're probably right,' Jack agreed slowly. He and Lizzy had been friends a long time, and if anyone was going to guess that he and Ellie weren't a normal happy couple it would be her. He looked at Ellie. 'We'll have to pretend that we're in love.'

She coloured. 'Would you mind?' she asked awkwardly. 'I...I know how difficult it would be for you.'

'And for you,' he pointed out.

There was a tiny silence. Ellie couldn't look at Jack. He wasn't to know that the hardest thing for her would be to pretend that she was just pretending.

'It would only really be for the wedding,' she said, unsure whether she was reassuring him or herself.

Jack's eyes rested on her profile. 'I think I could manage that,' he said. 'If you can.'

The question in his voice made Ellie glance at him sharply. He was watching her with an unfathomable expression in his brown eyes, and when she would have looked away again she found her gaze trapped. She couldn't speak, couldn't move, could only stand and look helplessly back at him, while her heart boomed into the suddenly charged silence, so loud that she was sure that Jack must be able to hear it.

He knew, she thought in sudden panic. How could he not know when the truth of how she felt about him must be written all over her face? What if that odd expression in his eyes was really embarrassment? Or, worse, pity?

With an enormous effort, Ellie wrenched her eyes away and moistened her lips. 'I...I'll try,' she said, hating the huskiness in her voice.

'Ellie,' Jack began abruptly, then stopped, as if unsure how to continue.

Oh, God, he was going to tell her that he had guessed! Ellie steeled herself for his awkward kindness as he explained that there was no point in her hoping, but before he could finish Alice threw her mug across the verandah with a shout of triumph that made them both jump as if a gun had gone off.

Trembling, intensely grateful for the reprieve and for

the excuse to hide her face, Ellie bent to retrieve the mug and took her time about placing it very carefully on the folding table.

By the time she straightened, Jack had scooped his daughter up into his arms. 'What do you think you're doing, young lady?' he demanded with mock sternness that didn't fool Alice one bit. Beaming with satisfaction, she tugged at his hair and squealed with laughter when Jack yelped in pain.

'Hey!' he complained, tickling her in revenge, which only made Alice laugh louder.

He looked so normal that Ellie began to wonder whether she had imagined the intense look that had passed between them. He certainly couldn't have guessed that she was in love with him, or he wouldn't be able to stand there, holding Alice and laughing as if nothing had changed.

Legs weak with relief, Ellie sank down into one of the chairs. She was just being stupid.

She could even smile when Jack sat down beside with Alice on his knee. 'What will you tell Gray and Clare?'

Jack didn't answer immediately. 'I think I'd like to tell them the truth,' he said eventually, his eyes on Alice. 'I wouldn't want Clare to think that I'd forgotten Pippa so soon. You don't mind, do you?'

Ellie shook her head. 'Do you think she'll understand why you're getting married?'

'Clare will want what's best for Alice, and our marriage will be.' Jack sounded very positive. 'She's very nice,' he added, glancing at Ellie. 'You'll like her.'

'I think it's more important that she likes me,' said Ellie.

'She will,' he said confidently. 'It's Alice's birthday next Sunday. She's going to be one.' A momentary sadness shadowed his face at the thought of how alone Pippa must have felt only a year ago. 'She's too young to understand about birthdays, but we thought we ought to mark the day in some way. Why don't you come over to Bushman's Creek and meet Clare then?'

He smiled persuasively at Ellie. 'You could do with a break from painting. Come over for lunch.'

'All right,' said Ellie a little doubtfully. She wasn't sure that Alice's birthday was the best time for her to meet Clare. She would be thinking of Pippa more than usual on that day. Jack had told her how much Clare had done for Alice, and she couldn't be expected to welcome anyone who seemed to be trying to take the place of her beloved sister.

Ellie was very nervous as she drove to Bushman's Creek the following Sunday. Normally she never thought about what to wear, but that morning she had dithered for ages before deciding to put on her only dress in honour of the occasion, and as she drove up the long track leading to the homestead she wished that she had stuck to her jeans.

It wasn't that it wasn't a nice dress, but she always felt very self-conscious in it. Lizzy had bullied her into buying it the last time Ellie had visited her in Perth. Ellie could see that dusky red colour brought a flattering glow to her skin, but she was always fiddling with the little straps or tugging at the hem, trying to reveal a little less of herself.

'I just don't feel like *me* in it,' she had complained to Lizzy, but Lizzy had been insistent.

'It's perfect for you,' she said firmly. 'Just relax and enjoy looking feminine for a change!'

The trouble was that she couldn't relax in it, Ellie thought gloomily, rattling over the last cattle grid. It had seemed a good idea to try and look feminine and pretty for Jack that morning, but what was the point when she couldn't behave naturally? She just wasn't any good at being feminine and pretty. Jack would just laugh at her.

But when Jack came out to meet her, he didn't laugh. He stopped dead as Ellie got out of the car and his cheerful greeting died on his lips. It was Ellie and yet somehow not Ellie at all. She was wearing a simple red dress that stopped above the knee and showed off long, slender legs while the tiny straps revealed the warmth of her skin and the pure lines of her shoulders and throat.

It was only a dress, but Jack felt as if he had been poleaxed. 'Why…Ellie…' he said in a peculiar voice.

'Hello, Jack.'

Ellie swallowed and folded her arms in an instinctively defensive gesture. He was staring at her with such a strange expression that she felt acutely uncomfortable. Why had she worn this stupid dress? Why hadn't she brought a coat or a cardigan or *anything* to cover herself up?

'You look…you look so different.'

She glanced shyly down at herself. 'It's the dress.'

'Yes.' Jack pulled himself together with an effort. 'I'd forgotten you had legs,' he tried to joke, although when she stood there in the sunlight with that dress outlining every curve of her body it was hard to remember when he had felt less like joking. 'I don't think I've seen them since you were six!'

Ellie smiled weakly. 'That's just what Kevin said when he saw me this morning. Lizzy's always telling me to make more of an effort and dress up more, but I'd rather just wear my jeans. I feel funny like this,' she admitted in a burst of honesty.

Jack didn't think she looked funny. He thought she

looked beautiful. But he couldn't help wishing that she had worn her old paint-splattered jeans instead.

'You look fine,' he said, almost curtly.

It wasn't much of a greeting for the poor girl, he realised belatedly. He should have gone over to give her a welcoming hug. But the mere thought of putting his arm around her shoulders and feeling the warmth of her bare skin beneath his hand was oddly disturbing.

Jack was conscious of a small spurt of resentment. Ellie had no business changing. He wanted her to stay the same—quiet, gentle, undemanding, the way she had always been. He didn't want to be knocked off-balance just because she had put on some dress. He didn't want to have to think about her differently, and he wasn't going to! Dress or no dress, Jack told himself, she was still just Ellie, and there was absolutely no reason not to behave just as he had always done.

'Come and meet Clare,' he said instead, and turned on his heel to lead the way to the homestead before he changed his mind.

CHAPTER FOUR

CLARE wasn't at all as Ellie had imagined her. Slight and dark, she had beautiful, shining grey eyes and she wore her clothes with an effortless style that made Ellie glad she had put on a dress after all. Jack might not like it, but at least Clare did.

They found her in the kitchen where she was putting the finishing touches to a birthday cake for Alice. She looked up with a smile as Jack brought Ellie in, and put down the icing bag to greet her with a warm hug.

'I've been so looking forward to meeting you,' she said. 'Jack's told us how hard you've been working at Waverley Creek. Alice is obviously pleased to see you, too,' she added as the baby spotted Ellie with a crow of recognition.

She was ensconced in a highchair, and when they came in she was patting a piece of dough on her tray and examining her sticky fingers with interest, but the sight of Ellie with her father made her beam with pleasure.

Her brown eyes were so like Jack's and her smile was impossible to resist. Ellie didn't even try. Smiling back, she went over to drop a kiss on top of Alice's head, and smoothed down the fine blond hair that was just beginning to grow into wayward curls in an unthinkingly tender gesture.

She was still smiling as she glanced up to see Clare and Jack watching her. Clare was smiling, too, a little sadly, but Jack's expression was shuttered, almost unfriendly, and he turned away as if irritated by the sight of her with his daughter.

'I'll go and give Gray a hand with the barbecue,' he muttered, and strode out.

Clare saw the flash of hurt in Ellie's eyes, but she made no comment, breaking the strained silence that followed Jack's departure with a compliment about her dress instead. 'It's a fabulous colour.'

Ellie forced an answering smile. 'I'm not used to wearing dresses. Jack hardly recognised me with legs.'

She kept her voice determinedly light, but she was hurt and puzzled by Jack's behaviour. He obviously hated her dress. She could sense his discomfort, how careful he had been not to touch her and how quick to leave her.

He had looked at her as if he didn't like her. Jack had never looked at her like that before. Ellie stroked Alice's curls and fretted inwardly. It wasn't like him to be rude. Perhaps he was ill? A cold hand clutched at her heart. Perhaps he had changed his mind? Or perhaps she had said or done something to irritate him?

But what? All she had done was put on a dress! Jack was a practised charmer, always ready with the most outrageous compliments to melt the dourest of hearts. *You look fine.* That was the best he could manage for *her*!

'Sit down.' Clare appeared not to notice Ellie's struggle between hurt, concern and a stirring resentment. She picked up her icing bag once more. 'You don't mind if I finish this, do you?'

'Of course not.' Ellie made an effort to pull herself together and sat down at the table where she had sat with Lizzy what seemed like a lifetime ago.

'I'm so glad I've met you at last,' Clare was saying. 'I've heard lots about you from Jack, of course, and from Lizzy.'

Banishing Jack and his odd behaviour from her mind, Ellie gave Clare her attention. 'I'd forgotten that you knew Lizzy.'

'I was terribly jealous when I first met her,' Clare admitted. 'I knew she'd been engaged to Gray at one time, and she's so nice and such fun that I thought he was bound to be still in love with her. I was determined to dislike her, but I just couldn't!'

Ellie's face relaxed into a genuine smile. 'No, it's hard not to like Lizzy!'

'She's been a wonderful friend to Gray and to Jack, and to me,' said Clare seriously. She looked at Ellie with open interest. 'You don't look at all like her, do you?'

'No, we've always been quite different. Most people find it hard to believe that we're related at all.' Ellie sighed a little, remembering Lizzy's blond vivacity, her sparkling blue eyes and the warm charm that swept all before it. She loved Lizzy dearly, but it hadn't always been easy trailing along unnoticed in her shadow.

'Pippa and I were like that,' said Clare, to her surprise, and when Ellie looked at her she saw that there was understanding in the frank grey eyes. 'I was quiet and sensible, and she was the bright, bubbly one. She was always so full of life, so passionate about everything she did.' Her smile twisted slightly. 'There were no half-measures with Pippa.'

'I'm sorry,' said Ellie quietly. 'You must miss her very much.'

'Yes, I do.' Clare went back to her icing. 'But not all the time, not now. It was awful when she died, and for a time I thought I'd never be happy again, but I am, happier than I would have believed possible.'

She glanced at Ellie as she spoke, grey eyes shining with the thought of the love that she had found. 'It's a terrible cliché, but life really does go on. I think of Pippa often, but I don't see her ghost everywhere.'

'Jack does.' Ellie's head was bent, and she was apparently concentrating hard on drawing together a few stray crumbs on the table.

'He does at the moment, but he won't always.' Clare hesitated, picking her words with care. 'It's difficult for him being at Bushman's Creek. This is the only place he ever knew Pippa. It's full of memories of the time they spent together. It'll be different when he's at Waverley,' she added gently.

'Did...did he tell you about the arrangement we've made?'

Clare nodded. 'Yes, he did.'

'Do you mind?'

'Mind? No. I am a bit worried, though. From Jack's point of view, I can see that marriage makes sense. He needs a wife, and Alice needs a mother.'

'Are you worried that I won't look after Alice properly?' Ellie made herself ask, but Clare seemed genuinely appalled at the idea.

'Of course not! No, I'm worried about you.'

'Me?'

She hesitated. 'It's a very risky thing to marry without love. I know. It's what Gray and I did.'

'But you're happy!'

'We are now, but we weren't when we were first married. I didn't know that Gray loved me then, and he had no idea that I was desperately, desperately in love with him. We both believed that the other one just thought of our marriage as a temporary measure until Jack came home. I know how hard it can be to live with someone when you think they don't love you.'

'It's different for Jack and I,' said Ellie, still busy tidying up crumbs. 'I *know* Jack doesn't love me. He's still in love with Pippa.'

'Jack told us that you were in love with someone as well,' said Clare.

'Yes,' said Ellie dully.

There was a pause. 'It's Jack, isn't it?'

Ellie froze. She stared down at her fingers on the table, and with an odd, detached part of her mind found herself noticing a knot in the pine so intensely that afterwards she could have drawn it in exact detail.

Very slowly, she looked up to see compassion in Clare's grey gaze and knew that there was no point in denying it. 'How did you guess?'

'It was just something about the way you looked at him, something in your voice when you said his name. Don't worry, it's not that obvious. Maybe it's because I'm so in love myself that I'm more attuned to recognise it in others now.' Clare smiled a little. 'I think I used to look at Gray like that when he wasn't watching me. I know what it's like,' she added gently.

Ellie swallowed. 'You won't tell Jack, will you?' she begged, green eyes pleading.

'Of course not,' Clare reassured her. 'That's something only you can tell him.'

'I'm not going to do that,' said Ellie in a flat voice. 'Jack's only marrying me because he thinks that I'm in love with another man and won't expect anything from him that he can't give. He doesn't want anyone to take Pippa's place, and I'm not even going to try.'

'Ellie, Pippa wouldn't have wanted Jack to spend the rest of his life grieving for her,' said Clare. She had finished the cake and was sliding it carefully onto a plate. 'He won't ever forget her, but he will fall in love again. Pippa was wonderful, and I think he was very much in love with her, but that doesn't necessarily mean that they would always have been happy together.'

Straightening, she wiped her hands on her apron with a thoughtful expression. 'Pippa had a very strong personality, just like Jack. Maybe they were too alike. It would never have been a restful relationship, that's for sure.' She sighed a little. 'Who knows how long it would have lasted once the first fire and passion was over and they had to get on with the nitty-gritty of living together permanently?

'Jack will wonder that, too, sooner or later,' Clare went on. 'He's still a young man. Of course he'll get over Pippa and fall in love again, but...'

She hesitated, wondering how best to put it, and in the end it was Ellie who finished for her. 'But it won't be with me?'

'It might not be, Ellie. I wouldn't want you to build up your hopes and then be hurt. I think you'd be good for him, but we don't always fall in love with the people who'd be good for us.'

'I know that,' said Ellie with a trace of bitterness. 'If we did, I wouldn't be in love with Jack, but I am and I just have to live with it. I've faced the fact that he may fall in love with someone else eventually, and if he does, I'll let him go. He'll never know how I feel.'

'It'll be very hard, Ellie,' said Clare quietly. 'Are you sure you want to marry Jack, knowing that he doesn't love you?'

'I'm sure,' she said. 'It's my only chance to be with him, and I have to take it.'

Clare nodded, as if she had known all along that Ellie would say that. 'I hope it works out for you, Ellie. I really do.'

'I'm glad you don't mind,' said Ellie in a low voice.

'Of course I don't.' Clare smiled as she pulled off her apron and went over to wipe Alice's hands and face. 'I do feel sad about not being able to spend so much time with Alice, though. Gray and I are going to miss her horribly, but she needs to go with Jack and with you and be part of a family. Besides,' she went on with a sudden smile that lit her face, 'we're having a baby of our own. Having brought Alice up so far, I know I won't have too much time for feeling sad.'

'Oh, Clare, that's wonderful news!'

Clare laughed. 'We think so. Gray's beside himself. You'd think that no one had ever been a father before!' She lifted Alice out of the highchair and kissed her. 'We'll still miss you, though,' she promised.

Glancing at Ellie, she held the baby out to her. 'Will you take Alice?' she asked.

'Of course I will,' said Ellie, and Clare handed Alice over in a gesture that they both recognised as symbolic, although neither said anything. Ellie cuddled Alice's warm, solid little body and her eyes met Clare's in a moment of complete understanding.

Clare smiled. 'Come on,' she said. 'Let's go and find the others.'

Carrying Alice, Ellie followed Clare out to the garden at the back of the homestead, where Jack and Gray were standing in the time-honoured male position by the barbecue. They both looked round at the sound of the screen door.

Gray was a browner, quieter version of Jack, with a slow smile and an air of calm competence, but at the sight of his wife it seemed to Ellie that something lit up inside him. He didn't say anything, he didn't move, he just looked at Clare, and she looked back at him, and they might as well have kissed.

Ellie's throat tightened painfully and she felt ridiculously close to tears. If only Jack would look at her like that one day! But when she glanced at him he was just standing there with the barbecue tongs in his hand, his face empty of all expression.

Jack saw the longing in Ellie's eyes as she watched the exchange of looks between Clare and his brother, and he knew exactly what she was thinking about. It must be hard for her to see people so obviously in love with each other when her own love was so hopeless, he tried to tell himself, but it didn't stop him feeling edgy and irritable, the way he had been feeling ever since she had got out of the car in that red dress.

It wasn't Ellie's fault that he was in a bad mood, Jack knew, but somehow it felt as if it was, and she wasn't making things any better by standing there cuddling his daughter lovingly against her and thinking about another man. When he saw her glance his way, he jerked his eyes away and turned back to the barbecue to turn the steaks with a sort of controlled savagery.

'Hello, Ellie!' Gray's smile held surprise as well as pleasure as he spotted Ellie behind Clare. 'It must be years since I've seen you. You've turned into a beauty!' he teased her as he came forward to give her a hug.

Jack jabbed at the steaks. He didn't want Ellie to have turned into anything. He wanted her to stay exactly the way she had always been.

Out of the corner of his eye, he could see Ellie smiling back at Gray, shifting Alice onto her hip so that she could return his hug. He could have hugged her like that, if he hadn't been so thrown by that dress.

'I'm sorry I missed your wedding,' she was saying to Gray. 'And now I understand more congratulations are in order?' she added with a demure smile that had Jack hunching a shoulder angrily.

Where had she learnt all these feminine tricks? he wondered sourly. Put on a dress and she was suddenly Mata Hari! Where was the tomboy who had scrubbed floors on her knees and slapped paint onto walls with never a thought to her appearance?

Gray was doing a very bad job of concealing his delight. 'I've just been boasting about it to Jack,' he grinned. 'He's been longing for you to come out and rescue him.'

Ellie shot a quick glance at Jack, who was still scowling down at the barbecue. He didn't look as if he had been longing for her to come anywhere. He looked as if he wished she would go away as soon as possible.

Suppressing a sigh, she turned back to Gray and Clare. 'I'm so pleased for you,' she said honestly. 'It'll be lovely for Alice to have a cousin.' She tickled Alice's nose. 'Won't it?'

'Gah!' said Alice, so clear and unqualified a 'yes' that they couldn't help laughing.

It was Alice's day. She was too young to appreciate that it was her birthday, but she knew that the four people who meant the most to her were with her and she revelled in all the attention, showing off shamelessly. She had a whole piece of the chocolate cake that Clare had made, and showed her appreciation by sticking her fingers in it and proceeding to wipe them over her face and hair before sucking them with noisy relish.

Jack's ill-humour dissolved as he watched her. It was impossible to stay cross when Alice was peeping glances under her lashes with mischievous brown eyes, when she crowed with delighted laughter or tried to imitate Ellie clapping but couldn't quite manage to bring her chocolatey hands together at the same time.

He would do anything for her, Jack vowed. She was the reason that he was marrying Ellie. What did it matter if Ellie was in love with someone else as long as she was there for Alice?

He slid a sideways glance at Ellie. She was relaxed in her chair, laughing at Alice's antics, glowing in the red dress, her awkwardness forgotten. Jack felt something shift in his chest, and he looked quickly away.

Later, when Alice was asleep, exhausted by all the excitement, he walked Ellie to her car.

'I'm sorry I haven't been much company today,' he said abruptly, breaking the constrained silence between them.

'That's all right,' said Ellie. 'I realised that you were thinking of Pippa.' She hesitated. 'It must have been a difficult day for you.'

'It wasn't that,' he said honestly. 'I have been thinking of her, of course, but… I don't know what it was,' he confessed with a sigh. 'Maybe the whole idea just takes some getting used to.'

He glanced down at Ellie. Her lashes were lowered, guarding her expression, and it occurred to him that for all her familiarity there was something elusive about her. He had always thought of Ellie as being quiet and straightforward, but the more he saw of her, the more mysterious she seemed.

'We've got over the first hurdle anyway,' he said, striving for a lighter tone. 'I wasn't looking forward to telling Clare that I was marrying you, but she seems to approve. Now we just need to convince your family. Have you told them yet?'

'Yes.'

'How did they take it?'

'Mum's over the moon, and is already deep in plans for the wedding. Dad doesn't say very much, but I think he's pleased. Kevin and Sue were even more pleased—I think they were relieved to hear that I wasn't planning on staying with them for ever!'

'And Lizzy?'

She grimaced. 'Lizzy's suspicious,' she admitted. 'She knows how you feel about Pippa, and she knows me. She guessed the truth right away.'

Jack glanced at her. 'The truth?' he said, an odd inflection in his voice, and she stopped by the car to look at him in surprise.

'That you're just looking for a mother for Alice.'

'Did she guess the truth about you, too?'

Ellie's eyes shifted. 'She thinks I'll do anything to stay in the outback. I didn't tell her…anything else.'

'So did you tell her that she guessed right?'

'No.' Ellie shrugged, as if trying to shake off an uncomfortable memory. 'I don't like lying to her, but you know how romantic she is about marriage. She thinks that you should only get married if you're passionately in love and everything's perfect. I had to pretend that that's how it is for us.'

Jack leant against the bonnet of the car and folded his arms. 'Did she believe you?'

'I'm not sure.' Ellie bit her lip. 'I don't think so, not really. She asked when it had all happened, of course, and I said that we'd got to know each other better while I was helping you at Waverley, but that wasn't enough for Lizzy!'

Her eyes kindled with remembered indignation at the interrogation Lizzy had put her through. 'She wanted to know every detail!'

Jack could imagine Lizzy's reaction to Ellie's carefully understated story only too well, and swift amusement gleamed in his brown eyes. 'What sort of detail?' he asked.

'Oh, you know…' Ellie's gaze slid away from his, and she rested her hand against the car door, running her finger down the windowframe. 'How we fell in love. When we first kissed. What it was like. That kind of thing.'

'What did you say?'

When she risked a fleeting glance at him, she saw with a trace of resentment that there was still a smile lurking at the back of his eyes. It was all very well for him to find it funny. *He* hadn't had Lizzy on the phone for hours, asking awkward questions she couldn't answer.

'What about?' she asked almost snappishly.

'About our first kiss.'

'I said it was wonderful, of course,' said Ellie crossly. 'I couldn't very well say that I'd never kissed you, could I?'

'Not if you want her to believe that we're passionately in love,' agreed Jack.

'She says she's coming home from Perth next weekend to see for herself,' Ellie went on glumly. 'She's already asked Mum and Dad what they're doing about an engagement party. I tried to tell them that we were too busy at Waverley for a party, but I might as well have spared my breath! They're busy inviting half the district. Just because they love parties doesn't mean I do! Why can't they leave us alone?' she demanded wildly.

'Poor Ellie!' Jack couldn't help laughing at her expression. 'They just want to make things special for you. It won't be that bad.'

Ellie refused to be consoled. 'Yes, it will. It'll be *awful*. I won't be able to relax for a minute. Everyone will be there, looking at me, and Lizzy will be watching us like a hawk to see if we really are in love or not.'

Jack unfolded his arms and straightened from the bonnet. 'We'll just have to be ready to put on a convincing show, then, won't we?' he said.

'How are we supposed to do that?' she asked, still preoccupied by her grievance over the party.

'Well…' Jack pretended to consider the matter. 'We could kiss,' he suggested casually.

'K-kiss?' stammered Ellie, jerked out of her abstraction.

'It's usual at engagement parties, especially when you're the couple getting engaged.'

'I know, but…'

'It's not a problem, is it?'

She swallowed. 'No…no… At least…' She trailed off incoherently, unable to explain to Jack why the thought of kissing him threw her into such confusion.

'If it is, perhaps we should practise now,' said Jack, as if struck by a sudden thought.

'Practise?' she croaked.

'I'm going to have to kiss you at the party, and at the wedding,' he pointed out. 'I just thought it might be a good idea if I kissed you now so that it doesn't look as if it's our first time when we have to do it in front of everyone else.'

He made it sound so normal, so obvious, as if it would mean no more than shaking hands. 'What do you think?' he asked.

His face was perfectly straight, but there was a deepening of the creases around his eyes, a suspicion of a smile lurking around his mouth. Ellie didn't know at that moment whether she loved him or hated him for finding the idea of kissing her so amusing.

'I...don't know,' she said stiffly.

'At least then if anyone else asks you what our first kiss was like you'll be able to tell them.'

Her heart was slamming in slow, painful strokes against her ribs and her throat was so tight that she could hardly breathe. She stared uncertainly at Jack, half afraid that he would turn out to be joking after all. She longed to kiss him, but dreaded it at the same time, terrified of what she would reveal if she did.

'I won't kiss you if you don't want me to,' said Jack softly, and when she still said nothing, he made as if to step away.

'No,' said Ellie involuntarily, and he stopped, lifting his eyebrows. She had longed for this moment for years. How could she run away from it now?

'I mean...no, I think you're right,' she managed to croak as she struggled for composure. 'It's a good idea.'

It *was*, she told herself. If she was going to make a fool out of herself, it was far better to do it now, alone with Jack in the yard at Bushman's Creek, than at some party with the entire district looking on.

'We...we don't want to look silly at the party, do we?' she went on, mustering a brave smile from somewhere.

'No,' Jack agreed slowly.

The lurking smile evaporated from his eyes. Ellie's grumbling about the party had been reassuringly familiar, her awkwardness about the idea of kissing him endearing, reminding him that this was the same, safe Ellie he had always known and not some stranger in a red dress.

But now he was going to kiss her, and his indulgent amusement evaporated as they looked at each other in strumming silence. Jack felt absurdly nervous. He had kissed lots of women, but not like Ellie. Ellie was different.

He took her by the waist as hesitantly as the first time he had ever kissed a girl. He could feel the warmth of her body, the slight shift of her dress beneath his palms, the cool, smooth material slipping over her bare skin, and his throat dried.

Ellie was trembling. Her pulse boomed in her ears and her legs seemed to have disappeared so that the burning touch of his hands through her dress seemed to be all that was keeping her upright.

She had to help him. Desperately she tried to steady her spinning senses. It couldn't be easy for Jack to kiss her. She had felt his hesitation and knew that he must be thinking of Pippa, the only girl he really wanted to kiss.

Taking a deep breath, she put her hands on his shoulders. Beneath her wondering fingers, his shirt was soft over steel-hard muscles.

She had loved Jack for his reckless charm, for the faint, indefinable sense of danger that edged his lazy good humour and his kindness, for the warmth of his eyes and the way the sun rose when he smiled, but in that moment she was conscious only of him as a man.

She wanted to slide her hands beneath his shirt and spread her fingers over his bare chest. She wanted to explore the hardness of his body and burrow into his lean strength. Physical desire churned through her, leaving her sick and giddy and so afraid that she would simply succumb to it that she was about to step back when Jack pulled her closer and her last hope of resistance had gone.

Tightening one arm around her, he lifted the other hand to smooth the hair from her face before letting it slide down her throat so that he could caress the line of her jaw almost absently with his thumb.

Ellie stood stock-still, staring blindly at the pulse that beat steadily below his ear, quivering at the merest graze of his fingers against her cheek. She knew that she was lost.

'Look at me, Ellie,' said Jack, his voice so deep that it seemed to vibrate through her.

Slowly, unresistingly, Ellie lifted her eyes, and the breath snared in her throat. Jack was looking down into her face with an unfathomable expression, but his hand was sliding beneath her hair, holding her still at the nape of her neck, and anticipation shivered over her skin.

And then the long waiting was over and he was bending his head, and Ellie had time only to sweep her lashes over her eyes before his mouth came down on hers. It was a very gentle kiss, but the mere touch of his lips sent such a jolt of response through her that she gasped and her fingers curled instinctively into his shirt. When he lifted his head almost immediately she had to struggle not to cry out in protest.

So that was it. Disappointment gripped Ellie by the throat. Swallowing, she opened her eyes, but she couldn't have said anything if she had tried. She didn't know any tricks, any little way of letting him know how desperately she wanted him to kiss her again. She could only stare dumbly back at him.

Jack had meant to let her go at once. She hadn't wanted to kiss him, not really, he remembered. A brief kiss would have been enough. But the piercing sweetness of her lips had caught him unawares, and somehow, instead of releasing her as he'd intended, he found his arm sliding round to gather her closer, and before he knew quite was happening he was lifting her up to kiss her again, the way a girl in a red dress should be kissed.

Delight mingled with relief cascaded through her in a tumbling golden rush, and she melted into him, beyond fear that she would give herself away, beyond worry about the complications of their situation, beyond thinking about anything but Jack, the taste of him and the feel of him and the glorious knowledge that she was in his arms at last.

Her hands crept up from his shoulders to wind around his neck, and she abandoned herself to the honeyed pleasure spilling along her veins. His mouth, moving so warm and persuasive against hers, was intoxicating, the strength of the arm that held her fast encircled her with enchantment.

It didn't matter to Ellie that there were no stars, no romantic backdrop to their first kiss. She didn't care that she was standing in a dusty yard sheltered only by the straggly shade of a gum, that Jack had ignored her for most of the day, or that the kiss meant no more to him than an amusing rehearsal. She cared only that it was her turn, that his arms were around *her*, that his lips were on hers.

Ellie never knew how long the kiss lasted. It might have been a few seconds; it might have been an hour. All she knew was that it ended much too soon. When Jack let her go, she leant shakily back against the car door, heedless of the handle digging into her back, boneless and trembling. The world was still rocking around her and she had to lay her hands flat against the hot metal to steady herself.

Jack was the first to recover. 'Do you think that would have convinced Lizzy?' he asked, and although he tried to sound unconcerned he could hear the ragged edge to his voice.

'I hope so,' said Ellie huskily. It had nearly convinced her.

Unable to meet Jack's eyes, she fumbled for the door handle behind her. 'I...I'd better go,' she managed.

Jack watched as she scrambled into the driving seat and bent to insert the key with fingers that felt thick and clumsy. The sweetness of her kiss had caught him unawares, and his senses strummed with a new and disconcerting awareness of the softness of her lips, the pliancy of her body, the scent of her skin.

He had wanted to kiss her again, but her eyes had held a stricken expression and she had turned away so quickly that for the first time ever Jack wondered if she had enjoyed the kiss at all. She obviously couldn't wait to close the door between them and get away.

Acutely conscious of his gaze on her, Ellie became more and more flustered. It took ages to get the key in the ignition, but at last it slotted into place and she braced herself to look at him, certain that he would be laughing at her confusion.

But Jack wasn't laughing. He was just watching her with a faintly worried expression in his brown eyes. It lightened slightly as she wound down the window to say goodbye.

'You'll tell Gray and Clare about the party?' she said with stilted politeness.

'Of course,' said Jack, equally formal.

He hesitated, concerned by the paleness of her face, the over-brightness of her smile, the way she clutched at the steering wheel as if for support. 'Are you all right, Ellie?' he asked in a different tone, putting out a hand to rest on the open window.

'I'm fine.'

'You didn't mind me kissing you?'

'Of course not,' said Ellie with an unconvincing smile. 'It's me that wants to convince my family that we're in love. That was part of the deal.'

The deal. The reason they were getting married. The

reason she was there. The reason he had forgotten when he was kissing her.

'Oh, yes, the deal,' said Jack in a flat voice, and he stepped back from the car to let her go.

CHAPTER FIVE

JACK didn't want to go to any engagement party the following weekend. Especially not his own.

He had been in a bad mood all week. It was his own fault for kissing Ellie, of course. Jack knew that. It had seemed like a good idea at the time, but he hadn't bargained for the way the memory would stick like a burr in his mind.

He was disconcerted to find himself thinking about Ellie at odd times of the day. About the way she had looked in that dress, about the slender smoothness of her legs and the unexpected sweetness of her lips, and sometimes his palm would tingle as if he could still feel the silkiness of her dress slipping over her skin.

Whenever that happened, Jack would shrug the memory aside. It had only been Ellie, he reminded himself at rather too frequent intervals. He had kissed much prettier girls much more passionately. There was no reason for that particular kiss to leave him feeling restless and uneasy.

It wasn't even as if Ellie herself had been bothered by it. It had been part of the deal, as she had pointed out, and it annoyed Jack that he couldn't forget it as easily as she apparently had.

He was silent as they drove to the party, content to let Gray and Clare talk in the front while he sat in the back next to Alice. Firmly strapped into her car seat, she amused herself by playing with her toes until the monotonous vibration of the car lulled her to sleep.

Jack's eyes rested on her as her head lolled at an awkward angle onto her shoulder. Her mouth was slightly open, and the ridiculously long lashes fanned her rosy cheeks. Unsettled and out of humour, he had been on the point of ringing Ellie to cancel their engagement several times during the past week, but whenever he'd picked up the phone he had thought of Alice.

Alice, who was Pippa's daughter. Alice, who needed a mother. It was for her that he was marrying Ellie.

No, he reassured himself as he watched his daughter sleeping, he was doing the right thing. He just wished that he hadn't spoilt everything by kissing Ellie.

Jack was irritatingly aware that, in spite of all his misgivings, he was looking forward to seeing her again. It wasn't supposed to be like this, he thought crossly as Gray turned onto the sealed road. The idea had been that Ellie would be a gentle, undemanding friend, a restful companion, someone who would be there when he needed her but who he wouldn't really need to think about the rest of the time.

Jack scowled out of the car window. Ellie wasn't supposed to put on red dresses and confuse him like this.

His mood was not improved when they arrived at the party to find Ellie wearing the same damned dress and looking even prettier than he had remembered. She was giving an incredibly convincing performance of a girl happily in love, Jack noted with an obscure sense of resentment.

He should have been grateful to her for carrying off the pretence so well, but somehow he wasn't. He didn't like the way her eyes sparkled as she talked and laughed. He didn't like the way the men she had known all her life clustered around her. He didn't like the way they looked at her.

Jack glowered as he watched Ellie. He didn't have to be told that the man she loved was there. There was a glow about her today, and it certainly wasn't for him. He found himself studying the face of every man there, wondering which of them was responsible for her radiance.

She ought to have more pride, Jack decided austerely. She had told him that she had given up hope of having her love returned, but why else would she be smiling like that? Why else would she be wearing that red dress like that?

Across the room, Ellie saw the compressed line of Jack's mouth and suppressed a sigh. She had been horribly nervous about seeing him again after that kiss, hiding her apprehension behind an air of desperate gaiety.

It was very important that Jack should have no inkling of what his kiss had meant to her. He would be appalled if he knew how she had lain awake every night since then, reliving every second, remembered pleasure shuddering slowly down her spine

From the moment he had walked into the party it had been obvious that Jack's feelings were very different. Ellie had seen from his face how much he regretted kissing her, and guessed that he was terrified in case she had misinterpreted it.

Well, he needn't worry, thought Ellie, lifting her chin proudly. She had no intention of embarrassing him or of making a fuss.

She smiled brightly at Jack to reassure him, but he didn't respond. He managed a smile for her parents, but couldn't wait to get away and join the massed ranks of his ex-girlfriends, who were all eagerly awaiting the chance to greet him. He managed to smile at them, too, Ellie noted sourly, watching as he returned their hugs with unnecessary warmth.

As the party wore on, and Jack continued to avoid her, Ellie began to get cross. It wasn't her fault Jack had kissed her! If he didn't want to marry her, he could have said. He needn't have come today at all, but, since he had, he could at least make the effort to behave like a fiancé.

As it was, she was left pretending to be engaged single-handed! Uncomfortably aware of how much effort her family were making for her, Ellie resisted the temptation to march over to Jack, slap all those girls' hands off his arm and tell him he could look elsewhere for an unpaid housekeeper if that was all he wanted. Her parents were so delighted for her that she couldn't bear to disappoint them by letting her feelings show. They wanted her to have a wonderful time, and a wonderful time she would seem to be having!

Ellie put up her chin and fixed a glittering smile to her face. Jack could make it obvious that he wasn't in love with her if he wanted, but she would play the part of a deliriously happy fiancée if it killed her!

She had known almost everyone at the party her entire life, so it wasn't that difficult to enjoy herself—or it wouldn't have been if she could have ignored Jack as comprehensively as he was ignoring her. But whenever she looked at him he had some other girl hanging around him. They were all blond, all pretty, and Ellie was prepared to bet that they all knew just as well as her what it felt like to be kissed by Jack.

A sudden sense of hopelessness swept over her. Who was she trying to fool? It must be obvious to anyone with eyes in their head that she wasn't Jack's type. Did anyone in this room really believe that out of all the girls there who would have jumped at the chance of marrying Jack he had chosen her, quiet, ordinary Ellie Walker?

Of course not.

Ellie's carefully bright smile slipped from her face. All at once she felt exposed and humiliated, as if the entire room were sniggering behind their hands at her pathetic attempts to catch Jack for herself when he so obviously belonged with someone pretty and clever and fun. Someone unlike her.

She had to get away. Murmuring an excuse, Ellie glanced around her to make sure that no one noticed where she was going and slipped out of the room. From the kitchen she could hear the sound of cheerful voices as her mother and her friends prepared endless salads for the evening meal, and she turned the other way, escaping instinctively to the far corner of the back verandah, where she could hide behind the potted palms that helped keep the shade cool and green.

Ellie sank gratefully down into one of the old wicker chairs. The effort of smiling for so long had taken its toll, and she rubbed her aching jaw, savouring the silence and the blessed relief of being on her own.

'What are you doing out here?'

Ellie's head jerked up at the sound of Jack's voice. He was striding down the verandah towards her with a thunderous expression, and her stomach gave a great lurch that was partly shock, partly anger, partly exasperation with herself for loving him even when he was being cross and unreasonable.

'What does it look like I'm doing?' she retorted, thrown off-balance by his obvious fury. What did *he* have to be so angry about?

'Meeting this famous lover of yours?' Jack suggested in a deliberately offensive voice.

Ellie was so taken aback that she could only stare at him. 'What?'

'I saw you look around to check that no one was watching you before sneaking off,' he told her. 'It was perfectly obvious that you were going off to meet someone. I thought you told me there was nothing between you?'

'There isn't,' she said tightly, torn between relief that he hadn't, after all, guessed how she felt, and anger at his sheer obtuseness.

'Oh?' Jack didn't even bother to hide his disbelief. 'Then what were you doing sneaking out of the room like that?'

'I wasn't *sneaking*! I needed some air, and I just wanted to be on my own for a bit. I didn't want anyone to follow me,' she added pointedly, but Jack refused to take the hint.

He threw himself down in the chair next to hers and eyed her moodily. 'Why not?'

'I don't like parties.'

'You could have fooled me,' said Jack. 'I would have said that you were having a wonderful time in there.'

Ellie drew in a sharp breath. 'Why would I have been having a good time, Jack?' she asked, dangerously quiet. 'I've had to spend the day lying to my family and friends. I've had to pretend to be happily engaged to a man who's spent the entire time ignoring me. I've had to put up with pitying looks from all your ex-girlfriends, who are plainly wondering why on earth you're marrying me when you're clearly not in the slightest bit interested in me. What makes you think that I've been enjoying that?'

Jack scowled. 'I haven't been ignoring you. I just haven't been able to get near you all day. Whenever I saw you, you seemed more than happy to be the centre of attention.'

'It's called making an effort,' snapped Ellie. 'Mum and

Dad have gone to a lot of trouble to arrange this party for us, and they'd be really upset if they thought I was less than deliriously happy. Of *course* I've been looking as if I'm having a good time! What do you expect me to do? Stand there looking miserable?'

'Flirting with every man in sight seems a funny way of convincing your parents that you're happily engaged,' said Jack unpleasantly.

It was so unfair that Ellie was momentarily deprived of breath. *'Flirting?'* she gasped as she stared at him in gathering fury. 'I haven't been flirting with anyone! I wouldn't even know *how* to flirt!'

'Oh, I wouldn't say that,' he sneered. 'In fact, I'd say you had that wide-eyed, artless look down to a fine art! And nobody could say that you were picking on anyone in particular, which I'm sure was your object. I must be the only man here you *didn't* flirt with!'

'I might have done if you'd come anywhere near me,' said Ellie in a shaking voice. 'You obviously had much better things to do. I'm surprised you even noticed what I was doing!'

'Of course I noticed.'

Jack glared at Ellie, but even as he glared he was disturbingly aware of her. The red dress was like a flame in the dim shade, her eyes were green with anger and she looked startlingly, even shockingly, vivid. The memory of how it had felt to kiss her caught suddenly at Jack's heart, making it stumble, and he got abruptly to his feet to prowl over to the verandah rail and stand with his back to her.

'We *are* supposed to be engaged,' he pointed out.

'Oh, so you remembered?' Ellie had never, ever quarrelled with Jack before, and the realisation that she could actually be angry with him was curiously exhilarating.

'That would explain, of course, why you've been avoiding me and paying such close attention to all your ex-girlfriends instead!'

Jack shut his teeth. 'I've just been catching up with old friends,' he said, unwilling to admit how the sight of Ellie surrounded by so many obviously admiring men had thrown him off-balance.

'Funny how all your *old friends* just happen to be young, female and very pretty!'

It wasn't like Ellie to be sarcastic, and Jack didn't like it one bit. His mouth tightened as he swung round to face her.

'Don't be ridiculous! I've talked to almost everyone here today, which is more than you have. I've been polite to your aunts, said all the right things to your father and your brother and been grilled by your mother and Lizzy. I would have talked to you, too, but I haven't been able to get near you all day. It would have meant fighting my way through the throng of men who were all anxious to get an eyeful of you in that dress!'

There was a blistering silence. They eyed each other with dislike, although both were secretly appalled at the quarrel which had sprung up between them and which had already turned nastier than either of them would have been able to imagine.

It was Jack who turned away first. 'He's here, isn't he?' he asked in a different voice.

'Who?'

'The man you're in love with.'

Ellie looked at his back and sighed. 'Yes,' she said after a moment.

'I could tell,' said Jack without looking at her. 'It's as if someone switched on a light inside you. Pippa used to look like that. She said that it was just knowing that I was near.'

Ellie didn't want to hear about Pippa. She got to her feet and went to stand next to Jack by the verandah rail, although not close enough to touch him. 'Yes, that's what it is,' she said heavily.

'Is he married? Is that the problem?'

'I don't want to talk about it.'

'Every unmarried guy in the district was panting over you in there,' Jack persisted. 'There isn't one of them who wouldn't jump at the chance of unzipping that dress. All you'd have to do is lift a finger and you could have whichever one of them you wanted, so it must be someone else.'

'Jack.' Ellie gritted her teeth and spoke very distinctly. 'I do not want to talk about it, all right?'

'I wouldn't tell anyone. I just want to know.'

'It's none of your business.'

'The hell it isn't! We're getting married!'

'We had a deal,' she said stonily. 'I told you the situation, and you said that you understood. I'm not prepared to discuss it any further.'

'And that's it?' Jack eyed her set face with a mixture of bafflement and frustration. 'I'm supposed to stand by and watch while you light up every time this guy is in the same room as you?'

It was at this inauspicious moment that the sound of high heels clicking on the wooden floor announced the arrival of Lizzy.

'There you are!' she exclaimed as she came down the verandah towards them. 'What on earth are you doing hiding out here? I've been looking for you everywhere. We want to have the toast, and Dad's going to give a speech—'

She stopped as she took in the way Jack and Ellie were standing rigidly apart, their faces set.

'Uh-oh! I smell tension in the air! What's going on?'

'Nothing,' said Ellie.

'Just a little lovers' tiff,' said Jack at the same time. He bared his teeth at Ellie. 'Isn't it, darling?'

Ellie only glared back at him, and Lizzy's mouth twitched.

'Are you planning to kiss and make up, or shall I go and tell Dad the wedding's off?' she asked, opening her eyes innocently.

'Of course the wedding's not off.' The smoothness of Jack's voice was in direct contrast to the hardness of his grip as his fingers closed around Ellie's wrist. 'You can all get your glasses ready. We're coming.'

To Lizzy's evident amusement, he practically dragged Ellie back inside. Ellie had to almost run to keep up with him, and only just remembered in time to fix a brittle smile to her face before he jerked her to a halt beside her father.

Steeling herself to meet the embarrassed stares of everyone around her, Ellie was amazed to discover that there was not a single raised eyebrow in sight, and that they were all smiling fondly as her father launched into his speech. Couldn't they *see* that Jack's smile didn't match the cold anger in his eyes? That he was holding her hand in a punishing grip? That the air between them was fairly crackling with acrimony?

Only Lizzy seemed to be aware that anything was wrong, and instead of looking concerned, she wore a pleased smile. Ellie stared suspiciously at her. Lizzy had been the only doubter when she had announced her engagement to Jack, and had been clearly reserving her judgement until she saw the two of them together. Why, then, was she suddenly looking so satisfied?

Ellie felt as if she had been standing there for hours with Jack's merciless fingers around her own before her father eventually came to the end of his speech. Everyone laughed dutifully at his appalling jokes, and nodded sentimentally when he told them that Jack and Ellie were made for each other. Ellie couldn't bear to look at Jack then, but she felt his hand tighten so hard that she winced.

'So I'd like you all to raise your glasses—' her father was beaming as he wound up at last '—and drink to the future happiness of Ellie and Jack.'

'Ellie and Jack!' they all chorused obediently, raising their glasses with such goodwill that Ellie squirmed inwardly.

The arrangement she and Jack had come to had seemed their own business until she'd realised that it meant deceiving an awful lot of people she cared about. It would have been much easier if they had all ignored her engagement altogether, instead of overwhelming her with their delight and good wishes.

The cheers died away, and in the expectant hush that followed Ellie found herself the focus of all eyes. They were waiting for Jack to kiss her.

The realisation sent the air whooshing out of Ellie's lungs, and her bright smile faltered as she glanced nervously at Jack. He would make some excuse, she reassured herself. He couldn't possibly kiss her now, not with their quarrel still ringing in their ears.

But when she tried to tug her hand away, Jack wouldn't let her go. He pulled her towards him instead, turning to look down at her with a smile that made her insides jerk themselves into a tangled knot of apprehension and alarm, threaded through with the treacherous pulse of excitement.

Ellie opened her mouth, although she had no idea what she would have said, and in any case it was too late. Jack had jerked her roughly into his arms, and his mouth came down on hers before she had a chance to protest.

It wasn't how he had kissed her before. This time there was no sweetness, no drench of delight. This kiss was a challenge.

Jack's lips were fierce and demanding, his hands hard against the bare flesh of her arms, and the anger surged between them like an electric current. Ellie was riveted by the intensity of her response. She could feel it rocketing through her, jolting, explosive, terrifyingly uncontrollable, and yet edged with elation.

So Jack wanted to punish her, did he? Well, she was tired of being the dear, sweet little Ellie who would put up with all his moods without question! If his kiss was a challenge, she could meet it!

Curling her fingers into his shirt, defiant, even provocative, Ellie kissed Jack back. She had forgotten that they were surrounded by people who would all be watching them, forgotten the arrangement they had made and why they were there. Nothing mattered but the clash of wills and the undertow of a dark, dangerous excitement that ran between them.

Afterwards, Ellie couldn't have said when that turbulent kiss changed, but just as it seemed set to blaze out of control the fierce antagonism vaporised into pleasure so intense that her bones liquefied and she had to hold more tightly on to Jack to stop herself dissolving away altogether.

It was as if their mouths had been made to move together, urgently seeking the source of that whirling delight, as if Jack's hands had been specially designed to slide possessively down her spine, to gather her closer, as if her body had always been meant to melt into his unyielding strength.

'Hey, break it up!' a voice somewhere called. 'There are children here!'

The burst of laughter and cheering that followed seemed to Ellie to come from a thousand miles away. It was nothing to do with her or with Jack, and when she felt him begin to draw away she murmured in instinctive protest.

Jack hesitated, then ignored it. When he lifted his head, Ellie was disorientated to find that, far from being alone, a thousand miles from anyone else, they were surrounded by grinning faces. Swallowing, she blinked back at them with dark, dazed eyes.

What had happened? One minute she and Jack had been kissing each other furiously, and the next... Ellie didn't know why it had changed or what it meant. She knew only that she felt boneless and bewildered, and so shaken that she was afraid to move in case she simply collapsed into an untidy heap on the floor. Jack's hands at her waist were all that was keeping her upright.

Almost reluctantly, her eyes met Jack's. He was looking appalled, and they stared at each other in consternation, too shocked at first to wonder what their interested audience would think. That thought occurred to them simultaneously, and as if at some unspoken signal they stepped abruptly away from each other.

For some reason, everyone seemed to find their behaviour funny. There was laughter and cheering and good-natured whistles, and then the crowd lifted their glasses again as one.

'To Jack and Ellie!'

By the time they had waved off the last of the guests that evening, Ellie was exhausted. She had somehow managed to pull herself together and continue chatting brightly, as if Jack kissed her like that every day, but she had longed for everyone to go so that she could shut herself away somewhere and stop smiling.

She and Jack were very careful not to touch again. Jack took Alice from Gray, which gave him a good excuse not to have to hold her hand or put his arm around her waist as a real lover would have done. Ellie told herself it was better that way, but it didn't stop her feeling cold and confused and very alone.

They barely spoke to each other until Jack came to say goodbye with Gray and Clare. He was still holding Alice, and Ellie was able to make a big fuss of saying goodbye to her without once meeting his eyes.

'I was thinking of going over to Waverley next week,' Jack said awkwardly. 'What about you? Are you busy?'

Ellie wasn't sure whether he wanted her to pretend that she couldn't go with him or not, but her brother and sister-in-law were standing right beside her and they knew perfectly well that she had nothing else to do. Besides, wouldn't it be better just to pretend that nothing had happened?

'No, I'll be there.' She flashed a bright, meaningless smile somewhere over his shoulder. 'I've still got those windows to finish.'

'Gray and I are mustering tomorrow and Tuesday, so I won't be going before Wednesday,' said Jack with the same stilted politeness. 'I could pick you up on the way, if you like.'

'Fine.'

Jack hesitated, as if he wanted to say something else, but in the end he just nodded. 'I'll see you then.'

Hugging her arms together, Ellie watched as he settled Alice into the car seat and got in beside her without even a glance over his shoulder to where she was standing at the bottom of the verandah steps.

Long after they had gone, she carried on standing there, looking after them, and it was only when she turned that she discovered that Lizzy was there too, eyeing her with a very strange expression.

'What?' said Ellie defensively, even though Lizzy hadn't said a word.

'I was just remembering how appalled I was when you told me you were going to marry Jack,' said Lizzy. 'I thought that you were both getting married for all the wrong reasons, and when I saw how politely you greeted each other today I was sure of it, whatever you'd told me. But as soon as I saw you quarrelling I knew that I was wrong and you were right after all.'

'You did?' Ellie looked at her sister, wondering what on earth she was talking about.

'Oh, yes.' Lizzy nodded vigorously. 'You were having a real fight when I walked in, weren't you? That's a very good sign.'

'It is?'

'Come on, Ellie, you've never fought in your life, and I don't think I've ever seen Jack lose his temper like that. He's always been so laid-back. You wouldn't have been having an argument like that unless there was something special between you. You have to care about someone a lot to argue like that—and to kiss like that,' she added as an afterthought.

She smiled a little wistfully. 'I wish I could find someone who would kiss me like that, not caring who was watching or what they were thinking. I think you're very lucky, Ellie.'

'Lizzy,' Ellie began impulsively, then stopped. She had been about to tell Lizzy the truth, that there was something between her and Jack, but not what she thought it was. It was a deal, not love. But Lizzy was looking so pleased for her that Ellie couldn't face her reaction if she knew what they had agreed. Lizzy would tell her parents, and everyone would be bitterly disappointed and hurt that Ellie had lied.

No, Ellie decided, she couldn't do it. She turned instead to look back at where the lights of the car had disappeared into darkness, taking Jack with them.

Her lips still tingled from his kiss; her body still boomed where he had held her against him. It might not be the way she had wanted, but at least she had kissed him instead of spending her life loving him from afar and wondering what it would be like.

She could have been stuck in a city job by now, Ellie reminded herself, pining for the outback. She could have been watching tonight as Jack got engaged to another girl who would be a mother for Alice. She wouldn't have to face that now. He was going to marry her, and she would be able to stay at Waverley, with him.

It wasn't everything she wanted, but it was a lot. It was enough.

'Yes,' she agreed slowly, 'I'm very lucky.'

Jack picked her up on Wednesday at first light. Ellie was waiting for him at the airstrip, and he left the propeller spinning blurrily as she climbed in beside him.

'Hello, Ellie.'

'Hi,' she said brightly, making a big fuss about fastening her belt so that she didn't have to look at him directly.

She was determined to behave naturally. Ellie had done a lot of thinking since the party. Jack's kiss was seared on her memory, raw and disturbing. She felt sick and shaken when she thought about how treacherously her body had responded, but she had made up her mind.

She was going to marry Jack. Living with him was obviously going to be more difficult than she had thought, but it would be better than living without him. All she had to do was pretend that nothing out of the ordinary had happened at the party, that he had never kissed her and that she had never kissed him back with that aching hunger.

Easier said than done.

Ellie was agonisingly aware of Jack beside her as the little plane sped down the airstrip and lifted into the air. She felt the familiar drop of her stomach as the ground fell away beneath them, the same lurch of alarm and anticipation she felt whenever she saw Jack, whenever she thought about the way he smiled, the way he squinted against the sun, the way he tilted his hat on his head.

Jack seemed to be absorbed in flying the plane. Ellie took the chance to study him from under her lashes. He sat relaxed in his seat, his hands sure and steady on the joystick, his eyes intent as he checked the instrument panel.

Her gaze rested on his profile. Everything about him was so familiar: the creases at the edges of his eyes, the angular planes of his face, the long, mobile mouth. But now she knew how exciting those lips felt against her own. She knew the strength of his hands and the hardness of his body in a way she had only been able to imagine before.

Ellie's insides clenched, remembering. Now everything was different.

CHAPTER SIX

JERKING her eyes away from Jack, she moistened her lips and sought desperately for something to say.

'D-did you bring more paint for the bathroom?' Hardly the most sparkling of conversation openers, but the best she could manage.

'Enough to do that and to finish Alice's room, too.'

Jack was intensely grateful to Ellie for breaking the uncomfortable silence. They talked decorating for a while, and when that subject was exhausted, and the silence yawned around them once more, they talked about how much rain there had been and how high the creeks were running. They were even driven to talking about fixing the generator at Waverley and how much fuel they would need to order.

Their stilted conversation filled the silence, but it didn't stop the memory of the kiss they had shared strumming in the air between them.

In the end, Jack could bear it no longer. He broke off in the middle of telling Ellie what was needed to make the stockmen's quarters habitable to say abruptly, 'I'm sorry about the other day.'

'The other day?' said Ellie, thrown by the sudden change of subject.

'I was out of order,' he said. 'You were right. Your feelings for this other man are none of my business. I never meant to quarrel with you like that,' he went on awkwardly. 'I don't know why I was so angry. It just seemed to be a difficult situation, and I guess I was on edge.'

'I think we both were,' she said, trying desperately to keep her voice light.

Jack took a breath. 'It's not just the argument. I need to apologise about that kiss, too.'

'Oh, that,' said Ellie weakly.

'I don't know what was the matter with me,' he said, determined to make a full confession. 'I wasn't thinking straight, and somehow it all got out of control.'

She swallowed, remembering how helpless she had been to resist the soaring excitement, how hungrily she had kissed him back. It hadn't been all Jack's fault. The colour deepened in her cheeks. 'It doesn't matter,' she muttered.

'I didn't frighten you, Ellie, did I?' he said, shooting her a quick glance.

The only thing that had frightened her had been the power of her own response. 'No,' she said in a small voice.

'I was afraid I might have done. You looked...' Jack trailed off, remembering how dark and desperate her eyes had been. 'Upset...' he finished lamely.

'I was OK.' Ellie turned her face away to hide the colour burning in her cheeks. 'It caught me a bit off-balance, that was all.'

Off-balance. That was a nice, understated way to describe how she had felt as the world reeled around her.

Jack eased the joystick to the right, sending the plane into a gentle curve. 'Ellie, are you sure you want to go ahead with this?' he asked. 'I know I wasn't very understanding at the time, but that party made me realise how difficult it's going to be for you to be married to me and pretend that everything's fine when all you want is to be with someone else. I didn't make things any easier by carrying on like that, either. I wouldn't blame you if you'd changed your mind after the way I behaved.'

'Are you trying to tell me that you've changed *your* mind?'

'No.'

He had, of course, several times—and changed it back again as often. He felt uncomfortable whenever he thought about that party. His reaction to Ellie had disconcerted him. Clare and Gray hadn't noticed her with all those men, and it was obvious that they thought that he had been imagining it. But why would he do that unless he had been jealous, which he wasn't? He couldn't be jealous of *Ellie*.

No, he had been tired, edgy, confused, maybe, but definitely not jealous. Ellie was… Well, she was just Ellie. Or she had been until she'd put that dress on, he remembered darkly.

He cast a sideways glance at her averted face. When he had seen her waiting for him at the airstrip in her old jeans and a faded green shirt he had been relieved, but also more than a little embarrassed. It seemed hard to believe that he had got in such a state about Lizzy's little sister. Ellie was someone he looked out for, someone comfortingly familiar, not someone who drove him into a fury and then melted into his arms.

He hated the idea of her being hurt, of course, but that didn't mean anything. If he had a sister of his own, he would feel exactly the same.

'What I'm trying to say is that you don't have to do anything you don't want to do,' Jack went on after a slight pause. 'I know it might be awkward to cancel the wedding just after we've announced the engagement, but we could think of some excuse. We could pretend that we wanted to postpone it or something. People would soon forget.'

'I don't want to cancel the wedding,' said Ellie quickly, before he managed to talk himself out of the whole idea. 'I haven't changed my mind either.'

She drew a deep breath. 'I owe you an apology, too, Jack. It takes two to argue and two to kiss. When things got out of control at the party, it was my fault as much as yours. Perhaps we should just pretend it never happened?'

Jack shot her a grateful look. 'If you're happy to forget about it, Ellie, then so am I.'

Forget about the way he had kissed her? There was fat chance of that, thought Ellie.

'At least one good thing came out of that party,' she said, mustering a smile and hoping that she sounded suitably cool and composed, and not as if her heart was somersaulting around her chest at the mere thought of that kiss. 'It completely convinced Lizzy that we were a real couple.'

'Really?'

'I was surprised, too,' said Ellie. 'But Lizzy seemed to think that the fact that we were arguing was a very good sign—I'm not quite sure why. She even said that she envied us!'

Jack didn't feel as if there was anything about his situation for anyone to envy. 'She wouldn't say that if she knew the truth,' he said with the faintest shade of bitterness.

Ellie looked down at the land that rolled like an endless greenish-grey carpet out to the horizon and beyond, at the vast expanse of scrub where the cattle hid beneath the spindly gums and termite mounds rose like castles out of the red earth.

'No, I don't suppose she would,' she agreed dully.

There was a silence which for some reason felt awkward. It was Jack who broke it first.

'I thought Lizzy was a believer in waiting until you had found your soul mate and only getting married if everything was romantic and perfect.'

'She is.' Ellie kept her eyes on the bush below them. 'We obviously put on a better act than we realised.'

'We must have done.'

There was a strange note in Jack's voice and Ellie could feel him watching her. Her skin prickled beneath his eyes, and the colour rose in her cheeks as she imagined Jack wondering how she had been able to put on quite such a convincing performance of being in love with him.

'I asked Lizzy once if she had ever been in love with you,' she said, in a desperate attempt to steer the conversation away from her own eager response to his kiss.

At least she succeeded in diverting Jack. 'What did she say?' he asked, half-startled, half-amused.

'She said that she hadn't, but she didn't know why not. You're such good friends, and you've got so much in common. I always thought that you and Lizzy would end up together,' Ellie confessed, amazed at her own composure. She really sounded as if she hadn't really cared one way or another, as if it had been no more than a matter of vague curiosity.

'I've never thought about it before, but now you come to mention it, it *is* funny,' said Jack slowly. 'I guess I always knew that it was Gray she loved. I couldn't believe it when she broke off their engagement, although I can see now that she was right. I don't think it ever occurred to me that Lizzy and I would be anything other than good friends,' he went on after a moment. 'I don't know why. She's a very special person.

'Pretty, too,' he added, an affectionate smile touching the corners of his mouth. 'It's odd that I never fell in love with Lizzy, but I did with Pippa. Pippa wasn't blond, but she was like Lizzy in lots of ways.'

A shadow crossed Jack's face as he remembered Pippa. 'She was warm and funny and lively, just like Lizzy is, but I don't go weak at the knees when Lizzy touches me, and the sun doesn't come out when she smiles. Do you know that feeling, Ellie?'

Ellie thought about the way the earth seemed to shift beneath her feet whenever Jack so much as brushed a finger against her. She thought about how the world took on a dazzling clarity when he was near, how the stars would brighten and the air would crispen and all her senses would tingle just knowing he was there.

'Yes, I know that feeling,' she said. She looked at the horizon, faint and blue and blurry in the far distance. 'There's no accounting for why we fall in love with one person and not another.'

Jack glanced at her averted face and found his eyes resting on the pure line of her cheek, on the warm curve of her mouth and the way her hair curled softly behind her ear, and he felt an unaccountable tightening around his heart.

'No,' he agreed in a voice that sounded shorter than he'd intended.

There was another pause. He made an unnecessary adjustment to the plane's course and tried to concentrate on the instruments in front of him, but Ellie was tugging annoyingly at the edge of his vision. His eyes flickered sideways just as she risked a glance at him, and even though they both looked quickly away, Jack was left feeling a fool for some reason.

'What about your parents?' he asked a little too heartily. 'Did we manage to convince them as well?'

'I don't think it would ever occur to them that we might be pretending,' said Ellie frankly. 'They're not exactly suspicious types. Mum's already obsessed with wedding dresses and floral arrangements,' she went on, seizing the chance to move the conversation onto less dangerous ground. 'She's determined that it'll be a traditional wedding. We've already had a row because I won't get married in the church at Mathison.'

'What's wrong with the church?' asked Jack. 'I don't mind, if that's what you want.'

'Churches are for real weddings,' said Ellie a little wistfully.

'Isn't ours going to be a real wedding?'

She turned her clear gaze on him. 'You know it isn't, Jack. I think the wedding should be at Waverley Creek. Waverley's the reason we're getting married. You want to marry me so that you can live there with Alice, and I'm marrying you so that I can live there rather than in the city.'

'Very clearly put,' said Jack, a slight edge to his voice.

'I'm just being honest. Our marriage isn't going to be real in the way it would have been real if you'd married Pippa,' she said with a little difficulty, 'and we've agreed that the vows we make aren't going to be binding. It's Waverley that binds us together, isn't it? Don't you think it would be better if we had the wedding there?'

A muscle was beginning to twitch in Jack's jaw. 'If that's what you want,' he said curtly.

Ellie looked down at her hands. 'It's not a question of

what I want,' she said sadly. 'It's a question of what would be the most appropriate, given our situation.'

She stole a glance at Jack's profile, but there was something daunting about his complete lack of expression. 'I, er, thought we could clean up the old woolshed,' she went on hesitantly when Jack said nothing. 'It's a lovely building. It's still got a roof, and it would just need to be cleared out and swept. I think it would be a great place for a party.'

'Good idea,' Jack agreed, trying to summon up some enthusiasm.

The trouble was that he didn't feel very enthusiastic. He felt flat and oddly dissatisfied. It was something to do with the way Ellie kept reminding him of just why she was marrying him, with her bright, impersonal conversation as she chatted on about the plans she and her mother were making for the wedding.

Jack didn't want to talk about the wedding. He wanted to know whether the kiss had shaken her as much as him. He wanted to know what she had felt, if she had lain awake every night since then, reliving it and wondering just what had happened.

They finished painting the homestead that weekend. 'I'm borrowing a couple of men from Bushman's Creek next week,' Jack told Ellie as she rinsed her paintbrush under the tap. 'We'll fix up the stockmen's quarters first, then we can make a start on the cattleyards.'

'Great,' said Ellie, trying not to notice how polite and distant Jack always was now. 'What time do you want to pick me up?'

Jack didn't quite meet her eyes. 'It's OK,' he said, 'We can manage. Things have been a bit busy at Bushman's Creek lately, especially with me spending so much time over here, but Gray's said he can spare Jed and Dave for a month or so, until I can find some men to work here for the new season.'

'I could help, too,' she offered. 'I don't mind what I do.'

'I think you'd be better sorting out the wedding,' said Jack. 'It's not that long now, and there's still a lot to organise.'

'Mum and Lizzy seem to be happy to do all that.'

'Still…' He hesitated. 'There's no need for you to be here just yet.'

What he meant was that he didn't want her there. Ellie felt as if she had been slapped. Jack obviously thought she was only good for women's work, for cleaning the house, for making the home. He had no more use for her until he needed her to look after Alice.

Refusing to let him see how hurt she was, she put up her chin and flashed a brittle smile. 'Fine,' she said. 'There's no point in me being here if you don't need me, is there?'

So Ellie was stuck at home, bored and restless, trying to show an interest in bouquets and tablecloths, while her mother and Lizzy fussed daily on the phone about who was wearing what and what everyone would eat.

She was ordered to Perth, where Lizzy swept her off to buy a wedding dress, but being in the city only made her feel more lonely and out of place. Ellie stood obediently and let herself be bullied in and out of elaborate confections, but all she wanted was to be back at Waverley, where the station was coming to life without her, and where she wasn't needed.

The thought of Waverley kept her going. She longed for the wedding to be over. When the dress had been worn and the flowers had died and the guests had gone, she would be at Waverley, with Jack, and with Alice, and she would be needed. Everything would be all right then.

They were married a month later.

'I cannot *believe* my little sister is getting married before me!' Lizzy pretended to grumble as she walked around Ellie, inspecting her with a proprietorial air and twitching the folds of her dress into perfect place. 'I'm obviously doomed to be the only spinster left in Australia!'

'You'll find someone Lizzy, and he'll be perfect.'

'If I don't, it will be your fault for insisting on having me as your bridesmaid,' said Lizzy darkly. 'This is the third time I've had to do this. You know what they say—three times a bridesmaid, never a bride!'

'Well, you're not really a bridesmaid,' Ellie tried to placate her. 'I just want you there for moral support.'

'I know,' said Lizzy with a grin. 'I'm just joking. Wild horses wouldn't have stopped me holding your flowers for you today—as long as you make sure that I'm the one who catches the bouquet!'

Picking up a spray of native flowers from the chest, she handed them to Ellie. 'There!' She stood back to admire the effect, and her face softened. 'You look beautiful, Ellie.'

Ellie turned almost reluctantly to look at herself in the mirror. Lizzy had insisted on making her up, and now it was as if a stranger stood staring back at her, a stranger with luminous green eyes and a warm, sultry mouth. Her brown hair was drawn back with jewelled clips to reveal a delicate bone structure that Ellie had never even known that she possessed, but her face felt stiff and unfamiliar, and she grimaced just to see whether her reflection would grimace back and convince her that it really *was* her in the mirror.

'It's a lovely dress,' Lizzy went on encouragingly. She had picked it out and had practically had to force Ellie to try it on, so she had a proprietorial interest in it. 'That ivory colour is perfect for you.'

Ellie glanced down at the dress a little dubiously and fiddled with the fringe of a sheer stole that Lizzy had draped artistically over her arms. She could see that it was a beautiful dress, long and sleeveless and cut with a stunning simplicity, but it just didn't feel like *her*, any more than the lipstick and the mascara and the pretty clips in her hair felt as if they belonged on her.

'I wish I could have got married in my jeans,' she said with a tiny sigh, and Lizzy looked shocked.

'Jeans! Honestly, Ellie, what is the matter with you?' she demanded. 'You're walking out that door to marry the nicest, sexiest, best-looking man in the district, and you want to wear *jeans*! Don't you want Jack to look at you and be bowled over by how beautiful you are?'

For a treacherous moment, Ellie let herself imagine what it would be like if Jack saw her and fell head over heels in love with her, just as she had always hoped that he would one day.

'Of course I do,' she said wistfully, wishing that she could believe that it might happen.

This was the day she had dreamt about for as long as she could remember. In a few minutes she would walk out through the door and marry Jack, but it wasn't the golden, laughing Jack of her dreams, Jack with the warm, dancing brown eyes and the smile that clutched at her heart. She was marrying a Jack whose eyes were wary, whose smile was rare, a Jack she had hardly seen for almost three weeks.

He had met her at the Waverley airstrip when she had arrived with her parents and Lizzy earlier in the day, and although he had smiled, he had made no effort to speak to her alone. He had said simply that he would let them have the homestead to get ready in and would see them at five o'clock. He might have been arranging to meet for a beer for all the sense of occasion he'd shown.

'Well, then.' Lizzy gave the folds of her dress a final twitch. 'Are you ready to go?'

Ellie took a deep breath. 'I think so.'

'How do you feel?'

'Terrified.'

It was true. The realisation of what she was about to do hit Ellie without warning with the force of a steam-roller, sending the breath whooshing from her lungs in a rush of sheer panic. She was wearing a wedding dress. She was going to get *married*.

But Lizzy only laughed. 'You'll be fine,' she said, picking up her own flowers and opening the door with a flourish. 'Just keep thinking of Jack.'

It was just after five o'clock when Ellie took her father's arm and walked across to the old woolshed.

Built in Waverley's glory days, its stone walls and curved roof had stood up to the years of neglect far better than the other station buildings, and now it had been transformed. Where teams of shearers had once worked their way through thousands of sheep, temporary tables covered with pale pink cloths had been set up and decorated with creamy-coloured flowers flown in specially from Darwin, and trays of glasses gleamed in anticipation of the champagne that would be opened as soon as the ceremony was over.

When Ellie and her father appeared, the woolshed was full of wedding guests. They turned as if one, parting to let her walk through them on trembling legs to where Jack waited with Gray at his side.

For Ellie, it was all a blur. She had a confused impression of smiling faces, but they seemed to be separated from her by an invisible curtain. She felt curiously detached, as if in a dream, and she found herself clinging to tiny details to convince herself that this was actually happening and that she really was on her way to marry Jack. She could feel the wiry strength of her father's arm, the hard wooden floor beneath her feet, the dull swish of silk against her legs as she walked.

And then, suddenly, Jack was there, turning to watch her approach, tall and devastatingly attractive in his formal suit, his expression so sombre that Ellie's heart turned over. Her step faltered and she would have stopped if her father hadn't borne her on regardless.

We shouldn't be doing this, she thought in sudden panic. I shouldn't marry Jack when I know he doesn't love me. He shouldn't marry me when he's still in love with Pippa. It's all wrong.

It *was* all wrong, but it was too late to do anything about it. Everyone was there, people she had known her whole life, all watching expectantly. Lizzy was behind her, her mother was already sniffling into a handkerchief, her father was beaming. And now they had reached Jack's side and her father was stepping aside, leaving her alone and stranded with no one to turn to but Jack.

With a sense of fatality Ellie took the hand he held out to her, and lifted her eyes to look into his face at last.

Jack had been feeling slightly sick. Waiting with Gray for Ellie to arrive, he had run his finger around his unfamiliarly tight collar and wondered what on earth he was doing there, about to marry a girl he didn't love—a girl, more to the point, who didn't love him.

He had thrown Gray a glance of desperate appeal, hoping that his brother could come up with some way to help him out of this mess he had got himself into, but Gray had been smiling at Clare, who was standing a little further along, with Alice in her arms. Jack had followed his gaze, and at the sight of his daughter, his nerves had steadied.

Alice was the reason he was here.

Behind him, the crowd stirred in anticipation, and he turned to see Ellie coming towards him on her father's arm. At least, he assumed it was Ellie. She looked so cool and so poised, so elegant in the long white dress, that Jack was shaken by sudden doubt that it was Ellie at all. She had done something to her hair, too, and the pure lines of her face and throat stood out with startling clarity.

Jack stared, gripped by sudden panic. He couldn't marry this stranger, walking towards him with her eyes demurely lowered!

She had reached his side and he put out his hand, hardly aware of what he was doing. Her fingers trembled in his, but when she looked up her eyes were clear and true and troubled. Ellie's eyes.

Almost giddy with relief, Jack smiled down at her. This was no cool, beautiful bride. This was the Ellie he had always known. Ellie who was hating this as much as he was. This wasn't the wedding she had wanted either, he reminded himself. Holding her hand tightly, he turned towards the celebrant.

It wasn't a long service. Ellie stared blindly ahead of her. The celebrant spoke about marriage, but the words seemed to wash over her, and then she heard her own voice, as if it belonged to someone else, making the right responses. Jack must have done the same, for the next moment she was holding out her hand, and he was sliding the ring onto her finger. Ellie could feel the warmth of his touch, the smooth, cool gold against her skin, as the celebrant pronounced them man and wife.

Man and wife.

Dazed, Ellie stared down at the ring on her hand. They were married. She was Jack's wife.

Slowly, she lifted her head, to find Jack watching her with warm understanding in his eyes.

'You may kiss the bride.'

Jack's smile was crooked as he looked down into Ellie's face. He had to kiss her, he thought, although after the last time it was probably the last thing she wanted. He couldn't *not* kiss her, not when all her family and friends were watching expectantly with sentimental smiles, but he could make it as easy on her as possible.

Taking her face between his palms, he touched his mouth to hers. It was only for a moment, hardly long enough to be called a kiss at all, but as their lips met Jack felt something unlock inside him, and he had an insane urge to gather Ellie into his arms and carry on kissing her.

The impulse was so strong that Jack had to wrench his mouth away. Oddly shaken, and unable to meet her eyes, he took Ellie's hand instead, and forced a smile as they turned towards their guests.

Ellie saw Jack smile and guessed at the effort it cost him to pretend that this was the happiest day of his life. She had felt his instinctive recoil as he kissed her, and her heart ached for him. He had hardly been able to bear to kiss her, the bride he had never wanted. She longed to comfort him, tell him that he didn't have to go through with it after all, but even as the words trembled on her lips she knew that it was too late.

It was done. They were married. And there was no time to do anything more than brace themselves for the flurry of congratulations that soon swept them apart.

The reception was almost as much a blur as the ceremony for Ellie. People kept telling her that she looked radiant, but she couldn't help thinking that they were just saying it because that was what you said to a bride, regardless of how she looked.

She didn't feel radiant. She felt disconnected and alone. Jack had Alice in his arms, and he held her close with his big, strong hands. Overwhelmed by the crowd, Alice clutched at her father, burying her face shyly in his neck, and Jack's expression as he bent his head to murmur reassuringly to her told Ellie everything she needed to know, if she hadn't known already, about why he had married her. He and Alice were two parts of a whole. They didn't need her to feel complete, not the way she desperately needed them.

Ellie's heart twisted, and she looked away to find that Clare was watching her with such understanding and sympathy in her expression that Ellie's chin came up. She didn't need anyone to feel sorry for her, and she wasn't going to feel sorry for herself. It wasn't as if she hadn't known exactly what marriage to Jack would involve. She had made her choice, and she was going to make the best of it.

She smiled at Clare, a bright, defiant smile, and she kept on smiling. She smiled through the photographs and the speeches, she smiled as she cut the cake. She even smiled when guests who had only just discovered that Alice was Jack's daughter commented on their closeness. Ellie was sure that she could read pity in their eyes, as well as a kind of satisfaction at having Jack's puzzling decision to marry her explained. Of *course*; he needed a mother for his baby daughter. Why else would he have chosen boring little Ellie Walker as his wife?

No one mentioned the matter outright, of course, but Ellie was sure that was what they were all thinking, and as the evening wore on her smile began to look strained. Not that anyone else seemed to notice. The party was well away and no one seemed to be watching her at all.

Finding herself alone, Ellie seized her opportunity. Drifting unobtrusively back into a shadow, where thousands of fleeces had once been stacked, she allowed the smile to fall from her face. Oblivious to her, the party spun noisily on, and the woolshed resounded with the sound of music and laughter and dancing feet.

Through the crowd, Ellie caught a glimpse of Clare and Gray. They were just standing, observing the dancers, not even touching but somehow a unit, perfectly balanced and complete. As she watched, Gray ran his hand down his wife's spine in a gesture that was at once discreet and yet so sensual that something inside Ellie twisted with an envy so intense it was painful.

She saw Gray murmur something in Clare's ear, saw the secret smile that curled Clare's lips as she put her arm around his waist and leant into him. There was something so intimate about the way they stood there that Ellie felt her face burn, as if she had been caught peeping into their bedroom, and she looked quickly away, only to find herself staring straight into Jack's eyes. Her heart seemed to stop.

He was on the other side of the woolshed, watching her with a grave expression, and as their eyes met and held the music faded and the dancers whirled into a silent blur, and the two of them were quite alone, staring at each other.

Without haste, as if unaware of the other people around

him, Jack made his way across the floor to where Ellie stood, a slender, dark-eyed figure, her ivory silk dress gleaming in the shadows.

Ellie was suddenly very tired. She knew that she ought to fix the smile back on her face, and carry on playing the happy, radiant bride, but she couldn't. She couldn't move or speak or even think. She could only stand there and wait for him.

Jack came to a halt just in front of her, shielding her from the other guests, and his smile was twisted as he looked down into her face. 'You've had enough,' he said gently, and he held out his hand. 'Shall we go?'

CHAPTER SEVEN

ELLIE didn't answer. She just nodded and took his hand, and they slipped out of the woolshed by a side door.

Outside, the night air was cool and starry. Ellie turned her face up to the dark sky and breathed in its deep, tranquil silence. 'Thank you,' she said quietly after a moment.

'I saw you watching Gray and Clare,' said Jack. 'I saw your face, when you thought no one could see you.' He hesitated, remembering the nakedness of her expression. 'I know what it cost you to keep smiling all day. No one could have guessed that it wasn't the wedding you wanted.'

'It wasn't the wedding you wanted, either,' she said in a low voice.

There was a pause. 'No,' he agreed.

He was still holding her hand, and Ellie was very aware of him, a dark, solid figure in the starlight. The whiteness of his shirt gleamed in the darkness, and as her eyes adjusted she was able to make out more details: his tie where he had loosened it, his collar open around his strong throat, the rugged line of his jaw.

Her gaze drifted on to rest on his mouth, and it was as if she could still feel its warmth and its firmness as he kissed her, as if his hands still cupped her face, and a tiny shiver snaked disturbingly down her spine.

Pulling her hand away, Ellie began walking briskly towards the homestead. 'Do…do you think anyone noticed us go?' she asked, hoping Jack wouldn't wonder why her voice was suddenly so high and squeaky.

He shook his head, his slow, rangy stride keeping up with her without difficulty. 'The party's well away in there,' he said. 'Nobody would think it odd even if they did see us leave,' he pointed out. 'We *are* married.'

'So we are,' said Ellie on a tiny gasp. 'I just can't quite believe it.'

'I know,' said Jack with feeling. 'I told Gray and Kevin we didn't want any fuss, so I hope we'll be spared the usual high jinks. With any luck, anyone who did see us go will just think we're desperate to get to bed.'

'I suppose they would.'

There was a bleakness to Ellie's voice that made Jack wish that he had chosen his words more carefully. Now the image of newly-weds longing to fall into bed together seemed to jangle tauntingly in the air between them.

Ellie had reached the bottom of the verandah steps, and on an impulse Jack put out a hand to stop her. 'You don't need to worry, Ellie,' he said abruptly.

She looked at him with a certain wariness. 'What about?'

'About sleeping together.' He hesitated. 'We'll have to share a room tonight. There are so many people staying in the homestead that it would look odd if we didn't. But it's only for one night.'

His smile gleamed a little crookedly through the darkness. 'I won't lay a finger on you,' he promised. 'And when everyone's gone tomorrow, I'll move into the room next to Alice.'

'I see.'

'I guess we should have talked about this before,' Jack persevered, a little daunted by Ellie's lack of response. 'I just assumed that you wouldn't want to sleep with me.'

There was the faintest question in his voice as he finished. What did he expect her to say? Ellie wondered with a small spurt of anger. Oh, no, Jack, I want you to make love to me all night, every night? I want to lie in bed beside you and to be able to run my hands over your body? I want you to kiss me until I can't breathe, and then I want you to kiss me some more?

She couldn't tell him the truth, but if she didn't say anything she might never get the chance again.

'Well, I…' She trailed off hopelessly, not sure how to continue, or even what she had been planning to say in the first place.

'I know it's difficult for you,' said Jack quickly, seeing that she was floundering. 'You're in love with another man. Of course you're not going to want to jump straight into bed with me. I just don't want you to think that I ever expected that you would,' he finished, wishing that he could have phrased it better.

'I never thought that.' Ellie picked up her skirt as she turned to climb the steps, away from Jack and his tantalising nearness, away from the temptation to cast pride to the winds and simply tell him the truth. The effort of appearing composed made her sound almost cold. 'I never thought that you would want to sleep with *me*.'

'Didn't you?'

The dryness in Jack's voice halted Ellie with her foot on the second step, and the air leaked out of her lungs as she turned slowly, almost fearfully, to look down at him. He stood at the bottom of the steps, rangy and apparently relaxed. His jacket was slung over his shoulder, and he wore a quizzical expression that confused and unnerved her.

'No, I…I mean… Well, we said we'd be friends…' she stammered.

Jack looked at her, poised uncertainly on the steps, her wedding dress gathered in one hand and falling in soft folds. The satiny shimmer of the silk was reflected on her skin, so that she seemed almost luminous in the starlight, her eyes dark pools in her pale face.

'Yes, that's what we said, isn't it?' he agreed, one corner of his mouth lifting in a lop-sided smile. 'And friends is what we'll be.'

Ellie eyed him uncertainly. Wasn't being friends what he wanted?

She hesitated, but before she had a chance to ask him what the strange note in his voice meant, Jack had climbed the steps past her and was holding open the screen door as if they had been discussing nothing more than the chance of rain or the price of feed.

'Lizzy wanted to know where we were sleeping,' Jack went on in the same brisk, impersonal way as he led the way down the corridor. 'She knows we haven't moved in properly, and I think she wanted to make sure the bedroom looked nice for you.'

He opened the door into the main bedroom and gestured Ellie inside. Desperate not to brush against him, or do anything that he might construe as an unwanted invitation, she practically edged around him and into the room.

It was one of the last rooms she and Jack had decorated. Ellie could remember painting the walls and wondering if it would ever be a room they would share. Well, now it looked as if it would be, even if only for a night.

The floor was wooden, the walls plain, and there were slatted shutters at the windows. In daylight, the effect was one of spare, uncluttered coolness, but Lizzy had done her best to create a romantic atmosphere. There were flowers on the chest of drawers, a lamp threw a soft yellow pool of light over the bed, and a lacy nightie was draped invitingly over the pillows.

They saw it at the same time. 'Oh,' said Ellie weakly.

'No one could accuse Lizzy of not making an effort for you,' Jack tried to joke, and she glanced at him.

'No,' she sighed.

There was an awkward silence while the nightdress lay on the bed and seemed to mock them and the loveless marriage they had embarked upon. Unable to bear the sight of it any longer, Ellie went over to the bed and picked it up with an unconsciously wistful expression. It was a lovely thing, she thought as she pulled it through her hands, no more than a wisp of silk and lace, and it must have cost Lizzy an absolute fortune. It was perfect for a bride.

For a real bride.

Ellie could feel pathetic tears prickling her eyes and she blinked them back fiercely as she folded the night-dress with jerky movements and almost shoved it out of sight in the top drawer of the chest. She cleared her throat. 'It's very nice,' she said with a fine assumption of unconcern, 'but not exactly the kind of thing one wears to sleep with a friend!'

'No,' Jack agreed. He turned abruptly on his heel. 'I'm going to check on Alice.'

Left on her own, Ellie wandered restlessly around the room. Her body was thumping with strain, and her brain buzzed with tiredness, but she knew she wouldn't be able to sleep. How could she, when Jack was going to be lying right beside her, warm, tantalising, close enough to touch?

What if she talked in her sleep? What if she rolled against him in the night? How would she be able to stop herself from clinging to him and begging him to make love to her?

How was she going to bear being just a friend?

She was just going to have to, Ellie decided, coming to an abrupt halt. It was only for one night. She was getting into a state about nothing, because nothing was what would happen. All she had to do was take off her dress, wash her face, find her own sexless T-shirt that she had brought to sleep in and climb into bed. And when Jack came back she would say goodnight, turn on her side and go to sleep.

It would be easy.

Having talked herself into being sensible, Ellie found herself baulked at the very first part of her programme when she couldn't undo the complicated fastening at the back of her dress. She wriggled and squirmed and contorted her arms over her shoulders, but she couldn't quite reach the top of the zip, and in the end she gave up and went along to the bathroom to try washing her face instead. Surely she would be able to manage *that*.

The door of Alice's room stood ajar. Jack was probably still in there, giving her a chance to get ready for bed in privacy. Ellie kept her eyes lowered and walked quickly past, her skirt swishing along the polished wooden floor.

She felt better when she had brushed her teeth and washed the make-up off her face, and she made her way back down the corridor to the bedroom with her head held high. She wasn't going to spoil everything by making a stupid fuss now.

A movement in Alice's room caught her eye as she passed the door. From this direction she could see how the light from the corridor angled into the room. It just reached the end of the cot, where Jack was standing, staring down at the framed photograph he held in his hands.

As Ellie hesitated, he looked up, and even in the dim light she could see that his expression was one of such unutterable sadness that her heart cracked for him. She didn't have to be able to see the picture to know that it was the photo of Pippa that always stood by Alice's cot.

They looked at each other in silence, while Alice slept peacefully. There was no need for words. There was nothing either of them could say. Ellie could only gaze helplessly, hopelessly back at Jack and long for some way to comfort him. When the only way she could think of was to leave him alone with his grief and his daughter, she turned and walked softly on.

Her own feelings were so trivial compared to Jack's. Ellie thought about the sombreness of his expression as he watched her walk across the woolshed towards him on her father's arm. The whole day must have been agony for him.

It should have been Pippa standing next to him, Pippa who held out her hand for the ring, Pippa smiling in the photographs and laughing as she tossed the bouquet. How had Jack been able to bear looking at his bride today? wondered Ellie. How had he managed to smile when he saw her standing there next to him with her quiet, ordinary face, instead of the vibrant, beautiful Pippa?

With a sigh, Ellie sat on the edge of the bed and smoothed the cover sadly with her hand. Poor Jack, poor Pippa. All that love, all that laughter, and now there was nothing.

'Are you planning to sleep in that dress?' Jack spoke from the doorway, obviously making an effort to keep his voice light.

'No.' Ellie got to her feet, willing to follow his lead

and pretend that everything was normal. 'I can't undo the zip, that's all.'

'Come here, and I'll have a go.'

Jack moved into the room and Ellie turned towards him, only to stop as if teetering on the brink of an abyss. She couldn't do it, she realised with a blinding sense of certainty. She couldn't pretend that everything was all right when Jack's heart was broken.

'Oh, Jack,' she said unsteadily, and her voice cracked. 'I'm so sorry...'

Jack stopped, too. He didn't say anything. He just opened his arms, and Ellie walked into them.

They held each other close, and it seemed to Ellie that she was taking comfort as much as giving it. 'It must have been so awful for you today,' she muttered after a while. Her arms were tight around his back, her face pressed into his shoulder, and she could smell his warm, clean, reassuringly masculine smell. He moved with an easy, even lazy grace, but he was like a rock she could cling to, his body firm and solid and inexpressibly reassuring.

'And for you.' Jack laid his cheek against Ellie's hair and tightened his arms around her in a warm hug. She needed comfort, too.

Pippa's photograph had caught his eye as he'd bent over the cot to check that Alice was sleeping soundly, and he had picked it up slowly. Pippa had smiled joyously up at him, and Jack had ached with a renewed sense of loss as he remembered her brightness and her beauty. Her laughter had seemed to echo in the darkness above their sleeping daughter.

He had thought about Pippa a lot that day as he prepared for his wedding. She was the mother of his child, the dazzling star who had lit up his life and then disappeared, leaving it in darkness, and on his wedding day, of all days, he owed it to her to remember the girl he should have shared it with.

'I'm getting married for Alice, Pippa,' he had murmured to her photograph, but as he'd lingered by the cot his memory of her had kept blurring, unbidden, into thoughts of Ellie. Of the unhappiness in her eyes as she'd walked through the woolshed to marry a man she didn't love. Of the naked longing in her face as she'd watched Gray and Clare. Of the way she had looked in the starlight, with her wedding dress gathered in her hand and her gaze dark and questioning.

Jack held her now, very conscious of her softness and her slenderness. She felt warm and pliant and disarmingly right in his arms. He could smell her perfume, light and elusive, and the silk of her dress was cool and smooth beneath his hand as he rubbed her back with a slow, gentle movement, soothing her distress as he would a frightened animal.

Gradually, the strain eased out of Ellie's body. She relaxed into him with a tiny sigh, and the only sharp edge to her was the jewelled clasp, which felt cold and hard against Jack's cheek as he laid it against her hair. Without thinking, he unclipped first one and then the other, and let her hair tumble softly around her face.

Ellie didn't protest, but she did pull back a little in surprise, and Jack found himself looking straight into her eyes. They looked at each other, both conscious that as the silence lengthened the companionable comfort was trickling out of the atmosphere and leaving in its place something new and infinitely more disturbing, something that jangled insistently in the air between them and seeped under their skins.

Very slowly, Jack opened his fingers and let the clasps

fall to the floor with a clatter that reverberated in the quietness, but Ellie didn't react. She stood mouse-still, her eyes never leaving Jack's, while a quivering began deep inside her.

Jack lifted his hands to tangle them in her hair. 'Ellie…' he said in a deep voice, 'Ellie, do you think that just for tonight we could be more than friends?'

Tongue-tied by his touch, tantalised by his nearness, Ellie looked dumbly into his face. Her heart was slamming against her ribs in slow, painful strokes. She knew what Jack wanted. He wanted to forget his grief, to stop thinking and remembering and to lose himself for a while where the past and the future faded into insignificance and only the moment mattered. She couldn't bring Pippa back, but she could do this for him.

Her arms had fallen from him when he'd pulled the clasps from her hair, and now she lifted her hands to spread them against his chest, finding her voice quite easily after all. 'Would it help, Jack?' she asked gently.

The corners of his mouth lifted in a slight smile. 'I think it would,' he said gravely, his warm fingers grazing her skin as they drifted tantalisingly along her jaw and down her throat.

'I'm not pretending it will make everything right,' he went on softly, 'but it might make it easier for us both to get through this night. What do you think?' he added, his voice so low that it seemed to shiver over Ellie's skin.

'I…think it would, too.' Ellie was dry-mouthed, her senses already drumming in response to his slightest touch.

His hand had curved around her throat, was sliding under her hair to caress the nape of her neck. 'I don't want to force you, Ellie. You can say no. You know that, don't you?'

'Yes, I know,' she whispered.

With an agonising lack of haste, Jack pulled her back into his body. His lips were at her temple, warm, tantalising, almost thoughtful as they drifted over her cheekbone, along her jaw, to rest on the very corner of her mouth.

'It's just for tonight,' he murmured again, and Ellie managed to nod.

'I know.'

'You need some comfort, too, don't you, Ellie?'

She could feel his breath against her lips, and she closed her eyes against the wrench of desire. 'Yes,' she said unevenly. 'Yes, I do.'

Jack's mouth brushed over hers. 'You don't want to say no, do you?'

'No,' said Ellie. 'I want you.'

Her voice was barely more than a whisper, but the words seemed to echo around them, bouncing off the walls and booming in the air. *I want you, I want you.* It was true, but Ellie hadn't meant to tell Jack that.

'Just for tonight,' she added quickly, before he could recoil, just so that he knew that she understood.

'Just for tonight,' said Jack, and then his lips possessed hers, and Ellie gasped with a mixture of relief and excitement and a strange, heady sense of having come home at last.

She wound her arms around his neck and gave herself up to the intoxicating pleasure of being kissed by Jack the way she had always dreamed of being kissed. She knew that it wasn't real, she knew that it wasn't for ever, but for tonight it was enough to be in his arms, to be able to kiss him back.

They had made a bargain to forget everything for this one night. Tomorrow, they could go back to pretending, but now…now there was no need to hold back, and no fear that Jack would guess the truth. This was comfort; this was allowed. Jack needed it and wanted it as much as she did.

Jack gathered her tightly against him, his hands insistent as they slithered over the silk, and Ellie melded into his hard body, beyond thinking about anything but the taste of him and the feel of him and the trembling need inside her which grew stronger and more urgent with every kiss, every caress.

'You wanted me to undo your dress, didn't you?' Jack murmured seductively against her throat, his mouth so warm and his lips so enticing that Ellie tipped back her head with a tiny gasp at the desire that clutched savagely at her in response.

'I did,' she said breathlessly, and shivered anew as she felt Jack smile against her skin.

'I'll have to see what I can do.'

His hands slid caressingly over her shoulders and met at the top of the zip, where he found the fiddly hook-and-eye fastening. It took him longer than he had thought to undo it, but then his fingers weren't quite steady, and Ellie wasn't making things any easier by kissing his throat and fumbling with the buttons of his shirt.

Jack's senses snarled with mingled anticipation and frustration. On the point of giving in and simply wrenching the fastening impatiently apart, he muttered in relief when he somehow managed to get the thing undone, and he felt Ellie quiver with responsive laughter.

Kissing his way down her neck to the alluring curve of her shoulder, Jack took the zip between his finger and thumb and eased it with a luxurious, provocative lack of haste all the way down to the base of her spine. The slow, swishing sound of the unfastening zip seemed to sizzle erotically in the lamp-lit hush. Once it had gone as far as it would go, he traced his way back up to the nape of her neck with warm, enticing fingers that stroked and circled and teased until Ellie felt as if she was afire and would shatter in the spinning, searing delight.

Murmuring something that was half-protest, half-pleading, she clutched at Jack, but he was intent on sliding the straps of her dress off her shoulders. Slowly, he drew the dress down, until it slithered over her hips and puddled onto the floor with a sigh of silk, and then he reached round her to unclip her bra and let it drop beside the dress.

'Ellie…' He caught his breath, unprepared for the way she looked. She stood before him, slender, wide-eyed, her body softly curved, her skin glowing in the lamplight.

Jack felt as if a powerful force had slammed into him, lifting him off his feet and leaving him reeling and helpless. 'Ellie…' he said again in an unsteady voice, then stopped, unable to go on, unable to find the words to tell her how she made him feel, unable to do anything but gaze at her in wonder.

His stunned disbelief was so obvious that Ellie was conscious of a surge of exultation at her own power. She stood quite still, smiling at him, until with hands that were not quite steady he reached for her, and she lost all sense of time. He secured her against him with a new urgency and the fire between them exploded into a blaze. Kissing frantically, they pulled at his clothes, shedding them as they went, until they were both naked and Jack could draw her down onto the bed.

His hands moved possessively over her, very strong and sure against her softness, and he explored her with wonder, dipping and curving, gliding lovingly over the satiny warmth of her skin, his lips following his hands in searing patterns of desire until she arched beneath him, gasping his name.

He was so firm, so exciting. Ellie ran her own hands over him with a kind of desperation. She couldn't touch him enough, couldn't press herself close enough against him. She rolled over him, glorying in his strong, supple body, in the taste and texture of his skin, in the ripple of muscles beneath her questing fingers.

Caught up in the whirl of sensation, Ellie gave herself up to the timeless beat of desire, where nothing mattered but the hardness of Jack's body, the sureness of his hands and the wicked pleasure of his lips as he discovered her secret places, opening her up, unlocking her until she soared free.

Ellie had never known such an intensity of feeling. It was exhilarating, entrancing, electrifying. It was terrifying. Sobbing Jack's name, she dug her fingers into his back, and he murmured reassuringly to her as they moved together in an irresistible rhythm that bore them up to heart-stopping heights before it sent them tumbling and breathless at last into a dazzling explosion of release.

It was a long, long time before they slept. Reluctant to waste the night they had, they lay entwined in the shadows, learning each other anew, and later they made love again, slowly, tenderly, drenched in enchantment. They didn't talk. Words might have broken the spell. So they just held each other, and at last Ellie fell asleep in the curve of Jack's arm, her cheek resting on his chest where she could feel the steady beat of his heart.

Sunlight striping through the shutters woke Ellie the next morning. She lay drowsily for a while, eyes closed, emerging reluctantly from sleep and dimly aware that she didn't want it to be morning. Morning meant that the long, sweet night was over.

Turning her back to the window, Ellie squeezed her eyes shut against the light, but it was no good. She was awake, and the enchantment had evaporated with the dark. 'Just for tonight,' Jack had said.

'Just for tonight,' she had promised.

And now the night was over.

Lying in the morning sunshine, Ellie ached with the memory of the sweetness they had shared. She would never forget it, and never regret it, but she had to accept that it would never happen again.

The door opened and Jack came in, carrying Alice. He was wearing jeans and a sweatshirt, and he held a mug in his free hand. He set it down by the bed as Ellie pulled herself up onto the pillows, taking the sheet with her.

'Oh, good, you're awake,' he said, as if he had never whispered endearments into her skin. 'I've brought you some tea.'

'Thank you.' Ellie felt ridiculously shy in the bright morning light, and she was glad when Jack swung Alice down onto the bed. She could smile and hold out her arms to the baby at least.

Crowing with delight, Alice clambered onto Ellie, who welcomed her with a tight hug. Jack turned abruptly away and went over to open the shutters. 'There's no sign of anyone else,' he said.

Ellie made a heroic effort to match his conversational tone. 'They're probably all sleeping it off.'

'It must have been quite a night.'

Ellie concentrated on Alice, holding her little hands wide apart so that she could stand, gurgling proudly at her achievement. 'It must have been,' she agreed in a voice quite without inflexion.

Jack had been standing by the shutters, running his finger along one of the slats, but at that he came back to sit on the edge of the bed. 'It was quite a night for us, too,' he said quietly, and the breath dried in Ellie's throat.

'Yes,' was all she managed to say.

Ignoring Alice, who had lurched from Ellie's hold to clutch at his shoulder, he took Ellie's hand. 'I don't know how to thank you,' he said.

His fingers were warm and strong around hers. Last night they had curved around her breasts. Ellie swallowed and looked away. 'You don't need to thank me, Jack.'

'I do. Last night…' He hesitated, trying to find the words to tell her what it had meant to him.

'I know,' she said quickly before he could remind her that she shouldn't take it seriously. 'Last night we comforted each other.'

She drew her hand out of his, and when Jack made no attempt to hold onto it she lifted her chin proudly. She wasn't going to beg for something he couldn't give. 'I'm grateful to you, too, Jack. It would have been a long, lonely night without you, but you needn't worry. I'm not going to make a big deal out of it. We both know exactly where we stand, don't we?'

'Yes,' said Jack, deflated by her composure.

He wished the situation seemed as straightforward to him as it apparently did to her. She had been so sweet and so warm, and he could still feel the silkiness of her skin, the wildfire that had burnt between them. He had told her that he wanted comfort, but somehow comfort had become delight, and delight had blurred into passion, and passion had spun in its turn into something else, something fiercer and more urgent, something awesome in its power.

'Yes, of course we do,' he said again more firmly, in case Ellie suspected that he *didn't* really know where he stood any more. He had started to try and tell her that when he took her hand, but she had withdrawn it so quickly that he had lost his nerve. It was obvious that last night had been a one-off as far as she was concerned. She would be appalled and embarrassed if he said something now, and the last thing Jack wanted to do was to make Ellie uncomfortable.

'It was just one night,' Ellie continued, determined to make sure that Jack understood that she wasn't going to embarrass him by misinterpreting what had happened.

She couldn't look at him, though, finding it easier to watch Alice, who was happily oblivious to the awkward atmosphere and was using her father as a support, her tiny fingers clinging onto his sweatshirt as she edged her way round him on unsteady legs.

'Yes,' said Jack again, too conscious of Ellie's bare shoulders and her nakedness beneath the sheet to pay much attention to his small daughter's triumphant if somewhat wobbly progress.

Ellie stared down at the shiny new wedding ring on her hand as she twisted it nervously around her finger. 'It's not that it wasn't…it wasn't…' Oh, God, how could she tell him how wonderful it had been without convincing him that she was panting for more? She drew a shaky breath. 'I mean, it was good for me,' she said with difficulty, cringing at the pedestrian inadequacy of the words, 'but I think we should leave it at that, as we agreed.'

Jack was conscious of a spurt of irritation. There was

no need for Ellie to go on about it. He had got the point that she had no intention of sleeping with him again the first time.

Opening his mouth to snap back at her, he was diverted by Alice, who was taking a wild lunge back towards Ellie. Unable quite to make it without a step, she staggered, wavered and then lost her nerve, sitting down abruptly on her bottom. The bedclothes made a soft landing, but her face was a picture of frustration and determination as she took the easy option and crawled the rest of the way over Ellie's legs.

Jack felt something in himself relax at the sight of her clambering so trustfully over Ellie. He had forgotten Alice last night. She needed Ellie to stay and be a mother to her, and Ellie wasn't going to do that if she felt that he was trying to renegotiate the agreement they had made.

Ellie was right. They should draw a line under last night and pretend that it had never happened. It was much better not to complicate matters.

'Of course,' he said after a moment, and he even managed a smile. 'Shall we go back to being friends, the way we were before?'

Ellie forced an answering smile without quite meeting his eyes. 'Yes, we'll be friends,' she agreed.

She would be his friend, and he would be hers, and it would be fine, she told herself. It just wouldn't be like it was before.

Jack got to his feet and scooped Alice up from the bed. 'Time for your breakfast, young lady,' he told her, his voice just a little too hearty.

He stood for a moment, Alice squealing and wriggling with excitement under his arm, and something in his silence made Ellie lift her head and look up at him. As their eyes met Jack made a small movement, as if he were about to say something, but whatever it was, he seemed to change his mind.

'Drink your tea,' was all he said, and then he had gone, leaving Ellie staring after him.

CHAPTER EIGHT

THEY both tried, but somehow being friends was much more difficult than it had been before.

Jack was very glad that there was so much work to do. Gray's men were needed back at Bushman's Creek, but he had hired three more men for the season at Waverley, and they spent all day outside on the station, mending fences, checking watering points and making sure that the yards were ready before they began mustering in the stock to see exactly what they had and what kind of condition the herd was in.

The first muster gathered in dozens of horses that had run wild over the years when Waverley had been neglected. Separated from the cattle, they were corralled, and then Jack, who loved horses, spent hours working with them, coaxing them to the stage where they could be ridden.

Sometimes Ellie took Alice down to the yards after her afternoon nap to watch him. It was a favourite excursion for both of them. Alice liked to look at the horses, and Ellie liked to see how gentle Jack was with them. He would stand in the middle of the enclosure, talking softly to them as they laid back their ears and shied nervously away, looking utterly at home in his jeans and his boots and his battered cattleman's hat.

Her eyes would rest longingly on him. He was her husband, but the only time she could look at him properly was when he was absorbed in his task. Her gaze drifted hungrily over his lean figure and up to his face. His hat shaded his eyes, but she knew exactly how they creased at the corners, how white his teeth would flash if he turned and caught sight of Alice balanced safely on the wooden rail before her.

Ellie watched him, and squirmed with the need to touch him again. The memory of the night they had spent together was a fire that smouldered away inside her. She tried to keep it banked down, but it was hopeless when all Jack had to do was lift his hand or turn his head and it would blaze into life again.

Ellie dealt with it the only way she knew how. She was cheerful and friendly, but she was very careful not to touch him or to appear eager for his company, and she made no attempt to stop him disappearing into the office every night as soon as the men had gone.

Hiding her loneliness and frustration behind a show of activity, Ellie made a point of keeping herself busy. She would have liked to help Jack and the men, but there was more than enough to do around the homestead, what with looking after Alice, providing three meals a day for four hungry men, and keeping up with the normal washing, cooking and cleaning.

Desperate to get out of the house, even if only as far as the garden, she planned to grow vegetables, and she spent long hours digging and preparing a plot. It was hot, heavy work, but somehow soothing, too. Ellie would rub her back at the end of a session and contemplate the neatly tilled earth with satisfaction and a new sense of calm.

She had known it wouldn't be easy, but at least she was here, at Waverley, with Jack. It was what she had wanted, wasn't it? Jack might not be ready to think of her as more than a friend, but if she just got on with doing what she had agreed to do, and didn't alarm him or embarrass him, he might get used to her presence. He might change his mind. Ellie told herself that she just had to be patient.

The day Alice took her first step, Ellie was as thrilled as if she had been her own daughter. Exclaiming at her cleverness, she caught her up with a kiss and was about to rush down to the yards to find Jack when she stopped and put Alice carefully back down on the floor.

'I think Daddy will want to see you take your first step himself, don't you?'

'Dada!' agreed Alice obligingly.

Ellie hoped that Alice might show off her new skill when Jack came in to bath her that evening, but she just carried on stubbornly cruising around the pieces of furniture that she could reach, dropping down to a crawl if there was too big a gap to cross on her two legs. Ellie could almost have sworn that Alice was deliberately holding back until Jack was in the proper mood to appreciate her achievement.

She didn't show him what she could do until two days later. Ellie was back in the vegetable plot, while Alice sat nearby in the shade, almost enveloped by an enormous floppy hat. Ellie had given her some water in a bowl with an old plastic cup, and she was absorbed in her own experiments, chirruping with interest and pleasure when she saw what happened when she poured water onto the red dust around her.

When Jack found them, Ellie was sitting back on her heels, watching Alice with a smile. Neither of them saw him at first, and as his eyes moved from his grubby daughter to where Ellie crouched, her face shaded by a straw hat, her hands as dirty as Alice's and a gentle smile curving her lips, his throat tightened.

'You both look like you're having a good time,' he said, his voice absurdly dry.

Ellie's heart missed a beat, the way it always did when she saw Jack, and she straightened instinctively as he moved towards her with that lazy grace that was so typical of him. Taking off her hat, she made a show of wiping the back of her hand across her forehead, just so that Jack realised that the colour in her cheeks meant that she was hot and not that she was suddenly, ridiculously, shy.

'Alice certainly is,' she said, hating the effort she had to make to keep her voice light and controlled. 'That water has kept her happy for ages.'

'It doesn't take much to amuse her, does it?' Jack hunkered down beside Alice and tickled her nose. 'It would be nice if all we needed was a bowl of water to make *us* happy.'

He glanced up at Ellie as he spoke. His tone was joking, but beneath his hat his expression was serious, and when their eyes met, the air seemed to evaporate between them, leaving Ellie's mouth dry and her heart hammering.

'It would,' she agreed a little breathlessly. 'But things are never that simple, are they, Jack?'

Jack thought of his own confused feelings, of how he lay awake torn between loyalty to Pippa's memory and wanting to do the best for Alice, between grief and regret and the unsettling way Ellie made him feel, just as she was doing now, as she stood there with her face smudged with dirt and a trowel in her hand.

'No,' he said deliberately, 'they're not.'

A peremptory tug on his jeans made him look down at Alice, who preferred to be the centre of attention and was not at all impressed by the way the two of them were staring at each other and ignoring her. Grunting with the effort, she used his leg as a support as she pulled herself upright and stood, clutching at her father with one hand and with a rather uncertain expression on her face, as if she was not quite sure what to do with herself now that she had got there.

Not sorry for the excuse to break eye contact and look away, Ellie put down her trowel. 'She's almost ready to walk,' she said as coolly as she could. 'Why don't we see if she'll go to you?'

Keeping her fingers crossed that Alice would take the opportunity to show off, she lifted her away from Jack and crouched behind her, steadying her at the waist. Jack knelt on one knee, just out of Alice's reach, and held out his hands.

'Come on, Alice,' he said. 'Come to Daddy.'

Alice hesitated. 'Dada,' she echoed a little doubtfully, but Jack's smile was encouraging and she could feel Ellie's hands supporting her, so she took a step, and then another, too intent on reaching her father to realise that Ellie had let her go. And then Jack's hands were there, sweeping her up triumphantly, his face ablaze with an expression that made Ellie's heart contract.

'Did you see that?' he demanded. 'She was walking!'

Alice beamed, and looked so pleased with herself that in spite of the ache around her heart Ellie couldn't help laughing.

'She's a very clever girl,' she said. 'And she knows it!'

Jack was thrilled with his daughter's achievement. 'Let's see if she'll do it again,' he said, the slight awkwardness between them dissolved in the excitement. He set Alice down, and this time she went into Ellie's waiting arms. Her gait was decidedly unsteady, and sheer momentum got her most of the way, but she was undoubtedly walking.

'Look how good she is!' said Jack proudly. 'Her first steps, and she's got the hang of it already!'

Ellie smiled, intensely glad that she hadn't spoiled his pleasure by telling him about the steps Alice had taken earlier. 'There'll be no stopping her now!' she agreed.

Alice was very pleased with herself, and with all the attention that she was getting, and the almost imperceptible tension in the atmosphere faded as Jack and Ellie laughed together at her self-important expression. Everything would have been all right if they hadn't made the mistake of looking at each other again instead of at Alice.

Ellie was very conscious of how close Jack was. She could see the dust on his skin, the faint prickle of golden stubble on his jaw, the way his smile creased his cheeks, and she was shaken by a gust of such desire that her smile faltered and she got abruptly to her feet.

'It's getting late,' she said, and her voice sounded high and thin even to her own ears. 'I should go and get Alice some tea.'

Jack rose to his feet more slowly, swinging Alice up with him. 'We'll come with you,' he said. 'It's been a big day.' He tickled her on the nose until she chuckled and tried to bat his finger away with her hand. 'When I came to look for you, you were baby and now you're a toddler!'

He smiled proudly at his daughter, and Alice clutched her arms around his neck and buried her face in his neck, which was the closest she could get to a hug. Watching them, Ellie felt her heart constrict with love for them both so sharp and intense that she could hardly breathe.

'Did you want anything special?' she managed to ask,

wrenching her eyes away and beginning to walk back to the homestead.

'Oh, yes,' said Jack, reminded. 'I'm planning to muster the top end next week. It's difficult country up there, and you can't do much from the air. There are so many little gullies and places for the stock to hide that the only way to get at it properly is on horseback, but it'd be a long job with just the three of us.

'I've just spoken to Gray on the phone, and he's going to come over and help, but that would still only make five. He suggested that he brings Clare with him. She could stay here and look after Alice and you could come with us.'

Jack hesitated slightly. 'It would be useful if you could give us a hand, but you don't have to come.'

Ellie's face lit up. 'I'd love to,' she said, too thrilled at the prospect of getting out onto the station to object to being thought of as an optional extra, someone handy but not essential.

It would have been even better if Jack hadn't needed his brother to point out that she might be some use outside the kitchen, but at least she would be out, getting to know Waverley and doing a job she loved.

If she could show Jack how useful she could be if only he would let her, he might include her more in the running of the property. They would be able to fill up the ghastly silences when they were alone with talk about the station, and gradually they would get back to the way they had been before.

Ellie's imagination ran on unchecked. They would be friends, partners, easy in each other's company, and then maybe, if she was very patient, Jack would get used to her being there. He might even come to need her.

Suddenly life seemed full of possibility, and there was

a new spring in her step as she turned to Jack with a smile. 'I can't wait!' she told him.

Jack blinked a little at her smile. Her eyes were green and shining, and her face was vivid, as if he had offered her the moon instead of a chance to ride for hours in the hot sun and sleep in a swag on the hard ground.

He felt an odd tightening in his throat as he looked at her. There was a smudge of dirt on her forehead where she had wiped her hand, and her fingernails were encrusted with mud. Her hat was battered, and her shirt shabby, but when she smiled like that somehow you didn't notice all those things.

She wasn't beautiful, thought Jack, his eyes dwelling on the curve of her cheek before drifting down inside her collar, to where a pulse beat in the shadowy hollow at the base of her throat. The sight of it gave Jack a sudden, shocking memory of how it had felt to press his lips there, and he jerked his gaze away.

She *wasn't* beautiful, he insisted to himself. Not really. Not at all. She was just Ellie.

It had taken him weeks to put the memory of their wedding night behind him. He wanted to be friends with Ellie, the way they had agreed, but it wasn't easy when she kept intruding on his notice in ways he hadn't anticipated. Before the wedding, he had imagined them sitting companionably together in the evenings, talking about the day and their plans for Waverley, but that had never happened. Instead he had found himself noticing little things about Ellie that he had never registered before: the tenderness in her face as she straightened the teddy bears in Alice's cot when she kissed her goodnight, the straightness of her back, the way she pushed her hair behind her ear.

Once, he had thought of Ellie as someone quiet and

restful to be with, but not any more. Now she made him distracted and uncomfortable and vaguely irritated.

It wasn't her fault. Jack knew that. *She* was fine. She was as cheerful and friendly as she had always been, but she never gave any indication that their wedding night had changed anything between them. That should have made Jack feel better, but it didn't. It made him feel worse.

It wasn't too bad during the day, when he could lose himself in sheer physical work, or when Alice and the presence of the men at meals kept the silence at bay, but at night…at night it was much harder. Harder not to remember the pearly translucence of her skin, the silken length of her thigh, and the feel of her lips teasing their way down his throat.

Jack would lie in bed and stare at the ceiling, willing himself to forget the exact curve of her body that his hand had learnt as it swept possessively from her breast, dipping down to her waist and smoothing over her hip. He was trying his best to treat her as he had always done, but he hadn't found it easy.

He hadn't found it easy at all.

As the weeks passed, though, Jack's sense of vague unease had faded and he'd begun to think that he was overreacting. Everything was going well. Alice was happy, Ellie seemed content, and the men certainly appreciated her cooking. Gray's suggestion that Ellie join the muster had come at a time when Jack had been wondering how to get their relationship back onto the old footing.

It had seemed the perfect solution, and everything would have been fine if Ellie hadn't smiled at him like that and knocked him off-balance again.

What was it about her that was so disturbing? Jack felt

as if he had to be constantly on guard, and then felt ridiculous for feeling like that about someone who had never pretended to be anything other than an old, familiar friend.

He was preoccupied as he bathed Alice that evening. She was overexcited by her new-found skill at walking, and it took him longer than usual to quieten her. He stood by the cot, his hand on her tummy, remembering her face as she had realised that she could walk, remembering the laughter in Ellie's eyes as she opened her arms and let Alice stagger into them.

Jack frowned. He hadn't meant to start thinking about Ellie.

His eye fell on Pippa's photograph, and he touched it sadly. He wished they could go back to the way they had been when she was alive and everything had seemed simple. He had known exactly what he wanted then. He had wanted Pippa, with her beauty and her passion and her fire.

Pippa had pushed him to extremes—of happiness, of fury, and of bitter regret when she had gone. But even when things were at their blackest, he had always known exactly what he felt. There had been none of the confusion and unsettling doubt that he felt now.

Jack didn't even know what he was confused *about*. He just knew that he felt ridiculously hesitant about joining Ellie in the kitchen.

Ellie was standing at the stove when he went in. She looked up from the gravy she was stirring. 'What's the matter?' she asked after a single glance at his face.

Jack had taken considerable effort to compose his features into an expression of cool unconcern, and was annoyed to discover that it had been a complete waste of time.

'Nothing,' he snapped.

Ellie didn't say anything. She just looked at him with those clear eyes and Jack felt the inexplicable irritation fizzle out of him as if from a punctured balloon.

He sat down at the table and looked at his hands. 'I was just thinking about Pippa,' he said in a different voice.

Ellie bent her head over the gravy once more. 'You miss her, don't you?'

Jack sighed. 'I miss what might have been,' he said heavily. 'I miss what it would have been like if she'd been able to hear Alice say her first word, or if she'd been here today to see her take her first step. She shouldn't have died,' he finished, as if the words were wrung out of him.

'No, she shouldn't,' said Ellie quietly. 'It wasn't fair.'

Jack's chair scraped over the floor as he pushed it back and got to his feet, unable to settle. 'I thought it would be easier away from Bushman's Creek,' he said, prowling around the kitchen. 'There are no memories of her at Waverley, but somehow that just makes it worse.

'Pippa would have loved it here,' he went on. 'She would have been so happy with me and with Alice, just the three of us. Sometimes I can imagine it so clearly that I think I can hear her laughter.' He glanced almost defensively at Ellie. 'Does that sound stupid?'

'No, Jack. It just means you loved her and that you're grieving for her.'

Jack gripped the back of a chair, so hard that the knuckles showed white under his skin. Ellie wasn't even sure that he'd heard her.

'I just feel…' He groped for the right words. He wanted to explain to Ellie how the echo of Pippa's laughter was fading, how her image was blurring, how he clung to her memory because he felt guilty at letting it go. Pippa had given him Alice and he owed it to her to keep her memory as sharp and clear as it had been the day she had left.

'I feel as if she should be here,' he tried again. 'At times like today, when Alice walked for the first time, I imagine what Pippa would have done, how she would have looked, how happy she would have been, and she seems so close that I can feel her. But when I look, she's not there. *You're* there...'

Jack trailed off, unable to explain how she made him feel, how the ground that had seemed so firm seemed to shift beneath his feet and everything that he had taken for granted was suddenly uncertain.

There was a tight band around Ellie's throat as she stirred the gravy blindly. How stupid she had been to hope that Jack's memories of Pippa would fade eventually. How unfair to think that it would get easier for him to see her in Pippa's place.

She had been so eager to join the muster, so convinced that it would mark the start of a change in their relationship, so certain that she would be able to replace Pippa in Jack's life eventually. How crass of her to think that he could forget someone like Pippa!

He had turned to her for comfort on their wedding night, but comfort was all he had needed. She had known that, but it hadn't stopped her feeling hurt that he had avoided her since then. Of course he had avoided her, when every time he looked at her he saw Pippa's ghost hovering by her side with everything that might have been.

'I'm sorry, Jack,' she said with difficulty, knowing that there was nothing she could do to help. 'I wish things could be different. I really do.'

The soft brown curls swung forward, hiding her face, but Jack could hear the sadness in her voice, and it reminded him that Ellie had her own unhappiness to bear. He had forgotten the shadowy figure of the man she loved and who didn't love her back.

Jack wished that he had remembered him sooner. All the time he had been worrying about the disturbing effect that Ellie had on him, she had been dreaming of someone else and wishing, like him, that things had worked out the way they were supposed to! Jack was just glad he hadn't told Ellie how aware of her he had been. That would have made things really awkward.

He had hoped that realising Ellie's mind was elsewhere would make him less conscious of her, but it didn't work like that. He just carried on noticing the way her hair curled or the unselfconscious grace with which she moved, and pretending that he didn't. And the more he pretended not to notice, the more distant and disagreeable he became.

Frustrated, faintly humiliated by his inability to behave naturally with Ellie any more, Jack told himself that Ellie's indifference to anyone except the man she loved didn't bother him in the least. He was still in love with Pippa...wasn't he?

Wasn't he?

The very fact that he needed to question it made Jack uncomfortable, and the more uncertain he felt, the more he talked about Pippa to Alice, deliberately reminding himself of her liveliness and her spirit and all the ways she had been different from Ellie, holding onto her memory like a talisman against his doubts.

Ellie listened to him reliving his memories and told herself that she should understand. Jack was still grieving, and he needed to talk about Pippa, but it didn't stop her hurting at the way he shut her out.

Once, taking a bottle of milk into Alice's room, she saw Jack showing Alice Pippa's photograph. 'That's Mummy,' he was saying as he shifted her on his knee.

Alice looked up at her father. 'Mum-um,' she repeated obligingly, and Jack smiled.

'That's right. Mummy. She was beautiful, wasn't she?' He kissed the top of Alice's head. 'Just like you're going to be one day.'

Very conscious of intruding on a private moment, Ellie put the milk down on the chest and left without a word. Shaking, she went to stand outside and stood hugging her arms around her to stop herself crying. It was wrong to feel so jealous. Alice was Pippa's daughter. She needed to grow up knowing all about her. Ashamed of her own resentment, but tired of being made to feel second best, Ellie grew cooler and quieter, and hung on to the prospect of the muster.

Much as she loved Alice, she hardly ever got further than the homestead creek, and she longed to be out under the vast outback sky where she felt most at home. Ellie counted the days until they left, and as soon as she swung up onto her horse, her doubts fell away and she felt steadier, more balanced, herself once more.

It took them two days' hard riding to reach the foot of the range. It was wild country up there, with looming rocks and hidden gorges, but Ellie loved it. She sat easily in her saddle, savouring the space and the eerie stillness of the air, and the light that beat down around her.

When they stopped at last, they built a fire and heated the stew that Ellie had brought. Jack made damper, and they put the billy on the embers to make tea. At night, they rolled themselves in swags and slept under the stars, and Ellie was perfectly happy.

She was in the saddle again at first light, winkling out the cattle that had strayed deep into the gorges, chivvying them back to join the main herd that was being driven, rumbling protestingly, onto the plain. By the time the homestead came back into sight the herd had quadrupled in size and was a huge mass of heaving, snorting, bellowing beasts, half hidden in the thick cloud of dust raised by their hooves as they blundered on towards the yards.

Ellie was stiff and saddle-sore when she slid off her horse at the end of the last, long day, but she felt happier than she had for weeks, and Alice's obvious delight at seeing her again was balm to her sore heart.

Jack might not have come near her once while they were away, but Alice needed her. Ellie held her small, warm body and kissed her baby-soft cheek, and thought that as long as she had Alice and she had Waverley, that would be enough.

Ellie might have enjoyed the muster, but Jack hadn't. He wished he hadn't asked her to come. He'd tried so hard to ignore her, but it had been impossible when every time he'd looked round she was there, eyes shining, absolutely at home on her horse, in her element against the harsh landscape.

Jack pulled the saddle off his horse with a sigh. He had sat as far away from Ellie as possible around the campfire, but that had been a mistake, too. From where he'd sat he hadn't been able to keep his eyes off her as she'd talked quietly with the men, or gazed pensively into the flames, or leant forward to lift the billy off the fire.

It would have been easier if he could have told himself that she was just decorative, or disruptive, but of course she hadn't been. She had slotted easily into the team. She knew instinctively what to do. She could outguess a rogue bull and outride any of them. She had been one of the most useful people there.

He should have thanked her for her help, instead of curtly dismissing her to the homestead as soon as they got in. Irritable with guilt, Jack slapped his horse on the rump and watched it canter off into the paddock, kicking its heels.

'Muster went well.'

He turned at the laconic voice to see Gray, leaning his arms against the fence. 'Yes,' he agreed unenthusiastically.

'What's the matter?'

'Nothing.'

Gray raised his brows, but didn't pursue it. He waited until Jack had closed the gate behind him and fell into step beside him as he carried the saddle back to the shed.

'Ellie's a good person to have around, isn't she?' he commented.

Jack grunted.

Gray cast him a sidelong glance under his hat. 'She's pretty, too.'

Jack made a noncommittal noise. He wished Gray would shut up. It was all right for him, with an adoring wife waiting for him back at the homestead. Gray didn't know what it was like to live with someone who was a friend, someone it was getting harder and harder to think about in a friendly way, someone who was in love with another man and who had made no secret of the fact that she had married him for Waverley.

'You know, Jack, you're lucky to have her,' Gray went on, and Jack swung round, goaded beyond endurance.

'What do you know about it?' he snapped.

'Only what I can see with my own eyes.'

'Well, you can't see everything, all right!' said Jack savagely, and strode off with a thunderous expression.

His bad temper lasted well into the next week, long after Gray and Clare had returned to Bushman's Creek, and Ellie's hopes that the muster would mark a change in their relationship soon faded. Jack gave no sign of being prepared to involve her in the running of Waverley. He hardly spoke to her, except to tell her what time she could expect the men in for meals.

Hurt and bewildered by his attitude, Ellie would have welcomed even a return to the careful friendliness that had felt so uncomfortable before. Anything would be better than being treated as a mere housekeeper.

The sense of rightness she had felt after the muster had quickly evaporated. *Was* she doing the right thing? Ellie wondered. Yes, she was at Waverley, instead of stuck in some city office. Yes, Alice was adorable. But it *wasn't* enough, she realised at last, no matter how much she tried to convince herself that it was.

She didn't want to be a housekeeper. She wanted Jack to treat her like a partner.

Like a woman.

Like a wife.

CHAPTER NINE

BUT the more Ellie wanted it, the less likely it seemed that Jack ever would. She was appalled to find herself growing increasingly resentful of him, and threw herself into the household chores as if all the sweeping and scouring would somehow ease the loneliness and disappointment inside her.

She was scrubbing the floor in the living area one day when Jack came to find her. It was the first time that he had sought her out deliberately since the muster, and she was furious to discover that in spite of everything, her pulse rate still quickened at the sound of his voice.

'What are you doing?' Jack frowned irritably as he saw Ellie on her hands and knees. The corners of his mouth were turned down and he looked cross and ill at ease.

'What does it look like?'

After one quick glance, Ellie bent back to her scrubbing and sighed inwardly. What was it about Jack? He ignored her, he hurt her, he was grumpy and ungrateful, and still she loved him.

Everything would be so much easier if she could just stop loving him, she thought ruefully. If she could stop caring that he was obviously as unhappy as she was, stop hoping that he would come to love her in the end.

'There must be more important things to do than wash the floor in here!'

'Yes, there are, Jack,' Ellie agreed tightly, 'but not that I can do inside, right now.' She might be hopelessly in love with him, but it didn't stop her being exasperated by the way he left her with all the household chores and then had the nerve to criticise the way she organised her time!

'Alice is asleep,' she went on between clenched teeth, 'and I need to stay somewhere I can hear her if she wakes. If I have to be stuck in the homestead, I might as well get on with some of the jobs I can't do when she's awake.'

The edge in her voice was lost on Jack. He grunted something that might have been an acknowledgement, and propped himself on the edge of one of the chairs, digging his hands into the pockets of his jeans. He was frowning down at his boots, lost in thought, and had clearly lost all interest in what she was doing anyway.

Typical, thought Ellie sourly, and vented her feelings on the floor, sloshing water out of the bucket and scrubbing with ferocious energy.

The sound of the brush grated in the silence, and Jack looked up with a frown. 'Can you stop that a minute?' he said irritably. 'There's something I need to talk to you about.'

Ellie sat back on her heels and looked at him warily. 'What is it?'

'You're not going to like it,' he warned her.

Apprehension clawed at Ellie's stomach. This was it, she thought in panic. He was going to tell her that he couldn't stand living with her any longer and wanted to end the marriage. He wanted her to go, and leave him and Alice and Waverley behind.

She swallowed. 'Tell me.'

She saw Jack hesitate, and braced herself for the worst, her fingers tightening around the scrubbing brush.

'I've just been talking to Scott Wilson.'

The relief was so great that Ellie dropped the brush. It

clattered unheeded to the floor while she stared at Jack, torn between a hysterical desire to laugh at the contrast between what she had been dreading and the innocuousness of Jack's remark, and the bizarre conviction that she had completely misheard what he had said.

'Scott?' she echoed cautiously.

'You know him, don't you?'

She wiped her hands on her jeans to give herself time to adjust to a conversation which was turning out to be very different from the one she had been expecting. 'Of course I know him,' she said carefully, still not quite convinced that she hadn't missed something important. 'He was at the wedding.'

'So he was.' Jack gave her a sharp glance. 'He was at the engagement party, too, wasn't he?'

'Yes. Why? Nothing's happened to him, has it?'

'He's coming to stay.'

'To stay? Here?' Jack nodded and Ellie blinked at him as she struggled to make sense of a conversation that seemed to be getting stranger and stranger. 'When?'

'Tonight.'

'*Tonight!* Why?'

'We're mustering those paddocks in the west tomorrow. It's ideal country to use helicopters and Scott's built up quite a business contracting for work like that. With him in the air, and the three of us on the ground, it shouldn't take too long. Scott said he'd fly up tonight and then we can start first thing tomorrow. I thought I should let you know that there'd be one extra to feed tonight.'

All this, just to tell her that she needed to peel a couple of extra potatoes! The exquisite relief Ellie had felt when she realised that Jack wasn't trying to find a way to tell her that their marriage was over was rapidly dissolving, leaving her with the dull realisation that absolutely nothing had changed. She hadn't even known that he was planning to muster those paddocks. She could have helped him there, too, but, no! All she was good for was providing meals!

'Fine,' she said in a flat voice.

'The thing is, Scott's coming up as a favour,' Jack went on. 'He's got several men working for him now, but they're all busy, so he said he'd come himself. He said I could consider it as a wedding present,' he added thinly. 'In the circumstances, I think we should offer him a bed in the homestead.'

Ellie eyed him in some puzzlement, wondering what he was leading up to. 'OK.'

Jack got restlessly to his feet. Clearly there was more to come. He went over to the window and stood looking out, his shoulders stiff with tension. 'You know what Scott's like,' he said. 'I've never known anyone talk the way he does. He keeps the local grapevine going single-handed.'

'So what?'

'So if he gets any inkling of the fact that we're not living as normal newly-weds, it'll be round the district in no time,' said Jack impatiently.

Ellie climbed stiffly to her feet, brushing down her jeans. 'I see,' she said slowly.

'You don't seem very bothered,' he accused her as he turned round. 'I thought you'd be concerned about your family hearing that things aren't quite as perfect as we've gone to so much effort to convince them they are.'

She met his eyes steadily. 'I am concerned,' she told him. 'What do you suggest we do about it?'

Jack dropped his gaze first. 'I think we should try and pretend that we're just like any other married couple,' he said. 'It will mean putting on a show, but we did it before and convinced everyone, so there's no reason why we shouldn't do it again.'

'You mean we should pretend that we're in love?'

The brown eyes flickered. 'Yes. Do you think you could do that?'

'I expect I could manage.'

Jack took a breath. 'I think we should sleep together tonight, too.'

Vivid colour surged into Ellie's cheeks and the air was suddenly charged with electricity. 'You know what I mean,' he said testily, swatting mentally at the memories crowding around him, memories of the silkiness of her skin, the taste of her lips, of the tantalising drift of her hands. 'I'm talking about sharing a room, that's all.'

'Scott may like to chat, but he's not the kind of person who goes around prying into bedrooms,' objected Ellie, equally unnerved by the memories jangling in the air between them. It seemed imperative to convince Jack that she was no more eager for them to sleep together than he was.

Jack shrugged. 'It's up to you. You're the one who wants to convince your family this is a proper marriage.'

It was true. If her parents got so much as a whiff of the fact that she wasn't as happy as she claimed to be, they would be there, demanding to know what was wrong, and Lizzy would be on the phone from Perth. The last thing Ellie wanted was to upset any of them. She had made her choice, and she would have to live with it.

'All right,' she nodded after a moment. 'That's what we'll do.'

When Jack had gone, Ellie finished scrubbing the floor, but her arm moved mechanically while her mind was on the night ahead. A slow shiver of anticipation tiptoed down her spine at the thought of lying in the dark next to Jack. What better chance would she have to rediscover the closeness they had once had?

Ellie didn't know what she could do to improve things, but she knew that she had to do something. The current situation was miserable for both of them. Being friends hadn't worked, so perhaps it was time to take her courage in her hands and ask Jack if he would consider being lovers instead.

He might say no. He probably *would* say no, thought Ellie, remembering his grim expression and the guarded way he held himself when he was near her, but it was worth a try. It wasn't as if she would be asking him to forget Pippa, just to recognise that she was a woman, too, and not just someone who peeled potatoes and scrubbed floors and changed Alice's nappy when he wasn't around.

Was that so much to ask?

It was the way she looked right now, Ellie decided as she washed her hands afterwards. In the mirror above the basin, her reflection stared despondently back at her, red-faced, grimy, hair lank and sweaty with effort. She looked awful.

No wonder Jack had sounded so unenthusiastic about the prospect of pretending to be in love with her again! Ellie grimaced at the mirror. What was the point of complaining that Jack only ever thought of her as a housekeeper when she never made the slightest effort to look like anything else?

Perhaps it was time she did.

Alice was asleep. The meal was ready. *She* was ready. All Ellie had to do was walk through the door and join Jack and Scott on the verandah. Instead, she dithered around in her room, trying to pluck up the courage to face Jack, terrified that he would know immediately what she was trying to do, terrified that he wouldn't even notice.

All she had done was change into a simple, soft swirl skirt in a pretty shade of blue, with a plain white sleeveless top. Her hair was washed so that it fell in soft, shining waves around her face, and she had put on one of the many lipsticks Lizzy had forced upon her over the years and which she normally never wore. It was hardly a show-stopping outfit, but Ellie felt ridiculously self-conscious as she hovered behind the screen door.

Taking a deep breath, she pushed it open before she had a chance to change her mind and went out. Scott and Jack were sitting in the old chairs drinking beers, but at the sound of the screen door they both looked round and got to their feet.

'Ellie!' Scott greeted her with a big hug. 'You look fantastic!'

Ellie smiled nervously as she hugged him back. 'Thank you,' she said, but her heart sank when she risked a glance at Jack. He was looking grimly unappreciative, his brows drawn together and his mouth compressed into a thin line.

'It's great to see you again,' Scott was saying, holding her at arm's length so that he could admire her. 'I didn't get a chance to talk to you properly at the wedding. When was the last time we had real chat?'

Very aware of Jack's set face, Ellie forced herself to concentrate. 'It must have been a few years ago. Before I went to the States, anyway.'

'That's right! Remember, I took you to the Bachelors and Spinsters ball just before you left?' Scott grinned. 'That was a great night, wasn't it? It's hard to believe how much everything's changed since then. You heard that I was married?'

'Yes, Mum wrote and told me,' said Ellie, turning a little so that Jack wasn't looming at the edge of her vision. 'I didn't realise that you and Anna were that close.'

'We weren't. We never even liked each other that much, and then one day...bang!' Scott snapped his fingers and laughed. 'It was like a bolt from the blue! I can't believe I never realised before how fantastic Anna was,' he confided. 'And when I found out that she loved me back... Well, I guess I don't need to tell you two what that's like!'

'No,' said Jack, but there was so much irony in his voice that Ellie hurried into speech.

'I'm so glad you're happy, Scott.'

'Oh, I am. I never knew a man could be this happy! You know all that romantic stuff about finding the other half of you? Well, that's how I feel,' said Scott, beaming. 'You know what I mean, don't you, Ellie?'

Ellie's smile wavered. 'Yes, I know,' she said quietly.

Watching her, Jack saw her eyes darken with anguish, and everything suddenly fell into place.

Ever since Ellie had been startled into dropping the scrubbing brush at the sound of Scott's name he had had his suspicions. Scott seemed an unlikely person for Ellie to fall in love with, but it *could* be him.

The more he thought about it, the more convinced Jack became that he had stumbled upon Ellie's secret. The few clues she had dropped all pointed in the right direction. She was obviously much closer to Scott than he had realised, and Scott's marriage to Anna could well have been the reason she had decided that her feelings for him were hopeless. Scott was based in Mathison, where Ellie had wanted to stay so that she could be near him. *I just thought it would be easier being in the same place.* Wasn't that what she had said?

And Scott had been at the engagement party. Jack remembered how he had asked Ellie if the man she loved was there, and her face as she had nodded. 'Yes,' she had said.

It must have been a shock for her to hear that Scott was coming to Waverley, he realised. No wonder she had seemed upset when he'd told her! If he had known, he would never have asked Scott to help, helicopter or no helicopter. Seeing him, being with him, pretending to be happy, must be agony for Ellie.

It wasn't his fault, though, Jack's thoughts ran on, obscure guilt shading into disgruntlement. He wasn't telepathic. If Ellie didn't want to see Scott, all she had had to do was tell him.

Except that she clearly *did* want to see him. Jack's face darkened as he looked at Ellie and saw what an effort she had made to dress up for Scott. The sight of her when she walked through the screen door had been like a blow to his stomach. She never wore revealing tops or lipstick that drew attention to the warm curve of her mouth for *him*!

Jack wanted to stalk across the verandah and punch the cheery, complacent smile off Scott's face before dragging Ellie along to her room and forcing her to change back into jeans and a shapeless shirt that would cover her bare shoulders and hide her from Scott's appreciative eyes.

Instead, he turned abruptly on his heel. 'I'll get you a beer,' he said to Ellie.

Ellie watched him go in despair. It was all her fault. She couldn't carry off a feminine look, she thought miserably as she sank into a chair and summoned a smile for Scott. She should have just stuck to her old jeans. It must be blatantly obvious that she was doing her damnedest to seduce Jack, and not succeeding. No wonder he was looking so disgusted!

At least Scott thought she looked nice, Ellie tried to console herself. *He* didn't seem to think that she looked ridiculous. His cheerful friendliness and obvious pleasure at seeing her again were balm to her wounded feelings, and she turned gratefully towards him. Somebody had to make the effort to make him feel welcome, anyway, and it obviously wasn't going to be Jack. Without that baleful stare on her Ellie could relax and enjoy herself, talking to Scott about times when everything had been so much simpler.

In the kitchen, Jack heard her laugh and slammed the fridge door shut. They seemed to be quite happy out there without him! *Scott Wilson*, he thought in disgust, wrenching the top off the beer bottle. What in God's name did Ellie see in him?

It wasn't that he cared *who* she loved, but after all she had had to say about how much she loved him Jack had expected it to be someone a bit more special than Scott Wilson! Scott was the kind of bloke who talked too much and laughed too loudly at his own jokes, Jack thought disparagingly. Ellie would never be happy with someone like that. She needed someone to cherish her, someone like… Well, someone *not* like Scott, he finished to himself, unable to think of anyone worthy of her.

Not that Ellie seemed to think so. When Jack got back to the verandah she was looking relaxed and happy, with her legs curled up beneath her and her body turned invitingly towards Scott. Grimly, Jack set the beer down on the table next to her.

She glanced up at him and he noticed bitterly how she tensed at his nearness. 'Thank you,' she said.

Something about the way she flinched away as he pulled up a chair beside her caught Jack on the raw. He was supposed to be her husband, for God's sake! Very deliberately, he reached out and slid his hand beneath her hair. The nape of her neck was warm, the skin tender, her hair soft and silky against the back of his hand, and his fingers circled slowly in an instinctively possessive gesture. No harm in letting Scott know who she belonged to now.

'I'd do anything for you, darling,' he said provocatively, baring his teeth in a smile.

Scott gave a shout of laughter. 'I see you've got Jack just where you want him, Ellie.'

Burningly aware of Jack's lazily circling fingers, Ellie sat rigid and trembling, fighting the terrible urge to simply close her eyes and lean back into his touch. 'I wouldn't say that,' she said unsteadily.

'Wouldn't you?'

Jack's hand drifted down from her nape to the edge of her top, almost absently tracing its outline, from the narrow strap at her shoulder, down the scoop of the neckline and up to the other shoulder, and Ellie was unable to prevent a shiver as desire shuddered down her back and clenched at the base of her spine with such intensity that she had to bite back a gasp.

'No,' she managed with difficulty, and Jack jerked his hand away, consumed by a sudden fury—with Scott for his stupid comments, with himself for the way he was behaving, but most of all with Ellie for the way she flinched with distaste whenever he touched her.

'I see,' he said.

'Jack knows who's really boss,' chuckled Scott. 'Marriage is a wonderful thing, eh, Jack?'

'Wonderful.'

'You're a very lucky man to have Ellie.'

Jack wanted to hit him. 'I know,' he said, only just managing to unclench his teeth. He didn't feel lucky. He felt raw and confused and inexplicably depressed.

Ellie shot him a warning look. It had sounded as if the words were forced out of him. Hardly the way to go about convincing Scott that they were happily married! It had been Jack's idea to invite Scott, she thought crossly. He could at least make *some* effort. Scott was no fool. She could see his bright eyes flicking assessingly between the two of them. He was bound to guess that something was wrong.

'I hope you've bought a new car since I last saw you, Scott,' she said quickly, in an effort to change the subject.

At least she'd managed to divert Scott. 'The first thing Anna did when we got married was to make me get rid of it!' he told her ruefully. 'She said either the car went or she did.' He laughed. 'Remember that time we broke down on our way to the races?'

With that, they were off. Jack drank his beer morosely, forced to sit and listen as they reminisced. He hadn't realised that Ellie and Scott had known each other that well. For the first time, Jack felt his age. They were both eight years younger than he was, and they seemed to have spent a lot of time together. He listened glumly as they talked about parties and races and rodeos they had been to. He must have been at most of them, too, but they had clearly been too busy having a good time to notice *him* there.

It was a new experience for Jack to think about Ellie having friends of her own, a life of her own that had nothing to do with him, and he didn't like it. He took a savage pull of his beer. He was used to considering Ellie as part of *his* life, not of anyone else's and especially not of Scott Wilson's!

By the time Scott finally decided to go to bed, Jack could hardly bring himself to say goodnight. He was fed up with hearing about the parties the two of them had been to, parties where they might have kissed, where Ellie might have fallen in love. He was fed up with watching the way Ellie smiled at Scott, the way she laughed with him, the way she'd leant her elbow on the table and propped her chin in her hand, careless of what the other men would think of her flirting. She certainly didn't care what *he* thought, Jack decided sourly. She had hardly glanced at him all evening.

He had hoped that when the stockmen went back to their quarters Scott would take the hint and retire as well, but, no! Ellie had offered him another cup of coffee, another glass of wine, and Jack had had to sit for another hour listening to their interminable reminiscences.

At last Scott had let slip a yawn, and Jack had leapt to his feet. 'You must be tired, and we've got an early start in the morning,' he'd said, practically hustling Scott out of his chair. 'I'll show you to your room.'

He waited until he had seen the bedroom door shut firmly behind Scott before he went back to the kitchen, where Ellie was washing dishes with a kind of controlled fury. 'Sorry to break up your cosy little tête-à-tête,' he said nastily, 'but I want Scott working in the morning, and if it was up to you he'd never have got any sleep.'

Ellie crashed a saucepan onto the draining board. 'What cosy tête-à-tête?' she demanded. 'It's hard to imagine anything *less* cosy than the evening we've just spent, with you sitting there with a face like concrete! Why were you so rude to Scott?'

'I wasn't rude.'

'You hardly said a word all evening! You just sat there glowering and making everyone else uncomfortable.'

'I didn't notice you looking uncomfortable,' said Jack, scowling. 'You seemed to be having a great time!'

Ellie drew in a sharp breath. A *great time*? One of the worst evenings of her life, and Jack thought she had been having a great time? She controlled herself with an effort. 'Well, let's hope Scott thought so,' she said sweetly.

'I don't think there's any doubt about that!'

'In case you've forgotten, Jack, you were the one who said that Scott was doing us a favour, and as you made absolutely no effort to be pleasant I thought it was up to me.'

'Being pleasant?' he jeered. 'Is that what you call making a fool of yourself by tarting yourself up and flapping those eyelashes of yours at him? God, I don't think I've ever seen anything so pathetic! *Oh, Scott, remember when we went swimming?*' he mimicked cruelly in a falsetto voice. *'Oh, Scott, remember what a cute little girl I used to be?'*

Jack snorted. 'Do you have any idea how boring you both were? Remember this, remember that... Couldn't you have found anything more interesting to talk about?

'Like what?' Ellie was so angry at the injustice of it that she could hardly speak. 'Believe me, Jack, I would have *loved* to have had something else to talk to Scott about! But I don't suppose he would have been very interested in hearing me talking about cooking or washing or tidying up after you and Alice, and since that's all I've done since I married you. It was reminiscences or nothing. I dare say my past *is* pretty boring to you, but I can assure you that it's a lot more entertaining than my present. Do you have any idea how boring *that* is?'

Jack's mouth tightened. 'What's wrong with it?'

'I do nothing but cook for you, clean for you and look after your daughter for you, Jack, and I get no thanks for it. I'm stuck in the homestead all day. I never get to go anywhere or see anyone or do anything.'

'It never bothered you before,' he pointed out.

'Well, it bothers me now,' she said flatly.

'You knew what was involved,' he accused her. 'If you don't like being a housekeeper, you shouldn't have offered to be one.'

Ellie went white. 'I offered to be your wife, Jack, not your housekeeper,' she said in a frozen voice.

'It's the same thing.' Jack prowled irritably around the kitchen. 'We had an agreement. You wanted to stay in the outback and I wanted someone to help me look after Alice. That's what happened.'

'We agreed that we would be partners!'

'You own half of Waverley, Ellie,' he reminded her coldly. 'How much more of a partner do you want to be?'

Ellie pulled out the plug and watched the soapy water drain away like all of her hopes. What was the point of arguing? Jack just didn't understand. 'I want to be involved,' she said hopelessly. 'You never tell me what you're doing.'

'I can't come running back to the homestead every time I decide to do anything,' said Jack impatiently. 'There's no point in whining now, Ellie. That's just the way things are. You knew how it would be when we got married, didn't you? *Didn't you?*' he repeated savagely when she only shook her head.

'Yes,' said Ellie in a voice devoid of all emotion. 'You're right. I did.'

For some reason, her agreement only made him even more angry. The trouble she had taken to make herself look beautiful for Scott, the warmth of her smile, the way she had leant towards him, all had left Jack raging and confused, and now he lashed out, not knowing why, knowing only that he wanted to hurt her.

'In that case I suggest you get on with what you agreed to do,' he said bitingly, 'instead of whingeing that you're not involved, exchanging your dull stories with your dull friends, and dreaming about your pathetic little love affair that never even happened!'

Ellie stared down at the tea towel she was using to wipe her hands. It had a pattern of blue-and-red checks, faded through frequent washing, and there was a stain in one corner. She felt cold and very sick.

So that was what Jack thought of her. *Dull. Whingeing. Pathetic.*

Was that how she was?

There was a black mist swirling around her. Very carefully, Ellie hung the tea towel on the back of a chair and turned blindly for the door.

'Where are you going?' Jack demanded furiously.

'To bed.'

'You can't just walk out in the middle of an argument!'

'Yes, I can.'

Jack glared at her in frustration. 'I haven't finished!'

Ellie didn't even look back. 'I think you've said enough,' she said, and walked away down the long corridor to her room.

Jack's jaw worked furiously. He hated the way Ellie did that. He hated the way she just went away rather than face anything she didn't like. She didn't even have the decency to storm and shout back at him. She just left.

He caught up with her at the bedroom door. 'You're going to have to talk to me,' he said angrily. 'We're going to be sleeping in the same bed. You can't just ignore me.'

Ellie turned with her hand on the door. 'I don't think there's any point in us sharing a room, do you, Jack?'

'What about Scott?' Jack was appalled to find himself blustering. 'What's he going to think when he sees us coming out of separate rooms tomorrow morning?'

'It doesn't matter now,' said Ellie, and she closed the door in his face.

She lay awake all night, too numb to cry. Why hadn't she realised how much Jack disliked her? His cruel words echoed endlessly in Ellie's head.

Dull.

Whingeing.

Pathetic.

Ellie burned with shame and humiliation when she remembered how hopefully she had dressed for him that night. She should have known that it would take more than a skirt and a dash of lipstick to change Jack's mind. All she had done was make herself look ridiculous.

Jack was right, she *was* pathetic. It had been pathetic to hope that he would come to love her, pathetic to believe that if he ever looked for another woman after Pippa it would be her, pathetic to waste all those years dreaming about something that could never be.

Well, now the dreaming was over.

Jack was never going to forgive her for not being Pippa; Ellie knew that now. It was time to put an end to a situation that was making them both miserable. They had tried, but their marriage hadn't worked, and she loved him too much to stay and keep on hoping that things would get better. Jack needed a chance to be happy, and he wasn't going to be with her.

The only thing she could do for him now was to go.

CHAPTER TEN

ELLIE was giving Alice her supper the next day when she heard the sound of boots on the verandah and she tensed. She knew that she had to talk to Jack, but she wasn't ready, not yet. She couldn't face him now, when she was numb with misery and exhaustion, and too desperate to explain calmly and clearly why she had to leave him.

They had barely spoken that morning. Jack had left early with Scott and they had been mustering all day. For once, Ellie had been glad not to be out there with the men. She'd needed to be alone to think about what she should do. But in the end she hadn't been able to think about anything but the longing to fall into a deep sleep and wake up to discover that this had all been a bad dream.

'Ellie?'

With a rush of relief, Ellie realised that it was Scott, and not Jack, and she got to her feet, Alice's empty bowl in her hand. 'Back already?' she asked, summoning a smile.

Scott nodded as he came into the kitchen. 'The other guys are bringing the herd in now,' he told her, 'but I need to get back to Mathison before dark, so I came ahead to get my bag and say goodbye to you and Alice.'

Ellie wondered whether to ask Scott not to say anything about the obvious tensions between her and Jack, but in the end it didn't seem to matter that much. Everyone would know soon enough that their marriage was over. 'Thank you for coming,' was all she said instead, as she carried Alice out onto the verandah to see him off.

'No worries.' Scott put his hat on his head and hesitated. 'Are you OK, Ellie?' he asked in concern. 'You don't look too good.'

'I'm fine.' Ellie's voice was tight, her smile brittle. 'Everything's fine.'

Only everything wasn't fine. Numbly, she watched Scott walk away towards the airstrip. He stopped at the junction of the two tracks, and she saw that he had met Jack, coming up from the yards. They stood for a moment, talking, and even from a distance Ellie could see the tension in Jack's lean, rangy figure and the grimness in his expression.

Her heart cracked at the sight of him. It was hard to remember now his lazy good humour or the effortless charm that had been so typical of him. Once he had been carefree and relaxed, once there had been a devastating, daredevil glint in his brown eyes and his smile had been irrepressible. No more. Marriage had turned him into a dour stranger with shuttered eyes and lines of strain in his face. *She* had done that to him.

She saw him lift his hand in unsmiling farewell to Scott, and continue on his way to the homestead. Alice wriggled in her arms. 'Dada!' she said, pointing excitedly.

'I know.' Ellie's throat was unbearably tight as she watched Jack walk towards her and knew that the decision she had made last night was the right one. She would have to go to give him any chance to be happy…but how could she bear to leave him, and Alice? Everything she loved most in the world was here at Waverley Creek. Somehow she was going to have to find the strength to turn and walk away.

Jack halted at the bottom of the steps and looked up at where Ellie stood with Alice in her arms. Her eyes looked enormous in her pale face, and they held an expression of such anguish that his heart stumbled.

'Did you say goodbye to Scott?' he asked, his voice rough with concern.

Ellie couldn't trust herself to speak. She nodded dumbly instead, and Jack hesitated, feeling inadequate to comfort her. He had suspected that she loved Scott—she had practically told him, hadn't she?—but he hadn't realised just how much until now, when he saw in her face what it had cost her to watch the other man leave.

'Are you all right?' he asked gruffly.

Why did they keep asking her that? Of course she wasn't all right! Ellie tried to say that she was fine, as she had said to Scott, but the words wouldn't come out, and to her horror she felt her mouth begin to wobble. She clapped her hand over it to hide its treacherous weakness, and stared back at Jack with appalled green eyes. She never cried. She couldn't cry now. If she let herself cry now, she wouldn't be able to stop.

Without thinking, Jack came quickly up the steps towards her. 'Ellie—' he began, but Ellie couldn't face him any longer. Thrusting Alice into his arms, she pushed past him and stumbled down the steps.

'Ellie!' he cried, but she was running now towards the creek, and with Alice protesting at her undignified transfer into his arms, he could only stare impotently after her.

There was a sick feeling in the pit of his stomach. He had been furious with Ellie the night before. The marriage had been her idea, after all, and it was too late now for her to start complaining about being bored. Her resentment had caught Jack on the raw, and although the anger had continued to churn through him all day when he'd thought about the things that she had said, it had been edged with a peevish sense of guilt. He *hadn't* treated her as a partner, Jack had realised uncomfortably, but that had only made him feel worse.

He had been bracing himself for another stilted evening with Ellie, but the moment he had looked up into her face and seen the naked misery in her eyes all the rage and turmoil inside him had evaporated. He had thought only to comfort her, but Ellie hadn't wanted anything from him. She had run away rather than tell him how she really felt, and Jack was left looking after her with a terrible feeling that he had taken a wrong turn somewhere and lost something precious along the way.

When Ellie finally made her way back from the creek, Jack was bathing Alice. Or rather, he was crouching by the bath, his sleeves rolled up and one hand hovering somewhere behind Alice's back in case she toppled backwards. Alice objected on principle to anyone trying to help her, and insisted on being left to wash herself, which made the whole process not only lengthy but nerve-wracking, at least as far as Jack was concerned.

Ellie was much better at dealing with Alice, Jack acknowledged to himself. By the time he came in she usually had his daughter fed and bathed, and he was left with the easy part. Today, he had had little choice but to carry on with Alice's normal routine as much as possible, and it was proving an uncomfortable lesson not only in how much Ellie did but in how guilty he was of taking her for granted.

He would make it up to her, Jack vowed. He glanced up when Ellie appeared in the doorway, and tried to smile, but she looked so awful that it never quite reached his lips. Her skin was blotched and her eyes red and swollen where she had obviously been crying. Jack's heart twisted. He had never seen Ellie cry before.

Ellie sat down on the edge of the bath and pushed her hair wearily behind her ears. 'I'm sorry about earlier,' she said in a low voice.

'Don't worry about it,' said Jack, shocked by her distress. The look in her eyes reminded him of the way he had felt when Pippa died. Did Ellie feel the same sense of hopeless despair when she had to watch Scott walk away to his nice wife and his life that had nothing to do with her? If she did, she must love him more than Jack had realised. More than he had wanted to realise.

'You were...upset,' he added, trying to show her that he understood.

Ellie looked down at her hands. *Upset.* It seemed a funny word to describe the tearing despair that had been clawing at her ever since she had realised just how peripheral she was to Jack's life. 'I'm just tired, that's all.'

Oblivious to the tensions above her head, Alice was smacking her hands into the water and chortling at the splashes she could make. Jack retrieved the flannel she had discarded earlier and handed it back to her in the hope that she would use it to wash herself, but Alice only threw it back in the water. 'No!' she said firmly.

Sighing, Jack fished it out again. Mindlessly, he wrung it out and wondered how best to help Ellie. At least he could start by apologising. 'I'm sorry about last night,' he said, looking up at her.

'No, it was my fault.' Ellie avoided his eyes. 'We both knew what the situation was when we married. I thought that things would be all right...but they're not, are they, Jack?'

Jack hesitated, then shook his head. There was no point

in trying to pretend that everything was OK. It would only make things more difficult for Ellie. 'No,' he said, 'they're not.'

Ellie took a shuddering breath and willed herself to get through what she had to say next without giving in to tears again. 'Jack, do you remember the agreement we made before we were married?'

Remember it? How could he ever forget it? Jack wondered a little bitterly, but he nodded and waited for her to go on.

'You made me promise that if I ever wanted to leave, I would tell you.' She paused. 'I want to go now, Jack.'

The room seemed to darken around Jack and he stared blindly at Alice. 'Why now?' he asked in a voice that seemed to belong to someone else. 'Nothing's changed.'

'*I've* changed.' Ellie paused, groping for the words to make him understand why she had to leave without telling him the truth that would only make things more difficult than they already were. 'I thought I could bear it, but I can't.'

'We could make some changes,' Jack offered with an edge of desperation. 'I haven't involved you in the running of Waverley the way I should have, I know that, but I'll try harder,' he promised. He couldn't believe that Ellie was sitting there, calmly talking about leaving him. How could he possibly manage without her?

'I'll get a housekeeper,' he hurried on before she could refuse. 'A girl who could help with the cooking and with Alice so that you could spend more time outside, the way you want to. That would make a difference, wouldn't it?'

'Oh, Jack…' Ellie looked at him helplessly. 'I know I complained about being stuck in the homestead, but that's not really the problem.'

'Then what is?'

'It's…the way I feel,' she said inadequately.

There was a desperate silence. Jack lifted a protesting Alice out of the bath and wrapped her in a towel on his knee. He didn't look at Ellie.

'You're still in love with him, aren't you?'

Taken aback by the abruptness of his voice, she stared at him. 'With who?'

Jack couldn't bring himself to say Scott's name. 'You told me you'd always loved someone,' he reminded her in the same harsh tone. 'You said it was hopeless. That was why you were prepared to marry me.'

'Yes.'

'*Are* you still in love with him?'

Ellie looked at Jack. She could draw his face in her sleep. She knew exactly how many lines creased the corners of his eyes, how the hair grew at his temples, the precise length of the tiny scar on his jaw. They were part of her in a way she couldn't explain.

'Yes,' she said.

'And he's the reason you want to go?'

Ellie drew a shaky breath. 'Yes.'

She wished that she could make Jack understand that it was for his sake that she was going. The truth hovered on her tongue, but she couldn't bring herself to say the words. The very thought of the appalled disbelief in his expression if she told him that she loved him made her cringe. It would only make things worse for him. No, better by far to let him believe, as he seemed to, that she loved someone else.

'I thought it would help that neither of us could have what we really wanted,' she went on carefully, 'but it doesn't. It just makes things twice as bad for both of us, and they'll only get worse. I'm never going to be Pippa, Jack. I'm never going to have what I really want either, and I know now that nothing else will do. The longer I stay, the more bitter and resentful we'll both get.'

She glanced at Jack's face, but it was closed and cold. Didn't he understand? Couldn't he *see*?

'I'm sorry,' she finished drearily.

Sorry? What use was sorry? thought Jack bitterly. 'What about Alice?' he said. It was unfair to use Alice as emotional blackmail, but he didn't feel very fair at the moment.

Ellie bit her lip. 'I won't go immediately. Of course I'll wait until you've found someone else to look after her.'

'Thanks.'

The bitter irony in his voice made her wince. 'I'm doing this for you, too, Jack,' she pointed out. 'It'll be better for both of us in the end.'

'And Alice?'

'It'll be better for her, too. It's not good for her to grow up in an unhappy house.'

'It doesn't have to be unhappy,' said Jack stubbornly.

Why was he making it so difficult for her? 'It's what it has been,' said Ellie, her voice cold with the effort of not crying. 'It's what it will be.' She swallowed hard. 'I'm not the right wife for you, Jack. You promised you would let me go if I asked.'

Jack was mechanically drying Alice's toes. 'Yes, I did,' he agreed dully, without looking up. 'Of course you can go, if that's what you want.'

It wasn't what she wanted, but it was what they both needed. Ellie had to remind herself of that again and again over the next ten days. Every nerve in her body screamed at her to throw her pride to the wind, tell Jack the truth and beg him to let her stay after all, but she knew that she couldn't do it.

Better to make a clean break now than to let the situation drag on and on. No matter what Jack said, he would meet someone else eventually, someone he could love the way that he had loved Pippa, and Ellie couldn't bear to be there then. She would be a burden to him, making him feel guilty and resentful for not needing her the way she desperately, desperately needed him.

No, it was better to go now.

Better, but hard. Oh, God, it was hard…

Jack made no attempt to persuade her to change her mind. He treated her with a distant courtesy that hurt Ellie more than his anger had done. He had rung the agency in Darwin the very next day, and asked them to send out a housekeeper as soon as possible.

'They haven't got anyone suitable immediately available,' he'd said when he told Ellie what he had done. 'In the meantime,' he had gone on stonily, 'I suggest we carry on as normal.'

'Of course,' Ellie had said quietly, but how could she behave normally when there was a cold, leaden weight inside her, dragging her down? When it was an effort just to breathe, and she moved slowly and stiffly, like an old woman hunched over her pain?

She did her best. She cooked and she cleaned and she watched Alice grow daily more confident in her steps. She heard her try new words, and her heart splintered to think that the baby would turn into a little girl and she wouldn't be there to see it. Someone else would pick Alice up when she fell and kiss her bruises better. Someone else would cuddle her on their lap and read her a bedtime story, and watch her lashes droop with sleep.

Someone else would water the garden, and cook the

vegetables that she had sown. Someone else would serve the meals and listen to the stockmen as they talked in their slow voices about bull-wrestling and rodeos and what could be done about the dam over at Coollee Bore.

Someone else would sit on the verandah with Jack and watch the stars. She would be gone. She would be far away in the city, learning to live without him all over again.

Every time the phone rang Ellie braced herself for the news that a housekeeper had been found. Every day she dreaded the moment when Jack would tell her that he didn't need her any longer and that she could go. But as day followed day, and nothing happened, she began to long instead for the worst. The waiting, the not knowing when she would have to face saying goodbye, was agony. Terrified that her resolution would fail if she stayed any longer, Ellie prayed that the agency would find someone soon and put her out of her misery.

But when it happened, she was still unprepared. She was peeling potatoes for the evening meal when Jack came into the kitchen.

'I've just been talking to the agency,' he announced without preamble. 'They've found a housekeeper. She's about fifty, but she says she likes children, and she's got good references as a cook.'

Ellie stared down at the potato in her hand. This was the moment she had been preparing herself for, and now it was here and all she wanted to do was to shout that it was too soon, she wasn't ready. There was a cruel, icy grip around her heart, its talons clawing, tearing, squeezing so agonisingly that she had to close her eyes against the pain.

It took a moment for her to be able to speak, and when

she did her voice seemed to belong to someone else. 'She sounds ideal.'

'Her name's Wanda,' said Jack. 'She's worked in the outback before, so she knows what to expect.'

'Good.' Ellie's hands were shaking so much that the peeler kept slipping off the potato. 'When can she come?'

'The day after tomorrow.'

It was too soon, thought Ellie in panic. She swallowed. 'So that will be it.'

'Yes,' said Jack heavily. 'That will be it.'

'I...I can think about going, then.'

Jack tensed. 'You'll stay and meet Wanda, won't you?' he said, clutching at any excuse to keep her longer, but Ellie was already shaking her head.

'I think it would be easier for all of us if I went before she arrives.'

'But that means going tomorrow!'

The weight of despair inside Ellie was so great that she almost buckled beneath it. 'I... Yes... I...I guess it does,' she said unevenly.

She was going.

Jack stared at her as she stood at the sink. Her back was completely familiar to him, he realised, and it would be the last he would see of her the next day when she turned and walked away from him.

He had known that she wanted to go, but it was only now that he understood what it was going to mean. She was going to go, and he would be left here on his own. The homestead would be empty and echoing without her. When he came in she wouldn't be there, moving around the kitchen, carrying Alice on her hip, turning to smile at him. Jack thought of all the times he had taken her warm, quiet presence for granted, and cursed himself for a fool.

Ellie was just standing there, peeling potatoes. She wasn't even looking at him, but for Jack it was as if the world had suddenly shifted around him, spinning everything that was familiar into a pattern that was at once new and dazzlingly clear. Jolted, jarred by the abrupt transformation, he could only stare at her back.

He was in love with her.

It was so obvious, he thought, shocked at his own stupidity. Why hadn't he realised it before? All those weeks he had been fighting it, refusing to acknowledge how much he needed her, and now she was going to go, and it was too late.

'Ellie—' he said urgently, and then stopped.

She turned from the sink, a potato in one hand and the peeler in the other, and something in his expression made her eyes widen. 'What is it?' she asked in concern. 'What's wrong?'

Everything's wrong! Jack wanted to shout. I love you and I'm about to lose you! The temptation to jerk her into his arms and kiss her until she promised to stay was so strong that he had to clench his hands by his sides to stop himself striding over to the sink.

Nothing had changed just because he knew now what he should have known weeks ago, he realised bleakly. He might be in love with her, but Ellie was still in love with Scott. Jack knew that if he begged her she would probably stay, for Alice's sake, but what use was that? He didn't want her to stay because she felt sorry for him. He didn't want her to stay for Alice. He didn't want her to be *kind*.

He wanted her to stay because she loved him, because she needed him the way he needed her. He wanted her desire, not her pity.

And he wanted her to be happy, Jack realised. She was

right; she would never be happy here with him, any more than he would be able to accept being second-best. It was better for her to leave and make a fresh start where she could try and forget Scott, where she wouldn't have to see him or listen to him telling her how happy he was with Anna.

'Jack?'

'Nothing,' he said curtly. 'Nothing's wrong.'

'We should talk.'

It was Jack who broke the silence in the end. They were in the kitchen, washing up the dishes as they always did after an interminable evening meal. They moved carefully around the room in case they touched each other accidentally. They always did that, too.

The chink of crockery was deafening in the strained atmosphere. Ellie kept her head bent and concentrated on washing the pots, scrubbing each one with an obsessive attention to detail.

'I suppose we should,' she muttered as she laid the last saucepan on the drainer.

Jack picked it up and began to dry it. 'If you're leaving tomorrow, we need to sort out a few practicalities,' he said, the tightness in his throat making it hard to keep his voice level. 'I'll pay you for your share of Waverley, of course, but I may not be able to do it immediately. It will take some time to arrange, and in the meantime I'll give you an allowance.'

Mindlessly, Ellie wiped around the sink. 'I don't want any money, Jack,' she said, trying to ignore the pounding behind her eyes. 'I don't want anything.'

'We had an agreement,' he insisted. 'You're my wife and you're legally entitled to my support. You've spent all this time here, looking after Alice, and you haven't got anything out of it.'

Ellie thought of the times she had watched the sun set over Waverley Creek. She thought of seeing Alice take her first steps, of the sound of Jack's boots on the verandah. She had memories that she would treasure for the rest of her life, memories of Jack's lips, of the feel of his body, of the touch of his hand.

'Yes, I have,' she said quietly.

'You'll need some money to start again.' Jack set his jaw stubbornly. 'It's the least I can do for you.' He hesitated. 'Have you told your parents yet?'

Unable to clean anything else, Ellie wrung out the cloth and draped it over the drainer. She hadn't thought about what her family would say. She hadn't been able to think about anything except how she was going to bear leaving him, and Alice, and Waverley Creek.

Wiping her hands on her jeans, she took a steadying breath and turned to face Jack and forced a smile. 'No,' she said. 'Not yet.'

Jack looked at her. There was an air of fragility about her now, as if the slightest blow would shatter her into a thousand pieces, but her head was tilted at a gallant angle and his heart ached at the bravery in her smile.

'What are you going to do, Ellie?' he made himself ask, instead of doing what he wanted to do and putting his arms around her to stop her being hurt ever again. 'Where are you going to go?'

Ellie's careful smile faltered, and her eyes slid desperately away from his. 'I don't know exactly,' she confessed, wishing that she could lie to him, 'but I'll be fine. There's no need to worry about me.'

'But, Ellie—'

All at once Ellie couldn't bear any more. 'I…I'd better

go and pack,' she muttered, desperate to get out of the kitchen before she started to cry.

Jack saw her turn and head for the door. This was what it was going to be like the next day, when she would turn and walk away from him for good. 'Ellie, don't go!' he blurted out before he could stop himself.

The urgency in his voice stopped Ellie at the door, but she didn't turn round. 'I can't talk now,' she admitted in a shaky whisper.

'No... I mean...don't go, ever,' said Jack desperately. 'Don't go now, don't go tomorrow. Don't ever go.'

Ellie stayed very still, eyes squeezed shut, afraid that he was going to ask her to stay for Alice's sake, terrified that she wouldn't have the strength to refuse.

'Please, Ellie.' Jack walked over to stand behind her, but although his hand went out he let it fall again without touching her. 'Please stay,' he said, no longer caring that he was pleading with her. He didn't care if she stayed out of pity. The only thing that mattered was the knowledge that he couldn't bear her to go and leave him alone.

'I know you want to go,' he said. 'I know I ought to let you go. I thought that I could, but I can't. I didn't mean to say anything,' he stumbled on, 'but when you turned and walked away just now, I knew I couldn't cope without you.'

'You'll find someone else,' said Ellie with difficulty. 'Alice will be fine.'

'*I* won't be.' Jack hesitated, struggling to find the right words. 'I need you, Ellie.'

'It...it's not as if we'll never see each other again,' she managed to say. 'We'll always be friends.'

'I don't want to be friends!' Jack's voice rose to a shout and he stopped, forcing himself to sound calmer. 'Being friends isn't enough.'

There was a moment of intense silence while his words seemed to echo around the kitchen, and then, very slowly, Ellie turned round. Her eyes were green and enormous in her white face, and their expression of disbelief made Jack's sudden rage evaporate. If he hadn't felt so desperate he would have smiled at her shock. How could she not have known?

'I'm in love with you,' he told her, quite simply after all.

Ellie stared at him, unable to move or to speak or to let herself believe what she had heard.

'I know you don't feel the same,' Jack hurried on before she could recover enough to tell him it was hopeless. 'I know you're in love with someone else, and that I haven't done anything to make you love me instead.' His smile twisted. 'I just took you for granted. I let you do everything for me. I let you make my house a home, and care for my daughter, and work until you were ready to drop, and never once did I do anything for you.

'I never showed you how much you mean to me,' he went on more slowly. 'How could I when I didn't know myself? It wasn't until you said that you were going that I realised how empty my life would be without you.'

Ellie swallowed. She felt very strange, almost disorientated, as if this were just a terrible, wonderful dream. 'But…but you love Pippa,' she stammered, surprised to find that she could get the words out at all.

'Yes, I did love her,' said Jack. 'But I didn't love her the way I love you. Pippa was fun and exciting. What we had was wonderful, but somehow never quite real.' He realised it for the first time. 'Perhaps if it had been that stupid argument we had wouldn't have been enough to make her leave, and everything would have been different.'

He sighed. 'I don't know if the love we had would have lasted. Now, it seems like a dream. All I know is that what I feel for you *is* real.'

Still he made no move to touch her, sensing that she was not yet ready to accept what he was saying. 'I wasn't expecting to fall in love with you, Ellie. I don't even know how it happened. You were so close that I couldn't see you for a long time, and then one day I looked and there you were, part of my life, as necessary to me as breathing.

'I'd got used to thinking of you as a friend, but that night we made love it was like coming home. I knew then that I didn't want you as a friend; I wanted you as a lover. I wanted you to belong to me and no one else. I wanted to punch Scott every time he so much as looked at you.'

Jack paused, and when Ellie still didn't say anything he went on quietly, 'I don't deserve another chance, Ellie, but I'll go down on my knees and beg if you'll just say that you'll stay—not for Alice, not because you love Waverley, but because you want to be with me.'

It was a dream. It had to be a dream. Ellie shook her head to clear it, and Jack took an urgent step closer. 'Don't say no!' he pleaded. 'At least think about it! I know you love Scott, but he's got Anna. He doesn't need you, and I do.'

'Scott?' said Ellie in a peculiar voice. 'You think I'm in love with Scott?'

It was Jack's turn to stare. 'You mean you're not?'

'No.'

He had been so sure it was Scott. Now he had to struggle to readjust all his ideas. 'You're in love with someone else?' he said carefully.

She nodded, a smile trembling on her lips.

Jack's first surge of relief at discovering that it wasn't Scott evaporated. What if it was someone who wasn't married, who might just look at Ellie one day and suddenly realise, as he had done, just how beautiful she was?

'You said you'd never have a future with him,' he reminded her. 'Why not stay here with me instead? I'll make you happy,' he promised. 'I'll spend the rest of my life helping you to forget him.'

Ellie found her voice at last. 'I'll never be able to do that, Jack,' she said with a wavering smile.

'You could try, couldn't you? You could learn to love again.' There was a note of desperation in Jack's voice. 'You could change your mind!'

'No, I won't.' Ellie's smile shimmered through her tears. 'He's the only man I'll ever love.'

Her eyes were luminous with love, and Jack turned away, sick at heart that it wasn't for him. Well, he had tried. He had begged her to stay, but it wasn't any good. He should have known that she wouldn't change her mind. Ellie would always be true. She was a one-man woman. He just hoped that the man she loved knew just how lucky he was.

'I see,' he said heavily. Leaning his arms on the table, he stood with his head bowed as he tried to master the bitterness of disappointment. 'Well,' he managed with difficulty, 'that's that, then. You'd better get on with your packing.'

He sensed Ellie's warmth beside him before he felt her hand on his shoulder, and he averted his face, unable to bear the pity he knew would be in her eyes. 'Just go,' he muttered.

'Jack,' she said softly. 'Jack, it's you.'

Jack didn't know what she was talking about. He rubbed his face tiredly. 'What?'

'Look at me, Jack.'

Lifting his head, he stared at her uncomprehendingly.

'It's you,' said Ellie again with an unsteady smile. Her hand slid from his shoulder down to his elbow, curling round to drift lovingly down the inside of his bare forearm and lace her fingers with his. 'It's only ever been you.'

'Me?'

'I've loved you all my life, Jack,' she said simply. 'I could never love anyone else.'

Hope warred with disbelief in his brown eyes. 'You love me?' he asked incredulously, and she smiled tenderly, hardly able to believe herself that she could tell the truth at last.

'I always have. I always will.'

Jack's grip on her hand tightened convulsively. 'Say that again,' he demanded, and pulled her against him so that he could bury his face in her hair. 'Oh, God, Ellie, say it again.'

'I love you, Jack,' she said, her voice breaking as the tears spilled over.

Tangling his fingers in the soft brown hair, he tilted her face up to his. 'Again,' he insisted.

Half-laughing, half-crying, Ellie told him what he wanted to hear. 'I love you, I love you!'

He kissed her then, his lips coming down on hers hungrily. They kissed with a kind of desperation born of the knowledge of how close they had come to losing each other. Ellie put her arms around his neck and gave herself up to the enchantment spilling through her in a golden rush of joy as she began to believe that he loved her as she loved him.

'Why didn't you tell me?' Jack asked breathlessly at

last, kissing her eyes, her cheeks, her nose, her mouth once more.

'I couldn't. I was so sure that you would never love anyone but Pippa. Whenever you talked about her she sounded so wonderful, and so different from me, that it seemed impossible that you could ever look at anyone else. I knew that I could never rival Pippa's ghost, and I thought that if you knew how much I loved you, you would be embarrassed and it would spoil everything. I told myself that it was enough to be married to you, just to be near you. That was all I'd ever wanted.'

Jack lifted his head to look down into her eyes. 'Then why were you going to leave?' he asked, holding her face between his hands and running a thumb along her cheekbone in a tender caress that made Ellie shiver with pleasure.

'Because in the end being near you wasn't enough. It was fine at first, but the more I was with you, the more I loved you, and the more it hurt that you didn't love me back.'

'And I was so jealous of Scott!' Jack shook his head at his own stupidity, and then he smiled, the old, brilliant smile that Ellie had loved for so many years. 'You mean I've spent all this time being jealous of myself?'

Ellie laughed and buried her face in his throat, succumbing to the sheer joy of being able to kiss him and hold him. She clung to him, shivering with pleasure as his arms tightened around her. It was a dream, a wonderful, glorious dream, a happiness so intense that it hardly seemed real.

'I thought it was obvious how much I loved you,' she told him. 'I couldn't believe that you would ever come to love me back.' Drawing back slightly, she looked up into the brown eyes that were warm with love. 'I still can't believe it,' she confessed. 'Not really.'

Jack smiled as he drew her out of the kitchen. 'Then I'll just have to prove it to you,' he said.

'Now do you believe me?'

Ellie stirred at the honeyed pleasure of Jack's hands moving with warm possession over her body. Jack was leaning over her, looking down into her face with an expression of such tenderness that her heart melted with love.

'I believe you.' She wound her arms around his neck and pulled him down for a long, sweet kiss. 'That's not to say that I won't need regular reminders, though!'

'There's no time for that,' said Jack with mock sternness. 'We've got work to do!'

'Yes.' Ellie stretched blissfully at the thought. 'We'd better ring the agency in the morning and tell them that we don't need a housekeeper any more.'

Jack twisted her hair around his finger. 'I've got a better idea,' he said. 'We'll have her here to help in the homestead, and that will give you more time to work outside with me. We've got a lot to do still, Ellie, but this time we'll do it together,' he promised.

Ellie sighed happily. 'This time we'll do it right.'

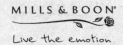

Tender
romance™

0406_AUDIO_BOOKS

Look for these exciting new titles on Mills & Boon Audio CDs on sale from 5th May 2006

The Greek's Chosen Wife by Lynne Graham
Wife Against Her Will by Sara Craven

A Practical Mistress by Mary Brendan
The Gladiator's Honour by Michelle Styles

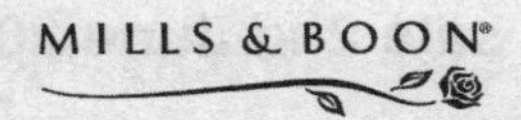

www.millsandboon.co.uk

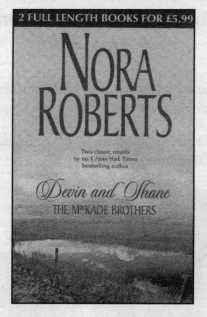

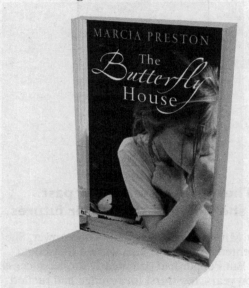